# SHATTERED

by

## Diane Bridenbaker

Bloomington, IN  Milton Keynes, UK

authorHOUSE®

*AuthorHouse™*
*1663 Liberty Drive, Suite 200*
*Bloomington, IN 47403*
*www.authorhouse.com*
*Phone: 1-800-839-8640*

*AuthorHouse™ UK Ltd.*
*500 Avebury Boulevard*
*Central Milton Keynes, MK9 2BE*
*www.authorhouse.co.uk*
*Phone: 08001974150*

*First published by AuthorHouse 12/13/2006*

*ISBN: 978-1-4259-6114-5 (sc)*

*Library of Congress Control Number: 2006908725*

*Printed in the United States of America
Bloomington, Indiana*

*This book is printed on acid-free paper.*

For my grandchildren,
three wonderful blessings God saw fit to bestow upon me,
each one possessing their own unique personality and special
talents. Live happy, kids!

# Acknowledgements

Once again, I would like to extend heartfelt thanks to those people who have encouraged and inspired me, and in many cases imparted their knowledge or applied their special talents:

My grandson, Brandon, for his input on the title and cover of the book. His insight made the decisions easy.

My sister, Judith Drezek, who was pressed into service as full-fledged editor this time around. Her contribution is invaluable.

Laura Schwartz Martin for again creating a fantastic painting for the cover of my book.

LeeAnn Hughes and Kathleen Luce for their valuable information regarding the testing done when breeding Newfoundlands.

Wendy Lippert, R.N., who answered all my medical questions.

Patty Sepull for being my "in-house" source of information on Newfie character and personality. I'd also like to publicly thank her for making her restaurant, The Fireside Inn, a most welcoming place where I love to go and unwind.

Roger Lunde, retired FBI Special Agent, for providing any law enforcement assistance I needed.

Patricia Lunde for who she is, although she defies explanation.

Jere Hoisington who was unintentionally left out of the credits in *Tricked* after he had contributed valuable information in that book and again in this one. The thing of it was, he did it via his wife, Jackie, so I gave her the credit because it was she I talked to and besides, she's my buddy. To make amends, Jere has since been dubbed Director of All Things Pertaining to Hunting, Transportation, and Fire and Rescue.

Jackie Hoisington for acting as go-between and my own personal barometer and testing ground.

Laury Miller who at the risk of life and limb pursued her quarry, which was a truck by the way, to get the information I needed. Anything for the book, right?

Joanie Hussar for providing instantaneous answers to any questions I threw at her concerning dog shows.

Stephen Aszkler, D.D.S., for getting on the Internet and finding information whenever I just happened to pose a question in the office.

Rick Aber, Carolyn Comilla, James Schwartz, and of course, my children and their spouses for being there whenever and for whatever I needed them.

My canine pals, Spike and Libby, for providing me with new material through their crazy antics.

And lastly, Josh, Ch. Darbydale's All Rise Pouch Cove, for being the outstanding champion and consummate showman that he is.

To continue on as in *Tricked*, this novel is loosely based on some truths and real places, but is in actuality a work of fiction as evidenced by the fact that the shop depicted within these pages is still in business!

# Prologue

***Early October***

The noise kept pounding at her, harder and harder, louder and louder. It felt like the blow of a sledgehammer against her body. How could these people stand it? They were all behaving so normally, like they couldn't feel it. How could they not? It was making her sick, but those around her were talking and laughing as though they were oblivious to the debilitating racket.

She was getting lightheaded and felt sweat break out on her forehead. The clamor kept bouncing off the walls and ceiling, slamming into her. Her head felt like it was going to shatter into a million pieces. The building she was in was cavernous, every sound reverberating innumerable times. She was going to be violently ill. She had to get out of there. *Now!*

Close to being in a full-blown panic, she searched desperately for a sign for the ladies' restroom. With darting eyes she finally spotted one on the other side of the room, unconsciously whimpered in relief, and ran over. Locating the entrance to the bathroom, she quickly ducked inside. There was an immediate respite from the outside din. She hurried to an empty stall, gagging as she went, and locked herself in. She turned to the toilet just in time to empty the contents of her heaving stomach into the white porcelain bowl. She continued to vomit until there was nothing left to bring up. Then she dry-heaved until her stomach felt like it was twisted into a tight knot, her throat strained and raw. Finally, she was able to straighten her doubled-over body and leaned weakly against the metal door. Her entire body was spent. She was drenched in a cold sweat and trembling uncontrollably. Her mouth tasted foul and she was gasping for breath.

She closed her eyes and unbidden images sprang into her mind. She saw their black heads looming over her, their crazed eyes peering into hers, their open mouths flecked with foam, their lips curled back in a snarl, and their teeth, those god-awful teeth, so brilliantly white in the sunlight were dripping with blood. *Her blood!*

She sobbed twice before her hand flew up to cover her mouth, muffling the sound. She forced her eyes open and willed herself to concentrate on something, anything other than what she was reliving in her mind. She looked blankly ahead and stared at the wall behind the toilet. There was nothing else to look at. She blinked rapidly and tried to center all her attention on the wall.

It was painted glossy beige. Must make it easier to clean, she thought dully, the painful images threatening to break through once again. She fought for control; she couldn't let her mind wander back to the terror. Think about the wall, she commanded herself. *Focus on the frigging wall!*

With a monumental effort, she did. The wall was made of blocks, concrete blocks. She knew that people still called them cinder blocks, but they weren't. Cinder blocks hadn't been made in a very long time. Why this information was being dredged to the forefront of her brain at that precise moment was a mystery and yet she was thankful; it was keeping the horror at bay.

Regardless of what they were called, there were a lot of them. Her eyes moved restlessly over the wall. Then, her body jerked in response as she suddenly realized the answer to her dilemma was right in front of her. The distraction she so desperately needed to push away the memories was staring her in the face. She could count the goddamn blocks! She grabbed onto the idea as if it were a lifeline. Her eyes immediately traveled upward toward the ceiling and she started to count, starting at the left-hand corner, one…two…three…With painstaking slowness, she silently mouthed the numerical progression while her eyes tracked her journey back and forth across the wall, immersing her mind in the steady mathematical trek.

After what seemed like an interminable length of time, she was able to bring her body back under control. Her breathing returned to normal and she stopped shaking. Her skin dried, although her blond hair still clung damply to her forehead. The muscles in her midsection and throat loosened and relaxed. After another minute or two she felt a little stronger and was able to stand upright away from the door, her gaze dropping away from the wall. She stood there placidly, not moving for a moment, and then grabbed some toilet paper and wiped her mouth. Discarding the used paper into the toilet, she got some more and blotted her forehead, lifting her hair away from her face as she did. She threw the now damp and sticking paper into the toilet and flushed. She watched as the water and its contents swirled and disappeared. She continued to take slow, even breaths, gathering her composure before she attempted to leave the stall.

"Are you all right?" someone asked from the other side of the cubicle.

She jumped, then froze for a second, startled by the voice. She hadn't heard anyone come in.

"Do you need some help?" asked the disembodied voice.

"No... no, I'm fine," she answered, forcing herself to respond calmly.

"Are you sure? I couldn't help but hear that you're in some sort of distress. I can get medical help if you need it."

"No... really. It must have been something I ate. I'm... I'm feeling much better now. Thank you."

"Oh, well, okay. I'm glad you're feeling better. Hey, I've been there, you know; I know just what you're going through. The same thing happened to me not too long ago and it's a real bitch, isn't it?"

"Yes... yes, it is. But thank you for your concern."

"You're quite welcome. If you're sure you're all right, I'll just use the facilities and then be on my way. I have to show my Maltese in fifteen minutes. I needed to take a bathroom break before I went in the ring. Nerves, you know."

"Yes...I know. Well... good luck."

"Thanks."

She listened to the sounds of the woman closing the door to another stall, and then soon after heard the toilet flushing. New noises indicated the woman had come out of the cubicle and was at the sink washing her hands. She listened closely for the paper towels being dispensed and waited anxiously for the woman to leave. She stayed where she was until she heard the outer door close. Only then did she step out of her stall.

She looked around. Thankfully, she was once again the lone occupant of the restroom. She walked over to the row of sinks, chose one, and washed her hands. Then using her hand as a cup, she scooped some water and rinsed her mouth. She reached for the paper towels and dried her hands. She took some more and got them wet under the cold-water faucet. She wiped her pale face and stared at her reflection in the mirror that ran the full length of the wall.

God, how she hated that face! Framed by silky, short blond hair that hugged her head and curled on her neck, her heart-shaped face looked back at her through eyes that were a brilliant azure blue. Her eyes were large and striking; her light brown lashes full and long. Her delicate eyebrows, the same color as her lashes, were at the moment pulled together in annoyance as she studied herself. Her nose was small and tipped slightly at the end. Her cheekbones were high and her skin soft and unblemished. Her mouth was a perfect pink bow with the bottom lip just a tad fuller than the upper. The face that looked back at her was beautiful and she loathed it. It wasn't hers.

Her gorgeous face was the result of numerous operations and seemingly unending pain. The operations had started when she was but thirteen and had continued for many years thereafter. There had been too many years of hospitals and bandages and feeling like a freak. Instead of parties and dances and sleep-overs, her adolescent years had been spent recovering from surgeries, bearing the countless taunts of her classmates, and having endless sessions with her psychiatrist.

In the end she had been left with this face, her own ravaged and long gone. *She* was long gone. When she'd come of age, she'd even legally changed her name, ridding herself of the last vestige of who she had once been. Sheri Compton didn't exist in any way that mattered anymore. She was now Moira Spenser, changing her first name to one that in Celtic/Gaelic meant the "bitter one". She could easily live up to that. She hadn't cared about her last name. She'd just wanted it to be something other than what she'd been born with. She'd picked it out of the phone book.

She was all grown up now, no longer the young, innocent child who had been lost forever on that warm summer day so many years ago when she had lain bleeding and alone on a sidewalk in her affluent neighborhood. She still wished they had let her die that day; it would have been kinder. No child should ever have to be subjected to the pain and nightmares that she had since had to endure.

Oh, God, the nightmares! She still had them. She probably always would. After all the so-called "help" she'd received from her psychiatrist, they were still there, haunting her sleep, ready to strike and send her into the terror of that long ago day. Her only peaceful sleep was achieved through pills or liquor, sometimes a combination of the two. She'd do just about anything to have a night free of those horrible memories. A night that was free of startled awakening because her own screams had dragged her out of slumber, her body completely soaked with sweat and shaking violently. Her fear so real, she could smell it. Once awake, she would be terrified to go back to sleep, unwilling to chance another nightmare that same night. So she would lie motionless in her bed, eyes wide open, and plan, focusing on the only thing that mattered anymore— her overwhelming need for revenge. To pay back those that had caused her so much misery.

She'd been planning it for what seemed like forever. At first she had been too young to do anything other than hate that which had so changed her life. But the seeds of her retribution had taken root in those early days of recuperation and had served as a guiding force in everything she'd done as the years rolled by. Now, she finally had the tool necessary to achieve her vengeance.

Three years ago she had graduated Magna Cum Laude in chemical engineering from Cornell University. Since then she'd spent all of her spare time and almost all of the money left to her in a trust fund by her wealthy and now deceased parents building her own lab where she was free to experiment and develop a formula for a rather unique food additive that would prove to be the instrument of her revenge. She had met with success two weeks ago. It was ready. She could begin.

But she had to get control of herself first. She had to be able to function when it was time to act. She had to be able to be around the very thing she wanted to destroy without falling apart. She couldn't afford to get physically sick just from the noise they made.

She stared harder at the image in the mirror. The hatred and anger she saw reflected in those beautiful blue eyes was enough to empower her for the moment. She straightened her shoulders and threw the paper towels in the trash. She opened her purse and took out a brush, then ran it over her short hair, paying special attention to the wisps that framed her face. She exchanged the brush for some lipstick and blush and repaired her makeup. Satisfied with the results, she stepped back from the sink, tossing her purse over her shoulder.

She gathered her resolve around her like a mantle and started for the door. She told herself that she could do this; she would do this. It was payback time and she had to be up to the task. She swore an oath to herself that she would not fail. She opened the door and determinedly stepped out onto her killing ground.

# Glenwood is setting for second novel

Local author Diane Bridenbaker has just released "Shattered," the highly anticipated second installment in her exciting new series of self-published novels. As with its predecessor, "Tricked," "Shattered" features many of the same beloved characters, most notably Emma Rogers and her trusty companion, Cole.

Well on its way to selling 1,000 copies, "Tricked" has not only become a favorite of Western New Yorkers, but for dog lovers everywhere. And "Shattered" begins where "Tricked" left off.

Just when life in Glenwood had seemingly gotten back to normal for Rogers and friends, things start to heat up again. It's not long before the girls find themselves, and their canine counterparts, back in the thick of an adventure that is sure to have readers turning the pages.

"My goal when I wrote 'Tricked' was just to entertain whoever read it. I never imagined it would have been so popular," said Bridenbaker. "It's very natural to write about what you know and love. And for me, that's dogs. I truly believe fans of 'Tricked' are going to love 'Shattered.'"

Bridenbaker will be appearing at dog shows and book signings throughout Western New York to promote the book and meet fans. Fans of the book can also purchase the book at several websites (*Amazon, AuthorHouse, Barnes & Noble*) or e-mail the author herself at *thistle99@earthlink.net*.

Bridenbaker has had a life-long love affair with dogs and has been involved with her canine friends in one way or another for over 35 years. She's experienced in both conformation showing and obedience training and was fortunate enough to successfully assist in the delivery of several healthy litters of puppies.

She recently moved to West Seneca after closing her country gift shop in Glenwood. In addition to writing, she works part-time as an orthodontic assistant.

Bridenbaker is the proud mother of three grown children and loving grandmother to their three offspring.

# ...TORIAL.

## Out Of Control

# Chapter One

"Is that what I think it is?" Sally asked, gaping at what Joanie held in her hands.

"I don't know; is it?" Joanie answered, a look of total innocence on her face.

"*Joanieee...* is it?"

"Could be."

"Tell me now. Is it?"

"Maybe."

"Come on, smart-ass. Is it?"

"Might be."

"I think it is."

"You do?"

"Yeah."

"Okay, you tell me; what is it?" Joanie asked, a wicked grin replacing the faked innocence. She deliberately smoothed her hands provocatively over the object she held in her grasp.

Emma, who was doing a piece count, kept her head down unable to contain a snicker.

"You know what I think it is, dammit! Geez, will you stop doing that?"

"Doing what?" Joanie asked as she continued caressing the wood. Emma turned away; she knew Joanie was going to milk this for all it was worth.

"That. Stop touching it that way."

"What way?"

"That way."

"Which way?"

"Christ! You're enough to drive a saint crazy."

"I am?" Joanie waggled her eyebrows and grinned devilishly. "I'm flattered."

"Don't be, you ass. You know damn well what you're doing. Stop it."

"Why? Is it bothering you?" Joanie asked as she continued stroking the piece.

"Yes, dammit. It looks like you're making love to the stupid thing for cripe's sake."

"Maybe I am." Joanie couldn't help herself; she leered at Sally.

"Oh, no. I am *not* going there, Joanie Davis. No way. It's too sick... Geez, how many of those things are there?" Sally's eyes had fallen on a stack of wood whose pieces all looked exactly like the one that Joanie held in her hands.

"There's six, one for everybody who's here tonight. It's part of the project, you dope. We've got a winner here, don't you think?"

"Shit, we're going to be surrounded by 'em. How can I take this seriously now?"

"What're you talking about? Take what seriously? Hell's bells, girl, you're not here to be serious for pete's sake. Get real, will you? You're here to have some fun, get crazy. This is all part of it... I think it's great."

"You would."

"You're damn right. This little baby right here," Joanie said, admiring the object of so much attention, "is just an added bonus."

2

"You are so sick."

"Yeah, thank God."

"Look at this thing. It's not like you have to use much imagination to see what it looks like. This thing's pretty graphic."

"I know. It's terrific, isn't it? Who'd have thought when we cut it out that we'd end up with this beauty?"

"Joanie, you need help."

"Nah, I need more of this." Joanie wiggled her eyebrows at Sally, who gave her an oh-my-God-please-don't-say-any-more look. Sally quickly looked to Emma for help, but there wouldn't be any coming from that quarter. Although Emma's back was turned toward her, Sally could see that she was shaking with uncontrollable laughter. *Great!*

"You're a big help, Emma."

"I try to be," Emma gasped between giggles.

"And just what's your take on this… on this…thing?"

"I think it's a perk."

"God, you're as bad as she is."

"Yeah, ain't it great?"

"You two are brutal. I'll never be able to look Santa in the face again."

"Sure you will. You'll just have a big grin on your face and your mind in the gutter when you do."

"Shit."

Emma Rogers and Joanie Davis, friends and partners in The Whistling Thistle, a gift shop they'd owned for the past ten years, were distributing the wood pieces the ladies would need for the project they were making. It was a Tuesday evening in early November and the class was just getting started in the back room of their establishment. The girls held painting classes almost every Tuesday and Thursday night during the fall and winter months. Sally and the five other women who made up the class were arranging themselves around the table, eager to get started.

Sally Higgins, owner of the Hearthmoor Inn, a restaurant that was five miles south from the shop on Route 240, was the third member of the girls' triumvirate. Sally had owned the popular eatery, which was housed in a converted 120-year-old farmhouse for the last twenty-five years and it was the girls' favorite meeting place. If Emma and Joanie wanted to relax and kick back, they got their butts up to Sally's.

The three fifty-something ladies had been friends for over twenty years and had shared plenty of life's up and downs while members of their exclusive sorority. Joanie was the only married one of the group; both Emma and Sally were divorced. They'd raised their kids together, gone through the hell of having teenagers together (although Joanie was still in the last stages of that particular torture), and were now enjoying their grandchildren together with the exception of Joanie who had informed her two boys that she'd better not see any grandchildren for a few years yet if they knew what was good for them, which was probably a valid threat since they weren't anywhere near being married.

The one staple in all of their lives had been their love of dogs and showing them, whether it was in the breed ring or obedience. Over the years, their individual breed of dog may have changed, but that was about all. They loved to show and no matter if they won or lost, they always went back for more.

Now Sally didn't usually take a class, preferring to buy what she wanted rather than having to make it due to time constraints resulting from the demands of the restaurant. Sound good? Sally thought it was a good excuse. But she'd wanted this four-foot Santa to decorate the entranceway of her restaurant for the holidays and Emma and Joanie had bullied her into taking the class. How'd they do that? They'd refused to sell the finished product to her! If she wanted it—she had to make it. Now she wished she'd just stolen the stupid thing; she'd probably never be able to look at it again without having trashy thoughts. She should have known, she thought, nothing was sacred with those two.

The girls' three dogs were in the shop too. Cole, Emma's big Newfoundland and Tank, Joanie's Parson Russell Terrier were a mainstay. Barring injury, sickness, kidnapping, or natural disaster, they were always at the shop with the girls. To a lot of their customers the two charismatic dogs *were* the shop. The fact that Sally's yellow Labrador Retriever, Kirby, had joined them that night was a bonus for not only Cole and Tank, but the customers as well.

Naturally, besides being their treasured companions, all three dogs were shown in the ring; Cole and Kirby in conformation and Tank in Obedience. Cole was already an AKC champion and being shown as a Special. Even though he was shown irregularly and just for the fun of it, he had three Best In Shows to his credit. Kirby was within two points of her championship and Tank only had to qualify one more time to get his Companion Dog (CD) certification.

Emma had predicted that Kirby would have her title by Christmas and she could very well do it. Tank, on the other hand, could take forever to get his. He could be a bit of the devil in the ring (oh hell, let's get serious, he could be a holy terror) and totally unpredictable. No, that wasn't quite right. Joanie knew exactly when he was going to screw up; the surprise was in finding out what methods he'd use to do it. So when and *if* he'd get his title was pretty much up for grabs.

Having been dislodged from their usual playground in the back room, the dogs were in the main part of the store behind the counter in the girl's private space. There was plenty of room for them, enough so that they were currently playing their own form of hide-and-seek. Tank was the smallest of the three and he was the one in hiding. The fact that he wasn't all that well hidden, seemed to be unimportant to the game. It was the chase that counted. It was up to Kirby and Cole to find the little rascal and then beat him back to the front of the shop. As usual, they'd added their own twist to the game. The trick was to do it without knocking anything over. So far they'd been successful.

While the dogs were busy entertaining themselves, class was getting underway. The five other women, two of whom had come together and were obviously friends, were now staring at the one piece of wood that Sally had found so remarkable. As a matter of fact, they had each picked up that particular piece from the pile of wood that was sitting in front of them and were, well, examining it with more than a little interest. They were downright fascinated.

"It looks an awful lot like you know what," one of the two who had come together said.

"No, what?" her sidekick asked.

"You know."

"No, I don't."

"You don't know?"

"Nope. Don't have a clue." The sidekick covered a smirk with her hand.

"Come on! You'd have to be from another planet not to know what it looks like."

"If you say so."

"Aw, come on. You do too know what it looks like. You just want me to say it."

"Yeah, I dare you."

"Forget it. I'm not saying it out loud."

"Why not?"

"You know darn well why not."

"Hey, there's nobody here except us women. You can say it."

"No, I can't."

"Chicken."

"You said it. Just call me Henny."

"Joanie? What's the name of this project?" asked another woman who was getting a kick out of the repartee of the other two.

"Santa's Coming Soon."

"You've got to be kidding," the woman laughed.

"Nope."

"Honest to God?"

"Would I lie?"

"That's a dumb question," Sally mumbled under her breath.

"That's really the name?" the woman asked.

"Yep."

"I don't believe it. You guys are absolutely nuts."

"Hey, that's the name of the thing. We didn't have anything to do with it."

"Yeah, right."

"I swear." Joanie held up her right hand to emphasize the fact. Emma nodded.

"Well, all I can say is, if this piece of wood is any indication, old Santa here will be coming really soon. Like within the next thirty seconds."

"Oh, my God!" the two friends who had come together exclaimed before they burst into giggles.

"Oh, poor Santa. What a thing to say. Don't you people have any respect?" asked another woman who was a first-time student and obviously not used to the usual banter that got tossed around during class.

"Nope." Sally and Emma both replied with proud looks on their faces. The girls would have liked to tell the woman right then and there to loosen up, but refrained from doing so. They would not, however, attempt to change the direction the conversation was going. This was the way they ran class, and if you didn't like it—don't come back. The whole objective of the evening as they saw it, in addition to making something with your own hands, was to let your hair down and have a good time. And if it got a little off-color— all the more fun! Where was the harm?

"You two had a lot of fun getting this ready, didn't you?" asked Pat Shanahan, another student. This was her third class with the girls so she knew a little about what direction these sessions were bound to take.

"Oh, yeah." Emma and Joanie were laughing outright.

By then Sally figured what the hell, she might as well get down and dirty with the rest of them. It would be a losing battle to try and remain on a higher level anyway. Besides, why bother taking the high road when it was so much more fun taking the low. She jumped into the swing of things and suggestively fondled her wooden piece. "My God," she said. "Talk about having a woody!"

All of the ladies gave it up then, including the one who appeared to be a little straight-laced, and any sense of dignified decorum was blown to smithereens. The piece in question was actually one of Santa's arms that happened to have a rounded bulge at the end for it's fur cuff and that met up with a mittened hand minus the thumb. Knowing how Emma's and Joanie's minds worked, how could they not have fun with this one? It would be against everything they stood for if they didn't make the most of it and then drag everybody else in with them.

After a few more pointed comments on the wood's striking resemblance to that part of the male anatomy, which they all seemed to have an intimate knowledge of, the class got down to business.

First, they needed to sand the edges of all those wood pieces and don't think for a minute there wasn't even more snickering going on when it came time to sand that arm. A wicked smile even crossed the face of the uptight woman whom the girls had dubbed, Miss Priss. Give the girls long enough and they'd have her right down in the dirt with the others and loving every minute of it. It was a knack they were very skilled at. They certainly should be; they practiced all the time.

Secondly, the ladies had to trace in any lines or features they needed, which in itself was not a hard job, but for some women it took on the impossible dimensions of a complex architectural drawing. That particular night everybody was able to pull it off without any gnashing of teeth or suicidal tendencies.

Next came the actual painting. Students were always advised to wear old clothing and for good reason. Between the painting and the staining, they usually went home with some type of souvenir on their clothes. That night would be no different. After instructing the newbies in the proper technique, they had at it and very soon the ladies had the obvious telltale signs of paint-streaked fingers and hands. There were a few who were already sporting splashes of white and burgundy on their clothing and more paint smudges were sure to follow after the ladies used black and fleshtone. One or two even had a smear of color on their face, but so far everybody's hair had been spared.

Once the painting was finished, there was a break in the action while they waited for the paint to dry and the girls served up the wine they were famous for. Nothing like a little wine to get the ladies in a buying mood! The ladies sipped from their glasses as they strolled about the store and leisurely shopped. They all found at least two things to buy and made little piles of their purchases on the floor next to the counter. Emma and Joanie kept the wine flowing.

The next step was the staining and the girls took appropriate measures to safeguard the room and its contents. They'd had enough merchandise ruined over the years from flying stain to take precautions akin to transforming the back room into their own version of a "clean" room. Drop cloths were laid over everything that could be covered and the floor was covered with large sheets of clean newsprint.

The table was doubly secured with another plastic cloth over the one that was already down and then that was covered with newspaper.

Why the women always went kind of crazy with the stain, God only knew, but they did. Overly enthusiastic would be the nice way to say it, but the reality of the thing was they went a little bonkers. No matter how many times the girls showed the class how to apply the stuff, they invariably resorted to their own method, which was always way beyond messy. They were forever flinging it around with their sponge brushes. And now that they had a little wine under their belt? Look out, mama!

The ladies pulled on their latex gloves and set to work. Emma and Joanie had put on gloves *and* smocks, having learned the hard way that they were not immune to having stain flung in their direction. It probably wouldn't have hurt to wear safety goggles as well since the girls had had stain slapped on their faces on more than one occasion. Come to think of it, wearing a full HAZMAT suit might just be the ticket!

It took less than an hour and the ladies, for better or worse, were finished. Their project pieces were grouped and labeled by name and laid out on the papered floor to dry. It took another half hour before they were cashed out and on their way.

It was going on 9:45; Emma and Joanie still had to clean up. Sally offered to stay and help.

"Thanks for the help, Sal. Class always goes a little longer than the two hours we plan for each session on the first night. It's probably because we have to wait for the paint to dry." Emma was rolling up the newspaper from the table, making sure the stain-soaked brushes were tucked safely inside the bundle.

"Yeah, that and some of the ladies really don't know what they're doing. You know, they're kind of like you, Sal."

Sally gave Joanie a look that should have shrunk her a foot in height. "Stuff it, Joanie."

"Hey, I was only kidding," Joanie said, faking an injured look.

"Like hell you were."

"All right, I wasn't, so sue me." Joanie stuck her tongue out at Sally. "I can't help it if this isn't your forte."

"Well, you guys are the ones that bullied me into taking this stupid class."

"Oh, yeah… I forgot."

"Well, I didn't."

"Doesn't matter, Sal. You still suck at it. I mean the proof is on your face."

"What? What proof? What are you talking about?" Sally touched her face, feeling for exactly what she didn't know.

"You've got a big streak of white paint on your cheek," Emma said, helping her friend out.

"I do?"

"Yeah. Come here. I'll get it off." Emma turned to the sink and wet a paper towel.

"At least I try," Sally said as Emma wiped her face, easily removing the paint, "even if it is under duress."

"I'll give you credit for that, but you still suck."

"Joanie…" Emma shot her partner a warning look.

"What? I speak the truth and she knows it. She can't help it if she's got two left hands when it comes to this stuff."

"Joanie, it's a good thing I like you," Sally said.

"Hey, who doesn't?"

"Emma, want to help me draw up the list?"

"It would be my pleasure. I don't think we have enough paper though."

"Very funny, guys. I'm killing myself laughing."

"Maybe if we work together you could help me take her down, Em. Then you could hold her while I beat the hell out of her."

"I kind of like the sound of that. Could be fun. What do you think, Joanie?"

"You don't want to know what I think, but this will give you an idea." Joanie shot them both the bird and everybody laughed, all the teasing done without any rancor.

"Hey, you guys, stop right there." Emma's attention had been diverted to the doorway where three inquisitive canines stood shoulder to shoulder. "Don't come in here. You have to stay out. Go on now; back it up. Git."

The dogs had gathered at the entrance to the back room, hoping to gain entry. But with the ladies' projects spread out on most of the floor, Emma had been quick to declare the room off-limits to the four-footed hellions. The dogs weren't any too happy about that; all their toys were in there, although right now they couldn't see hide nor hair of them. Nevertheless, that room was their territory and they wanted in.

At Emma's words they'd stopped dead in their tracks and looked at her with pleading eyes.

"Sorry, guys. You have to stay out. There's too much stuff on the floor."

The dogs looked from Emma to Joanie to Sally. It didn't look like anybody was going to give them the green light. So, having received their marching orders in no uncertain terms, smart dogs that they were, they resignedly gave it up, at least for tonight. They didn't have much choice in the matter, but come tomorrow, watch out. They'd be damned if they wouldn't retake what was theirs.

With Sally's help, they finished the cleanup in fifteen minutes and were locking the door a few minutes after ten. Sally and Joanie with dogs in tow piled into their separate vehicles and waved goodbye to Emma. She waved back and switched on her flashlight, turning with Cole to walk up the hill toward home.

* * * *

Emma and Cole lived in the woods directly behind the shop and about two hundred yards in from the main road of Route 240 in a small town named Glenwood. They lived in what was known as the infamous "snow belt" of Western New York, about twenty miles south of the city of Buffalo.

Their cedar-shingled house, which was trimmed in cranberry, was a two-bedroom ranch that boasted an open floor plan and was furnished with comfortable over-stuffed furniture, colorful area rugs, and the antique furniture Emma had collected over the years. Her many collectibles, which included teddy bears, pottery, and rug beaters graced the walls and shelves; her hoard of books, which could fill a small library, was present everywhere. The beautiful fieldstone fireplace located at one end of the living room was huge and known to get a lot of use in the cold weather months. The house had many well-placed windows designed specifically to capture any ray of sunshine that happened to appear, but at this end of the state it could stay hidden for long stretches of time, especially during late fall and winter.

The porch that covered the front and one side of the house merged with the back deck and both were presently decorated for fall with cornstalks and mums. Emma had been religiously bringing the pots of mums indoors at night to prolong their somewhat short life. There had already been some heavy frosts and the plentiful flowers in Emma's numerous gardens were long gone. Many of the summer blooms, however, gained a second "life" in the bundles of dried flowers she had hanging throughout the house.

Upon reaching the house, Emma let herself and Cole in. Cole dove for his "Froggy", a favorite toy that he loved to play with. Emma's granddaughter, Sydney, had given the green stuffed frog its self-explanatory moniker. Cole tossed the plaything in the air several times and brought it over for Emma to throw. She reluctantly took the plush toy, which now had a thin coating of dog saliva slobbered on it, and gave it a toss. The toy sailed from the living room into the kitchen and slid under the antique claw-footed oak pedestal table. Cole streaked across the hardwood floor and nimbly retrieved it, bringing his prize back to Emma and dropping it at her feet. With a look that asked her to do it again, Cole waited. Gazing into his big brown eyes that were nothing more than voluminous limpid pools of love, how could she refuse? Emma picked up the somewhat tattered toy and threw it again. This time it sailed clear across the kitchen and landed on the floor butting up against the cupboards. Cole followed after it and ended up sliding into the cupboards himself when he made a grab for it. With a triumphant expression on his face he swaggered back to Emma and dropped Froggy.

"One more time, Cole, and that's it. I've got a few things to do yet and you still have to be fed. Okay?"

Cole gave her a "woof"; he really did seem to understand everything she said. He waited patiently for the throw, although his eyes never stopped dancing. Emma gave him a sly look and thought she'd fool him. She pivoted quickly and threw the toy into her bedroom. It landed in the middle of her antique sleigh bed. Cole shot past her and in one leap landed right next to his cherished toy. He plucked Froggy up in one swift movement and stood there looking at Emma like he had just crossed the finish line at Indy in first place.

"Aren't you the good boy? Way to go, Cole!" Emma gave him an ovation, then motioned for him to come down off the bed. "Come on, hero; let's get done what we have to. You must be getting hungry."

Cole jumped down, carefully placed his toy next to Emma's favorite chair and faithfully followed her around the house as she finished up the few things she had to take care of. Emma served Cole a meal of kibble and leftover pork roast and watched while he wolfed it down. She'd be amazed if he'd tasted even a fraction of what he'd just inhaled with the speed of light.

After he'd licked his chops with a satisfied air for about the sixth time, Emma put Cole out in his kennel run for the final nature call of the day. She brought the mums into the mudroom, and got ready for bed. After the 11:00 news, Emma turned off the lamp on the oak commode that sat next to the bed and clicked off the television with the remote. Having already assumed his rightful position on the bed after he'd given a sniff to the ever-present flowers that were arranged in a vase sitting on the oak cabinet, Cole snuggled down next to his owner and within a few short minutes they were both dead to the world.

# Chapter Two

The next morning Cole woke Emma at the appointed time as was his custom. The exact nature of their routine was very simply this: Emma's normal wakeup time was at the ungodly hour of five o'clock, unless she specified otherwise, and it was Cole's job to get her up. There was no need for an alarm clock; Emma merely told Cole what time she had to get up and he did the rest. It would appear that in addition to his many other talents Cole had been blessed with a remarkable sense of time.

Now Cole, ingenious dog that he was, had developed various means of carrying out his sworn duty and used them with undisguised fervor. The basic tools of his trade were: the kiss (receiving a full facial wash with his very wet tongue), the full-body press (having your entire body squished under the weight of an 150-lb. dog to the extent it was hard to breathe), the nudge (getting a poke somewhere on your person with his nose), or a combination of any of the above. This morning he'd opted to use the nudge, placing it in the middle of Emma's back. Emma loved the nudge; it was such a nice amiable way to wake up, although this morning it seemed like Cole was putting a little extra oomph into it.

Not fully awake yet, Emma mumbled, "What's up, big guy? You in a hurry?"

Cole woofed and gave her another nudge, this time in her ribs. He jumped off the bed and stood in the doorway, waiting.

"Okay, okay. I get the message; I'm up. I'll be there in a minute." Emma threw the covers off and plunged her feet into the sneakers she always kept strategically placed near the side of the bed. It was her variation on the fireman-readiness theme. If she could somehow get her jeans to stand up by themselves she'd do that too.

But that morning, having already decided not to waste time putting on those same jeans, she only grabbed the sweatshirt she had laying at the foot of the bed and whipped it over her head, pulling her arms through as she made for the doorway. Cole by now had made his exit and was waiting at the back door of the mudroom somewhat impatiently for her as evidenced by his prancing feet. He'd already stabbed his nose into the center of several mums, inhaled their pungent fragrance, and had streaks of pollen on his nose. He was nuts for flowers of any kind; he *loved* to smell them.

Emma shivered the minute she opened the door and felt the blast of cold air that greeted her. Well, *that* sure chased away any remnants of sleep that might have been lingering. She quickly walked out to the kennel run and put Cole inside. He'd only taken about two steps before nature was not to be denied.

"Guess you had to go. Sorry about that, big guy. Speaking of which, this cold air is speeding things up for me too. I'll be back in a few minutes." Emma hurried back to the house and took care of her own needs, grateful that she was still fast enough to make it in time. Pressure relieved, she brushed her teeth and washed her face before getting Cole back in.

She gave him a few biscuits and filled the water dish that was hanging in his elevated dining stand. He chowed down the biscuits and then took a big drink, downing more than half the water that had been in the bowl.

"Guess you were thirsty, but keep that up and you'll have to go out again in ten minutes," Emma said, wiping the water and drool that was dripping from his mouth with the ever-present towel.

Cole gave her a look that suggested she didn't know what she was talking about and left to take up his post. Emma changed into her workout clothes and put the exercise tape into the VCR. Bless Leslie Sansone and her *Walk Away the Pounds* videos! Cole had stationed himself out of range of any misguided kicks, but he was near enough to keep tabs on her as she did her workout. He'd catch her if she tried to skip something. Emma had only done each of the tapes about a hundred times or more so he knew them practically by heart, and he'd bring her up short with an accusatory bark if he caught her slacking. It was a two-way street; she watched over his workout and he watched over hers. They both had to be in great shape for the show ring.

Forty-five minutes later Emma had finished with her three-mile workout and was more than ready to devour food in any shape or form. She moved quickly to the kitchen to make her breakfast, although she didn't have a lot to do to get it ready. The total work involved was getting a plate from the cupboard, a fork from the drawer, and opening the tin that held her preferred meal. This morning's menu had only one thing on it: a scrumptious, Texas-sized, homemade banana chocolate chip muffin. It was so moist, undoubtedly from the cup of sour cream that had gone into the batter, that no butter was necessary. It simply melted in her mouth as is. Mmm, heaven! She washed the muffin and her Vitamin E capsule down with a glass of orange juice and that was it. Breakfast was over and she was good to go.

Now about that Vitamin E. Emma took it religiously every day, 100 I.U. It was her cure for hot flashes. It didn't completely eliminate them, but did reduce their frequency and intensity. God help her if, for whatever reason, she did forget to take one; she'd be flashing all day.

Troublesome little buggers those hot flashes. They always seemed to happen at the most inopportune times, like when you're putting on makeup. You can't exactly do a good job when your face is bathed in a sheen of sweat and actual drops are beginning to form and run down your face. The makeup tends to clot and ends up in streaks. It's not a good look. Or how about when you're ready to dress for the day and your back is so wet your shirt sticks to your body and you can't pull your arms through the sleeves. The only solution then is to 1) stand in front of a fan with the speed on high; of course, there goes the hairdo, or 2) if it's winter, run outside and stand in the cold air. If that doesn't work, you can always roll around in the snow. You get a little wet, but the hot flash is almost always instantly gone.

Now, if you've run outside in your underwear, and this is only advised if you live in a secluded area, then it should be noted that there is some risk of developing pneumonia. This concern, however, should be a secondary consideration. Getting rid of the hot flash takes precedence over anything and everything, even the risk of the local wildlife fleeing in terror to parts unknown caused by the sight of a nearly nude fifty-plus female body.

Ready to get cleaned up, Emma slipped into the bathroom, locking the door behind her. Cole had recently added opening knobbed doors to his repertoire and Emma didn't want any uninvited guests to join her in the shower, which Cole would do in a heartbeat. He was a little off the wall for water. Plus, he adored Emma and wanted to be with her at any given moment, whether it be on land, sea, or in the air.

Once Emma was showered, made-up, coiffed (well, that was stretching it), and dressed, she loaded Cole and her bike into her red Ford Explorer and headed up to the local county park called Sprague Brook, which was about two miles down the road. It was here that Emma exercised or "roaded" Cole on a daily basis. With Emma on the bike and Cole trotting alongside, they went out a distance of three miles, u-turned, and came back the same three miles to complete their run. Emma knew their routine would change soon enough what with winter coming on.

Once the snow was flying, and the good Lord knew she hated that stuff, the bike would be unusable and Emma would cut the distance in half and walk with Cole on the three-mile trek. She was a very fast walker, so much so that her three children, who were all grown and married now, used to be left in her dust when walking through a parking lot on the way to a store. They were forever complaining and asking her to slow down. Their pleas fell on deaf ears; Emma only had one speed—fast. So she'd yell for them to catch up and they'd have to run to keep up with her. Such motherly compassion! It's a wonder they still talked to her.

Anyway, Cole would still get a good workout even with Emma walking and since they didn't attend too many shows in the winter they could afford to slack off a bit. Regardless, the shortened distance would be good enough to maintain Cole's conditioning and wouldn't hinder his performance in the ring.

When they returned to the house, Emma got ready for work and very soon she and Cole were heading down the hill to the shop.

\* \* \* \*

Emma arrived before Joanie and opened up. After she had applied herself to the usual start-up procedures, she directed her energies to the back room. Cole was pacing anxiously just outside the doorway, impatient to get inside.

"Don't go in yet, Cole. I'll have it cleaned up in a minute."

There was no mistaking the pointed look he gave Emma; she'd better hurry it up. His patience was quickly nearing its end. Today was reclamation day, after all, and delays were unacceptable.

While Emma started to pick up the now-dry wooden pieces off the floor, keeping them organized according to name, Joanie and Tank showed up and joined their friends at the back room. Joanie walked through the doorway, ready to help Emma and told Tank to stay outside with Cole. Never one to pass up an opportunity, Tank looked the situation over and decided to make good use of his time since this avenue of fun was still unavailable. So he did the first thing that came into his head and jumped on Cole, butting his head into the big dog, thereby issuing an immediate invitation for a game of chase.

Well, why not? Cole figured it was still going be a few minutes before they could get to their toys and chasing Tank was better than standing around waiting.

With Tank already moving back down the aisle, Cole turned and took off after his buddy. They streaked down one aisle and then the next. They had to slow a little on the turns and at one point Cole's legs shot out from under him. He recovered quickly and charged after Tank who was now nothing more than a blur. Cole didn't stand a chance of catching him, but he liked to humor the little devil. Having lost sight of his quarry momentarily, Cole was nearing the end of one aisle where a large display of stationary products sat when Tank came out of nowhere and ambushed him.

Tank had been hiding behind the display and when Cole appeared had launched himself off the floor and sailed onto Cole's back. God, he was an agile little shit! Cole let him have his moment of triumph for a split second and then rolled, bringing Tank down to the floor. Taking advantage of Tank's temporary disorientation, Cole quickly hunkered down and pinned him to the ground with his very large body. Now on his back, Tank looked up into his pal's big brown eyes and smiled. Oh, yeah, he could smile, although it really looked more like a sneer. Cole wasn't impressed; he gave Tank a piercing stare that told the little pipsqueak that the contest was now a draw.

Meanwhile, the two girls had about finished picking up the room and setting it to rights. The projects had been put on shelves, the papers taken up, and Emma was breaking out the dog toys. The sound of squeaky toys, balls, and Frisbees hitting the floor brought both dogs into the back room at a dead run. Each grabbed a favorite toy and were soon totally engrossed. Seeing that the dogs were happily occupied, the girls set out fresh bowls of water and then went out on the sales floor. It was time to get this show on the road; they'd already accomplished a lot this week, but they still had a long way to go before they were ready to open the doors on Friday for their big weekend.

This coming Friday, Saturday, and Sunday was the shop's Fall Open House and there was much to do in preparation. Not only did the girls have to make sure everything was sparkling clean, which was no easy task what with sawdust constantly flying around from the wooden primitives they made, but last-minute orders were still being delivered and the girls had to get them checked in, inventoried, priced, and out on the sales floor. Today and the next were going to be very busy just as the two previous days had been.

The shop was generally closed on Mondays and the customary day off for both women. But this week they had used the day to decorate their business inside and out. Even though this was the Fall Open House, the girls had dismantled and removed all traces of fall decorating, including pumpkins that had turned to mush after being frozen a few times (you know, the ones that still look good, but when you go to pick them up your fingers sink into slimy goush. Well, those—they'd had about twelve of them).

The upcoming weekend was their official kick-off for the madness known as holiday shopping and they had decorated for the Christmas/winter season. They'd turned the porch, which ran the full length of the front of the dove gray building, into a wonderland of white lights and evergreen trees and pine boughs.

The four six-on-six double-hung windows, already draped in tiny lights and grapevine, had had rectangular wooden antique boxes added to their wide sills. Arranged in the boxes were evergreen branches, pinecones, bright red wax apples, and silk baby's breath. The door had been adorned with a large balsam wreath and lighted wire reindeer had been placed among the rusted watering cans and baskets that were arranged on the floor. Primitive Santas and snowmen had been hung on the wall and a few large standing figures had been scattered about. The girls had draped the railing with garland and the flags that flew from each of the six support columns had been changed to reflect the holiday spirit.

The final touch was the live Douglas firs that they'd set out. Four of the smaller trees had been placed in baskets and decorated with lights and rusted ornaments. They were placed on top of overturned wooden crates and had been strategically added to the wintry scene the girls were creating. The two largest trees had been put in copper boilers and arranged on either side of the door. The lighted trees were about six feet tall and cozily bracketed the entranceway. Shoppers coming through the door would be enveloped in their fragrant, fresh pine scent.

Inside, the girls had again started by removing any traces of fall festooning and packing it away. They'd gone around the shop three times to make sure they had it all, but wouldn't have been surprised if after all that they'd still failed to spot something. There were just too many places to look and after a while their eyes neglected to see things. Heck, it wasn't but a month ago that Joanie had found a bunny that belonged with the spring displays. Unbeknownst to Emma, instead of packing the little guy away (which would have required some effort on Joanie's part, digging out boxes and all), she'd tucked him back into the niche where she'd found him and he was still there. If Emma didn't spot him for herself, Joanie wasn't about to enlighten her. Who knows, he could very well stay there forever or until some lucky soul finally discovered the little treasure and bought him.

The next order of business had been to set up three 7-foot-tall artificial trees in different locations throughout the store, skirting them with dark green and cranberry plaid wool fabric. They'd trimmed them out in white lights and ornaments that ranged from resin birds, to skiing snowmen, to polar bears, to whimsical Santas, to galloping horses, to klutzy moose, to heavenly angels, to antique vehicles, to circus animals, to just about anything you could think of. They were all for sale and the customers could pluck them right off the trees.

Next on the list had been the windows, which they'd draped in evergreen and pinecone garlands, intertwining the grapevine that had been previously in place. There were already electric candles on each sill and the girls had surrounded them with red berry branches, Spanish moss, and small white tin snowflakes.

There were several wrought iron jar candleholders on the rough cedar walls that the girls filled with scents of the season and burned throughout the day. They'd replaced all of the current jars with candles that were holly green in color and gave off a pine tree fragrance.

Included in their holiday/winter décor was every kind of primitive Santa and snowman imaginable whether they were hanging on the wall, sitting on a shelf, or standing on the floor. They were wooden, soft sculpture, tin, resin, and ceramic.

The girls had also decked the walls with beautiful wreaths in various sizes and embellished with a wide variety of ornamentation. To say the place was stocked to the gills was putting it mildly.

However, in addition to the housekeeping duties, decorating, merchandise concerns, and crafting of their decorative wood, the girls had yet another job they had to perform. This one took place after hours, at home in their kitchens. They had to bake and they had to bake a lot.

The first year they'd held the open houses (they had one in the spring too), their business wasn't what it is now naturally, and the girls had naively baked homemade, from-scratch goodies for their customers. They'd had plenty of time to do it and thought the desserts added a nice homey touch. Well, the shoppers had absolutely loved the scones, brownies, and apple crisp the girls had dished up. Emma and Joanie had even ended up giving out recipes. They'd had no idea at the time what they were getting themselves into.

Over the years the baked goods had become an expected part of the festivities. In fact, they were the main reason some of the people came. Who could pass up free eats?! The tasty snacks were now not only a well-entrenched tradition, but a very big, time-consuming job for the girls. Thursday night would be dedicated to making all the desserts their customers would be expecting this coming weekend. Both Emma and Joanie would be dead on their feet by Friday morning.

"Hey, Em. I just remembered something," Joanie said. They were taking a lunch break, stuffing warmed up leftover-from-Joanie's-dinner-the-night-before spaghetti and meatballs into their mouths. That's probably what triggered her memory. "I forgot to check our supply of paper plates and cups. I don't know about napkins or plastic eating utensils either. Have you checked?"

"Kind of. I know we need more plates and cups. Napkins, I think we're okay on. I don't have a clue about forks or spoons though."

"We'd better write it down on our 'to do' list or we're sure to forget."

"No kidding… Why don't I just go and check now; then we don't have to worry about it anymore."

"Oh, finish your lunch first."

"That's okay. I'll do it now while the thought's still there. I'll lose it otherwise." Emma went to back room, stepping over numerous toys and Frisbees, not to mention the dogs on her way to the cupboards. "We need silverware too," she reported after a quick perusal.

"One of us is going to have to run to Wal-Mart then," Joanie said.

"Yeah? When?" Emma sat back down to her lunch, shoving a meatball into her mouth.

"Good question. I think it'd have to be either tonight or early tomorrow morning. We're pretty much tied up after that. I won't feel like going in the wee hours of Friday morning after being up most of the night baking."

"Yeah, me neither. I'll be a little too bleary-eyed by then."

"Geez, we sure don't want you on the road if you're bleary-eyed. It's bad enough when you're bright-eyed and bushy-tailed."

"Cute, Joanie."

"Cute nothing. I'm only stating the facts and you know it."

"Yeah, well, we can't all be ace drivers."

"No, but it sure would be nice if we were all competent drivers."

"Joanie, I'm competent."

"Oh, no, you're not," Joanie said, shaking her head.

"I am too."

"No, you're not."

"Yes, I am." Emma was contemplating what a quick flick of her wrist would yield. The fork she held was loaded with twirled spaghetti. If she could do it really fast she was sure to smack Joanie right in the face at this distance.

"No, sorry, Em, you're not. Quit arguing with me. Think about it a minute and be honest with yourself."

"Joanie..." Emma could feel her wrist moving backward in preparation of the forward thrust. It was like it had a mind of its own. She had no control over the movement. Her hand was moving on instinct alone.

"Do it."

Do it? Emma blinked and opened her eyes wide, all wrist movement suspended. Was she hearing correctly? Did Joanie just give her permission to fling spaghetti in her face? This definitely needed further clarification.

"You want me to do it?"

"Yeah."

"You're sure?"

"Yeah, think about it."

"Think about it?"

"Yeah."

"Think about what?"

"Where the hell have you been? I asked you to think about if you really think you're a good driver for cripe's sake."

"Well, crap..." Emma forced her hand to relax and return to her plate where she pushed the spaghetti off the fork, thereby unloading her ammunition. "All right... if I have to be honest…I guess I'm not quite up to your skill level."

"*My* skill level? You call that being honest? You don't even come close."

"Joanie…" Emma was wondering if she'd been too hasty and should go ahead and reload.

"How *did* you ever get your license anyway?" Joanie asked.

"What do you mean, how'd I get my license?" Emma asked, a defensive note creeping into her voice.

"I mean how'd you get it? How'd you ever pass the test?" There was no way Joanie could ever imagine Emma successfully parallel parking. A three-point turn was a stretch. Hell, the day she got her license she pulled her car into a parking spot and rammed the front of the car into a brick wall.

"I don't know. I just passed it, that's all."

There was a beat or two of silence before Joanie snapped her fingers, then pointed at Emma. "I know. I know how you did it. The examiner felt sorry for you, didn't he?"

"Joanie…" Emma's voice had become subdued. She had to admit to herself, but would admit it only to herself, that that was probably the reason she had passed. She'd been so pathetic, the guy had all but said he felt sorry for her and was giving her a break. But she'd die a thousand deaths before she'd let Joanie know she'd guessed the truth of the matter. That was way too much ammunition for her friend to have at her disposal.

"All right, all right," Joanie said, giving in and letting Emma off the hook. She did, however, pretend to need something from behind her, giving her reason to turn her back to her friend while she made a face and mumbled under her breath, "It's not my fault you're one of the worst drivers God ever put on this earth."

"What'd you say?"

"Nothin', just thinking out loud," Joanie said, turning back and relaxing her features. "Getting back to the Wal-Mart thing… maybe I can get Sam to take me tonight. I still have to check and make sure I have all the ingredients I need for baking, so after I do that we might as well take the ride. I'm sure I'll need something." Sam was Joanie's husband of twenty-eight years and a retired FBI Special Agent.

A warning bell that had rung many times in the past went off in Emma's head. It had a familiar clang. "Whoa! Wait a minute, not so fast."

"Hmm?"

"You haven't checked to see if you have all the ingredients yet?"

"Ahhh…no."

Crap! Emma knew what was coming next, God help her. "Joanie, do you even know what you're going to make?"

"Well…"

"Do me a favor. Just this once, okay?"

"Sure, if I can."

"Oh, I'm sure you can. It's a matter of will you."

"Geez! What's the favor?"

"I'm going to ask you a simple question and I want an honest answer."

"Sounds easy enough."

"Oh, it is, but the hard part for you is going to be the honest part."

"I'm not sure, but I think I should I be insulted by that."

"No, you shouldn't. *I'm* just being honest."

"I'm not going to try and follow that. What's the question?"

"Are you ready?" At Joanie's nod, Emma continued. "I want you to watch my lips very carefully now, okay?"

"Okay."

"All right." Enunciating very slowly, Emma asked, "Do-you-know-what-you're-making-for-the-open-house?"

Joanie looked at her strangely for a second before answering. "Correct me if I'm wrong, but didn't you already ask me that?"

"Yeah, and if *I* remember correctly, I didn't get an answer yet."

"No?"

"No."

"Really? I thought I answered that one."

"Well, you didn't and I want an answer now. A truthful one."

"Truthful?"

"Yeah."

"As in honest?"

"You've got it."

"Do I have to?"

"Yeah."

"Well, if we're going for truthful…"

"We are."

"Then I have to say…no."

"Dammit! I knew it. I just knew it."

"What? What'd you know?"

"You know what I knew."

"I do? What?"

"Don't play games with me, you ass. I knew you hadn't figured out what you were going to make yet."

"Is that what you knew?"

"*Yeees.*"

"Oh… Well, so you knew. So what?"

"Well, don't you think it's getting a little late in the game for you not to know. I mean you do have to bake tomorrow night."

"Yeah, so?"

"Joanie, just once couldn't you make this easy."

"Em, you should know by now that I fly by the seat of my pants on these things."

"Yeah, I know and every time you do it you give me heart failure."

"Just relax. Everything will work out. It always does."

"Yeah, but, Joanie, one of these times—"

"I know, I know. It might not work out. Well, if it doesn't, you'll be the first to know, won't you?"

"Yeah, and that's exactly what I'm afraid of."

"Don't worry. There isn't a better person around who can deal with a huge screw-up like you can."

"Oh, God."

"No, not Him. You. You can do it." Joanie laughed wickedly, scooped up the dirty dishes and remnants of their lunch, and walked away.

Good thing. Emma felt her hands rising of their own volition again, forming claws that were reaching to get themselves around Joanie's neck. One little squeeze, just one little squeeze! Cripe! She could drive you nuts! Emma thought she'd better get busy with something constructive and in the opposite direction than the one her friend had taken or The Whistling Thistle might find itself with one less owner.

# Chapter Three

Thursday at the shop went pretty much along the same lines as the rest of the week already had except that Angie Newmann, one of their faithful customers, stopped in. Mind you, she wasn't there to shop; no, she would wait for the weekend to do that. She was there for only one thing, the thing that seemed to be her sole reason for being on this earth—to talk. And God, could she talk and talk and talk! It was the girls' lamentable misfortune that they were the captive recipients of so much of that talk. It had also been irrevocably demonstrated in previous encounters that Angie, while being an insistently irritating thorn in Joanie's side, was proving herself to be Emma's own personal Waterloo. She simply could not hold it together for the duration of one of Angie's marathon conversations.

Once they spotted her coming through the door, the girls' mournful groans along with a few muttered "Oh, shits" almost drowned out Angie's greeting.

"Hi, Emma. Hi, Joanie."

"Hi, Angie," both girls chorused with about the same amount of enthusiasm you'd expect when being led to your own death.

Cole and Tank had been behind the counter playing with some squeaky toys, but when they'd heard Angie's voice they'd snatched up their toys and beat a hasty retreat to the back room. They weren't any more enamored of her long dissertations than the girls were. Emma and Joanie watched them go, green with envy.

"What're you doing?"

"Getting ready for the Open House, Angie."

"Really?"

"Yep."

"It starts tomorrow, right?"

"Right, Ang." Drawing from past experiences, the girls were taking turns answering her. They figured that way maybe they could outlast her, or at the very least stay even.

"It continues all weekend, doesn't it?"

"Yep."

"That means it's still going on all Saturday and Sunday, right?"

"That's what it means, Ang."

"I don't know which day I'm coming yet. I've been thinking about it, but I still haven't decided. Which day is better?"

"What do you mean? I don't get ya," Joanie said.

"You know."

"No, I don't think I do."

"Well, what's the best day to come?"

"The best day for what?"

"To come."

"For what?"

"The stuff."

It was Emma's turn to field this response and she spoke with all the sincerity she could muster. "They're all good, Angie. We have a lot of people here on all three days. The 'stuff' is here for the whole weekend and you know what else? I'll tell you a little secret." Emma motioned her closer with a crook of her finger. Angie leaned in. "The 'stuff' is here right up until after Christmas. But don't tell anybody, that'll be just between us." Emma raised one eyebrow and gave her a conspiratorial wink.

"Oh, I won't," Angie responded in all seriousness.

"Good. I knew I could trust you." Emma derived such pleasure screwing with Angie's mind. And it was so damn easy.

"Oh, you can trust me. I won't breathe a word. But what's the best day?"

Shit! They were back to square one. "Whatever day you want to come is the best day," Joanie said, getting a tiny bit exasperated. Emma had already passed her on that score.

"Yeah? You think so?"

"Definitely."

"Okay, then I think I'll come on...Saturday!"

Halleluiah! They'd won! She'd finally committed to a day. It was all the girls could do not to break out in cheers.

"That's the best day then, Angie." Joanie could barely keep a straight face.

"What do you think, Emma?"

"Oh, I agree. That's the best day."

"You're sure?"

"We're sure." Both Emma and Joanie were nodding their heads in the affirmative with solemn looks on their faces, although they didn't know how long they could hold on to it. Emma had to stick her tongue into her cheek so as not to laugh and Joanie was pinching herself hard to maintain her somber expression. She'd probably end up with a bruise, but it'd be well worth it if they could now get Angie out the door.

"Did you get a lot of new stuff in?"

Damn! They'd been so close, but that question dashed all hope. She wasn't going to leave. She was still on a roll and she was back to "stuff".

Resigned to their fate, Emma answered the query, "Yeah, quite a bit."

"What'd you get?"

"What do you mean what'd we get?"

"The new stuff, what did you get?"

"You mean you want to know what all the new stuff is that we have in the shop?"

"Yeah."

"Right now?"

"Well, yeah. You know, just run down what's new since the last time I was in."

"Since the last time you were in?"

"Yeah. You can do that, right?"

"Let me see if I understand you." Emma was staring at Angie as though she had two heads. Scratch that, she barely had one. "You want us to list everything that's new since the last time you were in. Is that correct? Am I understanding you right?" Emma's voice was getting an ominous tone to it. Joanie, knowing the danger signs with her partner was inching a little closer to Emma.

"Yeah. It shouldn't be too hard, should it? It seems simple enough, at least to me. Hey, I have an idea. You could walk around the shop with me and point everything out. That would work, wouldn't it?"

Emma looked at Joanie and Joanie looked at Emma. Then they both looked away because the same thought was going through each of their minds: *Angie, you'd better get the hell out of here now before we kill you.* Joanie kicked Emma's foot, knowing she could easily give voice to the thought. There was a beat or two of silence before a greatly restrained Joanie answered their perilously-close-to-death customer.

"Angie. We would love to do that for you, but we're extremely busy right now and can't take the time. We will happily do it for you at another time."

"Why can't you do it now? Why are you so busy?"

Emma put both hands up to either side of her head and rubbed her temples using hard little circular strokes. Maybe if she applied enough pressure she could keep intact a brain that was sure to blow if she had to listen to Angie for much longer. They'd come full circle once more, as every conversation with this woman seemed to do. Gathering every bit of civility that she possessed, Emma answered Angie's questions.

"We can't do it now because we're busy getting ready for the Open House that starts tomorrow."

"Oh, yeah. Tomorrow, that's Friday. I wonder if I should come then."

Joanie grabbed Emma before she could vault over the counter, although *she* was ready to get the staple gun out and start shooting. Thank God, higher powers intervened and the UPS man arrived and defused the situation. He brought in a total of eight boxes and deposited them in the back room. Joanie signed for the delivery and ran—she did not walk—to the back of the shop, leaving Emma alone with Angie. Emma would have to get even with her for that later.

Emma decided to take a bold step, the only one that could possibly save Angie's life. She had no choice really, especially now that her partner had left her to her own devices. The coward! Besides, if she was in jail for the murder of Angie Newmann this weekend, there was no way Joanie would be able to handle the Open House by herself. So, for the sake of the business and her friend's peace of mind, she decided her only course of action was to be rude and leave Angie "hanging" as it were.

"Sorry, Ang. Got to go. Big delivery to unpack. Can't talk any more. We'll be busy the rest of the day. See you this weekend." Emma was talking a mile a minute in short little bursts, throwing the words over her shoulder as she quickly moved away from the counter and toward the back room, leaving Angie standing there by herself. She wasn't going to give the lunatic any choice but to leave the store.

Even so, it took Angie a full three minutes (the girls knew this because Joanie timed it from where she'd hidden behind the stack of cartons) before she realized the conversation was at an end and maybe she should leave. Finally, she got the hint and called out a cheery "goodbye" to the girls. When no return salutation came from the back room, she hesitated another second or two, but then shrugged and left the premises.

Emma and Joanie breathed a sigh of profound relief when they heard the front door open and then close. They took one look at each other and decided they didn't care what time it was; they were having a glass of wine. They'd been snatched back from the brink of committing a heinous crime only by sheer will and rude behavior. Thank God for giving them their well-honed talent for being obnoxious!

* * * *

After the shop closed, and it closed a little later than usual because the girls had had so much to do, Emma went home to start the baking. But first she needed a break and figured Cole did too. After opening up the house, she flipped the yard lights on and they went back outside for a little fun. She roughhoused a little with the big dog, and then sent him out to retrieve the balls she'd thrown. The air was cold, but not bitterly so and it rather invigorated the both of them. The skies were free of clouds and the stars were already twinkling brightly in the nighttime darkness. The wind was calm; not a branch was stirring on the maple and birch trees that dotted Emma's property. There wasn't so much as a puff of wind whispering through the pines. Conditions were perfect for the temperature to plummet by morning. The chrysanthemums' days were sorely numbered.

Cole had a lot of energy to expend, regardless of his forays with Tank all day, so he was happy to race all over the yard chasing the balls and bringing them back to Emma. For Emma, it was a chance to clear her head, take a breath, and just enjoy her dog.

Half an hour later, Emma dragged the mums back into the mudroom while Cole performed his sniff test on each and every pot. Satisfied, he gave his attention to the ice cubes that Emma had placed in the water bowl in his dining rack. He licked and crunched away while she made herself a quick dinner. Tonight there was no time for fussing so she simply made a sandwich of ham and Swiss on rye bread, topping it with lettuce, tomato, and a little ranch dressing. She plucked a dill pickle from the jar to eat with it and dug in. She gave Cole a slice of cheese and promised him dinner in a little while.

Once Emma had finished, she cleared her dishes, grabbed a Diet Pepsi (the caffeine would, she was sure, help get her through the night), made sure Cole was set, and prepared for the next round.

The first thing she did was to load the CD player with her musical selections for the evening. Her choices included Frank Sinatra, Jimmy Buffet, Alan Jackson, Buddy Guy, and the Vaughan Brothers. That eclectic mix should keep her hopping! Nothing like good music to keep you company when you're working (not to mention keeping you awake). So while "Old Blue Eyes" started off the night's concert, Emma organized her baking.

She was going to make five things: Chocolate Chip Sour Cream Scones, Apple Crisp, Pumpkin Raisin Cookies, Chocolate Peanut Butter Brownies, and Cranberry Orange Muffins. She'd start with the scones because they took the hottest oven and work her way down from there. It was going to be a very long night. Emma hoped that Joanie had at least figured out what she was making by now.

\* \* \* \*

During the wee hours of the morning, while Emma was elbow-deep in baking and hopefully Joanie was too, Moira Spenser, who lived in Pittsford, on the outskirts of Rochester, New York, woke up screaming. Bolting upright in her queen-size bed, her body was quaking, her nightgown soaked through with sweat. Dragging air in through her open mouth, she frantically pulled herself out of the nightmare and into the reality of her bedroom. Blinking her eyes rapidly to bring the room into focus, she fought to regulate her breathing and swallowed down the urge to throw up.

When she'd steadied herself somewhat, she turned the bedside lamp on with fingers that were still shaking and allowed her eyes to adjust to the soft illumination of the low-wattage bulb. She scanned the room, taking in the pale yellow flocked wallpaper, the cream colored throw rugs scattered over the hardwood floor, the golden oak dresser and armoire, the bedside chair upholstered in fabric embroidered with tiny yellow flowers on an oyster white background. She let her eyes rest on the *Southern Living* magazine lying on the seat of the chair and read a few words on the cover, forcing her mind to fixate on the here and now.

After a few seconds she swung her legs out of the bed and carefully placed her bare feet on the floor. She pulled herself up on shaky limbs and walked unsteadily to the adjoining bathroom. Holding on to the doorjamb with one hand, she reached inside and to the right with the other and flipped the light switch on. She let her eyes adapt to the brighter light and then crossed over to the white pedestal sink, grabbing hold of it with both hands. She fastened her eyes on the Peerless faucet and scrutinized the chrome fixture with an intensity that suggested her very existence depended on it. Minutes ticked by. She finally broke her tunneled concentration and slowly lifted her head until she was looking into the mirror hanging above the sink. Her fear-stricken face stared back at her. She turned away in disgust and ran the cold water. She splashed water on her face with both hands and then with her eyes still closed, she reached for and found a towel. Bringing the towel up to cover her face, she held it in place and stayed that way for nearly five minutes. When she at last brought the towel down and opened her eyes, her fear was gone, replaced by a simmering rage as the nightmare faded.

She looked at the clock that hung on the wall to the right of the mirror. It was 3:30 in the morning. She knew she wouldn't be getting any more sleep that night. That was okay; she could deal with it. She breathed in deeply and then exhaled; she did it again. She leaned back against the wall, closed her eyes once more, and sorted through her thoughts.

She had to remember to stay focused, to let her fury drive out the paralyzing fear. She couldn't let the nightmare gain control. The time had finally come. She was going to start to exact her revenge this coming weekend. She was ready to punish those who had taken away her face and self. She'd done all her homework; she knew what to expect. Everything was in place. It was going to be so easy. All she had to do was keep herself together. That's all she had to do—just keep herself together. She repeated that thought over and over like a mantra, chanting it in a singsong manner. *Just keep yourself together... Just keep yourself together... Just keep yourself together...*

After a few minutes, she felt more in control and opened her eyes. Moira stood upright and walked over to the bathtub, pushed the curtain aside, and ran the shower. She adjusted the water, stripped off her wet nightgown in one fluid movement, and stepped into the tub. The hot water sluiced over her naked body. She stood there like a statue with her head thrown back and her arms crossed beneath her breasts letting the pounding water wash away any remaining remnants of her torment and infusing her with the strength she was going to need.

# Chapter Four

Friday was a miserable, wet, windy, cold, raw day. The temperature was in the low forties, the wind was howling at a steady twenty-five miles per hour with gusts up to forty-five, and the ice-cold rain was coming down in buckets. Forecasters were predicting a good chance of wet snow especially in the higher elevations later that night when the temperature dropped to the low thirties. That meant the area where Emma lived was probably going to have snow on the ground in the morning; she wasn't at all happy about it and that was an understatement. It was far too early in the season for the white stuff as far as she was concerned. She actually didn't want to see snow until December 24th and then only for a day. What more could any sane person possibly need or want? Forget those damn skiers and outdoor enthusiasts; they were all certifiable.

On that less than perfect morning, Emma had skipped her exercise and Cole's roading. She was too darn tired and since Cole had kept her company most of the night, she guessed he wasn't any more energetic than she was. Besides, they'd be getting enough of a workout waiting on customers all day.

Emma had to make two runs down to the shop in the Explorer. She'd brought Cole down the first time and had deposited him safely inside. On her second trip she delivered all the baked goods she'd been up most of the night making. Dashing through the wind-driven rain she managed to get everything inside although it had taken several trips back and forth to the car to do it. By the time she'd gotten the last of it in, she was dripping wet and cold to the bone. She hurried to crank up the furnace.

The shop's heating system was forced air and, along with the modern heating ducts that conveyed the hot air, there was a large old-fashioned grate in the hardwood floor near the sales counter where an abundance of welcomed heat came up. It was to there that Emma gravitated as soon as she had relieved herself of her burdens. Legs spread wide on either side of the grate, Emma stood over the billowing heat, letting it take the chill away. Granted, the position was none too graceful or ladylike, but it got the job done. It only took a few minutes and then she had to move; she was getting too hot. Of course, it might have helped if she'd first divested herself of her coat, but she'd been too cold to even do that initially. No matter, now the rain had been dried off her coat as well.

She called Cole over and had him straddle the thing too. He was used to dryers blowing on him to dry his coat, so this was perfectly agreeable to him. For little Sydney—now that was another matter altogether. She didn't take kindly to it in the least. In fact, she avoided the grate like the plague, making a wide circle around it whenever she heard the furnace roar to life. There were monsters down that thing, didn't you know, and the hot air rushing out of it was from the fire coming out of their mouths. She wasn't going to be fooled by any silly explanation her Grammy gave her either. No way, uh-uh!

Joanie and Tank arrived just as Emma was finishing getting everything turned on, and up and running. Emma waited just inside the door and relieved Joanie of the various containers that housed her contributions to the refreshment table. Joanie was able to shuttle back and forth to her truck quickly and the two of them made short work of it using the relay method. As soon as Joanie was in for the last time, she too took a turn over the grate, soaking up the heat and drying out.

Then it was a mad flurry of activity to get the refreshment table set up, the desserts cut up and on serving platters, the coffee brewed, and the cider poured. It was 9:38 when the first customers came through the door. Ready or not, this was it!

There was never a break in the action the entire day in spite of the weather, which could sometimes have a noticeably adverse affect on business. There was a steady stream of customers flowing through the shop and the girls were on the go pretty much like they were running a marathon. Neither one of them had had more than three hours of sleep and they were operating on fumes of energy. It was a miracle they were clear-headed enough to ring sales up and have the transactions come out correctly. Thank God a lot of what they did was so ingrained after ten years in business that they didn't have to think twice about it.

One of the bright spots of the day was the appearance of Emma's Aunt Agnes and Uncle Lou. Uncle Lou was attired in his usual black suit, white shirt, and black socks and shoes. The Open House was an informal affair, so he was without his black tie. Hence, his casual look. He was as dressed-down as he ever got.

Aunt Agnes, on the other hand, was a whirling dervish of sparkling gold and silver. All 4'10" of her was bedecked with enough jewelry to open her own store. It was a good thing she was almost as wide as she was tall because if her center of gravity were any higher she would have fallen flat on her face from the sheer weight of her jewels. How she managed to wear that amount of watches, bracelets, necklaces, rings, pins, and earrings was anybody's guess. It must take her forever just to get all her jewelry on, much less decide where it was all going to go, especially those pins.

Last June she'd gotten her nose pierced (Aunt Agnes was in her very late seventies, quickly approaching eighty) and Emma had made it a point to talk to Uncle Lou about reining her in a little bit. Uncle Lou had assured Emma that he'd handle it. Yeah, well, from what Emma could see as she hugged her aunt in greeting, he either hadn't been fast enough or he'd failed completely because staring Emma right in the face was a bright, shiny gold hoop going straight through her aunt's right eyebrow.

Over the top of her aunt's head Emma shot her uncle an I-thought-you-were-going-to-take-care-of-this look. He merely shrugged and lifted his hands in a gesture of defeat. Emma could only hope that Aunt Agnes would stop now with the piercings. If she got anymore Emma really didn't want to know about them or where they were, particularly if they weren't readily visible to the naked eye.

"Why, Emma, you've got yourself quite the turnout, don't you?" Aunt Agnes observed, looking around the shop.

"Yeah, we've got a good crowd."

"I hope tomorrow and Sunday are just as good. If they are, you should do very well."

"Saturday will be even busier, Aunt Agnes. It always is. Sunday's usually a little lighter, but we should still do really well."

"Do you and Joanie need any help? I'd be glad to stay."

"No, I think we're all set. We've got Tammy coming in tomorrow to help, but we've got everything under control today. Joanie and I'll be fine, but thanks for offering."

"Anytime, sweetie… Tammy's coming in tomorrow?" Tammy Brochton, in her mid twenties and cute as a button, worked part time at the shop.

"Yeah, we'll have her restock when things get low and she'll keep an eye on the dessert table for us."

"Did you know that I've kind of taken her under my wing?"

"*Nooo*, didn't know that." Emma did a mental uh-oh. "When did this happen?"

"Oh, I don't know. I guess it was a month or two ago. It was one of those times we watched the shop for you."

"Which one?" Emma asked, immediately suspicious.

"I'm sure I don't remember exactly, dear, but one of them."

"Is there anything I should know, Aunt Agnes? Did anything happen that was… shall we say 'eventful' when you decided to take Tammy on?"

"Oh, no, dear. Nothing. Nothing at all." Aunt Agnes couldn't quite meet Emma's eyes.

Emma waited half a beat, then forced her aunt to look her in the eye. "You're not going to tell me, are you?"

"Nothing to tell."

"Uh-huh. Just tell me this. Was there any physical injury involved? Are we going to be sued? Are we going to have to go to court?" *Are we going to lose everything we own*?

"Oh, no, dear."

"You're sure?"

"Yes, sweetie."

"I don't have to worry about anything?"

"No, dear."

"You're positive?"

"Quite."

"You promise?"

"On your dead mother's grave."

"All right." Emma couldn't argue with that one. "So... how is this 'under your wing' thing working out or should I even ask?"

"Oh, no. That's fine; ask away. I think it's working very well. She's a lovely young woman, you know."

"Yes, she is lovely." That's not all she is, Emma thought.

"She just needs a little direction."

"You could say that."

"We simply need to keep her earthbound."

"That's a unique way of putting it, Aunt Agnes."

"Yes, well... she does tend to leave this plateau for another."

"I think she leaves it for more than one."

"Emma, dear, don't be unkind."

"Sorry, Aunt Agnes, I thought I was being honest."

"Yes, well, we're working on it."

"I think it'll be a long process."

"I'm afraid you might be right, but then nothing worthwhile is ever easy."

"I guess, but I think you've got your hands full."

"Yes, you're probably right, but I'll persevere."

"I have no doubts. But I'll put you on the prayer list just in case, although I don't know exactly what I'll say the problem is. Maybe... well, I'll think of something."

"I'm sure you will and thank you, dear. By the way, Grace and I are all set for next week. You and Joanie don't need to worry about a thing. I'm sure we won't have any problems."

Grace Foster, another long-time customer, was an elderly woman who embodied the picture of wealth and propriety. She and Aunt Agnes, upon meeting several months ago, had somehow been attracted to one another and had formed an unholy alliance. An odder combination you never saw, but together they were two very tough little old ladies who didn't let their advanced years get in the way of anything they wanted to do, including expanding their knowledge in the latest in sexual gratification. In fact, much to Emma's surprise, it was her aunt who'd played a major role in bringing her up to speed at a sex ed party Joanie had hosted when Emma was getting back in the dating game. It had been a little disconcerting for Emma—and that was putting it mildly!

"I'm sure everything will be fine. We have every confidence in you."

"Well, thank you, dear. That's very nice of you to say. Who's going to take the weekend?"

"My cousin Jackie."

"Jackie… Jackie… oh, of course, Jackie McCoy. I don't know where my head is sometimes. She's on your father's side of the family, isn't she?"

"Mm-hmm. That's right. She'll come out after work on Friday and stay at my house. She's very good. We don't have to worry when she's here either."

Emma and Joanie, along with Sally, were going to a dog show next week, namely the Fall Leatherstocking Cluster, and had to get coverage for the shop for Thursday, Friday, Saturday, and Sunday. They'd divided the time between the elderly women working as a team and Emma's competent cousin.

"Well, if she needs any help, Grace and I would be happy to come in."

"I know you would, Aunt Agnes, but Jackie should be fine. She's helped us out before and never had a problem."

"Well, just in case, you should let her know that we're available. Leave our phone numbers with her, all right?"

"Sure. I'll do that." Emma turned away from her aunt, trying to hide a grin. Whenever the two older women helped out in the shop, they very quickly took it over and were extremely reluctant to give it back. The girls, most times, had to negotiate to regain control. There was no doubt in Emma's mind that poor Jackie would have lots of company and "help" on the weekend.

Having spied her husband sampling the wares on the refreshment table, Aunt Agnes excused herself and joined him. She'd wait to shop until after her sweet tooth had been satisfied and then look out, she'd be on a tear. Uncle Lou would be pressed into service as a pack mule and the charge cards would be smoking. God, she was a kick!

Another bright spot, probably the best one of the day, was that Angie Newmann *didn't* show up. With the girls' lack of sleep, their patience levels were at the non-existent level and she could have very well been maimed for life once that mouth of hers got going. It would have been an ugly scene what with Emma and Joanie going ballistic in front of witnesses. There would have been no holding them back and prison bars would have loomed in their immediate future.

Joanie chalked Angie's absence up to divine intervention. She liked to invoke that whenever she could. If she was honest though, she'd admit that she'd helped things along a little by saying several prayers while baking, asking that they be spared Angie's presence that day. Hopefully by tomorrow the girls would be rested enough to be their usual civil, if not diplomatic, selves and able to deal discreetly with the woman who was fully capable of out-talking a United States senator filibustering on the legislative floor.

The day was over before they knew it and the girls were both exhausted and hungry. They could only eat so many desserts before real food was needed and there hadn't been any time for that. So by the time six o'clock rolled around, they were ravenous, but too tired to do anything about it. With gritty eyes and drooping eyelids, bed seemed a much more attainable goal than decent food, especially if they were supposed to make it themselves. And that just wasn't going to happen. Imagine how thrilled they were when Sam and Ben showed up with pizza and beer ten minutes after they closed.

Ben Sievers, also a retired FBI Special Agent, had moved back to the area earlier that year from Massachusetts and had been dating Emma for the last six months. They were wildly attracted to one another and had an oh-so-wonderful relationship. Ben matched Emma in age, which is to say he was fifty-five, was over six foot tall and had curly black hair with just a touch of gray at the temples. He had a moustache that drove Emma wild and a physique that made her heart flutter. Ben had fallen for Emma the first time he'd seen her and had been putty in her hands ever since,

Even so, Emma's son, Mack kept a protective eye on the situation to ensure his mother was treated well. Regardless of the fact he lived in Connecticut, he managed to get regular reports of the goings on between Emma and Ben. Seems that he employed a network of spies made up of friends he went to high school with to get the job done. Eric, Scott, and Bob were only too happy to keep tabs on Mack's mother. She'd kept enough tabs on all of them while they were growing up. They all took quite naturally to the role reversal and with three against one, Ben didn't stand a chance of getting away with anything. Fact is, if Ben mistreated Emma in any way he'd be answering not only to Mack, but to his three friends as well. It was a wonder he stuck around what with being constantly put under a microscope and all. Must be he liked Emma more than just a little bit. Oh hell, let's not beat around the bush; he was nuts about her.

The girls managed to get things cleaned up and shut down as quickly as their sleep-deprived bodies would allow. They passed out paper plates and napkins while the men got extra chairs. Joanie brought the wine and glasses out; the men popped the tops of their beer cans. Joanie poured and Emma gratefully sipped. Both girls sank thankfully into their chairs and then dove into the food. The cheesy pepperoni, mushroom, and banana pepper pizza was distributed quickly and after the girls had taken their first bites they were making noises comparable to Meg Ryan in her famous restaurant scene in *When Harry Met Sally.* The moans of appreciation and satisfaction emanating from Emma and Joanie had both men checking to make sure that the only activity the girls were engaged in was eating pizza.

"Oh, God, this is good. Mmmm," Joanie said, her eyes closed in ecstasy.

"Lord, I needed this," Emma breathed, her eyes at half-mast and with a faraway look.

"I need more." Joanie reached for another piece. "I am *sooo* hungry."

"This feels so good going down." Emma's head dropped back as she savored the taste. "Mmm, Mmm, Mmm." Both girls looked like their bones were melting they were getting so relaxed. Big glasses of wine and hardly any sleep will do that to you. If they stayed where they were, they'd probably be asleep in the next ten minutes, regardless of the food they were shoving in their mouths.

"Hey, girls? If Ben and I weren't so confident of our masculinity we might be jealous over your present involvement with this pizza. You're making quite the fuss. It is only food, you know."

"Maybe to you it's only food, but to us it's heaven. We haven't had anything decent to eat all day."

"What are you talking about? Look at all the food you two made."

"Sam, desserts don't count. We get sick of them real fast. Besides, after a person spends all night making 'em, they kind of lose their appeal."

"Not to me they don't."

"Yeah, but you didn't make 'em, you only smelled 'em."

"Ben, let's see if we can disprove their theory, at least the part about getting sick of them real fast. Where should we start?" Sam's eyes got big and his mouth watered in anticipation.

"Oh, no, you don't," Joanie protested, putting a halt to their dessert fantasies. "You can each have one thing. This stuff has to get us through the weekend. If we have to bake any more we're going to press you boys into service."

"Oh, God, not that! Anything but that!" Sam had put his hands up as if to ward off evil spirits. "All right, girls, you win. We'll only take one thing."

Sam and Ben made their solitary choice after much deliberation, but they made extremely short work of eating it. The dogs had been hanging around, waiting for scraps, but were now getting a little impatient. Through minding his manners, Tank was doing vertical springs on his back legs and kind of looked like a jack-in-the-box every time his head cleared the table. Cole was being a little more passive, but making his point nevertheless. He'd put his big head in Emma's lap and his ever-abundant drool was soaking her jeans. The girls got the message; it was definitely time to give them their share. With the banana peppers stripped off, the dogs were given several bites of the pizza. They deserved it; they'd put in a full day too.

Cole had performed his usual task of carrying bags for the ladies out to their cars. Every once in a while he'd even carried someone's purse so they'd have two hands free to shop. Nobody ever complained about the bit of drool that was left on their handles. Tank, well, he had entertained. He was too short to do much of anything else. Besides it was his God-given talent; he was a natural clown, although at times an evil-minded one and he didn't have to exert himself a whole hell of a lot to get people laughing.

When everyone, dogs included, had eaten their fill (not exactly a true statement—the dogs would have eaten until they exploded, but their owners had decided that they'd had enough), the girls cleaned up the remains of dinner and closed up. Out in the parking lot, goodbyes were said amongst the four with Joanie and Sam taking off for home in their separate vehicles. Ben walked Emma to her SUV and once Cole was safely inside, took her into his arms and gave her a kiss that curled her toes.

"Mmm, that was nice," Emma said when she came up for air. God, he still affected her just like the first time he'd ever kissed her—she turned to instant mush.

"If you liked that, I've got plenty more where that came from," Ben grinned.

"I have no doubts about that," Emma smiled. Ben kissed her again and Emma started to float, forgetting just how tired she was. Were her feet even on the ground anymore? "Would you like to come up to the house?"

"You know I'd love to, but aren't you too tired?" Ben nuzzled her neck, his wondrously sexy moustache brushing against her skin. He planted small quick kisses along her jawline. Emma went completely limp.

"I was extremely tired until a few minutes ago, but I think I've been inspired to rally. Hop in, I'll drive you up."

Ben didn't need a second invitation; he was around the car and inside quick as a wink. Emma put the Explorer in gear and they took off for the house.

# Chapter Five

On Saturday, Emma woke refreshed, but wary. Ben hadn't stayed too late, much to Emma's regret, and once she'd gotten into bed, to sleep that is, she'd been totally relaxed and had instantly gone off to dreamland with an exceptionally satisfied smile on her face. She'd been giving an excellent imitation of a comatose person until five o'clock that morning.

The wariness came from what she thought she might find when she looked out her bedroom window as predicated by the forecast from the day before. She got out of bed very slowly after Cole awakened her with his version of a kiss and approached the window on tiptoes. Like whatever was out there was going to hear her? Cole, having jumped down to the floor from the bed, was cocking his head from one side to the other trying to figure out what she was doing. This wasn't how things usually worked in the morning. Emma gave him a quick look and held up one finger. "Hang on a minute, big boy. I've got to see if it's here."

Cole wondered what she was talking about and a second later he knew.

"Ohhh shit! There's snow on the ground. Damn!" Emma was, in a word, pissed. She actually stomped her feet and a surprised Cole backed up, thinking, "Whoa, she's lost it."

Emma stopped her tantrum when she realized her dog was looking at her like she'd lost her mind and rightly so. Pushing her pajama bottoms off, she pulled her jeans on and stepped into her sneakers. "Might as well get this over with, Cole. Damn. I can't believe that crap's out there. It isn't fair, guy; it's way too early."

They made it as far as the mudroom before Emma stopped. "Hang on, Cole. I've got to get my friggin' boots on. Give the flowers a sniff while I find 'em."

Cole gave her a look that said she was acting like a maniac and gladly switched his attention to the mums that looked like they were probably on their last legs.

Intent on finding her boots, Emma dropped to all fours. As she searched the floor of the planked pine closet, she mumbled to herself, "Son of a bitchin' snow! Where are the damn things? Oh, here. Hell, I'd better pull out my winter jacket too."

Once she was finally booted and jacketed, Emma led the way outside. She put Cole in his kennel run, guessing she was walking through approximately two inches of wet, slushy, cold snow. It was enough to make you want to puke and Emma hated to puke. Cole, on the other hand, was quite happy with the white stuff. He was eating it like there was no tomorrow, pushing his nose through it like a plow. When he had enough bunched up, he chomped on it and after rolling it around in his mouth for a second or two, swallowed it down. If he keeps that up, Emma thought, he'll have to pee non-stop all day.

With determined steps, she strode back into the house and took herself off to the bathroom. When she next appeared, she had a somewhat brighter outlook, probably because her snow-and-cold-jolted bladder had been mercifully relieved. Emma snapped the radio on for the weather report. Two songs later, she got it. The forecast for the day was temperature in the mid thirties with wet snow and winds between fifteen and twenty miles per hour. The good news was there wasn't supposed to be any accumulation. Yeah, Emma thought, tell me another one. I've already walked through two freakin' inches of the stuff. Emma closed her eyes and wished herself off to the Hawaiian Islands. Lord, she'd give just about anything to be there. Someday, she promised herself, but first she had to live through another winter. Damn the luck!

Emma got Cole in; he was so happy he could hardly stand still. Never mind that his feet were soaked from the wet snow and he was dripping wet right up to his belly. What did he care? He'd had a great time in all that slush. Hurrah for him! Emma thought; now I get to clean up the mess. She grabbed a couple of towels from the closet and went to work. They were soaked in no time; he was a lot of dog to dry off. But she'd gotten the worst of it; at least he wasn't dripping all over the floor any more. For the time being she wasn't going to worry about the mess in the mudroom; that could wait until later.

Next she hustled Cole downstairs to the basement, the door to which was conveniently in the mudroom, and put him in his crate. She was moving to pull the dryers over when she stopped dead in her tracks. Shit! It'd dawned on her at that moment that she was going to have to do this all over again after their run. Double shit! Geez, she didn't need this today. Ranting about what she'd like to do with the snow in the bluest of terms, she turned the two big dryers on and left them to finish the drying job. This whole snow mess thing had not been on the agenda and was going to wreak havoc with the morning schedule. Wouldn't you know it was on a morning they had to be at work a little early.

Snow cleanup could be way worse than rain cleanup a lot of the time. With rain you simply mopped up the water, whether it was on the dog or the floor, and you were done. Even if mud was involved, you either rinsed it off and dried the dog, or let the mud dry and then brushed it out. Snow cleanup seemed to go on forever because the stuff kept melting and creating more water. At least wet snow didn't form those hard little balls that clung to the fur and in between the dog's toes, and could take what seemed like forever to melt. Those little balls of hard-packed snow were practically impossible to remove manually, so you had to wait for them to liquefy on their own. Although wet snow could get lodged in between the pads of the feet, it didn't take nearly as long to turn to water once it was exposed to the warmth of a house. In addition to the snow though, Emma also had to deal with the road salt and grit that mixed in with it. The combination made a dirty mess that coated Cole's feet and legs, and splashed up onto his belly. And that meant that when they got back from their run, Emma was going to have to rinse off Cole's affected body parts on a day when she was really pressed for time. Nevertheless, It was especially important to get the corrosive road salt off Cole's foot pads because it could cause burns to the tissue if not removed.

Emma went into power mode and decided to launch into her exercise while Cole dried off. She opted to do only a two-mile workout, so she could finish in half the time she originally thought she'd have. Uppermost in her mind was that they had to be down at the shop by 9:30 at the latest; the ladies never waited, as evidenced by the day before, until the official opening time of 10:00 to start coming. Not on Open House weekend!

Emma checked on Cole, found he was still wet and left him where he was, the dryers blasting away. She ran back upstairs, threw some cereal in a bowl, splashed it with milk, and gulped it down. She flew into the bathroom, took a five-minute shower, dressed, did makeup and hair, and went to get Cole. He was dry, thank God.

Emma bundled up and headed out to the Explorer. Cole jumped in when she opened the back, Emma threw the bike in, and they were off in nothing flat. It wasn't until they were down the hill and going through the parking lot that Emma gave any thought to the roads. One quick look told her they'd been cleared; the plows had already been out. Thank you, Lord! Now if only the road up at the park was clear, she'd be all set.

Five minutes later, she was pulling into the Sprague Brook parking lot and saw that her wish had been granted. There was no snow on the roadway. Hallelujah! She and Cole quickly disembarked and set off on their hike. Some of that forecasted non-accumulating snow started to come down and by the time they were finished, both Cole and Emma wore a blanket of the white stuff. Emma brushed herself off and had Cole give himself a few good shakes before she got him back in the car. Non-accumulating my ass, she thought as she brushed off the windshield.

\* \* \* \*

By the time Emma and Cole got down to the shop, which was at 9:31, they were met by total chaos. Joanie was there, but what she was doing was anybody's guess and how she had lost control so quickly was up for grabs. Emma waded through a throng of excited shoppers and finally corralled Joanie near the coffee pot.

"What the hell is going on?"

"Don't ask me."

"Well, who should I ask?"

"Maybe somebody other than me."

"I think you're the only one here I can ask. I doubt that little old lady over there will be any help. What happened?"

"I don't know. I got here, I opened up, I started the coffee, and the next thing I knew we were being overrun with crazed shoppers."

"All of these people came at the same time?"

"Yeah. It was like the dike broke. They just flooded in here all at once."

"Well, hell. That's great, but we better get on top of things. You take the register. I'll get the baked goods and cider out."

"Okay, but don't take too long. I'm going to need you to wrap and bag. If everybody decides to leave at once we'll be in deep shit. The line will be out the door."

"All right, I'll be quick. Is everything else done? Everything on?"

Joanie nodded and Emma was off and running. As soon as she had the refreshment table set up, she went to join her friend at the register. As predicted, the group was all leaving at the same time.

They must have come on a bus or something, Emma thought, although she hadn't seen one in the lot when she'd come in. Maybe the driver had gone and had breakfast at the little restaurant down in Colden, the town that was a mere three miles up the road. That was probably it; otherwise they would've had to get there via Scotty beaming them down because there were not enough cars in the parking lot to accommodate all these people. Hmmm... Now that was a thought Tammy, their oftentimes air-headed employee, could wrap herself around. Emma bet she would just love to hook up with old Scotty. It would most likely be a dream come true for the girl.

It took them thirty-five minutes, but they finally cashed out the last of the supposed bus group and had them out the door. Meanwhile, however, other shoppers had been coming in and there was no end in sight. The shop was full of people and Emma and Joanie had no choice but to stay at their stations. There was a constant line of people waiting to be checked out and at times the line wound through the store all the way to the front of the building.

Thankfully, Tammy had appeared in the midst of the bus group's leaving and was already restocking some of the merchandise. Her entrance had caused Joanie to do a double take and she in turn gave Emma an elbow nudge. Emma took one look, closed her eyes to the spectacle before her, and groaned.

"Oh, Lord, help me," Emma prayed. "She said she took her under her wing but I didn't think she meant this."

"I don't know if I can handle it," Joanie said, rubbing her forehead.

"This better be a trade-off for Tammy staying in sync with the world around her."

"If it's not, I quit."

"You can't quit; you own the place."

"I don't care. I'll gladly deed everything over to you."

"Well, I don't want it if you're not here."

"Fine, we'll give it to Aunt Agnes."

"Okay by me…Oh, Lord, look at her."

Tammy was neatly dressed in a baseball cap, which seemed to be a permanent part of all her ensembles, a royal blue turtleneck sweater, tan Dockers, socks and sneakers. All pretty normal. What wasn't normal was the amount of jewelry she was wearing. Tammy usually only wore one pair of earrings, a watch, one or two rings, and a bracelet. If she was really spiffed up, she added a necklace.

What the girls were looking at now was an Aunt Agnes clone in training! Tammy was decked from head to toe in gold and silver, the quantity only slightly less than her mentor's. It was probably only the constraints of her wallet that had prohibited her from looking like an exact replica of Emma's relation. But she had a good start! Emma counted two additional ear piercings in each lobe, there were at least four necklaces around her neck, and every finger had a ring, Emma could make out five bracelets on her right wrist, and there were—oh, my God!—three watches on her left arm. Bring her up to speed with pins, increase the number of the other pieces, add a few more piercings, and she'd be a dead-on duplicate for Emma's eccentric aunt. Holy shit!

Joanie snapped back first to the possible implications this newest development posed. "Is your Aunt Agnes bringing Tammy in to work with her and Mrs. Foster?"

"She didn't say."

"You'd better find out."

"Do we really want to know?"

"I think that would be smart."

"I think you're right."

"If she is, we'd better lay down some rules."

"Like what?"

"Like Tammy better not get near a sales book. No way do I want to have to decipher her receipts."

"I think they're supposed to be working on that."

"Well, until it's perfected I don't want her near the register."

"All right, I'll let Aunt Agnes know."

"Okay, but make her take a solemn oath just to make sure."

"How's this— I'll tie her up and torture her until she promises #1 not to abandon her post at the register and #2 to guard the sales book with her life. Failure to do either will result in a hideous death."

"Sounds good to me."

"You've gone over the edge. You know that, don't you?"

"Hey, I'm just trying to safeguard what's left of my sanity. You know what her receipts do to me."

"God, do I know! Don't worry. I'll make sure Aunt Agnes keeps Tammy away from the sales counter if she brings her in." Emma stole one more look at Tammy and decided against mentioning anything to her about Scotty.

Time seemed to go by at warp speed for the girls, Tammy, and the dogs. While Emma and Joanie attended to matters at checkout and Tammy was running around in eight different directions at once restocking the shelves and the dessert table, Cole was doing his thing—helping customers with their bags. He must have carried sacks out to the car for fifty people or more.

Tank was employing his usual talents at entertainment, but he'd added another duty for that weekend. He was patrolling the aisles, putting to good use his uncanny ability to spot a shoplifter. Cole wasn't as suspicious in nature and so was a little slow on the uptake when someone attempted to steal something. Not Tank. Maybe it was his own devious nature that alerted him to those of the same ilk. At any rate, once the alarm went off in his little head, he was like an avenging angel swooping down to right the wrong.

He always stopped the crime in progress very politely, but most effectively. Whether tipped off by scent or intuition, he would flush out the wrongdoer. Then with nothing more than an unwavering stare and a menacing growl combined with a curled lip he'd manage to reform the would-be thief on the spot, at least in their store. The crook-to-be quite naturally beat a hasty retreat and never attempted to enter the establishment again. There'd been only a handful of alleged shoplifters during the extended time the girls had been in business, but since Tank had been on the job, none had gotten away with so much as a 15-cent T-light. So far that weekend, Tank hadn't spotted anyone suspicious and was actually a little disappointed. He loved to give his impression of a vicious Rottweiler.

The girls knew it had to happen sooner or later, but were still unprepared when Angie showed up. They had hoped to fortify themselves with a glass or two of wine before facing the mouth-that-wouldn't-stop, but with it being as busy as it was they hadn't had a chance. Besides, it was only 11:45 in the morning when she chose to darken their door.

Emma saw her first; Angie had just come into the store and was heading over to one of the candle displays. Emma gave Joanie the "Angie Alert" which was a quick elbow to the ribs and Emma's fingers making like a talking mouth. Joanie knew immediately who was there and said a few choice words under her breath. Between the two of them, they kept her on radar while they took care of other customers.

Somewhere between forty and fifty minutes passed before Angie joined the group of shoppers waiting to check out. She was about fifteenth in line and already trying to get the girls' attention. Emma and Joanie steadfastly refused to look in her direction, but at the same time knew exactly where she was and how many places she'd moved up. It was like the countdown to a bomb going off.

Angie kept getting closer and closer, moving ever onward toward the cash register until she was second in line with only one body left between her and the girls. All too soon the buffer zone was gone, checked out; and then, there she was, front and center. It was a full frontal attack.

"Emma! Joanie! Hi!"

"Hi, Angie." From the tone of voice the girls used, a bystander would have sworn they were at a wake, consoling a member of the departed's family.

"How's it going?"

"Fine, Angie."

"Have you been busy?"

Emma and Joanie just stared at her and slowly blinked. Then they looked around the shop, wondering if all the people they thought they saw were a figment of their imaginations. They couldn't both be imagining the same thing, could they? They looked back to Angie. Yep, she was still there too.

"We've been a little busy, Ang," Joanie said, her facial expression indicating that she was concentrating *really* hard on getting the right words out. You know, the polite words, the civil words, the non-swearing words. To put it bluntly, she was trying not to rip her up one side and down the other.

"Really? I thought there'd be more people here."

Emma, her face devoid of any expression, looked at Angie and then turned her head slowly and looked at the next person in line. She got a sympathetic look back. Emma returned her stare to Angie and tried to dig down somewhere, anywhere, for some patience. There wasn't any; she was tapped out. It wasn't any use; she was going to have to let it rip. Leaning slightly forward, speaking deliberately and in a hoarse whisper, she said, "Get-the-hell-out."

"What? I didn't hear you, Emma. There's too much noise in here."

Joanie reacted like she'd been zapped with a cattle prod. She threw herself at Emma and just about tackled her, shoving her backward before she could repeat what she'd said. "Emma said she's glad you came out. Yep, that's what she said. She's so sentimental, just loves to see you. I wouldn't be surprised if she started crying. She's so emotional."

"Oh, Emma! You're so sweet," Angie said, her eyes having gone all soft and doe-like. The smile she beamed at Emma was of the 100-watt variety. Emma felt sick to her stomach.

"She is, isn't she? She's just a love. But you know what, Angie? We've got to look after these other customers right now, so how about we talk next week. Sound good?"

Angie looked around like she was just now noticing how many other people were waiting to be cashed out. "Oh, well, I guess so."

"Okay, good. We'll see you then. Bye, bye."

"Uh…Bye, Emma, Joanie."

As Angie faded back from the counter, the next in line moved up quickly to take her place. The girls gave the new customer their full attention while keeping their radar on full alert until Angie had made it through the front door and closed it behind her. It was only then that they breathed a sigh of relief. God only knows she could have doubled back. Several of the customers who were closer to the register and had overheard the conversation started to laugh. There were a few smart remarks as well; the girls weren't the only ones who had ever been subjected to the mouth-that-runneth-over.

While Joanie had been busy giving Angie the bum's rush, a stunned Emma had been focusing on the bullshit that had come out of Joanie's mouth when she'd been covering up what Emma had said. Damn! Joanie had made it sound like Emma considered Angie one of her best friends. She'd made it seem like Emma really liked her. Oh, God, the woman would be even more insufferable now. Heaven forbid, she'd probably *cling!* There was only one thing to do—Joanie had to die, slowly and with a great deal of pain. Emma gave her a veiled look that promised total retribution.

\*   \*   \*   \*

That night in a room at the Econo Lodge Motel located near the fairgrounds in Bloomsburg, Pennsylvania the young woman was alone and celebrating. She'd picked up some Chinese food and a bottle of wine on her way back from the dog show and was now indulging. As she sipped from one of the glasses that had been neatly wrapped with supposedly sterile paper the hotel supplied with each room, her eyes strayed to the tiny vial that sat next to her purse on the dresser and tipped her glass in homage.

The vial was nearly filled to the top. What she had used today hadn't made much of a dent in her supply. She didn't have to use much; a few drops was all it took to get the job done. Moira smiled, pleased with herself.

It had been so embarrassingly easy; there hadn't been any real challenge to it at all. These people were way too trusting and she had used it to her advantage. God, how they loved to talk about those damn dogs! Once they got started there was no stopping them. They were impossible to shut up. They'd just gone on and on. It was enough to make you sick and she held each and every one of them in scathing contempt. Their weakness, however, proved to be her silver lining. Inadvertently, their obsession with the beasts had provided her with an unfettered opportunity to accomplish the mission she'd been planning for years.

She'd watched, waited, and then picked on exhibitors who were getting ready to go into the ring. When their bait was out, either on their grooming tables or in their tack boxes, she'd made it a point to go over and inquire about their dogs. After she'd asked the first question, the owner or handler had been unstoppable in extolling the virtues of their breed. All she'd had to do was wait for the opening when the exhibitor was distracted enough not to notice her hand hovering over the bait container for just a second.

Concerned with last minute grooming, getting the dog leashed, gathering towels and toys, making sure the correct armband was on, getting the bait into a pocket, and talking to an interested bystander, the exhibitor's attention had been pulled in too many different directions at once to suspect anything untoward was going on. She'd been able to add her little additive, which was in the tiny vial concealed in the palm of her hand, with a quick flick of the wrist and the hurried, flustered exhibitor had never been any the wiser.

This had been her trial run, so she'd wanted to start out slowly. She'd not only had to make sure she wouldn't fall apart under the pressure, but she'd had to actually execute her until now only mentally choreographed movements. She'd approached four exhibitors and had successfully administered her additive four times. By tomorrow morning there should hopefully be four dead dogs, although if the tainted bait hadn't been used immediately, the results wouldn't be readily apparent. She'd tried to drip the poison on the very top pieces, but it wasn't like she'd had a lot of time to make sure she was accurate. God, how she wanted those dogs dead by tomorrow!

Feeling herself sliding into a panic, she worked to stay calm, to remain rational. There was nothing left to do except wait for morning, she told herself. She couldn't allow her anxiety over what might happen to push her into going off the deep end, inventing all sorts of problems and worst-case scenarios in her troubled mind. She had to stay grounded and relaxed. Although she wanted nothing more than to walk into the arena and find that four of those miserable creatures were no longer breathing, she couldn't let her desperation send her spiraling into chaotic dysfunction. She needed to be lucid and in control. She wanted to witness the fruits of her labor and the stunned reactions that were sure to follow. She knew deep down that she had to get at least one of them.

And if she was even the tiniest bit successful, then the next time out she wouldn't hold back and the count would be higher. Moira managed to smile again, poured herself another glass of wine, then saluted her hated reflection in the mirror that she'd made sure was directly across from where she'd chosen to sit. One glance was all the reminder she needed to reinforce her determination and grip on reality.

# Chapter Six

Customer traffic was a little lighter on Sunday as anticipated and the girls didn't need Tammy's help, but they were still pretty much on the go all the time. The weather had improved appreciably and the sun was actually shining, warming the air to about forty-five degrees. The wind had died down considerably and the breeze that fluttered the decorative flags was only blowing at about ten miles per hour. And that non-accumulating three or four inches of snow that the weatherman said they wouldn't get? It was melting.

Sally came in around noon, shopped for a little more than half an hour, and issued an invitation to the girls to have dinner at the restaurant.

"Sounds good to me," Joanie said. "God knows I won't be feeling like making dinner for my crew."

"I don't have anybody to feed but myself, but I know I won't have the energy to do more than make a peanut butter and jelly sandwich tonight. Dinner at the restaurant sounds way better than that."

"You don't have plans with Ben?"

"No, he's gone out of town to visit relatives."

"Not a hard choice then, huh, Em?"

"Nope, not at all. I think you can plan on us being there within minutes of closing this place down."

"Great! We need a 'girls only night' anyway. It's been a while since the last one. Joanie? Sam'll be all right with this?"

"Sam? Sam who? No, not to worry. He won't care. He'll take the boys out for pizza and wings. They can do a male-bonding thing."

"All right then. I'll see you later."

"Have the wine poured and waiting for us, okay?"

"Will do. Who's driving?"

"Me," Joanie supplied.

"Good. Emma can indulge herself beyond her usual two glasses then."

"Yeah, she might need three after yesterday. She just discovered she's got an emotional thing for Angie Newmann."

Emma immediately speared Joanie with a look that could nail her to the floor. "Stuff it, Joanie, or you won't live out the day."

"Am I missing something here?" Sally asked.

"No, not a thing," Emma answered quickly.

"I beg to differ, Em. I'll tell you all about it tonight, Sal."

"I can hardly wait," Sally said, giving Emma a questioning look, but getting nothing in response from her friend. "All right I have to go. See you later."

"Yep, see you later."

Aiming a final look toward her partner that could have taken down a bull moose, Emma directed her energies to the customers who had come up to be checked out. Joanie, grinning like the nitwit she was, deftly dodged the look and resumed her duties at the cash register.

The rest of the day provided no surprises and no problems. Thankfully it was business as usual, even if it was at a little faster pace. By four o'clock the dogs had had enough and figuring they had contributed plenty to the success of the weekend, retired to the back room. They each found their favorite spot and settled down for a little snooze.

Now as to the matter of finding their favorite spots, it worked like this: Cole would take the lead and find his spot first. He'd amble over to the place that he preferred, which was under the long worktable, and give it a good look. He'd bat away any toys that were in the way with his big paw and clear the area. After he circled a few times in both directions, he would lie down and scooch his big body around a little bit until he was comfortable. Once he puffed out a big sigh, indicating that he was settled and ready for a nap, Tank, who would have been watching and waiting patiently, would make his move to get to his most favorite spot. He'd walk over to where Cole lay and climb up onto his broad back. He'd lie down, stretch out, and burrow his head into Cole's fur. Content with the accommodations, he would yawn, close his eyes, and commence to drift off. With both of them happy as clams, they'd catch their forty winks.

\* \* \* \*

It was almost 7:00 by the time Emma and Joanie showed up at the Hearthmoor. For open house weekends, Sunday's normally shorter hours were discarded and replaced with the same ten to six schedule the shop had operated under for Friday and Saturday. The girls had had a few customers who'd lingered till after 6:00, and then the cleanup and shutdown had taken them another half hour. Sam had picked Tank up, but Emma had had to take Cole home before they went to the restaurant. Tonight they hadn't wanted to bother with anything other than themselves; all they wanted to do was veg out. They were tired, hungry, and really, really thirsty. They hoped Sally had the wine waiting.

Upon entering the entranceway of the restaurant, which was always lovingly decorated by Sally's own hand for whatever season or holiday was in progress, the girls found themselves surrounded with the final vestiges of fall. Cornstalks, hay bales, pumpkins and gourds of every size, and mums of rust, burgundy, and yellow coloring greeted them. The pungent fragrance of the flowers filled the space and allowed at least the essence of the dying season to prevail.

Upon entering the barroom, their eyes were immediately drawn to the two glasses of wine sitting on the polished cherry wood of the L-shaped bar. Hell, it was like twin laser beams zeroing in for the kill. Condensation had formed on the outside of the glasses and small rivulets of water were slowly running down the sides and onto the stems, soaking into the napkins beneath their base. Looks like they'd been sitting there for a while, Emma thought. Didn't matter, it'd still taste just as good. Joanie and Emma scooted onto the bar stools in front of the drinks and after a clink of their glasses each took a healthy gulp. Sally came out from the kitchen at that point and while she fixed herself a manhattan, asked about the success of the weekend.

While the two friends were taking turns filling Sally in on the goings on of the open house, Sally continued to wait on other customers at the bar and fill the waitresses' drink orders. There were six additional people who were either sitting or standing at the bar that could have easily accommodated more, and a glimpse into the dining room showed that most of the tables were occupied.

When Joanie started talking about the Angie Newmann incident, Emma tuned out and took notice of her surroundings. She looked up at the apple branches intertwined with white lights that hung over the bar and for fall had been decorated with colored leaves. She noted a few small pots of mums scattered about on the bar's shiny surface and the little pumpkins that had been interspersed amongst the liquor bottles on the shelves that hung on the opposite wall from where she sat. Next to the cash register there was a large, colorful ceramic turkey seemingly waiting patiently for the celebration of his special day.

Her attention was brought back to the ongoing conversation when she heard Sally say something about their plans for the dog show.

"Em, what do you think?"

"Sorry, I was admiring your decorations and blanking my mind on the Angie thing. What was the question?"

"How much food do you think we should take?"

"About fourteen million pounds."

"No, really. Be serious."

"I am."

"Em, how much?"

"Fourteen million pounds. We're pigs."

"Come on, Em. Really, how much?"

"As much as we can. You know how we are. We eat anything that isn't nailed down. Hell, we're like a horde of locusts where food's concerned and you know it."

"Yeah, but we're going to eat out for dinner. So what? Just breakfast, lunch, and snack food?"

"I guess and anything in between. We'll have our hot food for dinner at some kind of restaurant, so we don't have to worry about that. But the rest? Let's load up and take the usual. We'll have the ice chests and there'll be a refrigerator in the room. It should work."

"Okay. Let's divvy it up... Emma, you get the food for breakfast. Joanie, how about you get lunch. I'll get all the snacks. Is that all right with everybody?"

"Sounds good to me," Joanie said.

"Fine with me," Emma chimed in. "We do the usual with the alcoholic beverages?"

"Need you ask, Em? Only remember, guys, we'll be there for…" Sally thought a minute. "We'll be at the motel for three days, so let's make sure we bring enough."

"You got it. We in no way want to run out."

"Oh, God forbid," Emma said, smiling over the rim of her glass.

"Hey, we need it to keep our strength up and soothe our rattled nerves," Joanie retorted and Sally nodded her agreement.

"What rattled nerves?" Emma asked

"The ones we get watching you win Groups and Best in Show."

"You? What about me? I'm the one in the ring."

"Our job is harder," Joanie said. "By the time you get the win, we're exhausted. You only have to tag along with Cole. Hell, after the demonstration you put on in September, we know you were telling the truth when you said you're only along for the ride. Cripe, we have to do all the work.

"First, we have to bear up under all the tension. It's nerve racking to watch you in there, ya know. Secondly, we have to hope and pray that you'll win the entire time until the judge makes his decision and that, believe you me, takes a ton of energy. It must be because we're so fervent in our appeal, don't you think, Sal? Then when you do win, why the amount of cheering and clapping we do is unbelievable. And I'm not even going to mention our victory dances."

"Yeah, let's not mention 'em, Joanie."

"Why not?"

"I'd rather not say."

"What's wrong with 'em?"

"I refuse to answer on the grounds that I have to travel with you two."

"Hey, we're getting famous for those dances."

"I wouldn't be bragging about it if I were you."

"Listen, people look forward to those dances. They never know what we're going to do, but they can't wait to see what it is. As soon as you win, they forget all about you and Cole. Their attention zooms right over to us, doesn't it Sal?"

Sally looked dubious.

"They love us," Joanie insisted.

"Are you sure about that?" Emma asked.

"Yeah. What's not to love? Actually, they probably wish they *were* us. They're jealous of our ability."

"You think so, huh?"

"Yeah. Right, Sally?"

"If you say so, Joanie." Sally rolled her eyes and gave Emma a can-you-believe-what-an-ass-she-is look. It was true Sally participated in the dances, but she at least would admit how bad they were.

Emma closed her eyes, shook her head and blew out a breath. Then she gave  Sally a what-are-we-going-to-do-with-her look

Joanie caught it. "What?"

"Nothing."

"No, no. It's something. What?" Joanie looked from Emma to Sally and back again.

"Sally and I were just agreeing that you're our cross to bear."

"Yeah?"

"Uh-huh."

"Hell, I thought you were agreeing on what an ass I am."

"That too."

"Good. Then everything's normal. Let's eat."

The girls slid off their stools and Sally came out from behind the bar. Her bartender Hank took over for her and the three friends walked into the dining room. They went to the table that had been reserved for them in front of the twelve-foot long fieldstone fireplace with its raised hearth, and seated themselves.

There was a crackling fire burning and its warmth had drawn Emma like a moth to a flame. She'd managed to grab the chair closest to it and was already feeling its toasty heat along her back. There was a beautiful fall arrangement made up of pumpkins, dried and silk flowers, twigs, Spanish moss, and cinnamon tapers in pewter candlestick holders, extending from one end of the mantle to the other. Every table had a vase of fresh fall flowers sitting atop it and there were baskets of every shape and size filled with dried florals hanging from the exposed center beam. It was beyond easy for the girls to relax and get comfortable.

Sharon, their waitress and friend, came over and after the usual pleasantries had been exchanged, the first thing the girls did was order another round of drinks. Once the beverages had been delivered, it didn't take them long to settle on the day's special for their dinner choice.

That was the normal way of it because if Tom Ferrelli, the Hearthmoor's chef, knew that Emma and Joanie were coming, he invariably made the day's special a taste treat that he knew they would enjoy. His offering of epicurean delight this particular evening was Scallops Pesto, which was running a close second in Emma's opinion to her number one favorite, Chicken Olivia. The dish consisted of sautéed scallops and mushrooms, diced tomatoes, and bowtie garden pasta mixed with a homemade pesto sauce and sprinkled with shredded mozzarella. Emma's mouth watered just thinking about it. If she wasn't careful she'd be drooling just like Cole.

"Hey, where's Kirby? I just realized I haven't seen her." Emma swiveled in her chair trying to locate the yellow Lab.

"Yeah, where is she?" Joanie asked.

"She's upstairs having a major time-out."

"Kirby?"

"The one and only."

"Really? Kirby?"

"Yep."

"You gave her a major time-out?"

"Yeah, one that might stretch into infinity."

"Uh-oh. That doesn't sound good at all. What'd she do?"

"Let's just say she got a little too enthusiastic in her constant quest for food."

"Come on, give," Emma said. "What'd she do? I can't believe she did anything *that* bad."

"You'd better believe it," Sally grumped.

"All right, Sal, spit it out," Joanie demanded.

"Well, if you must know, earlier this evening she wasn't satisfied with her usual garlic bread and stole somebody's steak right off their plate."

"She did? Holy shit!" At first Joanie was rather surprised, then she was in stitches. "Way to go, Kirby!"

"Oh, God, you're kidding," Emma laughed.

"No, I wish I were and it's not funny, guys." Sally's pained expression didn't bode well for Kirby.

"Sorry, Sal, but yeah, it is. Hey, she made a good choice, steak over garlic bread? My kind of girl!"

"Why did I know you'd take her side?"

"'Cause you know me, you dope. Was it a regular customer?" Joanie asked, trying hard to stop laughing, but so far it wasn't working.

"Yes, thank God. Can you imagine if it had happened to somebody who'd never been here before? I don't even want to think about how bad it could have been."

"Yeah, it could have been nasty," Emma giggled.

"Let's give Kirby some credit here. She was smart enough to know who to steal it from, after all. Face it, Sal;

she's got the makings of a talented thief. There's no telling where this will lead."

"Oh, please."

"How'd the people react?" Emma asked, trying her darndest to keep a straight face, although she wasn't succeeding very well.

"Well, they were a little stunned. I mean one minute there's a lovely steak sitting on your plate and the next it's taking a hike via a four-footed eating machine." Sally couldn't help it; she joined in the laughter. "I don't think the lady had taken more than two bites out of the damn thing."

"What'd you do?"

"What could I do? I apologized profusely and got the woman another steak."

"But the people were okay with it?"

"Yeah, they were great actually. Good thing they're dog lovers. It probably saved my butt and my restaurant."

"Probably."

"So how long is Kirby going to be punished?"

"For the rest of her natural life."

"Come on, really. How long?"

"You think I'm kidding?"

"Yeah, we know you. What's the sentence?"

"She's got time-out for a week. It'll kill her."

"You're right. A week for Kirby without mooching food? She'll be in a bad way."

"It might cure her," Emma offered hopefully.

"Not a chance," Joanie said. "Take it from one who knows. It'll only make her more devious."

"Great. Just what I need, a Tank clone."

"Welcome to my world," Joanie said, lifting her glass in a commiserating toast.

"Lord, help me," Sally sighed, taking a bigger than normal sip of her manhattan.

The salads and garlic bread were delivered to the table and as they ate, discussion again zeroed in on the dog show.

"We should be able to be on the road no later than 7:00 Wednesday night," Sally said.

"That'll get us there around 10:00. That's not too bad. We should be able to be in bed by what? 11:30?"

"Yeah, that sounds about right, barring any problems."

"There will be no problems," Joanie stated emphatically, banging her fist on the table. "This trip's going to go smoothly. I forbid any problems." A few people from neighboring tables looked over, wondering what the commotion was about. Joanie gave them a mind-your-own-business look.

"You forbid any problems?" Sally asked. "And lower your voice, will you?"

"Oh, sorry," Joanie said, looking somewhat abashed, although not totally. "But don't even think about crossing me on this one, guys. We're going to have a problem-free trip this time. I guarantee it."

"If you say so."

"You're goddamn right I do," Joanie replied, starting to get worked up again.

"Joanie, hush!"

"*Weeell*... Listen, you guys. We've had our full quota of problems for the year. It's our turn for clear sailing."

"It'd be nice if you were right."

"I am; trust me." Emma and Sally exchanged a wary look. "Hell, aren't I the one who knows when we're jinxed or not?"

"Oh, shit, Joanie, let's not go into that again."

"Hey, I was proven right."

"In your mind. Well, in what little's left of it anyway."

"Hey, you two don't have any more left than I do. Don't worry. Everything is going to be great."

With those famous last words ringing in their ears, the girls turned their total attention to their food and dug into their main courses, which Sharon had just delivered. All discussion ended while they enjoyed their first bites and all three unwittingly did a mental review of the "problems" they'd experienced earlier in the year.

Emma had been stalked, Tank had suffered a severe sprain to his front leg, they'd almost been run off the road when they were traveling to a show, Sally had had to shoot a shotgun to save them, days later Emma had been shot and almost killed and finally Cole had been stolen.

When the three friends' spoke of problems, they tended not to be referring to the kind of everyday little problems that nag most people. Oh, no. When the girls mentioned problems, they were big, very, very big problems. And this was going to be the first show in which they were competing since the end of their so-called problems a few months ago; so it was natural that Joanie was shooting for the moon. They could only hope the trip would go according to plan.

Sally reopened the conversation after everyone had put a good size dent in their pasta. "What time do you want to load tomorrow? I'm going to pick the van up around ten." The girls were going to borrow Sally's son's full-size custom van for the show and stay in a motel instead of using the motor home.

"How would three o'clock be?" Emma asked. "That would give everybody enough time to get packed, run to the store, and get down to your place."

"That would work for me," Joanie said.

"Me too," Sally agreed.

The doors to the kitchen swung open and Tom came out, heading directly for their table. "Good evening, lovely ladies. Am I interrupting some high-level planning?" Tom asked as he approached.

"No, no, not at all. We were just talking about the show."

"Oh, right. The show's this week. I do believe that with the number of years' experience you all have that it would necessitate only a little low-level planning."

"Whoa, listen to him, will you."

"Oh, Tom. You are such a smooth talker."

"I am, aren't I?"

"My, yes. And to think you can cook too."

"Can't help it, ladies. It's a natural talent. It's called spreading the bullshit with aplomb."

"Well, you're one of the best at it. We'll give you that."

"Why, thank you, ladies. I appreciate the testimonial." Tom executed a formal little bow. "Now how is everything?"

All three women praised the meal lavishly and Tom's smile stretched from ear to ear. He loved to please the ladies—with his food, that is. He was a happily married man and dearly loved his wife. So, would he preen over the accolades of attractive women and bask in their compliments? Hell, yes. Where his food was concerned he was just plain easy.

"How did your open house go, girls?"

"I'm happy to say it was very successful, Tom."

"Glad to hear it, Emma."

"I think it could be the best one yet," Joanie announced. "I don't think we've ever been that busy for the full three days. What do you think, Em?"

"I think you might be right. It was constantly busy. We didn't have any down time at all."

"That's terrific. Listen, I'd love to stay and talk, but I've got things to do in the kitchen. Besides, I have to watch out for the interests of the boss. Make sure everyone's putting in an honest day's work. It's a huge responsibility."

"Is this more of your bullshit with aplomb?" Sally asked.

"Most certainly. How'd you guess?"

"It was off the meter."

"What meter?"

"The bullshit meter. I have one in my head. You may be a master at dishing it out, but I'm an expert at seeing right through it, although I will give you points for style."

"You're too kind," Tom laughed, "and with that I'll leave you, ladies. Enjoy your meal."

"Thanks, Tom, we will," the three women chorused.

After Tom left, the threesome finished making their plans and then sat back and enjoyed the rest of their dinner, a dessert of Sally's rice pudding with real whipped cream, another round of drinks, and each other's company.

At one point, Joanie had excused herself from the table on the grounds of having to use the bathroom. Emma knew better; she knew where she was really going. Sometime during the meal, Emma had caught Joanie palming two pieces of garlic bread and hiding them in the napkin on her lap. Sally was clueless; she hadn't seen a thing. Hell, half the time she didn't know what was going on till after the fact. Emma's intuitiveness came from working with her sicko friend every day.

At any rate, Joanie concealed the food when she left the table and once she'd bypassed the bathrooms, directed a look toward Emma that told her to keep Sally busy. Emma nodded almost imperceptibly, a small grin on her face. What the hell? They were partners, weren't they?

Joanie quickly made her way upstairs and into Sally's apartment. She turned the corner into the spacious country kitchen and looked through to the vaulted-ceiling living room. She took a quick look around the large, rectangular room with its wood stove in one corner and the tall windows that covered the back wall, which offered the perfect view of Sally's flower gardens and back acreage. There were two oval braided rugs on the cherry floor whose muted colors brought out the richness of the wood. The space was filled with several winged-back chairs and primitive antique pieces, among which was a 7-foot tall pine cupboard that dominated one of the walls. A flat-topped wooden trunk serving as a coffee table sat in front of an enormous high-backed colonial blue couch upon which the dog of the hour was lying.

Kirby looked about as dejected as a dog could look. She didn't even lift her head when she saw Joanie, but her sorrowful brown eyes gave a whisper of recognition. Her tail, however, did give one pitiful thump before she resumed her woebegone posture.

"Hey, Kirby. How you doing?" Joanie asked as she hunkered down to the dog's level.

Kirby gave a sniff; was that food she smelled? Her head came up off her front paws.

"Heard about your little coup there. Congratulations. You did a good job. I'd take steak over garlic bread any day too. Gotta tell ya, Kirb, Emma and I are proud of you and, to tell you the truth, your mother isn't all that put out with you either. Here, I thought I'd bring you a little reward."

There was definitely life in those big eyes now.

"I've got to hand it to you. Grabbing that steak was a masterstroke. Tank will be absolutely busting his buttons when I tell him what you did."

Kirby, at that point, wasn't worried about what Tank or anybody else thought. She was busy licking drool off her mouth and her eyes were riveted on Joanie's hands as she unwrapped the napkin.

"Here you go, girl. It's not steak, but it'll have to do. Enjoy."

Kirby inhaled the two pieces of garlic bread before Joanie had time to blink. There wasn't so much as a crumb left. Without any lingering evidence, Sally would never know Joanie had been there. Kirby certainly wasn't going to talk!

\* \* \* \*

Moira was almost home; only another hour or so and she'd be pulling into her driveway. As she drove, she kept going over and over what had happened that morning when she'd arrived at the show.

She'd turned up at the show site around 9:30, her objective being to make sure the deaths, if there were any, would be confirmed by that time. To her immense satisfaction and near jubilation, they were—all four of them! In fact, that's all anybody had been talking about. The activity in the rings had still been going on, but the interest it generated had definitely taken a back seat.

She'd walked around the rings and into the grooming area, listening to what people were saying. There'd been shock and concern and some people had been so overcome with grief, they'd been crying. It had been extremely difficult for her to mask her face in sympathy when all she'd really wanted to do was jump up and down and cheer. But she'd done it and had even offered words of condolence and support to those who'd seemed the most upset.

She'd been rewarded for her effort, and indeed been given a bonus. Not only were there four dead dogs, there was also one dead handler. Now wasn't that an extra dividend! Talk about beginner's luck! She'd had to dig her nails into the palm of her hand hard enough to draw blood to keep herself from giggling when she'd heard that juicy bit of news. She surmised that the handler must have been one of those who had the disgusting habit of placing the bait in their mouths.

During the day while she'd been observing and selecting her targets, she'd discovered that some of the exhibitors carried the piece of bait they used in their mouths when showing their dogs. She hadn't known about that, but that revealing piece of information had put a whole new spin on what toll her revenge could extract. Knowing the poison was so toxic that just holding a contaminated piece of bait in the mouth was enough to have it absorbed into the body, she realized the full implications of her discovery. Not only could she kill the damn dogs, but the fools who were so enamored of them as well. This was heady stuff. This was absolutely fabulous! She could get two for the price of one! After a brief bit of introspection, she'd found that indeed she hated the people who kept these animals almost as much as the dogs themselves.

So when she'd heard the additional news about the handler, she'd felt pure power surging through her veins and fearing that she'd no longer be able to maintain her guise of solicitude had walked purposefully, but unhurriedly from the building.

Alone in her car now, still giddy with success, she was already planning her next move. There was a big show in Syracuse, New York this coming week. She thought it started on Thursday, but she'd have to wait until the weekend to attend. She had a job she had to go to and she needed to keep up normal appearances. She couldn't very well start taking off a lot of time from work and not draw attention to herself. It didn't matter though. She didn't need four days at the show to work her "magic". She only needed one. She'd get to the grounds early Saturday morning and do her watching. By mid afternoon she'd know who her targets would be. Maybe she'd get lucky again and take out more than the dogs. On second thought, maybe she wouldn't have to rely on luck. Maybe she only had to rely on her own daring and determination.

Reflecting again on the outstanding results of her first attempt to seek recompense for her many years of suffering, she was a little overwhelmed. If she was honest, it had exceeded her wildest dreams. The fact that all the targeted dogs were dead was amazing in itself, but the fact that a handler was dead too blew her away because it meant that every piece of bait she'd poisoned had been used. What were the chances of that? There had only been time in each case to dribble a few drops of the poison onto the bait, which meant that only one or two, three pieces at the most were tainted. What were the odds that they all would be mindlessly grabbed from the container of who knows how many pieces by each handler? That astonishing fact served to cement the righteousness of the vendetta in her mind.

Ruminating further as the countryside sped by, another thought crystallized. It didn't matter if the dogs died at the show. Oh, yes, it filled her with a wild euphoria to witness firsthand the rewards of her handiwork, but if the poisoned bait was somehow not used at the show, it was still sitting like a ticking bomb in the containers that would be going home with the intended victims. The remainder of the bait was sure to be used as treats or whatever when the dogs returned to their safe haven. What better place to strike them down? And it would never be linked to the show, bettering her chances of not being connected to the deaths that were sure to come. Grinning hugely, she kept her eyes on the road ahead and contemplated what for her were pleasant thoughts.

# Chapter Seven

Monday was a crazy, bustling, hustling, I'm-never-going-to-get-it-all-done kind of day for the girls. But they did, of course, get it all done. So what if the effort took years off their lives! It was worth it; end goal was the show!

The weather, for a change, cooperated, which in "Emma-speak" meant that it didn't snow. She didn't care if it rained, she didn't care if it was foggy, she didn't care if the temperature was below freezing, and she didn't give a damn if there were gale force winds blowing. As long as it didn't snow, she didn't give a rat's ass what it did.

The morning hours, in addition to the normal everyday activities, were filled with packing and shopping, and for Sally, exchanging her SUV for her son's van. Once Emma and Joanie were packed and back from shopping, they had to load their vehicles. Sally had to get all her things out to the barn, which along with the restaurant sat on four beautifully landscaped acres. When she'd brought the van home, she'd parked it inside the outbuilding so they'd be out of the weather while they loaded their gear.

The dogs of each household were being more of a hindrance than help. While Kirby was merely underfoot, Cole had unintentionally complicated matters by carrying anything he could get his mouth onto as his means of helping with the packing process.

In Tank's case the hindrance had deteriorated to such a point that the wily terrier was simply being a major pain in the butt. Tank's behavior was causing Joanie to temporarily reconsider her deep attachment to the little dog. He was not only making every move she made more difficult by acting like a speed bump that she had to continuously step over, but he was undoing what she did as fast as she did it. Unlike Cole who was carrying everything he could handle over in the general direction of Emma's suitcase and duffle bag, Tank was taking Joanie's things anywhere but where she wanted them.

If Joanie packed a piece of clothing in her suitcase, he would take it out as soon as her back was turned and give her a merry chase with the article tightly clutched between his jaws the entire time. He'd only give it up once she was reduced to begging and threatening to cut his life short. Of course, that strategy only made him grin while evading capture, run back, and grab something else. The final straw came when after removing most of what had been in the suitcase, he'd laid down in it and wouldn't move.

No amount of cajoling, threatening, or promising him the world could remove that dog. He'd turned himself into dog Jell-O, a boneless lump of dog flesh. When Joanie tried to lift him out he was as limp as a wet noodle. From the angle she was at and because she had to bend down to reach him, she couldn't get a good grip and he kept slithering out of her hands. To make matters worse, he kept his eyes closed as if he were the most innocent of sleeping dogs when all along Joanie knew that behind those closed eyelids lurked the very devil himself. Evidence of such was the sick smile that was plastered on his face. He was fiendishly clever and seemed to be able to thwart her at every turn.

However, that was the operative word—seemed. Joanie was no fool—well, okay—maybe a little. It did take her longer than it should have to come up with a solution. And it wasn't a real hard one at that. So all right, she was at least a dork! Anyway, it only took one word, spoken with conviction and great volume, and Tank was up and scrambling for his crate. And what was that decisive idiom? Very simply, all Joanie had to do was open her mouth and bellow, "Sam!"

Tank's reaction was something akin to how children respond when mom threatens to bring their father into the confrontation. Undisputedly, this tactic has worked remarkably well down through the ages and will undoubtedly continue to do so in the future. Therefore, if it works for kids, why not use it on the dogs? Joanie wasn't about to debate the issue; it worked for her and she was going to take full advantage of it. As soon as Tank was up and running, she streaked after him and slammed the door shut to his crate the second he bolted inside. Now maybe she could get something done!

Tank peered out through the bars, and gave Joanie his version of the evil eye. Joanie lowered her chin and gave Tank an equally villainous glower right back. After a second or two of unwavering glares at each other, they both looked away and called it a draw.

Very obviously, all the dogs knew they were going to a show and the only thing they wanted to do was get on with it. Little did they know they wouldn't be leaving for another two days. Once they found out, the girls were again going to have to pay the price.

\* \* \* \*

Everybody managed to get to Sally's barn within three or four minutes either way of 3:00. Since the weather was dry, even though the cloudy skies made it gloomy, Emma and Joanie had brought the dogs so they could play with Kirby while they loaded the van. It was kind of like an impromptu doggy play-date. Emma and Joanie figured it was a surefire plan to spring Kirby from her long term time-out, at least for a little while. Cole and Tank did their part by making it virtually impossible for Sally to resist once they turned the full force of their soulful, pleading eyes upon her. She never stood a chance and went down gracefully in defeat. They put all three of the four-footed rascals in the big, graveled kennel area Sally had on one side of the barn and while they romped and cavorted, the girls got to work.

Once the three friends had everybody's gear in the barn, they stood with the van's doors open and assessed the situation. They didn't exactly look inspired. It had been early spring the last time they'd traveled in the vehicle and it was going to take a little thought as to how to load the darn thing. They had the routine down to a science with the motor home, but the van was a different matter. They didn't use it very often, maybe only three or four times a year, so the organizational plan was a little murky.

After a few false starts, however, the girls soon had the loading well in hand. Joanie and Emma were about to put Cole's big crate in when Sally stopped them.

"Hang on a minute, guys, I want to put something else in first." She walked over to the motor home and came back after a few minutes with what looked like a long leather case in her hands.

"Ohhh, boy, is that what I think it is?" Joanie asked, putting a little distance between herself and Sally.

"Yep."

"Crap." It wasn't hard to figure out Joanie's feeling on the matter.

"It's TFG, isn't it?" Emma asked, her eyes getting big.

"Yep. Where we go, it goes."

"But we've never had it in the van before, have we?"

"Nope, but there's a first time for everything. It was always in the motor home though, right from the start."

"Yeah, no shit. Only Emma and I never did know about it," Joanie said accusingly.

"Sometimes it's better if you don't know everything, Joanie."

"If you say so, oh wise one."

"Hey, if you would have known it was there, you probably would have freaked out."

"No kidding."

"Well, I didn't enlighten you for just that reason. I simply avoided your going bonkers until it was absolutely necessary."

"Thank you so much for your consideration."

"You're welcome."

"Don't be; I didn't mean it."

"I know."

"I was being a smart-ass."

"I know that too."

"Yeah, but did you know that you're a—"

"Hey, guys," Emma said, interrupting what had all the makings of a marathon exchange of remarks characterized by one-upmanship. Addressing herself to Sally, Emma inquired, "How come we're taking TFG with us now?"

"After what happened last June do you really have to ask that question?" Sally asked a little incredulously.

"Well… no, not when you put it that way," Emma said, looking duly chastised.

"Geez, you guys. I can't believe you're even questioning taking it. Not after what we went through. Who knows what would have happened if we hadn't had it."

"But, Sal, do you really think we *need* to take it?" Joanie asked.

"Yeah, Sal," Emma said, stuffing her hands in her pockets. "What are the chances of anything like that ever happening again?"

Sally's eyebrows rose about half a foot as she drew down on Joanie and Emma. "Ladies…stop, okay… Look, both of you, this is the first show we're going to since 'the ordeal', to quote Angie Newmann," Sally said, "and we aren't taking any chances. Do I make myself clear?"

Sally had slipped into fighter mode, Emma and Joanie knew to stand down.

"Clear," Emma said.

"Crystal," Joanie mumbled.

"All right," Sally continued, "So since we're changing vehicles, we have to transfer certain necessary equipment to our new ride and TFG is definitely on the list of necessary equipment now. You wouldn't have even thought about it if we were taking the motor home. It would've just been there. Right?"

"Well, yeah…right. It's just that, you know, it kind of creeps me out when I see the thing," Joanie said, giving herself a little shake.

"You've got a real case, you know that?"

"Can't help it."

"Who'd ever believe you are the way you are around guns, Joanie. It's so weird."

"It's not weird," Joanie snapped, her chin jutting out stubbornly.

"Yes, it is."

"No, it's not."

"Yes, it is. Isn't it, Emma?"

Emma looked like she wished she hadn't been asked that question. Darting a wary glance in Joanie's direction, she swallowed audibly before she answered. "Well…maybe a little."

Joanie spun on Emma and gave her a piercing stare, not quite believing that she wasn't going to back her up. Emma shrugged her shoulders helplessly; the truth's the truth after all. Seeing that there was no help coming from her supposed best friend, Joanie reluctantly confessed, "All right. I know it's weird, but I can't help it. Guns bother me."

"Yeah, but you're the wife of a retired FBI agent."

"So what? What's that got to with it?"

"Well, you'd think that you of all people would be used to the sight of a gun by now."

"I don't think that enters into it, Sal," Emma said. "It'd still be that thing from years ago."

"You're kidding."

"No, she still feels bad about it."

"Oh, Jesus, Joanie, let it go."

"There are some things you never get over and this is one of them," Joanie said, getting defensive.

"Oh, brother."

"Hey, how would you feel if you'd killed something?"

"Hello? Anybody home?" Sally lightly rapped her knuckles against Joanie's head. "I used to hunt, remember? I'd have to say I've killed a few things in my lifetime."

"Joanie, you didn't kill anything alive for cripe's sake," Emma said.

"They were alive. They were running, weren't they?"

"Well, yeah, until you got through with 'em."

"Nice, Emma, rub it in."

"Can't help it, that stove and refrigerator were top of the line until you shot and killed 'em."

"I know. It never leaves me," Joanie divulged. "I'm still haunted by it."

"They were beauts."

"God, don't I know it. I can still see them in my mind. They were just standing there, running, nestled in their spot in the kitchen doing their thing, minding their own business, and then out of the clear blue, I blasted 'em."

"You ass, get over it. It was an accident."

"We know you didn't intentionally kill two major appliances that, by the way, cost you a fortune to replace."

"I know, but I did it just the same. I really couldn't help it though. I thought I'd surprise Sam by practicing when he wasn't home, you know. I'd just finished loading the damn gun and was getting used to the feel of it in my hand when that blasted gust of wind blew through the house and slammed the bathroom door shut. It scared me so bad that my finger jerked and I squeezed the trigger. Then I just couldn't seem to stop, I just kept firing until I emptied the friggin' thing."

"Thank God nobody was home that day."

"No shit. I could have wiped out my whole family. Don't think that doesn't give me nightmares."

"Instead you murdered a top of the line stove and refrigerator. You're going straight to hell for that one."

"I was going anyway."

"Well, Emma and I'll probably meet you there, so don't feel bad."

"I still miss 'em. They were so beautiful."

"We know, but you've got to get over it."

"It's not easy.'

"We can only imagine," Emma commiserated.

Sally cleared her throat. " Ah…Let's get back to TFG, you guys. Seriously, I really don't think we should go anywhere without it after what happened, do you?"

"No, I don't suppose we should," Joanie agreed reluctantly.

"All right," Emma said, "Let's get it loaded. Where are we going to put it?"

"I thought we'd hide it behind Cole's crate. It'll be close enough to the back seat so that we can get to it if we need to. We can throw a blanket over it; nobody but us will ever know it's there. I'll put the box of bullets up in the glove compartment."

"Okay, let's do it." Joanie was finally resigned to taking the damn thing. Thank God! Now they might be able to get the rest of the loading done. "Wait!"

Emma and Sally stopped dead in their tracks. Now what? Emma wondered.

"What's wrong?" Sally asked

"Maybe we should take another one."

"Another what?"

"Another gun."

"Another gun?" Sally and Emma looked at Joanie like she was losing her marbles.

"Yeah."

"Do you mean a different gun or one in addition to what we have?" Sally asked, seeking clarification.

"An additional one."

"Why?"

"Because I think it would be a good idea."

"Why are you going from not wanting any gun along to wanting more than one?" Emma asked, giving Joanie a suspicious look.

"'Cause I just remembered something."

"And that would be…"

"We still have 'it'."

"Oh, damn," Sally sighed, "I thought that one was long dead."

"You've got to be kidding," Emma scoffed and walked a few feet away from her friend who she wanted to throttle right about then. "Didn't we have this discussion once before?"

"Yeah. So what?"

"Forget it. I'm not getting into it again."

"You don't have to. Facts are facts."

"Yeah, well, here's a fact for you. You're friggin' nuts."

"I am not."

"Yes, you are."

"No, I'm not. If you've got it, you've got it. It never dies; it's with you forever. And dammit, we've got it."

"Yeah, we've got it all right. We've got a lunatic for a friend."

"Hey, we're hot and you know it."

"Joanie, at this age, if we make it to lukewarm we're doing great—and that's on a good day."

"Speak for yourself."

"Girls!" Sally held up her hands to halt the ongoing exchange. "We're taking TFG and that's it." Joanie started to protest. "Not another word, Joan. One gun is all we need to protect ourselves and..." Sally rolled her eyes. "...our precious 'it'. Okay?"

"Okay," Emma readily agreed.

"Joanie?" Sally looked pointedly at her.

"Okay, I guess. But you guys had better learn to live with it. We're hot stuff and it's not going to go away."

"Lucky us," Emma mumbled as Sally stowed the gun along the side of the van.

TFG was the girl's acronym for Sally's shotgun. It was the one that had probably saved their lives when the bad guys had tried to force them off the road a few months ago. However, in the heat of the moment when the girls' panic had been escalating and tension inside the motor home had risen to towering heights, the shotgun had simply come to be referred to as *the fucking gun*. It had since been shortened to TFG since they couldn't exactly use that specific nomenclature on a regular basis around other people and still come off as the sweet, lovable little darlings they actually were. Well, all right, people who really knew them weren't fooled in the least and amongst themselves they frequently did use the original phraseology and didn't bother to apologize for it.

It took the three of them almost two hours, probably because they were fooling around so much, to get everything situated so that it all fit. They had to remember little things like to leave space so they could get crate doors open and to leave room for the coolers, food, and last-minute luggage that still had to be put in. By the time they left, the van would closely resemble a jam-packed junk wagon, something along the lines of the Clampett's jalopy on the *Beverly Hillbillies*. God help them if they had a flat tire!

The success of the loading deserved a reward to their way of thinking, so ladies and dogs adjourned to the restaurant for a quick drink. Sally took the dogs upstairs to her apartment for some water, while Emma and Joanie bellied up to the bar. Tom came out of the kitchen where he'd been doing prep work and served them some wine. While they were chatting, Sally returned with the dogs trailing behind and made herself a manhattan. The phone rang and she went to answer it. The conversation she had lasted about five or six minutes. Emma and Joanie could tell by the tone of Sally's voice that whatever was being said was serious.

"That was Stu Berger," Sally said, coming back to the bar and taking a sip of her drink. "He was at the Back Mountain show this past weekend and you'll never guess what he told me."

"What?" Joanie and Emma asked in unison.

"Something awful happened. One handler and four dogs died."

"What? Died?" Joanie had to make a supreme effort not to choke on the wine she'd just taken into her mouth. "They died?"

"Is he sure?"

"Yeah, he was there when they found out what had happened. He said he even saw the police and ambulance arrive on the grounds, but at that point he didn't know what was going on."

"He's not pulling your leg, is he?"

"Stu would never joke about something like this. He sounded really upset."

"Yeah, you're right. He wouldn't joke about this. My God, I wonder what happened," Emma remarked, not wanting to believe anything so tragic could have taken place at a show.

"They don't know. The handler and the dogs all showed on Saturday and by Sunday morning they were all dead."

"Geez, how awful."

"Did Stu know who the handler was?"

"Yeah, it was a guy named Tom Wilson."

"I don't think I know him," Emma said, trying to place the name.

"I don't think I do either," Joanie claimed. "His name doesn't ring a bell."

"I know I don't know him," Sally said, "but this is the weird thing. According to Stu, they weren't all his dogs."

"They weren't?"

"No. Only one dog was his. A Doberman."

"Well, who did the other ones belong to?"

"Stu didn't know for sure, but he thought they were owned by different owner-handlers."

"What were the breeds?"

"A black Lab and two Rottweilers."

"Cripe, this is terrible."

"I guess they found the handler and Dobe in his motor home. When he didn't appear at the ring where he was supposed to be, somebody went looking for him. The other people must have reported their dog's deaths to their friends 'cause Stu said that's all anybody was talking about on Sunday."

"Man, this is unbelievable."

"And they don't know what killed them?"

"No, at least not yet."

"I'm sure there'll be an autopsy on the handler. Probably necropsies on the dogs too."

"I wonder how long that'll take."

"I don't know."

"Shit, this is kind of…hell, I don't know what it is."

"It's kind of weird," Emma said, looking thoughtful.

"It's more than weird," Sally said, "it's downright scary."

"It's scary all right, but what I meant is that it's weird they were all black."

"Black? Oh, you mean the dogs."

"Yeah."

"She's right, Sally. They were all black," Joanie said, studying her wine glass. "I wonder if that means anything."

"I hope not," Emma answered, her mind already searching for known infectious or genetic diseases that were prevalent in the breeds that had died. She couldn't come up with any, but then what did she know. Her mind shifted in a flash to the one thing she did know— Cole was black.

"The Doberman could have been a red," Sally offered.

"Somehow I bet it wasn't," Emma said, worry lines forming on her forehead. "I've got a funny feeling the Doberman was a black."

"Well, there's no use speculating about it. We don't have enough information."

"I guess we have no choice but to wait and see what they come up with."

"I guess so."

"Anybody want another drink?" Sally asked.

"No, better not. I'm going over to Ben's for dinner. It's the last chance I'll have to see him 'til after the show."

"Uh-oh. We all know what that means." Sally waggled her eyebrows and grinned from ear to ear.

"Yeah, they'll be burning up the sheets tonight."

"Joanie…"

"Hey, make the most of it, Em."

"Believe me, I fully intend to."

"That's our girl," Joanie said. "Hell, once we got you started in the right direction, it's been full steam ahead, hasn't it?"

"You betcha."

"Hey, more power to ya. Have fun. I'll see you tomorrow."

"Will do. Come on, Cole. Let's go. Bye, Sally. Thanks for the drink."

"Don't mention it. I'll see you Wednesday after work."

"Okay. If you hear any more about what happened, let us know."

"Absolutely. You do the same."

"For sure. See ya."

# Chapter Eight

As soon as she got home, Emma beat a hasty path to the bathroom, took a quick shower, and got herself ready to go to Ben's. She'd changed out of her serviceable everyday underwear and had slipped into a bra and panties that six months ago would have been nowhere on her list of items to own. What a difference a man makes! The bra was lavender, sheer, and wired enough to lift her breasts up to where they were supposed to be and even gave her a little cleavage. At least with her clothes on, her breasts gave a good imitation of being not only lush and perky, but were positioned where any nubile, young thirty-year old's would be. Well…all right, if she was going to be totally honest, it probably wasn't a thirty-year old. It was more likely a not-so-nubile forty-year old, but it was still better than the actual fifty-five-year old pair that she was stuck with. Emma wasn't going to think about what happened when the bra came off. She hoped it didn't make too much difference when she was lying down. The trick was to get in that position before Ben noticed their deflation and descent to a lower region. So far she'd been able to keep him occupied with other body parts while her breasts made the transformation. Complete darkness helped.

Now the panties, they were something else. They matched the bra in color, fabric, and sheerness, but the totally mind-blowing thing for Emma was, they were bikinis. My God, she hadn't worn those since, well, since sometime after all the kids had been born. Damn! It'd been that long? We're talking probably more than twenty-five years here. Twenty-five years of wearing those comfortable, white cotton briefs. Hell, going to high-rise on the thigh had been a big deal. Why does that happen? Emma wondered. Why do you get so entrenched in the mommy role that you lose sight of being a woman and a seductive one at that? Seductive might be stretching it a bit in my case, Emma mused, but she thought she could pass for mildly sexy if she worked really hard at it.

Nevertheless, Emma felt like she was recapturing her youth. Well, making a return trip every once in a while anyway. Ben had even been hinting about a thong, but Emma was totally unconvinced about that one. She still didn't think a fifty-five-year old butt would look anywhere near good in a thong no matter how much exercising someone did. There were certain things in life that exercising just could not overcome and in this case it was that mound of gluteus maximus that was her middle-aged ass. Emma was going to try and hold him off on that one. Some fantasies at this age could turn out to be a real nightmare; better to leave well enough alone. The bikinis were enough of a shock for her to deal with for a while. They still felt completely weird whenever she had them on; she found she was constantly trying to pull them up every time she wore them. Imagine what she'd be doing to a thong! It would not be pretty.

Emma put on a pair of khaki pants and pulled a heathery purple angora turtleneck sweater over her head. The sweater felt wonderful next to her skin and she loved wearing it. She'd bet dollars to doughnuts Ben was going to like it too for however long it stayed on. She put on some knee-highs and slipped her feet into some shoes that would accommodate her nagging bunions. Cripe, those things were a pain in the you-know-what, but she wasn't in any hurry to have them removed. From what she heard about the operation, it was something to put off until she either couldn't walk anymore or she was near death. She'd choose death. Until then, she'd just buy wider shoes.

Those god-awful things were but only one of the lovely things she'd inherited from her grandmother. Thanks a lot, Grams, Emma thought, remind me to do the same for you! If only she could! The woman had been a bit of a bitch to put it mildly and never should have been allowed the title of Grandma. Grandmas were supposed to be warm and loving and gentle and tender. Those qualities had been nowhere to be found in this old woman. Hell, she'd been enough to scare a seasoned war veteran.

Not only had she been emotionally barren, but she'd been a behemoth of a woman to boot. She had to have been at least six foot tall and had probably weighed in around 250-275 lbs. And she hadn't been fat, dammit, she'd been all muscle or at least it had seemed that way when Emma had been small. Her upper arms had been the size of watermelons—big ones. And she'd been hard all over. There'd been nothing soft or squishy about her. She hadn't walked either; she'd stalked. She'd been—The Beast! When she'd been a child, Emma would have nightmares for a week after a visit with Grammy dearest. It wasn't enough that she'd tortured her while she was alive. Oh, no, now it was as if she'd reached out from the grave and grabbed Emma right through those damn bunions!

Ready at last, Emma took care of Cole and settled him in his crate. He wasn't all that happy about being left at home and gave Emma a look that told her so. On top of not leaving for the show after all the excitement the packing had aroused, he was being further disappointed by not being included in the evening's activities. He was not at a high point right now. So after visually delivering a telltale rebuke, he turned his head aside and gave her the cold shoulder.

Emma, having expected the rebuff ever since the dogs had become aware that they were not going to be jumping into the van and leaving, couldn't help but smirk at her dog. God, they were so predictable, at least as far as anything to do with leaving for a show was concerned. Joanie probably had her hands full right now with a miffed and vengeful Tank. Luckily for Emma, Cole would, in all likelihood, be fine by the time she got back home. Joanie, on the other hand, if established precedents were any indication, would not be so fortunate. Emma was sure she'd be hearing all about Tank's retaliatory payback tomorrow.

But right now it was time to go; so with a last goodbye to Cole, Emma left the house and got into her SUV to take the short ride down to Ben's. It took her all of one minute to reach her destination since Ben lived in the apartment building that was next door to the shop. She could have easily walked down the hill from her house, but didn't want to take the time. Geez, it would have taken her two or three minutes on foot and that was much too long. She had a hot, sexy man waiting for her! After exiting her car and locking it, she made her way upstairs to the second floor.

Ben had a comfortable apartment in the rear of the building, which housed eight units, so the view out his living room window was that of the woods that lay between his building and Emma's house. His apartment consisted of four rooms and a bath, with a balcony off the living room. The kitchen/dining room combination butted the far end of the living area and the two bedrooms and bath were off the central hallway.

Tweedy brown wall-to-wall carpeting covered the floors in the living room and bedrooms; the kitchen and bathroom floors had been laid with off-white tiles. The walls throughout were painted light beige; the ceilings were eggshell white.

The kitchen appliances were a utilitarian white and matched the spacious counter tops. The sink was stainless steel and the lighting fixtures in both the kitchen and dining areas were blasé enough to fit in with the rest of the apartment's basic color scheme.

The bathroom fixtures stuck to the same white theme and the tiles around the tub were gold-speckled squares with a white background. There was a single mirror that covered the medicine chest behind it hanging above the cabinet sink and the light fixtures were in line with the others that illuminated the apartment.

It was a very nondescript, aesthetically boring apartment as all apartments generally are. At least it had been until Ben had moved in with his personal belongings. He'd decorated his home to reflect his long time interest in sailing ships of old, which he'd developed while living in the Boston area when he'd been with the FBI. The area was rife with nautical history and Ben had succumbed to what had proved to be, for him anyway, its captivating lure.

In the living room there was a beautifully rich dark brown leather couch and two matching reclining chairs that were soft as butter. The coffee and side tables were made of highly polished bronzed oak with brass hardware. The lamps sitting atop the end tables were made from antique brass ship lanterns and had identical dark green shades. Across from the couch was an entertainment center and in the middle of the low coffee table that was between the two sat a perfect scale model of a 1700's tall sailing ship. There were two paintings on the wall of sailing vessels, one from the same era as the model and the other an early 1800's frigate. An oaken shelf above the couch held various relics from the sea and pieces of scrimshaw. A tall walnut bookcase held a collection of books, many of which were about sailing ships and nautical antiquities. Surprisingly enough, there were also several apothecary jars of colorful sea glass. The man had obviously spent a lot of time walking the beaches of New England.

The dining room held a black walnut oval table with six matching captain's chairs spaced around it. In the center of the table atop a runner with a nautical theme sat a ship's sextant of indiscernible age. The sideboard was made of matching walnut and it was home to a globe that pictured how the world was seen in the 18th century with the numerous trade routes clearly defined.

A massive king-size fruitwood bed dressed in blue and green plaid bed linens dominated the master bedroom. The accompanying chest-on-chest dresser, armoire, and nightstand were decidedly masculine and along with the matching blue draperies on the window lent the overall impression of the room to be one of seclusion and retreat.

The second bedroom was functioning as a study with bookcases, filing cabinets, and a large antique wooden desk that was at the center of the workspace. A computer sat in the middle of the desk and various seascapes decorated the walls. It was a no frills, get-down-to-business type of room, but the effect was softened as it was throughout the apartment with live houseplants, some of which were flowering.

Emma thought Ben had done a marvelous job of making a welcoming and homey nest for himself and was intrigued by the sensitivity it suggested. In her experience, most men didn't exhibit a flair for decorating much less concern themselves with creating a warm and cozy atmosphere. Let's face it; most of the male population couldn't care less about how their surroundings were decorated as long as there was a working television and a remote control within their grasp.

Emma rang the bell and almost immediately Ben was opening the door, a smile lighting his face. Emma drank in the sight of him for a total of two seconds tops before she stepped inside and found herself enveloped in his arms. The door was barely closed before Emma was receiving one of Ben's all-consuming kisses. Always one to participate in team sports, Emma returned the kiss with just as much gusto. God, they were like two little kids in a candy store. They never seemed to get enough of each other and it didn't seem likely that their supply of passion was going to run out any time soon. Emma had about fifteen years of it stored up and Ben—well, hell—he was a man, wasn't he? It went without saying he'd never run out.

They finally broke apart and walked into the living room. Emma thought Ben looked good enough to eat. He was dressed in faded jeans that didn't leave much to the imagination (of course, the kiss could have had something to do with that) and a red rugby shirt that hugged his muscular frame. His curly black hair, silvered only slightly at the temples was a little tousled like he'd run his fingers through it, and his glorious moustache was perfect as always. God, she loved that moustache and what it did to her when Ben kissed various parts of her body. Emma could feel herself getting turned on just thinking about it. Was this any way for a woman of her mature years to act? Yes, and if anybody didn't agree with her, they didn't know what they were missing.

Ben seated himself on the couch and watched Emma slide in next to him. The stirring blues of Buddy Guy were playing in the background. Ben already had a cold beer and a glass of chilled wine waiting on the coffee table. He handed Emma the wine and greedily soaked in every aspect of her appearance from her highlighted hair, to her flattering sweater and the lush form it covered, to her khaki slacks that hugged her firm hips and thighs, to her slender feet encased in brown leather flats. A vision if ever he'd seen one! She wouldn't agree with him, that he knew from previous compliments she'd batted away, but to him she was heaven on earth. God, he wanted her. She made him feel like a hormone-gone-crazy young boy. And if he didn't get his mind on something else, he'd take her right there and the hell with dinner.

With considerable effort, he picked up his beer and took a long drink before he spoke. "How did everything go with the loading today? Did you have any problems?"

"Just at first. We couldn't remember how to pack the van because it's been quite a while since we used it. But eventually everything came back to us."

"Is it all set? Is everything loaded now?" Ben stretched his arm along the back of the couch and let his hand rest on Emma's shoulder.

"Most everything. There are a few odds and ends yet, but other than us, the dogs, and the food it's all pretty much in there." Emma laid her hand on Ben's thigh.

"Sounds like you're ready to go." Ben's hand, involuntarily it seemed, started to rub small circles on Emma's arm.

"Yeah, we even packed TFG." Emma's hand slipped a little to the inside of Ben's leg.

"TFG?" Ben asked, his expression questioning, his hand momentarily still.

"Yeah, you know. *The shotgun.*" Emma moved her hand a little more to the inside of his thigh and lightly stroked upward.

"Oh…oh, right." Ben's voice hitched a bit. "I'm surprised you remembered to pack it." It was getting hard to have a coherent thought, much less speak it. Ben's hand resumed caressing Emma's arm, his fingers straying over to touch the outside of her breast.

"Well, Sally was on top of that one." Emma swallowed hard. She was starting to have the same problem. "She…she wasn't about to go anywhere without it."

"Good… I'm glad you'll have it with you. Better safe… than sorry." Ben abandoned Emma's arm and placed his whole hand on her breast. To hell with restraint! God, it didn't feel like there was much of a bra there. He could feel Emma responding, her nipple was rigid.

"Yeah, that's…that's what we th-thought." Emma shivered, not capable of thinking any more and speech was just about out of the picture. She shifted her hand and rubbed the front of Ben's jeans. Talk about full alert! There was standing room only behind that zipper right now.

Ben groaned and shifted a little under her touch. "How long… how long do you want to pretend we give a shit about this conversation?" Ben asked, his eyes nearly crossing.

"Not one second longer," Emma said, turning her head to press her mouth to Ben's.

"Thank God," Ben breathed against Emma's lips before he took control and claimed her mouth completely. When they came up for air several minutes later, Ben, his eyes fevered, asked, "Em, would you like to dance?"

Emma smiled, "Oh, God, yes." In Emma's opinion, Ben was about the sexiest dancer she'd ever encountered. God, could he move! To dance with him was in itself a sexual experience that she didn't think she'd ever get tired of. Dancing together, their bodies closely aligned and touching, her softness held against his hard muscular frame, had become a very sensual part of their lovemaking.

In one smooth movement, Ben brought Emma to her feet and into his arms. He guided her away from the coffee table and pressed her up close to his body. They fit together perfectly as they swayed to the music. Emma had her arms around Ben's neck and his were clasped behind her back at waist level, although they weren't there very long before his hands began to roam the length of her back, eventually sliding downward to her hips. Ben was quite a bit taller than Emma, he was 6'3" to her 5'6", so he had lowered his head and was kissing her neck, which she had helpfully arched to give him better access. Emma's hands were busy sifting through Ben's hair at the back of his head and her mouth had found an interesting spot just below his ear. His hands came to rest on Emma's bottom and he gently pulled her closer so that she felt his erection pressed against her stomach. She kissed his mouth hungrily and he wrapped her even tighter in his arms. Her breasts were flattened against his chest and she knew he could feel her hardened nipples. God, she loved the feel of him, every muscled part from his chest and arms to his thighs and calves. And then there was that tight, tight butt, not to mention that well-endowed evidence of his manhood, which was presently making itself known against her stomach. Lord, how had she ever gotten so lucky at this stage in her life?

Her mental question slipped away as Ben shifted slightly away and cupped her breast. His thumb had no trouble finding her nipple and he flicked it several times. Emma moaned and felt her legs start to give. He captured her mouth with his and continued to give attention to her breast as he slowly danced her into the bedroom. Before Emma knew it, her clothes, including her sexy underwear, were lying on the floor and she and Ben were soaring to the stars.

\* \* \* \*

It was quite a bit later, hours really, before Emma and Ben finally returned to earth. They'd both fallen into a sated sleep after their passionate lovemaking. They were in their fifties, after all, and it took a lot out of them. Not that they were complaining, mind you.

Once they'd awakened and played a little more (It's a rule: If you wake up naked in your lover's arms, you have to give him or her a parting shot of loving before you get out of bed.), they found they were ravenous. They dressed leisurely, Ben taking time to admire the underwear that before he hadn't even noticed. Well, geez, if given the choice what would any man worth his salt look at, underwear or a naked body? No contest. At any rate, that admiration cost them a little more time owing to what happened while he was admiring it. But eventually, they did make it out of the bedroom and into the kitchen.

Ben grilled New York strip steaks to perfection on the balcony while Emma fixed a salad. The potatoes had already been partially baked (Ben had planned ahead, that devil) and they hadn't needed much more time in the oven. The mixed vegetables had been zapped to readiness in the microwave during the last few minutes of everything else's cooking time and now all members of the major food groups were sitting on the table, including dairy which was represented by butter and sour cream.

"What time do you think you'll be getting back on Sunday?" Ben asked, his eyes on Emma's face. He didn't think he'd ever get tired of looking at her.

"Depends on how the showing goes. If Cole wins Group and then goes on to Best In Show, it'll probably be after six or six-thirty by the time we leave; add onto that a three-hour ride and that'll put us back at Sally's at nine, nine-thirty. Then we have to unload the van and reload our cars… It'll be late more than likely."

"Hmm…doesn't sound promising."

"For what?"

"For seeing you Sunday night."

"Oh…well, you never know. It might not go our way in Breed. Then we'd be done early."

"I don't think there's any chance of that happening."

"Ben, you never know what's going to happen when you step into that ring. It all rests on what the judge likes that day and how the dogs show. Cole could have an off day just as easily as any other dog. We've been extremely lucky."

"Oh, I think it's been a little more than luck."

"You're right. He's a great show dog, but still, you just never know."

"Well, even though I want to see you and for sure I'll suffer if I don't," Ben grinned, "I hope Cole takes another Best In Show on Sunday. In fact, I hope he takes the big win every day. That would really be tremendous, wouldn't it?"

"It would be fabulous, but a little too much to hope for I'm afraid. There's going to be a lot of great dogs at this show. Competition will be very stiff."

"Well, even so, I bet you can do it."

"Thanks for your vote of confidence, but I'll be happy with a couple of Group wins."

"You sell yourself short, sweetheart. If I were a betting man I'd put good money down on a sweep."

"Good thing you're not a betting man. You'd probably lose your shirt. Let me help you clean up. Then I'd better get going."

Together they took care of the food and dishes, then tidied up the kitchen. Ben walked Emma down to her car and couldn't resist laying a few big ones on her before she got behind the wheel. Emma in no way, shape, or form protested. What she did do was encourage those luscious lips and roaming hands. It was hard to tell there were two people standing there the way she'd plastered herself to Ben's mouth-watering body. It was with great reluctance that she finally peeled herself free and got in her car. He gave her one more guaranteed-to-make-you-hot kiss through the open window before she started the car and pulled away. Thank God she didn't have far to drive; with her mind not capable of stringing two coherent thoughts together, she would have never made it.

# Chapter Nine

The next morning, Emma walked down to the shop with Cole in a torrent of rain that was coming down so hard she thought it might have biblical proportions. It was going to be quite a day if this was a precursor as to what was to come. She'd no sooner had that thought than she stepped into a puddle that she hadn't seen and completely submerged her left foot. Well, crap! Where the hell had that come from? There was nothing quite like ice-cold water soaking through your shoe and into your sock to start the day. Dammit! Even the bottom of her left pant leg was wet and her other leg was pretty thoroughly splashed. She gave a quick glance over to Cole and found that he had very neatly sidestepped the offending water hazard and was giving her a look that let her know he was definitely laughing at her folly. Actually, he was just about bursting with it.

"You think this is pretty funny, don't you big guy?"

Cole gave her a big "woof" and wagged his tail, his stride breaking into a prancing high step.

"Oh, you just love this, don't you? Hmm? Don't you? I can tell you're in your glory right now, so don't try and deny it, you big goof. Is this part of your revenge for not leaving right away for the show? Huh? Come on, tell me the truth." Cole tipped his head up and gave Emma's hand a lick, mischief dancing in his eyes. "Well, I have to admit, it couldn't have worked any better if you'd planned it. Eeuw! That feels nasty. Come on, let's get inside."

Emma unlocked the door and they both stepped over the threshold. They were the first ones there so Emma started to turn things on as she walked, the shop springing to life bit by bit as she progressed through the store. Once everything was up and running, she shrugged out of her coat in the back room, and slipped out of her soggy shoe and sock. With one shoe on and one off, she went over to the grate and placed her sopping footwear over the heat that was already roaring up. She straddled the thing for a few minutes, making sure her bare foot was off the heated metal, and dried out her pants until they were only mildly damp.

Just as Emma was stepping away from the heat, Joanie came in with Tank tucked firmly under one arm. "Hey, Joanie," she called.

Joanie returned her greeting with a very short, "Em."

"Well, what's the matter with you?"

"Nothin'. Everything's just ducky."

"Right. What's wrong?"

"What could possibly be wrong?" Joanie's eyes were spitting bullets and Tank was squirming to get down, but she kept a tight grip on him.

"Umm…I don't know, but you seem to be a little out of sorts."

"You think?"

"Well, yeah! What's going on?"

"Not a thing. Not a damn, blessed thing…Tank, knock it off." Joanie gave him a little shake when he continued to wiggle.

"Uh-oh! I smell trouble."

"Yeah? Tell me about it."

"I bet I know what this means."

"You think so? Let me tell you something. You might think you do, but you have no idea."

"No, I think I know."

"Give it a shot then. Go ahead and tell me what put me in such a bitch of a mood."

"Well, taking my lead from past experience, there's only one thing that'll put you into this kind of bad temper. The Tankster has undoubtedly struck again. Right?"

"Oh, you could say that."

"Well, why don't you let him down and you can tell me all about this latest episode."

For the first time since she came in, Joanie really looked at Emma. "What the hell happened to you? Where's your friggin' shoe?"

"Geez! Aren't you in a mood."

"You're damn right. Now where's your friggin' shoe?"

"It's drying out on the grate along with my sock. I stepped in a puddle on the way down."

"Oh…well, that explains it."

"Joanie, calm down. You need to ease up before you break a blood vessel or something."

"I don't know if I can."

"Why don't you start by putting Tank down?" Emma laughed.

"Not yet and it isn't funny, goddammit. You don't even know what he did."

"That's true, I don't, but I have a feeling it was a good one."

"If you only knew…Oh, all right." Joanie took Tank's muzzle in her hand and turned his head so that he had to look at her. "Listen, you little monster. Be good or I'm going to send you to your maker. Pronto!"

Tank, not looking the least bit repentant over his alleged transgression, bounded out of Joanie's arms the minute she lowered him to the floor and raced to the back room. Cole, who'd been watching the goings on from the sidelines, followed his friend nonchalantly. He was sure he'd find out soon enough what had precipitated Joanie's ire. He already had a pretty good idea; he only needed the details.

"So spill it. What'd he do?"

"He hid."

"He hid?"

"Yeah. All night."

"And this has you ready to blow a gasket?"

"You better believe it."

"Why?" Emma couldn't help it. She was in full scale laugh mode now.

"'Cause I was worried about the little bugger! I thought something happened to him. You know how he is when he's after a squirrel or a chipmunk. There's no calling him off. I thought he'd gotten himself into trouble. I was up all night searching for him."

"*O-kaay.* Now I get the picture."

"I certainly hope so. It took you long enough."

"You searched all night?"

"Yeah, inside and out. You ever try to search sixty acres in the dark with nothing but a flashlight? In the rain?"

"Why didn't you call me? I would have come up."

"I know you would have, but I wasn't about to call you out in that weather. Besides, Sam was helping me, not that it did any good 'cause the little weasel wasn't even out there."

"Oh, shit. Where was he?"

"In the house."

"The whole time?"

"I'm pretty sure."

"Where?"

"I don't know where. I searched every nook and cranny before I went outside and I couldn't find him. Then this morning when I came back in he was just there, standing sweet as can be in the middle of the kitchen. He was just standing there, looking at me like *I* was crazy. He's the crazy one."

"I w-wonder where he w-was." Emma could barely talk she was laughing so hard.

"I haven't the foggiest idea and I'm so friggin' tired I can't think any more. God, he's going to be the death of me yet. And stop that damn laughing; it isn't funny!"

"Aw, geez! Y-yes, it is!" And Emma was off on another hoot.

"You're a big help."

"I kn-know!"

"What am I gonna do with him?"

"I d-don't know. He's certainly a ch-challenge."

"A challenge? That's a unique way of putting it. He's a friggin' disaster."

Emma's laughter slowly subsided as she wiped tears from her eyes. She was still composing herself when she went totally still. A sudden thought had just struck her. "That's what he did!"

"What'd he do?"

"It's so simple."

"What? What'd he do?"

"You're going to kick yourself in the ass when I tell you."

"If you don't hurry up and tell me, I'm going to kick *you* in the ass."

"I know what he did."

"Well, you better let me in on it real damn quick."

"He kept moving."

"Moving?"

"Yeah, in the house."

"What do you mean? When?"

"Boy, you must be tired if you can't figure this one out." Joanie shot her a look that told Emma her life was in danger.

"Okay, okay...When you were searching, I bet he moved from place to place after you'd checked it out. You know how he can move all quiet like when he wants to. He gets in that low body crouch and goes real slow and quiet. I bet that's what he did, Joanie."

Joanie stared at Emma a long moment before she switched her gaze to Tank who was staring at her from the back room. As the probability of Emma's deductions struck and eased into her exhausted brain, Joanie's eyes became narrowed slits and Emma thought she saw actual sparks shooting out. Emma switched her gaze to Tank who was giving Joanie a look that was downright smug. Uh-oh!

Joanie needed no other proof to know that Emma had hit the nail on the head. "Why, you little shithead. If I get my hands on you I'll strangle you. Do you hear me?"

Tank tossed his head and, if he could, would have more than likely stuck his tongue out. As it was his body language all too clearly shouted, "You lose!"

"Christ Almighty!" Joanie said, throwing her hands up in the air, both disgusted *and* defeated. "I don't believe it. He got me again."

"Looks that way."

"That dog's gonna be the death of me."

"Could be."

"Hell, I mean it. He's going to put me in an early grave."

"Hey, I don't doubt it. Really, not for a minute."

"Well, when he does...you'll notice I'm saying when, not if...when he does, you have to promise me something."

"What?"

"You have to promise me that you'll throw him in with me. If I go, he goes."

"All right. I promise, solemn oath." Emma raised her right hand in pledge. "But you know, it isn't over yet."

"What isn't over?"

"The torture."

"Oh, God, don't say that."

"But it's true."

"Why? Why do you think so?"

"Come on. You know why."

"Em, don't toy with me here. I'm not at my best. My thought processes are short-circuiting."

"It isn't over because we're not leaving 'til Wednesday night. That gives the little freak one more night to seek revenge."

"Oh, shit. I can't take another night." Joanie sounded totally done in.

"No, from the looks of you, I don't believe you can. That grave could be a whole lot closer than we think. Hmm... Well, how about if I take him home with me tonight?"

"What? You have a death wish?"

"Not really, but maybe he won't be so bad if he's with Cole."

"And what if he inspires Cole to wreak havoc? The two of them would be unstoppable. I can't let you do it. I won't let you sacrifice yourself. It's too high a price to pay." Secretly Joanie was praying that Emma would deliver her from another night of Tank-style torture, hence the dramatics. If she played her cards right, Emma would fall all over herself trying to help her out.

"Joanie, shut up. We'll be fine. Cole will keep him in line. You're the only one he likes to goad anyway, and you know it. It's because you're so darn easy and he can spot a sucker a mile away. He's a smart little shit."

"Yeah? Well, spot this." Joanie flipped Emma the finger. Damn, this was working perfectly! "Go ahead and take him. You think you're so smart. We'll see how you feel about the little bugger in the morning."

"He'll be fine, Joanie."

"Those words could spell the end of your cushy little life, you know."

"I doubt it. We'll manage. Don't worry."

"Me? Worry? About him? Not any more. I'll be worried about you."

"No need. Like I said, Cole will keep him in line."

"If you say so."

"Believe me, there won't be a problem."

"Fine. End of subject." Hallelujah! She shot, she scored! Emma had fallen for it hook, line, and sinker. She'd have a night of peace! Moving quickly to a safer subject, Joanie asked, "Hey, how was your dinner last night?"

"My dinner?"

Joanie quirked an eyebrow and gave Emma a sideways look. "Yeah, you know, your dinner with Ben—food, drink, eat, his apartment, last night."

"Umm…yeah, it was great."

"That's it? That's all you have to say?"

"Well…"

"Come on, out with the details. What gives?"

"Nothing gives. We… umm…had a great dinner."

"What else?"

"Nothing else."

"Don't give me that crap, Emma. What are you holding back?"

"Nothing, honest. It was just a little late by the time we ate, that's all," Emma said, looking a little sheepish.

"How come?" Joanie pushed. She knew that look. "You were over there around six, weren't you?"

"Yeah."

"Sooooo…Come on, give me the particulars."

"Well, we did a few other things first."

"Oh, yeah. Like what?"

"You know. Things."

"What things?"

"You know what things, dammit."

"Ohhh, okay…" Emma was blushing furiously under Joanie's scrutiny. "I see now. You were doing *those* sorts of things."

"Yeah."

"Things like the horizontal mambo."

"Joanie…"

"Yeah, yeah, I know. Well, what time did you finally get around to eating after you did those *things*?"

"I think it must have been around 10:30."

"Geez! You did an awful lot of things! Are you two going for a record or what?"

"*Nooo…*"

"You making up for lost time, Em?"

"Apparently."

"I guess so. Just be careful you don't wear yourself out."

"No danger of that. I pace myself."

"Well, you'd better and Ben too. You two aren't exactly youngsters anymore, you know."

"So we've noticed."

"Hmm, that sounds interesting. Could there be a story behind that statement?"

"Forget it, Joanie. I'm not explaining."

"Cripe, we've created a sex maniac. Whoda thought?"

"Not me, that's for damn sure."

"No shit, Miss-No-Sex-For-Fifteen-Years."

"What can I tell you? The flood gates have been opened."

"Yeah, and you're riding high on the wave."

"Yep."

"You've got to admit Sally and I do good work."

"Yeah, you did do good," Emma said, turning serious, her eyes suddenly filling with tears. "I owe both of you a lot. Thanks."

"Don't mention it. We just want you to be happy. And don't go getting teary-eyed on me now. We've got work to do." Joanie turned away from Emma quickly before she could see the tears that were filling *her* eyes now. For all their screwing around and good-natured ribbing, the three sentimental, middle-aged women cared a great deal about one another and their friendship meant the world to each of them.

Meanwhile off in a corner of the back room where the girls couldn't see them, Tank communicated to Cole in that doggy way they had exactly what he had done the night before. Cole "listened" attentively and had to give the little guy credit for inventiveness and high scores for deviousness. He wasn't about to pat him on the back, however. Tank was puffed up enough; he was strutting around like a peacock and it was that smug look on his face that told Cole he needed to take him down a peg.

Cole moved so quickly Tank never saw it coming. In an instant, Cole had brought his big paw up and pushed Tank over on his back, pinning him to the floor. He looked up into the Newfoundland's face and instead of getting what he thought would be an approving nod, he was greeted with a sobering look only Cole could dispense. Uh-oh, Tank thought, the big guy doesn't look real happy. It wasn't the reaction he'd expected; he'd anticipated Cole heaping accolades upon his wonderful self. That wasn't exactly what he was getting. Not at all! Cole locked eyes with the mischievous troublemaker and stared hard for a minute or so. Tank gulped, unable to look away. He got the message; he was to cease and desist. He gave Cole a baleful look and raised his front legs up over his head. He'd accept surrendering to Cole's wishes, for the moment anyway.

* * * *

Despite the rainy weather the shop was busy right up until closing time and the girls found they had a mere forty-five minutes to eat and set up for class. They ordered grilled chicken sandwiches from the pizza place that was diagonally across the street and started to get the back room in order. As the dogs' toys disappeared one by one into the storage unit, Tank and Cole's attitude became increasingly grumpy.

"Hey, you guys know the drill. We have to clean this mess up," Emma said, noting their sulking demeanor.

"Kirby will be here later and you can play with her. If we leave all this stuff out, somebody could break a leg tripping over it...Tank! Get away from that ball. Drop it!" Joanie made a quick lunge to grab the terrier but Tank was faster and bolted out to the front of the store with the ball held firmly between his jaws. "Damn him!"

"Oh, Lord! Here we go!" Emma said as she scrambled after him.

With Cole leading the charge, the girls bounded after Tank. Once they hit the main sales floor, they separated, trying to box him in. Well, that was what the girls were trying to do at any rate. Cole was just giving chase as he usually did when Tank threw down the gauntlet. To him this was an even better game than what they usually had going because the girls were involved. Both dogs were up for this one!

Up and down the aisles they went with Tank avoiding capture mostly because of his size and speed. Nevertheless, it didn't hurt that Cole was running interference at critical junctures. Joanie thought she had him at one point and ended up sprawled on her stomach after she missed him. Emma was laughing so hard she could barely walk much less run and her effectiveness was reduced to zero. She ended up collapsing on the floor and was content to just sit and watch the whole thing.

"We don't have time for this," Joanie shouted as she made another grab for the elusive little dog. "Come on, Tank. Give it up." Across the room and under a cabinet now, Tank gave her a triumphant look. "You've won, okay?" Joanie conceded. "Now let me have the ball, so we can finish up. Come on. Come here."

Tank glanced over at Cole who was standing a few feet away. Their eyes held for a moment and Tank came out from under the cupboard. With Cole at his side, they both walked over to where Joanie stood and Tank dropped the ball at her feet.

"Thank you. That's a good boy." As Joanie bent down to pick up the ball, Tank swooped in and grabbed it before Joanie could get hold of it. He was off like a rocket with Cole guarding his rear. "Shit! Goddamn that dog!"

Tank led Joanie on another lively chase for the next five minutes and it probably would have gone on longer if Emma hadn't finally trapped him beneath her legs when Tank had tried to run under them.

Joanie had been yelling for Emma to get up and make herself useful just moments before Tank made his fatal mistake. Emma might have looked like a useless lump on the floor to Joanie's way of thinking, but she knew exactly what she was doing. She knew Tank would never be able to resist seeing if he could get by her. All she had to do was wait. And wait is what she did until just the right moment. Tank never had a chance; he was stuck beneath Emma's legs and the ball was whisked out of his mouth before he knew what had hit him. Emma was extremely pleased with herself when she showed Joanie the offending ball clutched tightly in her hand. Joanie only gave her a disgusted look for her successful retrieval; Emma gave her the finger.

However, with the quest having been brought to a successful end, Joanie left and picked up dinner while Emma finished putting the toys away and laid out the students' projects. They were still eating when the first of the ladies showed up and the rest followed within the next few minutes. Kirby came in with Sally and, while the women adjourned to the back room, the three dogs stationed themselves behind the counter and got on with whatever game they were going to cook up for the night.

Putting the project together was always an interesting experience for the girls, especially if the student was a first-timer. Some of them had never used a hammer before much less an electric drill or screwdriver. Heck, some of them didn't even know the difference between a nail and a screw. It was total confusion if a staple was thrown into the mix!

Of the six women present, three were making their first project. Emma and Joanie were definitely going to have their hands full. Some of the ladies took to it like a duck to water—while some—well, some of them never got the hang of it and the girls ended up putting most of the thing together themselves. Miss Priss looked like she could very well be a candidate for the latter distinction.

An hour later, that particular prophecy had been confirmed. Emma was manning all the tools of the trade to assemble the woman's project, having to give her almost exclusive one-on-one instruction for all the good it did. God, the woman was a wimp! She wouldn't even pick up the darn drill. She kept making small whimpering noises and fluttering her hands every time Emma tried to give it to her. It was to Emma's credit that she hadn't backhanded her yet. Thank God, Joanie wasn't the one who was stuck with her. She probably would have drawn blood already. As it was Joanie had her hands full with the remaining five, but thankfully the other two first-timers seemed to be up to the task.

The wine had been brought out earlier and Emma, Joanie noticed, was keeping her glass full. Joanie speculated that Miss Priss must have been taking a very large toll on

Emma's patience. She shot Emma a look of sympathy and Emma rolled her eyes heavenward. Little did she know that Emma was giving serious thought to maybe letting loose with a few good swear words and seeing what the woman's reaction would be. If they were lucky Miss Priss might just run for the hills and they'd be done with her. Emma was sure that Joanie would approve, but abandoned the plan when the woman confided that she'd never had so much fun and was going to tell all her friends about the classes. Emma closed her eyes for a minute, clamped her mouth shut and kept working.

Everyone, by one means or another, had successfully finished their Santa by 8:30 and after the girls pronounced them all masterpieces, five of the ladies left for home thrilled with their accomplishment.

Sally stayed behind to help with the cleanup, which was an even bigger undertaking than on the first night of a project. There was sawdust, small pieces of fabric, broken grapevine, Spanish moss, and bits of wire all over the table and floor. The drills and bits, pliers, wire cutters, screws, staples, scissors, bottles of glue, coils of wire, yards of fabric, greenery, and unraveled lengths of grapevine were scattered from here to there. The back room looked like a marauding army had just torn through it.

While keeping the dogs at bay and out of the mess, the three friends wasted no time in setting the room to rights. Emma and Joanie had cleanup down to a fine art and Sally easily learned her part in it. They were finished in less than half an hour.

Sally left for home with Kirby at her side and her acclaimed work of perfection under her arm. Two minutes later Emma and Joanie parted in the parking lot. With Tank securely tucked under her arm and Cole next to her left leg, Emma started up the hill, her flashlight beam bouncing in the darkness as she walked.

* * * *

*Bright sunshine had warmed the early summer air to a comfortable 80 degrees. There was almost no humidity and the July sky was a brilliant blue. Narrow bands of thin, wispy snow-white clouds dotted the infinite expanse. The leaves on the trees rustled softly, their branches swaying languidly in the gentle breeze. Birds were chirping and the muffled sounds of children playing could be heard. Their innocent laughter and joyful shrieks floated over the wealthy neighborhood.*

*It was almost 4:00 and time for her to start heading home. Her parents were taking her out to eat tonight in celebration of her thirteenth birthday, which was tomorrow. A large family party was scheduled in observance of the big day, but tonight was just for her and her parents. It would be the first time she was permitted to go to the country club for dinner and she wanted to make sure she had enough time to get ready because this evening she wanted to look very grown-up. Her mother had surprised her with a new dress and shoes to mark the big occasion and she couldn't wait to put them on. She wanted everything to be sooo perfect.*

*She said goodbye to her best friend, Alison who had walked with her out from the backyard where they'd been lying in the sun near the pool. Still clad in her bathing suit and a hot pink cover-up that she'd hastily thrown on, she climbed onto her bike. With a few last parting words and shared girlish giggles, she started down the driveway and Alison, after giving her one last little wave, disappeared into the house.*

*Alison's house was at the end of the cul-de-sac in their heavily wooded neighborhood and she lived about ten houses away. She steered her bike out into the street and riding next to the curb on the right-hand side, headed for home.*

*The breeze felt good on her face and her long blond hair was streaming behind her. She was daydreaming about what color she was going to paint her nails, something to go with her dress, maybe pink. She had a couple of different shades of pink to choose from, or maybe she should use a white pearl like her mom since she wanted to look grown-up and besides, the country club was kind of formal. Maybe she should...*

*The sounds of barking dogs and running feet yanked her roughly back from her frivolous thoughts and she wobbled the bike. She looked behind her, still trying to steady the two-wheeler, and saw three dogs chasing after her. They were big and black and looked very mean. They were growling and snapping and showing all their teeth!*

*She shrieked in fear and turned her head away, trying to pedal faster. She had to get home where it was safe. She instinctively tried to call for her mom, but her throat was constricted with mind-numbing terror and nothing came out—nothing but a strangled whimper.*

*She hadn't gone ten feet and they were on her, one jumping on her back and the other two bumping hard into her left leg and the rear wheel. She could feel the dog's wet mouth on her bare leg and the scrape of his teeth along her skin. She felt the bike going down and her with it, the dog on her back tenaciously holding on. The bike hit the curb and fell into the grassy area between the road and the sidewalk. She tumbled off, going head over heels and landed on the sidewalk on her back, free for the moment from the dog that had attached himself there. He'd had to let go when she'd somersaulted.*

*Stunned, she was unable to get up and the dogs moved in quickly. They attacked ferociously and she was utterly defenseless. She brought her arms up, but they were useless against their onslaught. The dogs slashed and grabbed, biting into her tender flesh. She saw their eyes wild with savage bloodlust and they bored into her very soul. Their teeth were huge and they kept tearing at her face and body.*

*She heard their terrible snarling and growling, the sound of their jaws snapping. There was blood everywhere, all over her, all over them. They kept biting her over and over. Why wouldn't they stop?*

*From a long distance away, she heard a car horn blaring and brakes squealing. Suddenly, her tormentors were gone, the attack stopped. She was barely conscious, but enough that now she felt the pain. Oh, God, the pain...*

Moira bolted upright in bed, an agonized moan escaping her lips. For a second or two she could feel it, the pain, just like she had that day. Her sweat-soaked body shuddered, her stomach clenching into a knot. She gagged, her breathing loud and harsh in the quiet room. She lifted a shaking hand and pushed her hair off her forehead, then sat very still, getting her bearings after having lived through the nightmare yet once again. She allowed only her eyes to move and they darted to the clock, its illuminated face telling her it was 4:30 in the morning. At least she'd gotten through most of the night before she'd been plunged back in time and terror. She closed her eyes in thankfulness.

After a long while, she switched on the bedside lamp thereby insuring banishment of bad dreams and torments. She picked up a copy of a trade magazine from the nightstand next to the bed with hands that were still subject to quaking tremors and opened the periodical to the first article she came to. Mindless of its content, she began to read, doing so until her nerves had steadied, her sweat dried and she was able to face the day.

# Chapter Ten

"Well, I see you survived the night. You're here. How about Tank? Is he still alive? Maimed in any way?" Joanie threw her observation and questions out to Emma as she walked toward the sales counter the next morning.

"Hey, I'm fine and, believe it or not, so is he. He was good." Tank chose that moment to come out from behind Cole and jumped into Joanie's arms.

"It certainly looks like he's all in one piece," she said as she examined her wayward dog. "How about you? Physically you look all right, but how about any mental scarring?"

"No, no problem there. I'm not any worse off than I already was."

"What about Tank? Is he any more mentally twisted than he was before? Any more screws come loose?"

"It's hard to tell, but I don't think so. I think Cole put the fear of God into him. I caught a few looks passing between the two of 'em and it seemed like Cole had the upper hand."

"I might have to give the big boy a few extra biscuits as a reward for all his efforts." Joanie turned her attention to Cole. "Come here, big guy." Cole ambled over and Joanie lavished him with hugs and kisses. "My hero! If I had a medal, Cole, I'd pin it on ya."

"I'm sure he'll be happy enough with the biscuits. God knows he loves 'em. Tank even behaved when I gave him a bath."

Joanie's eyes widened in astonishment. "He did?"

"Yeah. I had to give Cole a bath last night, so I thought I might as well give Tank one too. He was great. He stood in the tub, nice as can be, and let me do my thing. Maybe he's seen the error of his ways. Could be he's reforming…" Joanie shot her an incredulous look. "…or not."

Joanie rolled her eyes. "Surely you're not serious?"

Emma didn't answer; she just gave her a sick look.

"Tank, reform? Are you really that gullible?"

"I never thought I was."

"Well, I've got news for you. If you think Tank will reform, you're not only gullible, you're bordering on stupid."

"Yeah, well…hell, you can always hope for a miracle."

"Don't waste your time. Not with Tank anyway. I'm sure this is but a small departure from the norm. He'll probably come back with a vengeance, won't you, Tank?"

Tank twitched his ears, cocked his head to one side, and gave Joanie a quick look that said, "You betcha!" and wiggled to get down. Joanie put him on the floor and he took off with Cole to the back room. They were knee deep in toys within two minutes.

"Did you see that look he gave me? He's already back to normal."

"Sorry, Joan. I was hoping the reformation would last a little longer."

"Maybe when hell freezes over… Well, what are you going to do? That's life," Joanie waxed philosophically. "Did you get everything packed?"

"Yeah, I didn't have that much to finish up. Everything but the food is in the car already."

"Same for me, but I brought my goodies with me and put them in the shop's refrigerator. I can go right to Sally's from here."

"Crap! Why didn't I think of that?"

"'Cause you're old."

"Yeah, I'm friggin' ancient."

"You're older than I am."

"You don't need to remind me."

"It helps on occasion."

"Oh, boy, here we go," Emma groused. "How?"

"It should be obvious."

"Well, it's not."

"Then I'm not telling you."

"Joanie…"

"What?"

"Where are you going with this?"

"Don't have a clue."

"Didn't think so."

"Then what'd you ask me for?"

"Blame it on a moment of insanity."

"Will do."

"You're just busting on me, aren't you?"

"Yep."

"Why?"

"Got sidetracked. Thought I'd pull an 'Angie' on ya."

"Oh, please… Can we get back on track?"

"Guess so, but that was kind of fun."

"Yeah, it was a regular riot. And knowing you, I'm sure we'll be doing it again sometime soon."

"Hope so. I'll be looking forward to it."

"I'm sure you will. Now, if you can drag your mind back to the trip—"

"Yeah, I'm there."

"Good—"

"Let's say you had a brain fart," Joanie interrupted.

"What?"

"You know, a brain fart."

"What about?"

"About the food thing."

"Geez, are we back to that?"

"Yeah, I thought you'd like it better if we blamed it on a brain fart instead of your age."

"Oh, for cripe's sake! Blame it on anything you want. I don't really give a shit. Now can we get back to the trip?"

"Sure, go right ahead. But I kind of like the brain fart thing."

"Good for you, Joan. I'm happy for you."

"Thank you."

"You're a total ass."

"No shit."

"Back to the trip?"

"Okay, I'm ready."

"Thank you, God," Emma said, looking upward. "Now, if everything goes right, we might be able to leave before seven."

"That would be great. Get there a little earlier. Go to bed a little sooner. Yeah, I could live with that."

"I think we all could. We're going to be whipped after working all day and then traveling for three hours."

"Yeah, and we'll be prime for plenty of brain farts."

"Joanie!"

"Well, it's true. We'll be tired *and* bored. We'll be traveling on *the* most boring part of the Thruway after all."

"At least it'll be dark and we won't have to look at the countryside."

"Now there's a blessing," Joanie said. The stretch of the New York State Thruway they were talking about, the part between Rochester and Syracuse, was undoubtedly the flattest and most boring part of any Thruway ride. There were no hills; there were no valleys. There was just flat land and swamps, the Montezuma Swamps to be exact, and they were not pretty. They were nothing but boring.

The phone rang right then, interrupting any more commiseration on the dullness of the scenery they were blessedly not going to be subjected to thanks to the darkness that would have descended by the time they were traveling through it. And to Emma's relief, any more talk of brain farts was abruptly abandoned.

The person calling was Peggy McAllister, owner of The Three Oaks Gift Shoppe on Route 16 in Chaffee and a long-time friend of Emma's. "Hey, how you doing over there?" she asked in greeting.

"We're great, Peg. Business is good. How're you faring?" Emma asked. She'd gotten to the phone first.

"Can't complain, I'm really busy most days."

"Good. Glad to hear it. Hey, did that lady ever show up the other day? The one we sent over for the witch's ball."

"Yeah, she did. Thanks for the referral. She ended up buying two of them in fact."

"Terrific. Glad we could help."

"Listen, the reason I'm calling is I've got some news that I'm sure you're going to love."

"Really? What is it?"

"You'll never guess in a million years who got fired."

"Who?"

"Are you ready?"

"Yeah, tell me."

"George Fleming!"

"You're kidding!"

"No, honest to God. I just heard from Marge over at The Red Caboose."

"Hot damn! Wow! Hey, hang on a minute. Joanie's about ready to come out of her skin wanting to know what we're talking about." Emma covered the receiver and turned to Joanie who'd been peppering her with numerous "whats?" while she'd been talking to Peggy. Before she could hit her with another one, Emma told her, "George Fleming was fired!"

Joanie's eyes seemed to widen to the size of half dollars. "Yes!" she screamed and immediately high-fived Emma. Emma's ears were still ringing when Joanie went into one of her demented victory dances.

Emma turned back to the receiver and heard Peggy say, "Guess Joanie liked the news."

"Geez, how could you tell?"

"My eardrums are still vibrating."

"Imagine how mine feel."

"No thanks, I'm just glad I had a little distance from her."

"Don't make me jealous."

"Sorry."

"So, how'd it happen?"

"Well, you know that after he was so rude to you I quit using him too. In fact, I haven't ordered anything from the company since." The last time George had been in The Whistling Thistle, he'd taken offense at what the girls had *not* been ordering and called Joanie a bitch. They'd taken exception and obviously so had Peggy.

"Yeah, neither have we."

"Well, it seems the higher-ups at Always Perfect Gift started making a few phone calls to George's accounts and it appears that we weren't the only ones with complaints."

"Well, wait a minute… Why would they start to investigate? It's not like losing our two accounts would really damage the company."

"Nooo, but after I made a little phone call to corporate headquarters, they were very interested."

"You're kidding! You made a phone call?"

"Yep, I sure did. Wanted to know if it was company policy for their reps to swear at their customers."

"You didn't."

If Joanie, in her excitement to know what was going on, kept pulling on Emma's arm much more it was going to be several inches longer than the other one by the time she got off the phone.

"Oh, yes, I did."

"I don't believe it."

"You better believe it 'cause that's exactly what I did and I guess it got the ball rolling. Shop owners started coming out of the woodwork to report their complaints."

"How come we never got a phone call?"

"I don't know, but from what Marge said the company found a lot worse things than George swearing at customers."

"No kidding. Like what?"

"Oh, like quadruple ordering with one shop. I guess there were four owners and he did separate orders with each one of them. They never realized what Fleming was doing until it was too late. They ended up having to take a loan out to pay the bill. True, there seems to have been a complete lack of communication between the four, but still—"

"He really took advantage."

"Yeah, big time. There was a lot of other stuff too, but the end result was that good ol' George got his butt canned."

"Hallelujah! Woo-hoo!"

"Like I said, I thought you'd like the news."

"Couldn't have happened to a nicer guy."

"My thoughts exactly."

"God, I bet he's madder than hell."

"I think that would be a real safe bet."

"This is great news, Peg. Thanks for the heads-up."

"My pleasure. I'd better run now, the shop's getting busy. Keep in touch."

"We will and thanks again for letting us know. You've made our day."

They both hung up and Emma readied herself to make full disclosure to her partner who'd been hanging on every word Emma said.

\* \* \* \*

The day seemed to drag on forever despite their preoccupation with Mr. Fleming's fall from grace and even though the shop was a hubbub of activity, time seemed to creep by. Actually, at this time of the year there wasn't a day that went by that wasn't filled with the hustle and bustle of customers trying to buy the ideal gift. And it would only get worse the closer they got to Christmas. To have a slow day during the holiday season was so rare that for all practical purposes, they didn't exist. Nevertheless this day, regardless of how swamped the girls were, was taking way longer than it should have to be over.

Even a visit from Mrs. Foster, who needed to pick up the keys and get instructions, failed to speed up the clock. The girls were sure that at least three quarters of an hour should have gone by when Mrs. Foster took her leave, but damn, only fifteen minutes had elapsed and she had been full of gossip. You would have thought it would have taken way more time to get the latest scoop.

Emma and Joanie's frustration was growing by leaps and bounds every time they looked at the clock, whose hands seemed to be practically frozen in place. Heaven help their customers if they reached their flash point, which was lurking ominously in the shadows nearly ready to bust out. Why the heck wouldn't this day just get over with?

Could it be that they were more than a little anxious to be on their way to a show? Had time seemed to slow to a crawl because they were near to bursting with excitement about getting back in the ring? After all, they hadn't competed in five months and that was a long time for the girls not to have stepped foot on what they considered hallowed ground. Or maybe it was the dogs who were themselves so excited they were barely behaving with their usual good manners. Joanie thought she might implode if she had to give Tank even one more warning and Emma had taken to ignoring Cole's constant prancing because he was making her so nervous she was having trouble breathing. All in all everybody's nerves were stretched to the limit; they needed to leave for the show. If only the damn day would end!

Finally it happened. The day was over. It was 6:00. It was time to close. After what seemed like three days rolled into one, the blasted day was done. The girls practically pushed the last customers out the door before they shut down and locked up. Joanie virtually ran to the refrigerator to retrieve the food she'd stored there that morning. Then she grabbed Tank, shot out the door, got in her truck, and headed for the restaurant.

Emma and Cole were right behind her and essentially sprinted all the way up to the house. A breathless Emma nabbed her stash of food and scooted Cole out the door; they ran to the SUV and jumped in. Castigating herself again for not bringing the car and food down to the shop that morning, echoes of Joanie's brain fart theory reverberated in her mind. Screw it, she thought; it was anybody's guess why she'd spaced out and there was no reason to contemplate it anyway. Who cared? Things happen. She'd just chalk it up to a "senior moment" and leave it at that. At any rate, Emma put the car in gear, revved the engine, and they were off.

Less than fifteen minutes had elapsed between the time Emma left the shop and drove into the Hearthmoor's parking lot. She pulled in next to Joanie's truck at the far side of the barn, parked, and jumped out. Joanie was already unloading; Tank was in the kennel area barking like a madman. Joanie didn't bother to try and shut him up. Why waste her breath?

Under these circumstances, she knew it was an exercise in futility. Tank was too psyched up; he knew they were leaving.

Emma put Cole in with Tank. Cole walked over to his buddy and gave him a little nudge; Tank shut up. Joanie stopped what she was doing and looked over at her nemesis, then switched her gaze to Cole. "I owe ya," she said.

Cole woofed, acknowledging the debt.

Emma and Joanie continued to unload. The girls transferred everything to the van and then went in search of Sally. They found her in the kitchen giving last minute instructions to Tom. Kirby had her nose in the air smelling the beef tenderloin that was cooling on the stove, hoping against hope that she was going to get some. She was out of luck; it just wasn't going to happen, especially after her steak-napping escapade.

"Hey, Sal. Hi, Tom."

"Hi, guys," Sally called, her attention momentarily diverted to her two friends.

"Hi, Emma, Joanie," greeted Tom.

"You ready to go, Sal?"

"Yeah, in a minute. I was just finishing up here."

"No rush. It's not like we have anywhere to go or anything," Joanie said sarcastically.

"Cute, smart-ass."

"Hey, at your service."

"Take your time, Sally. We'll be out at the bar," Emma said, dragging Joanie with her.

Sally joined them no more than ten minutes later and the girls helped her bring her gear out to the van. Once everything they could think to take was loaded, they got the dogs and put them in their crates. They each went back in for one more visit to the bathroom seeing as how it was a necessity at their ages, and yelled their goodbyes as they went out the door for the last time. They piled into the van with Sally in the driver's seat, Emma in the front passenger's, and Joanie in the back seat behind Sally. It was preordained where they sat, a carryover from the motor home.

With a hoot and a holler they pulled out onto Route 240 going north and then turned west onto Genesee Road, which would take them to the 219 Expressway. From there they'd hook up with the Thruway. Once they were through the Williamsville tollbooths it would be a straight shot over to Syracuse where comfortable beds awaited them at the Gate Post Motel, which was about a mile down the road from the show site on the New York State Fairgrounds.

As far as the weather was concerned, the girls couldn't have asked for better traveling conditions at this time of year. No precipitation was forecast for any part of their journey, winds were on the light side, and the temperature was supposed to hover in the mid thirties. So with all that going for them and dry roads all the way, it should be an easy ride.

They hadn't even made it through the Buffalo interchanges on the Thruway before they'd eaten the sandwiches that Tom had made for their dinner. It was impossible to smell the succulent aroma of hot sliced seasoned beef and grilled vegetables on fresh sourdough rolls and not dive in and eat. Besides, they reasoned, the sandwiches wouldn't be any good cold. So, they'd had to eat! And boy, did they. Each of them devoured two of the tasty concoctions and then topped their meal off with some rice pudding, which had been neatly packaged in disposable containers. *Now* they were ready to travel! Road trip here we come!

They had just passed Rochester when Sally asked Joanie if she would get her a bottle of water from the cooler and a couple of aspirin from her purse.

"Sure, just a minute. What's wrong?"

"Nothing much. It's just a little headache. It started around Batavia and I want to catch it before it gets too bad."

"Are you sure you're all right?"

"Yeah. I'll be fine once I get the aspirin." Joanie handed the water and medication up to Sally. "Thanks, Joanie."

"No problem."

"Do you want me to drive, Sal?" Emma asked.

A resounding "NO!" sprang from both Sally and Joanie's mouths. In fact their emphatic response was so loud, that startled, Emma jumped in her seat.

"Geez, you guys, take it easy."

"Sorry, Em," they both mumbled.

"Why can't I drive?" Emma asked, looking from one to the other.

"Em, you know why," Sally said.

"No, I don't. All I have to do is go straight, right? I can do that."

"That's true, you can go straight, but it's also dark."

"So?"

"Do we have to remind you that you can't see shit in the dark?" Joanie asked, giving Emma a look that said she ought to know better than to even ask to drive.

"What's there to see other than the road for cripe's sake?"

Sally caught Joanie's eye in the rearview mirror and shook her head. "*That* is precisely why you can't drive, Emma."

"What is?" Emma asked, truly puzzled.

"Your question."

"Sorry, I'm not following you."

"We know," Joanie said.

"Emma, you have to watch for deer. That's what you have to see other than the road."

"Oh."

"Yeah, oh. You never see them until you're practically on top of them. That won't work at 65 miles an hour."

"*Ohhh*. All right, I gotcha," Emma replied good-naturedly.

"And don't forget about other cars," Joanie stated.

"What about them?"

"You have to watch out for them too."

"No shit, Joanie."

"Well...you know, sometimes—"

"Can it, Joanie. I see other cars."

"Yeah, right. How about the time—"

"Never mind. That was a long time ago," Emma interrupted. "Sally? Do you want Joanie to drive?"

"No, I think I'll be fine. If my headache doesn't let up in the next fifteen minutes or so, I'll pull into a rest area and make the switch. Okay?"

"Okay."

"We'll let you drive from the motel to the fair grounds, Em."

"Gee, thanks."

"Don't mention it," Sally said, her grin hidden in the darkness of the vehicle.

Emma was thoughtful for a moment and then asked in all seriousness, "I won't have to back up, will I?"

"No, Em. We'll make sure you don't have to back up."

"Good. 'Cause you know I can't do that."

"Yeah, we know, Em."

"Especially in a van."

"Yeah, we know."

"I just can't seem to get the hang of it."

"We know."

"Mack tried to teach me, but I just couldn't do it."

"We know that too."

"I really tried, but no way could I do it."

"We know, Em."

"There's something wrong with my depth perception."

"We know."

"I can never tell where my wheels are."

"Yeah, we know."

"I can't seem to figure it out."

"Yeah, well, you've proved that time and again."

"I try to be safe though."

"We know that."

"I always park so I can pull straight out."

"Hell, we know that too, Em."

"It doesn't matter how far I have to walk through a parking lot to get to a store, I find a space where I can pull straight out."

"God, don't we know that."

"Well, at least I know my limitations."

"You certainly do and so do we," Sally said.

"What's that supposed to mean?"

"I think you know."

"Well, maybe."

"Maybe?"

"Oh, all right."

"But, Em," Joanie said tongue-in-cheek. "We want you to know we still think you're a hell of a good driver."

Emma gave Joanie a quelling look. "Hey, Joanie?"

"Yeah?"

"Bite me."

# Chapter Eleven

They pulled into the motel's parking lot at 9:45 with Sally still in the driver's seat, her headache having dissipated within the fifteen-minute time limit. She parked the van in one of the slots in front of the office, which was located at the end of the building closest to the street. Joanie jumped out to register and get the room key since she'd been the one who'd made the reservation. She was back in five minutes and directed Sally where to park so they'd be in close proximity to their room.

It appeared they were on the second floor since the room number on the key tag read 216. This was *not* good news.

"I thought you asked for a room on the first floor," Emma said as Sally parked in a space near the far end of the motel.

"I did."

"Are you sure?"

"Yeah."

"Well, it doesn't look like we got one. We'd better go find out exactly where the room is before we start unloading."

The girls locked the vehicle before they walked into the building. They entered the double doors located at the end of the motel and were immediately in an everywhere-you-

145

look beige-colored stairwell that ascended to the second floor. They marched upward and after going through the beige metal fire door, walked down the serviceable brown tweed carpeted corridor until they found room 216. It was about halfway down the hallway. Joanie fit the key into the lock and opened the door. She found the light switch and flipped it on. Sally and Emma stepped into the room and let the door close. Then all three stood there as if their feet were glued to the floor and stared. Nobody moved, nobody spoke; they just fixated on the only thing that had captured all of their attention.

It was the bed. The only bed. The one bed. Three women, one bed. It didn't compute. Pulling their eyes away from what they hoped was a hallucination, Emma and Sally turned slightly and redirected their now-accusatory gaze at Joanie.

"I asked for two beds," she blurted out, feeling a compelling need to defend herself before her two friends launched their attack.

"Right."

"I did!"

"Are you sure?"

"Yes!"

"Just like you asked for a first-floor room?"

"Yes!"

"Are you positive?"

There was a slight hesitation before Joanie answered somewhat timidly, "Almost."

"Oh, shit."

"Who did you deal with? Did they speak English? Did *you* speak English?"

"Of course I did. Don't be stupid. What do you think I am?"

"Don't make me answer that right now," Emma said.

"How hard can it be to get across that you need two beds?"

"You'd be surprised," Joanie grumbled.

"Well, this is just great. Nothing like starting off the whole weekend on the wrong foot."

"Stay here," Joanie said. "I'll go down to the office and get this straightened out."

"I hope so, or it's certainly going to be a long four days."

"You mean nights," Sally corrected.

"Whatever," Emma said. "We'll hardly be at our best if we all have to share a bed the entire time. It's going to be a little crowded, not to mention uncomfortable."

"Good thing we like each other," Joanie ventured.

"That may change sooner than you'd think."

"Oh, come on. We've always been close."

"We can all do without that much closeness, thank you very much."

"Joanie, don't take offense, but Emma and I would rather not be joined at the hip while we sleep."

"You guys are getting awfully picky."

"Joanie…" Both Emma and Sally fixed her with a no-nonsense glare.

"All right, all right. I'll see what I can do. Don't worry, guys. I'll get this fixed. I'll be back in a few minutes. Don't lose hope."

"We wouldn't think of it… Sally and I'll walk the dogs while you take care of business. They must have to go."

The three exited the room and while Joanie marched off to the office, Emma and Sally put the dogs on leads and took them off to a grassy area just beyond the well-lit parking lot so they could relieve themselves.

"So, what do you think?" Sally asked while they waited for the dogs to do their thing.

"About what?"

"You *know*, the room thing. Do you think Joanie's going to be able to fix it?"

"Nope."

"There isn't even a glimmer of hope, is there?"

"Not a one. A snowball's got a better chance in hell than she does."

"Yeah, that's what I kind of figured too."

Resigned to their fate, they walked the dogs around the lot a few times to stretch out any cramped muscles and exhaust some of the energy that had been stored up during the three-hour ride. This was especially important where Tank was concerned—the energy part, that is. If the girls were to get any sleep that night, most of Tank's get-up-and-go had to have got-up-and-gone.

Emma and Sally had just put the dogs back into their respective crates when they saw Joanie striding toward the van. She'd been gone a little more than half an hour; Emma and Sally were sure that didn't bode well for the outcome of Joanie's negotiations.

"Well?" Sally asked.

"That's all they've got."

"Damn, I knew it."

"They don't seem to know anything about a mix-up with the reservation. They're filled up; there's some kind of convention in town besides the dog show and they don't have another room."

"How about a cot?"

"Nope. Everything they've got is in use. We're stuck with what we have."

"Terrific."

"I really tried, guys."

"We know you did." If Joanie, with her blunt if not unique gifts of persuasion, couldn't get it changed, then nobody else could either.

"Well, it won't be the first time we're in less than ideal conditions, right?" Joanie asked, trying to put a more positive spin on the situation.

"Right," Emma said tiredly. "We'll make do."

"Don't worry about it, Joanie. We'll survive, I'm sure."

"All right then," Joanie said, ready to leap into action. "Let's get a move on and get everything up to the room."

They all pitched in and started the transference of gear from the van to the room. The two flights of stairs were a major pain because they couldn't use their dollies without making a god-awful racket, so they only used them for the heaviest pieces and carried the rest of the stuff up by hand. That made for more trips, more grumbling, and bodies that were already tired getting sore muscles. The term "happy campers" was not a label that could be applied to the threesome as they trudged up and down, back and forth.

The average-sized room was painted off-white and was furnished with the usual assortment of motel furniture, namely a bed and dresser, a table with two chairs, a nightstand, an armchair, lamps, and a television. The girls had to rearrange the furniture a bit to accommodate everything they were bringing in; by the time they were finished the room was extremely crowded. Floor space had been reduced to narrow pathways zigzagging through the room.

They settled Cole, Tank, and Kirby first and got them fed. The girls had brought their own supply of water for the dogs since a change in water could lead to bouts of diarrhea and that was the last thing they needed.

After the dogs had finished and seemed content enough to go to sleep, the girls got ready for bed. It was almost 11:30 and the lateness of the hour was beginning to show in the amount of yawning they were doing. They took turns in the bathroom and when the last of the three was done, they all gathered around the single queen-size bed.

"All right, how're we doing this?" Emma asked.

"Joanie gets the middle," Sally announced firmly.

"Why me?" Joanie demanded.

"'Cause you got us into this mess," Sally said.

"I didn't do it on purpose. How was I to know they were going to screw up the reservation?"

"It's the principle of the thing."

"Yeah? Well, screw that."

"We'll all take a turn," Emma soothed. "We're here for four nights, so we'll divide it up. You just get to go first."

"Okay, but promise me you'll take your turns."

"Promise. I'll take it tomorrow night."

"Yeah, and I'll take it on Friday night," Sally agreed.

"Okay. Let's go to bed."

The three girls piled into the bed with Joanie in the middle. Sally and Emma hid a covert look between them. They'd pulled one over on her and Joanie hadn't caught on yet. Thank God she was tired and her nimble mind wasn't processing information at its usual rate. With any luck she wouldn't realize she'd been duped until Saturday night.

Emma turned off the bedside lamp, which left only the bathroom light on behind a partially closed door. They didn't dare turn every light off; if one of them had to get up in the middle of the night, they'd kill themselves in the dark trying to maneuver around all the stuff they'd brought in.

The girls jostled around for a few minutes, trying to get comfortable. They each eventually found the perfect position and settled down. All was quiet and still, everybody was beginning to relax, muscles were losing tension, eyelids were closing, thoughts were starting to drift, when out of the blue Emma's voice pierced the silence.

"Joanie?"

"Hmmm?"

"I sure am glad we're not going to have any problems this trip, aren't you?"

Joanie didn't answer, at least not in words. But both Emma and Sally felt a sudden tenseness grip the body that lay between them. Neither one could prevent the snicker that escaped.

Then there was quiet again and all three women surrendered to the slumber that was fast claiming them.

* * * *

Her anticipation was growing; she could feel it building day-by-day, hour-by-hour. There were only two more days to go before she could go back to hunting and taking down her prey.

It was that expectation that was keeping her awake now. Her excitement was so extreme that it had banished the recurring nightmare to the furthest reaches of her mind. She had no fear of it appearing that night.

It was already 2:00 in the morning and she felt not the least bit sleepy. She was lying in her bed, cocooned under the sheet and blankets that had warmed with her body heat. The only sound she heard was the ticking of the bedside clock. It was an old-fashioned wind-up and sat next to the digital clock radio. She loved that sound; it was so soothing, so predictable, so ordered. It often served as a lifeline to her after a night of terror, but tonight it was simply omnipresent background noise.

Her agile mind wouldn't turn off; it kept churning out scenario after scenario of her future successes. How many would she be able to destroy this time? How many more times would she be able to do it? Would the number that died ever be enough? She didn't think so; she had a feeling her quest for revenge would be infinite and the thought made her happy.

She smiled in the darkness and took pleasure in the possibilities awaiting her. Her eyes closed for a moment to rest and when she opened them again, they glowed with insanity and a lust for revenge.

# Chapter Twelve

The wakeup call came at 5:30. The jangling telephone pierced the near-total blackness of the room and jolted the three bed buddies wide awake, their hearts hammering wildly in their chests. Since they were all kind of tangled up with one another, with legs and arms thrown all over the place, it was an instantaneous chain reaction going from one woman to the next that could be measured in milliseconds as they were wrenched from deep sleep to gut-clenching wakefulness. Needless to say, it was a pretty rude way to wake up as anyone who's had the same pleasure knows and the girls, never ones to hold back, voiced their displeasure quite succinctly. Emma was closest to the phone so she picked it up, not waiting to hear anything from the other end.

"We're up!" she barked none too pleasantly, slamming the phone back in the cradle. "I'd rather have Cole give me a full body slam," she moaned. Emma stretched and willed her heart to slow down.

Sally and Joanie had rolled onto their backs and were gazing at the ceiling, bringing the room into focus and slowly getting their bearings.

The three lay there for a few minutes not saying anything. Each of them was in her own way supposedly getting their bodies ready to move. It took some doing at their ages.

"Cole's in the ring at 10:00, right?"

"Yeah."

"What time do you want to get to the grounds?"

"Early."

"Then we'd better start hauling ass."

"Yep."

They lay there another ten minutes, contemplating what it would take to haul ass. It was the dogs whimpering that finally made them move. Some things just couldn't be put off. They rolled out of bed and grabbed their clothing from yesterday, which had been haphazardly discarded the night before. They each took a quick trip to the bathroom and threw on their dirty clothes. They leashed the dogs, grabbed some Baggies, and left the room. They lost no time in traversing the corridor, going down the stairs and out the door, then crossed the parking lot to a grassy area. They took advantage of a few well-placed trees and then strolled with the dogs while they picked out the perfect place to do their business. The girls put the Baggies to good use and deposited their packages in a garbage can that had been conveniently placed at the edge of the blacktop.

Other show people were staying at the motel and a few were out attending to their four-footed charges as well. It was natural to exchange greetings and chat with one another about what else but dogs. It didn't matter that they were all total strangers; their love of dogs crossed all social boundaries and formalities.

The girls were starting back across the parking lot to go to their room when Joanie suddenly screeched, "Hey!"

Emma's eardrum about ruptured from impact since Joanie had been a mere two inches from it when she'd yelled. "What the hell was that for?"

"That guy." Joanie pointed to a man walking away from the grassy patch. "Hey!" she yelled again. "Hey, mister!"

Emma and Sally both turned and looked in the direction of the man who, from all indications, was very shortly going to be on the receiving end of a Joanie-style tongue-lashing.

"What's he doing?"

"It's not what he's doing; it's what he didn't do."

"All right, what didn't he do?"

"He didn't clean up after his dog. I'm going to set him straight."

"Oh, shit," Sally said, closing her eyes.

"Joanie, hold on. He's kind of big, don't you think?" Emma asked, sizing up the intended quarry.

"Yeah, I guess. So what?"

"Well, what are you going to do if you piss him off?"

"What any red-blooded American woman would do."

"Oh, God," Sally murmured, knowing this whole scenario could go south at any moment.

"I don't know if that would be a particularly good move."

"Hey, a well-placed knee will bring down the best of them. Don't worry, Sam taught me really well."

"Yeah, well, let's hope you're better at that than you are with a gun," Sally muttered under her breath.

"I heard that."

"Do I look like I care?"

"No, not particularly. Don't sweat it. I've got everything under control."

"Yeah? I've head those words before and we're usually in deep shit afterwards."

"Sally, you've got to have more faith in me."

"Forget it; I know you, remember?"

"Joanie, be careful. Watch what you say. Use a little discretion, okay?" Emma knew there was no turning her back; she only hoped to appeal to her common sense. *Yeah, right!*

"Just don't go getting us into any trouble," Sally warned.

"No problem," Joanie grinned.

"Damn, we're doomed."

"Uh-oh, here we go," Emma said as Joanie moved off toward her target. Emma glanced over at Sally.

Sally shifted her attention back from the man Joanie had singled out to Emma and gave her an oh-shit-this-is-it look.

The man stopped when he saw Joanie approaching. She was pointing an accusing finger at him and had fire in her eye. Puzzled as to what she could want, he asked shortly, "What?"

"Clean it up."

"Clean what up?" the man asked belligerently.

"Like you don't know. Your dog's deposit. Clean it up."

"Yeah, right," the man sneered.

"I mean it, buddy."

"Yeah? Who are you?"

"Who am I? I'll tell you who I am. I'm the goddamn poop police."

"Right," He laughed and started walking.

Leave it to Joanie; she was on a mission. She stepped even closer and got right in the guy's face, forcing him to stop again. No matter that he outweighed her by about 100 lbs. and was taller than she by six inches. Add to that the man's dog was a Rottweiler and he looked like he might be starting to take exception to Joanie's presence. She couldn't have cared less; she gave the dog a look that would have brought down an enraged rhinoceros and stopped him before he'd taken even one step in her direction.

"Don't even think about it, you overgrown fleabag. Sit!" The dog sat immediately. That minor nuisance taken care of she turned her full attention to the man. "Listen, asshole. You go clean that up. It's jerks like you who ruin it for the rest of us. If we don't clean up after our dogs, motels won't want us staying here anymore and you can't blame them. So clean it up. Now!" She pulled a Baggie out of her pocket, shoved it toward him, and stood there tapping her toe.

The other people who had been out with their dogs had been drawn over by the confrontation and now surrounded the man. Boxed in as he was, he had no choice but to do as he was told. Clenching his teeth and with a noticeable tick under his right eye, he took the proffered Baggie and went and cleaned up his dog's mess. He threw it into the garbage can with an emphatic *thwack* and started to walk away. Don't you know, Joanie had to get in one last shot.

"Hey, buddy," she yelled.

The man stiffened, stopped, and turned to face her. "Now what?"

"Get yourself some Baggies today. You're going to need 'em. And just so you know—we'll be watching to make sure you do a good job." The man glared at her for a long moment, then turned away. "Oh, hey, one more thing." The man stopped, but didn't turn. "If we *should* happen to find any Rottweiler-size land mines on the grounds, we'll know right where to take 'em… You have a nice day now." The man's posture became even more rigid, if that was possible, and he stalked off. "Okay," Joanie said, turning to her friends, a big smile on her face, "I've done my good deed for the day. Now let's get this show on the road." Like the other two had been holding things up?

Emma and Sally shared a sigh of relief, Joanie strode off like the incident was an everyday occurrence, and the dogs, anxious for something to eat, marched up to the room, their guard only now lowered that the possible danger had dissipated.

Emma took to the shower first, and Sally and Joanie organized what they needed for the day. When Emma finished, Joanie took the bathroom and Emma moved to the sink and mirror to do teeth, make-up, and hair. By the time Joanie was done showering, Emma was through at the mirror. Sally moved to the bathroom and Joanie replaced Emma at the sink and mirror. They were once again operating like a well-oiled machine.

When everyone was groomed and dressed, they stopped moving long enough to have breakfast. They had a variety of juices to choose from, fruited yogurt, and homemade sour cream peach and almond scones, courtesy of Emma. Sally had brewed a pot of coffee, compliments of the motel, but as always she was the only one to partake.

The dogs nostrils were quivering from the smells they were picking up and they were all licking their chops. They'd already had a few dog biscuits, but this stuff was far better food than that. They each got half a scone and some yogurt after the girls noted that their drool was forming small lakes in the bottoms of their crates.

By 8:00, they had reloaded the van and were driving onto the State Fairgrounds. Conformation competition was being held in the Cargill Exhibition Center and Obedience was in the Pepsi International Pavilion. The girls were going to set up in Cargill. They'd walk over to the Pepsi building when it was time for Tank to compete.

Emma, as promised, was in the driver's seat. She'd taken over after Sally had backed the van out of their parking space at the motel. She found a parking spot not too far from the building and pulled in. She'd been at the controls for all of something like five or six minutes and hadn't had a problem. Sally and Joanie felt blessed. Now it was time to unload—again.

They pulled the hand trucks and four-wheeled dolly out first. They got the dogs out, put them on lead, and handed them to Sally. After the grooming tables were loaded onto the four-wheeler, Emma and Joanie broke the crates down and piled them on top. Everything else followed: tack boxes, coolers, and purses. When everything was secured, they each took their dog's leash in one hand and with the other either pushed or pulled their load.

They entered the huge building and were immediately hit with the familiar noises associated with a dog show: people talking, dogs barking, equipment being set up, hair dryers running, and PA announcements coming sporadically over the loud speakers.

The usual smells were there too. Shampooed dogs, grooming sprays, cologned men and perfumed women, early morning coffee, food smells from the vending booths, and of course, the odor from the strategically placed necessary relief stations for the dogs. It was all part of the game and the girls loved every bit of it. As they walked through the building looking for a place to set up, they feasted their eyes and drank in the smells and noise, happy to be back in the thick of it.

Indoor shows seem to be simply more of everything due to the fact that all show activity is confined to the inside of a large building which multiplies the intense activity tenfold because of the restriction to finite space. Due to the nature of the structure itself, usually a huge reverberant arena, the noise level far exceeds that of an outdoor show and the only place to escape it is the bathrooms where it filters down to a low roar.

Exhibitors who would normally set up either at their cars or motor homes at an outdoor event generally moved into the designated grooming areas at an indoor competition. It dramatically increases the number of people who make use of the area as compared to the number that use the grooming tent at an outdoor show.

So, you've got more people plus more dogs; add an enclosed area where every sound bounces off the walls and you've got the perfect combination for big noise and total congestion. The girls were in heaven!

They found an empty spot along the wall and quickly laid claim to it. The next half hour was devoted to setting up and getting organized. Then they took the dogs outside for some exercise and bladder relief if they needed it.

Cole, Kirby, and Tank were higher than kites. Their excitement at being back at a show was only too telling. They were barely controllable. The girls needed to bring them down just a little bit, so with the dogs at their sides they loped into an easy jog on the roadway that encircled the building. Emma ran Cole with the others, forgetting at the time that later on she'd be feeling the effects of running on blacktop through painful shin splints.

Mercifully, the weather wasn't a problem. It was cold, the temperature hovering around 40 degrees, but dry.

By the time they arrived back at the entrance, the dogs were more settled and under control. Joanie fervently hoped that was truly the case with Tank, but it was a toss-up as to the reality of the situation. With Tank's problematic history, she had good reason to wonder if he was faking a more complacent attitude and knew only time would tell. She hoped it worked in her favor; he was due to compete at 11:00.

Activity within the building had increased tremendously by the time they reentered. More exhibitors had arrived and even more were still expected. The early morning judging had already begun; the first dogs had entered the ring at 8:30. Spectators were streaming through the gate and had begun to line the outside of the rings as well as infiltrating the grooming area.

Emma started to groom Cole the minute they got back to their set-up. He was on the long table lying on his side with Emma sectioning his coat and brushing it out when Joanie became aware of an inordinate number of people pausing and looking in their direction before moving on. Emma, as usual, was clueless to anything going on around her when she was involved with Cole.

"What's going on?" Joanie asked Sally who'd just returned from getting a cup of coffee from one of the refreshment stands.

"Where?"

"Here. Don't you think an awful lot of people are passing by this way? Like they're looking for something."

"How would I know? I just got back here."

"Well, didn't you notice before you went and got your coffee?"

"No, I didn't notice anything."

"Well, notice now. Watch," Joanie commanded.

So Sally stood there like a sentinel, sipped her coffee and watched, at first doing so only to humor Joanie. But as she continued her vigil, she had to admit that Joanie was right. The people who were passing by did seem to be looking in their direction. A few of them even pointed and most of them were smiling. What the heck was that all about?

"You're right," Sally conceded. "What *are* they looking at? Is one of us missing an important piece of clothing or something?"

"Not that I know of. At least I don't think so." Joanie gave Emma and then Sally a quick inspection before she turned a cursory glance upon herself. "Nope, we're all decent."

"Well, what is it then?"

"I'll be dipped if I know." Joanie switched her attention from the passing onlookers back to Sally. "There's only one way to find out, though."

"Oh, crap, Joanie. Don't do anything rash."

"Who, me?" Joanie wiggled her eyebrows and schooled her facial features into their going-into-action expression.

"Uh-oh, I know that look. Be nice."

"Of course. When aren't I?"

Sally didn't bother answering that one; she just shook her head and looked away. She didn't want to see the carnage that could possibly be left in Joanie's wake. These people hadn't been schooled in the ways of "Joanieism"; they weren't equipped to handle the steamroller that was about to roll over them.

Joanie moved forward, singled out a young man who had shown the same kind of interest as everyone else, and engaged him in conversation. God, Sally thought, this poor kid could be scarred for life after an encounter with Joanie. He 'looks so innocent. Lord, she prayed, please keep him safe.

Joanie continued talking to the kid. Sally noted he hadn't paled and she didn't see any visible signs of stress. This was good; maybe she was going easy on him. He was smiling now and pointing in Emma's direction. Joanie wasn't trying to wrestle him to the ground, so everything should be okay. Finally the kid moved off and Joanie turned back to her friends.

"So, what?" Sally asked.

Emma had finished grooming Cole and he was now sitting on the table, looking as regal as any king propped upon his throne. Sally's question caught Emma's attention and she asked, "What, what? What's going on?"

"You aren't going to believe this," Joanie said.

"What aren't we going to believe?"

"You know what's been going on here all morning? These people?"

"What are you talking about? What people?" Emma asked, totally unaware.

"The people who've been parading past here all morning while you've been grooming Cole."

"I hadn't noticed."

"Yeah, well, that's obvious."

"So what are they doing?" Emma persisted.

"Joanie, if you don't spill the beans and tell us right this minute, I'm going to come over there and punch you one. Now *what* is going on?" Sally asked, her warning enough to jolt Joanie into revealing what she knew. Joanie knew firsthand that Sally's punch could pack quite a wallop.

"All right, all right. Listen. All these people who've been coming by…they wanted to see Cole. Judging from what the kid said, I guess word has spread like wild fire that he's here and everybody wants to take a look at him. You know, up close."

"What kid?" Emma asked, looking around.

"Never mind."

"Well, why do they want to see Cole?" Emma asked, her expression blank.

"Emma, no offense, but sometimes you're dumb as a rock," Joanie said.

"*O-kaaay…* no offense taken, I guess. But I still don't know why all those people are coming over here."

"Remember this past September? What you did to prove he was your dog?"

"Yeah."

"Well, word has since spread about the show you and Cole put on and all the circumstances behind it. People want to see him firsthand."

"Oh."

"Yeah, oh. You two are famous."

"Get out of here."

"Really."

"No way."

"I'm not kidding, Em. You watch. I bet there's going to be a big crowd around the breed ring and they'll all be there to watch Cole."

"I don't think so."

"She might be right, Em," Sally said. "There's been an awful lot of people passing by and they were all looking over here. See for yourself. They're still coming this way."

Emma did look then and to her horror, saw the girls were right. People were pointing in Cole's direction and smiling. Oh, crap, she thought. She didn't want all this attention. She just wanted to show her dog and have some fun. She didn't want a spotlight on them, at least not outside of the ring anyway. Damn! What could she do? Not a whole hell of a lot, she decided quickly. She'd just have to ignore it as best she could, she guessed. Hopefully people would find better things to do with their time and the whole thing would blow over. Maybe in another day or so they'd be considered old news; the novelty would have worn off. Emma turned to Cole who'd been watching her and gave him a hug. He gave her a kiss, put his head on her shoulder, and let out a big sigh. Emma figured he was letting her know that all the extra attention they were getting didn't faze him in the least. She'd be smart to take a cue from her dog. However, that was easier said than done.

They had thirty minutes till ring time, so Emma wanted to take Cole out for one more bathroom break before the competition started. As she walked him through the building, she was acutely aware of exhibitors following their progress as they passed by. The whole thing was making her very uncomfortable. Cole didn't seem to notice, probably because he couldn't have cared less. There was only one person's praise he needed or wanted and she was walking right beside him.

Once outside, Cole cooperated straight off and watered a tree. Emma let him snoop around the grass for a while to see if he was so inclined in that direction, but he quickly brought his attention back to her and let her know he was finished.

Emma walked him back inside and ran into some exhibitors she knew before she'd taken more than a few steps past the doorway. Pleasantries and good wishes for success at the show were exchanged before the parties went their separate ways. Emma came away from the encounter in much better spirits. It was a great relief to have been treated like one of the gang and not some kind of celebrity, which was about the farthest thing from what she was.

She rejoined the girls and made small talk while they watched the clock. At 9:58, they walked down to Ring Four where the Newfoundlands were assembling. As Joanie predicted, there were a lot of people gathered around the ring, way more than the usual number. It was hard to even get through to ringside, but Joanie went first and elbowed her way in, making a path for Sally, Emma, and Cole. Emma picked up her armband and settled in to wait, focusing her mental energies on keeping her nerves under control.

There were some excellent young dogs in and the three friends discussed their strengths and merits. There was a beautiful bitch shown from the Open Class that Emma fell in love with and she ended up taking Winner's Bitch. Joanie had looked her owners up in the catalog and found they lived over in Marilla on Four Rod Road, which wasn't all that far from their neck of the woods.

It was time for Best of Breed competition, and after getting the usual "good luck" from her friends, Emma, anxious to get started, strode into the ring with Cole. There were six Specials, four dogs and two bitches; Winners Dog and Winners Bitch completed the lineup.

Emma set Cole up, smoothed her hand down his back, took a deep breath to steady herself, and whispered in his ear, "It's been a little while since we've been in the ring, big boy, but let's see how good we can do. Okay?"

Cole brought his head up, looked into her eyes, and gave her face a quick lick; he was ready. Cole returned his head to proper position; Emma rechecked his stack, then dropped the lead, and stepped back. Cole stood like he'd been blasted out of granite.

Judge Evelyn Bridgton from Scranton, Pennsylvania entered the ring and took her first look. She gave the signal for the go around and dogs and handlers prepared to move out.

For indoor competition rubber mats or runners are laid down to cover the inside perimeter of each ring with another mat going diagonally from one corner to the one opposite. These mats give firm footholds for the dogs and handlers as they make their way around the ring and are something that young dogs need to be exposed to before their first time at an indoor show. Their initial turn on the mats can sometimes be unsettling to a youngster and they'll refuse to walk on them. Insignificant as it may seem to the outsider, it is yet another aspect of their show training that must be addressed and is usually done so at conformation classes held by the various dog clubs and private kennels.

Another important difference between an indoor and an outdoor show is that the rings are somewhat smaller indoors. The more limiting rings don't appear to affect the toy or smaller breeds since they rarely use the entirety of the outdoor ring when called upon to move. However, for the larger breeds and those whose natural gait covers a great deal of ground when in motion, such as the Pointers and Setters, the smaller rings can be a problem. If the handler and dog don't make the necessary adjustments, they can be around the ring and back in place and never have attained the stride that best showcases the dog's reach and drive. Once again it comes back to training, experience, and expertise.

Emma and Cole were fourth in line and Emma wisely waited for the first three dogs to start out. When there was enough room between the third dog and themselves, Emma slowly moved Cole out, gradually increasing in speed. They relaxed into their stride and moved powerfully around the ring. Once they were back in place, Emma played with Cole until they were second in line, the dogs in front of them having moved to the end of the line once their individual inspections were finished. She stacked Cole and waited for their turn.

The dog ahead of them was moving around the ring, so Emma moved Cole up to the first spot. Cole had walked himself into a perfect stack, so after Emma checked foot placement, she dropped the lead and stepped away. The judge turned toward them and approached. She examined Cole head to foot and asked Emma to do the down and back. Emma gathered her lead and with a pat to Cole, led him off on the diagonal mat. They moved like a dream. On the way back, Mrs. Bridgton gave the signal to stop when they neared, and Emma went out to the right while Cole came down on all four feet in a dead-on stack and focused all his attention on Emma.

The judge held them there for several seconds and then sent them around the ring and back to their place in line. The quiet that had invaded ringside while Cole was performing was broken by resumed conversations when Mrs. Bridgton went on to the next dog. Joanie gave Sally a nudge; they both had big grins on their faces. Cole was going to do it again; they had no doubt.

Their supposition was confirmed moments later when Mrs. Bridgton awarded Best of Breed to Cole. There was no quiet then; ringside erupted into a noisy volley of clapping and cheers. When Emma and Cole left they ring they were so surrounded with people offering congratulations that Joanie and Sally couldn't get near them. Maybe that was a good thing considering how over the top the two dynamos could be whenever Emma won. Emma knew her respite wouldn't last long; eventually her friends would push their way through and then only God knew what would happen. There was always an element of surprise involved in the girl's celebratory high jinks.

The crowd thinned a little and Emma moved Cole further away from the ring. She heard movement behind her and knew intuitively it was her buddies; she braced herself for impact. Good thing. They about climbed up her back!

Cole shot Emma a look that suggested he was really glad she was the object of their affection and not him, although he didn't get off scot-free either. They nuzzled and snuggled him until he couldn't take any more and sought relief. His only thought was to get back to the safety of his crate where he'd be able to escape their exuberant celebration. He pulled Emma in that direction; she gladly followed, leaving Joanie and Sally to their own devices. It only took a moment or so before they realized they were being deserted and quickly tagged after the departing duo. With a glance at her watch, Joanie realized they'd better get it in gear; Tank was due in the ring in twenty-five minutes.

# Chapter Thirteen

Their performance was not going to go well today; Joanie just knew it. She could feel it in the air; the vibrations were definitely not good. The premonition was not only tangible, it had a goddamn life all its own. Hell, all she had to do was look at Tank and it was clear what his intentions were. He was not going to make her proud, not one little bit. He was going to do the exact opposite; all the signs were blatantly there. Number one, he wasn't the least bit relaxed; he was like a coiled spring waiting to go *boiiing*. Number two, he wouldn't look her in the eye; he kept shifting his eyes to anywhere she wasn't. Number three, and this was the killer, he had that sick smile plastered on his face. Joanie had no doubt he was going to make a complete ass of her and have a wonderful time for himself while he was doing it. Damn the little bugger!

They'd hurriedly gotten him ready (there really hadn't been much to do other than give him a stern look and a warning to be good, which was itself, an exercise in futility) and walked over to the Pepsi Pavilion. On the way over he'd taken every opportunity to mark as many trees as he could in the general vicinity. Joanie let him do it, figuring it was better to go along with him at that point. If she had any kind of real smarts she wouldn't even put him in the ring today. She knew it was going to be a colossal fiasco, but that sick part of her personality not only *wanted* to know, but *needed* to know just how he was going to do it. They truly deserved each other.

Tank and the three girls arrived at ringside with scarcely two minutes to spare. Joanie grabbed her armband and had barely gotten it on when judging began. According to number, she'd be third in. At least she wouldn't have to wait long before she discovered the means by which Tank meant to insure her indubitable embarrassment.

The second exhibitor was finishing up in the ring and Joanie was preparing to go in when she turned to Emma and Sally. "Well, here goes nothing."

"You're a glutton for punishment; you know that, don't you?"

"Yeah, I know. If I was smart I'd pull him from competition today."

"You know he's up to no good."

"Yeah, it's written all over him."

"As plain as day," Emma said, taking Tank's measure. "I don't suppose it'll do any good, but I wish you luck."

"Yeah, good luck," Sally added. "I hope whatever happens in there won't be too painful."

"Thanks, guys. Come on, devil man. It's time to face the music, for me anyway." Upon hearing her number called, Joanie strode into the ring summoning all the dignity she could muster to meet her fate.

They got through the Heeling on Leash exercise and the Figure-8 relatively pain free. Then it was time for the Stand for Examination. Joanie set Tank up and moved away. As soon as the judge, Mrs. Gloria Lamotti from Saratoga Springs, New York moved in to do the exam, Tank broke from his stack and flopped down on the floor like he'd been shot. He flipped over on his back with his legs in the air, his front paws curled downward. His eyes were closed and there was a looseness to his body that was reminiscent of Jell-O dog. Joanie, a resigned expression on her face, sighed and rolled her eyes. Well, she thought, at least it's over with; I don't have to live in suspense any longer.

Mrs. Lamotti, not one to appreciate Tank's unique talents, told Joanie to return to her dog and promptly failed Tank on the exercise. She could have at least smiled, Joanie thought, it was kind of cute, evil, but cute.

Tank, however, wasn't at all ready to give up his charade. He wouldn't get up when Joanie told him to heel; instead he continued in his role of dead dog, a boneless lump of fur prone on the cement floor. Joanie gave a tug on the leash and succeeded only in moving him an inch or two. Tank never even opened his eyes, but if it was possible his grin had gotten considerably bigger. Cripe, his lips were even curling.

Now things were getting serious. The judge was glaring and waiting impatiently to do the off-leash heeling. Joanie gave another tug and got the same reaction. Tank remained in character. Joanie shot a quick look to Emma and Sally hoping they might enlighten her as how to proceed. They both shrugged their shoulders and shook their heads. They were clueless; she was on her own. Well, so be it.

With nothing to lose, because they'd already lost any chance of getting the final leg of the CD title, Joanie threw caution to the wind and got down on all fours next to her demon dog. She lowered her head to within an inch of Tank's ear and in so doing raised her butt into the air. Not an elegant posture to be sure, but at this point she really didn't give a damn. She spoke quietly, but in a tone that brooked no quarter.

"Tank, open your eyes." Nothing, no response. "Tank, you little shithead, open- your- eyes." Tank opened his eyes; he knew better than to ignore that tone of voice for very long.

171

"Are you listening? Do I have your complete attention, you little shit? Good. Now listen to me and listen carefully. If you want to enjoy life, as you now know it, you *will* get up this instant and finish the next exercise without incident. If you don't, you may not live for another five minutes. Do I make myself clear?"

Tank locked gazes with Joanie for a long moment. Then with an oh-what-the-hell shrug, rolled and jumped to his feet, giving himself a shake that went from head to tail. He went to heel position and with a bounce in his step walked with Joanie to the location within the ring where they needed to be for the off-leash heeling exercise. They made it through that, went on to do the Recall without a problem, and then exited the ring.

Knowing what was coming from her wisecrack-slinging friends, Joanie attempted to stop the comments before they even started. "Don't say a word. If you value your lives, don't say a word. I should be considered a danger to myself and others right now."

"But, Joan, he made such a fine showing. I'd be right proud of him if I were you," Emma laughed, sarcasm rolling with every word.

"Em, I warning ya, I could go off at any time."

"I liked the take-down myself," Sally said, ignoring Joanie's threat. "He did it with a lot of flair."

"Hey, Sally, you know what you can do with that flair. Proceed at will."

"I think I'll pass on that one."

"That would be advisable," Emma intoned gravely between bouts of laughter.

"I can't believe what a devious little monster he is. I never saw that one coming," Joanie admitted.

"If nothing else he is inventive. You've got to give him credit."

"Oh, that's not the only thing I'll give him."

"Well, all I can say is, I'm glad it's you in there with him and not me," Sally said. She shuddered a little just thinking about it.

"Yeah, it's a load of fun, all right."

"Well, at least it's over. He should be done with his high jinks, right?"

"He should be, but I don't know. He seems to be totally wired today."

"Well, what more could he do?"

Joanie gave Sally a blank stare before she answered. "You didn't just ask a really dumb question, did you? You, who knows what a holy terror this dog is. You should know better than to question what more he could do. The possibilities are endless."

"Sorry, I was only trying to give you hope."

"Don't bother. He's out to get me today. I can tell. It's all a question of who's going to have the upper hand once the dust settles."

"Who has it now?"

"It's a draw. He won in the ring, but I threatened his life. He chose to live."

"Sits and Downs ought to be interesting."

"Oh, yeah, I can't wait."

Joanie and crew had to wait forty-five minutes before the Long Sits and Downs took place. Tank was an angel on the Sit, which made Joanie all the more suspicious going into the Down.

The dogs were downed, the handlers were standing on the other side of the ring, and Mrs. Lamotti was timing. Joanie was just starting to think she might squeeze through the exercise unscathed when she heard a distinctive sound. Her eyes zeroed in on Tank and she saw his ears perk up almost at the same instant his head swiveled to the source of the noise Joanie had heard. Oh, shit, she thought, here we go; this is it. She switched her gaze over to the side of the ring.

It was cellophane, the unmistakable sound of crinkling cellophane that had drawn Tank's attention like the pull of a powerful magnet. Some woman sitting at ringside was opening a package of peanut butter crackers. Oh, Lord, lady, Joanie thought, you have no idea what you have just done. She hoped the lady really didn't want those crackers because they were pretty much done for.

Joanie looked back to Tank, willing him to stay in place even though she knew it was pointless. Tank gave her one quick the-devil-made-me-do-it look, sprang up, and raced over to the unsuspecting woman. He grabbed the package out of her hands before she knew what he was doing and ran out of the ring. He didn't go far, in fact he only cleared the traffic at ringside before he lay down and proceeded to crunch and munch his stolen booty. He didn't give a damn about the crackers as evidenced by the bits and pieces that were scattered in a wide area surrounding him. He only wanted that cellophane and God, was he enjoying it. He was one happy little dog!

Meanwhile, back in the ring, poor Joanie was still waiting for the three minutes to be up on the Long Down. She wasn't worried about Tank, she knew he wasn't going anywhere; besides, Sally and Emma were there to grab him if he should decide to take a hike. No, she was worried about how she was ever going to leave the ring gracefully now that her dog had made a complete fool out of her. It wasn't possible; there was no way to pull this off with any kind of social grace. It would be best to just slink out of the ring as quietly and as unobtrusively as possible.

The judge finally told the exhibitors to return to their dogs and Joanie followed the directive although she had no dog to return to. She returned to an empty spot and anxiously waited for Mrs. Lamotti to end the exercise. When she did, Joanie beat a hasty retreat and joined Emma and Sally who had corralled Tank in the interim. Standing with the posture of a victorious warrior even though he was covered in cracker crumbs, Tank met Joanie's stare head-on. She could only shake her head in frustration, taking in the resultant mess left after Tank's assault in one glance. There were shreds of cellophane mixed in with cracker debris all over the floor. Joanie swallowed her embarrassment and alerted the ring steward to the problem who then called for cleanup. Would the humiliation never end?

Next Joanie approached the woman whose crackers had been illegally appropriated. She apologized and offered to compensate the woman for her loss. Thankfully, the woman showed no signs of ill will and waved the matter aside. She did suggest, however, that Joanie do a bit more training before putting her dog into competition again. Emma stepped in and hustled Joanie off before she could tell the woman exactly what she could do with her suggestion.

\* \* \* \*

It was five minutes to one when the girls arrived at Ring Six for Labrador judging. They hadn't had time for a real lunch, so compensated by throwing some junk food down their throats. It would do until Sally was through in the ring; then they'd eat like the little piggies they were.

Kirby was primed and ready; her coat gleamed, her eyes sparkled, and her entire manner spoke of controlled excitement. She couldn't wait to get into the ring; neither could Sally. Too bad they had to wait through ten classes before theirs was called. Nevertheless, when Open Bitch, Yellow was announced they eagerly marched in and took their spot, anxious to show their stuff.

The Open class for Labrador Retrievers for both dogs and bitches was divided into three separate competitions as determined by color. In this particular class, yellow Labs were judged independently from the blacks and chocolates in both sexes.

Sally guided Kirby skillfully through the go around and brought her back to their place in line where they'd wait for their individual inspection, moving up as each dog advanced to the first spot. Teasing her with a squeaky toy, Sally held Kirby's attention, but kept her relaxed while they bided their time.

They were soon in the spotlight and Kirby held her stack as the judge, Mr. Peter Warren from Killingworth, Connecticut went over her. He signaled Sally to take Kirby down and back and they took off on the diagonal mat. Coming back, Sally stopped a few feet from Mr. Warren and Kirby went into her free stand. She held it nicely while the judge looked on and then he signaled for Sally to take her around. He gave Kirby a last look before turning to the next dog.

When all the inspections had been done, the exhibitors stacked their dogs. Mr. Warren moved down the line, then gave the signal to move the dogs out a final time. He gave Sally the number one nod when she went past and then followed with his second, third, and fourth choices.

Sally and Kirby stayed in the ring after the awards were given out and were then joined by the winners of the other classes. Mr. Warren did a quick review of the dogs presented and gave Winners Bitch to the Open Bitch, Black winner on the final go around. Sally stayed in for Reserve Winners judging and left with not even that in her pocket.

"Em, I'm still *swooooping,*" Sally singsonged, her disappointment obvious.

"I know, Sal. I thought you were going to sweep today. Honest, I did."

"The jinx is still in effect, dammit. I have to sweep soon, Em. This is the only show we're going to before the end of the year. You told me I'd finish Kirby by Christmas and I'm holding you to it."

"Yeah, I know and you will. There're three more shows to this weekend, remember. You'll be sweeping, trust me."

"Are you two at it again?" Joanie asked. "Enough with the sweeping and swooping; you'd better just start winning, Sal."

"Really, Joanie? Forgive me for not realizing the error of my ways. I'm supposed to win, you say?"

"Don't start," Joanie said, shooting her a leveling look.

"What? Win? I'm supposed to win?"

"Oh, so now you're getting smart, huh?"

"Who, me? Never," Sally said sarcastically.

"Right."

"Seriously, I am just so happy that you're here to keep me on the straight and narrow. I can't thank you enough."

"See. You are too getting smart, but I'll tell you what. I'll give you a straight right alongside your narrow if you don't watch it," Joanie laughed. "Now let's go get something to eat. I'm starving."

Food always won out. The girls headed back to where they were set up and made for themselves a small feast from fixings that magically appeared from the dark, cold confines of their coolers. Little did passersby know what treasure troves those innocuous coolers held.

The sandwiches they concocted were huge; the base of their gastronomical creation was a sesame seed soft roll whose bottom half was slathered with sweet mustard. Piled high upon it were paper-thin slices of ham, turkey, and roast beef. Topping that were slices of Muenster and provolone cheese, leaf lettuce, tomato, and kosher dill pickles. The top half of the roll was spread with mayo and a small amount of Greek Parmesan dressing. Men would, without a doubt, kill for this sandwich!

Then they pulled out pasta salad and chips and sat down wherever they could find a spot to plunk their butts to fully enjoy their little repast. With the amount of food these girls ate it was anybody's guess why they didn't each weigh 200 lbs. Another thing was their speed; they plowed through food like it was an eating contest. Could be a leftover from the days when their kids were babies and they had to shovel in food fast before their attention was demanded elsewhere, namely to a hungry, crying infant or an impatient, fussy toddler Some habits were hard to break even so many years after the fact that the girls really didn't want to count them. Besides, this ability to inhale food quickly still came in handy with the grandkids, not to mention dog shows.

# Chapter Fourteen

There were twenty-three representatives of the Working Group in the ring, including Cole. Emma and her young Newfie found a place about halfway down the line sandwiched between the Great Pyrenees and the Bernese Mountain Dog. Ring size had once again been doubled to accommodate Group judging. Spectators around the ring had amassed in force and almost total attention was focused on the nearly two-year old Newfoundland. Joanie thought it was fortunate that Emma was oblivious to what was going on outside the ring; she'd probably have a heart attack right where she stood if she realized the extent of interest in Cole.

The judge, Mr. Louis Archer from San Diego, California walked to center ring and took his first look; all the dogs were stacked, the handlers tuned in to the figure who was already evaluating what was in front of him. He gave the signal for the go around and the dogs moved out. Emma and Cole quickly settled into their natural rhythm and floated around the ring. Mr. Archer appeared to take notice.

The judge was not one to waste time, so Emma and Cole were at center ring for their individual examination in what seemed like a matter of minutes. Cole had walked into his stack perfectly and after giving him a quick chuck under the chin, Emma dropped the lead and stepped back. Mr. Archer approached and very efficiently conducted his inspection. Cole never moved and when the judge returned to his head Cole gave him a direct look.

Mr. Archer signaled for the down and back. Emma retrieved the lead and led Cole off. Their stride was synchronized and fluid; Cole's front and rear movement displayed to absolute perfection. When called upon to execute the free stack, Cole hit it with precision and then locked onto Emma. When the judge signaled for the go around, Cole tossed his head in Mr. Archer's direction and then set off with Emma, feet flying over the mats. People were applauding enthusiastically, but Joanie doubted that Emma even heard it.

Once back in line, Emma kept Cole loose and the drool sopped up. When examinations were finished, Mr. Archer moved down the line of stacked dogs and made his first cut. He pulled out eight and excused the rest; Cole was still in the ring.

He had the dogs move out individually and watched as they went through their paces. Back in place, they went into their stacks, and he reshuffled their order. The judge gave the signal for the go around and as they sped around the ring, he pointed and called, "One" to the Newfoundland, "Two" to the Akita, "Three" to the Saint Bernard and "Four" to the Kuvasz. Cole had done it again! Hot damn!

While Emma and Cole had moved to the awards area and were being congratulated by those in the ring, Joanie and Sally had gone into dance mode and were reaching a new level of embarrassment. Where *did* they get those moves from? Most respectable people didn't want to know. Meanwhile, the applause was thunderous.

After the picture taking was over and Emma and Cole had joined the crowd outside the ring, Joanie and Sally bullied their way through and launched their celebration attack.

Cole, knowing what was coming, stationed himself behind Emma and braced himself for impact. The girls hit and Emma bounced back on Cole; she was extremely thankful for his 150 lb. solid-as-the-Rock-of-Gibraltar support.

"Yahooeee!" Joanie screamed as she wrapped her arms around her friend. "You're number one again."

Emma checked her ears for bleeding and gave an appreciative pat to Cole for keeping her upright.

"You did great in there, guys," Sally said, grabbing Emma around the neck and giving her cheek a bruising kiss.

"Thanks, Sal." Emma blinked and tried to draw back a bit from her keyed-up friend; there was no telling what else she had in mind, better to put a little distance between them.

"Cole was fabulous!" Joanie shouted. Emma's ears were mindful of the fact that Joanie had downsized her voice from a scream to a shout and would be forever thankful.

"Yep, he did his usual great job," Emma said, scratching Cole behind his ears. "Let's get back and let him rest before Best In Show." Maybe if she got the girls moving they'd release their hold on her. It was worth a try.

"Good idea. Let's go."

They disengaged from Emma so fast she almost tumbled backwards. Thank God Cole was still braced behind her. He knew better than to give up position until the two wackos were a safe distance away. Emma followed his lead and stayed put until Joanie and Sally were several yards ahead; then dog and mistress, ever mindful of safeguarding their health and well-being, followed slowly behind, careful not to close the distance between them and the wrecking crew.

\* \* \* \*

The time between competitions was spent letting the dogs stretch their legs outside, grooming Cole, and fielding questions from interested spectators. Emma had no sooner finished downing a can of Diet Pepsi and it was time for Best In Show.

Emma, Cole, and her two-woman cheering squad arrived at ringside at about the same time as the other competitors. There was an impressive German Wirehaired Pointer named Moon from the Sporting Group that belonged to an old friend of Emma's, a low-slung Basset Hound representing the Hounds, a number one ranked Norfolk Terrier from the Terrier Group, a beautifully-coated Yorkshire Terrier from the Toy Group, a number two ranked Bichon Frise coming from Non-Sporting, an Old English Sheepdog was the winner from the Herding Group, and finally Cole, representing the Working Group.

The ring steward called them into the ring and Emma settled Cole behind the German Wirehaired Pointer. The rest of the line-up, led by the Old English Sheepdog was behind them.

The judge, Mrs. Luella Thackeray from Charleston, South Carolina entered the ring and went to center court to get her first impression. After taking time to scan each dog, she signaled for the go around. The Wirehair moved out smoothly and Cole followed with Emma letting the big dog glide into his dynamic gait.

Back in line, Emma stacked Cole while the Wirehair moved to center ring to be examined. While the Wirehair was starting on the down and back, Emma brought Cole out to the same spot where the Wirehair had been presented. She quickly stacked him, dropped the lead and stepped back. Cole went still as a statue and waited for the judge to approach.

Mrs. Thackeray, after finishing with the Wirehair, studied Cole from a distance and then walked over to where he stood. She ran her hands over the Newfie from head to tail and then came back to his head. She stood in front of him and he looked at her steadily, his big brown eyes capturing her attention. He blinked and raised his head a fraction of an inch, more or less saying, "Here I am; what do you think?"

She asked Emma for the down and back and the duo complied, moving rhythmically down the side of the ring; Cole finished with a perfect free stack at the end. When they returned to their spot in line after the go around, the judge was still watching. Cole slid into his stack and gave Mrs. Thackeray a long look across the distance that separated them as if he was judging her! It was several seconds before she tore her eyes away from the imposing black dog.

The individual inspections were over and the group stood stacked and anxious, although their outward appearance revealed no such emotion. The judge walked down the line, reviewing and evaluating the dogs against the standard for their breed. She moved back to center ring and asked for the dogs to individually do a go around. The Wirehair led off and when he was at the back of the line, Cole went out. The rest of the dogs followed in the same manner. When everyone was back in line and stacked, Mrs. Thackeray gave one last look and went to mark her book.

She came back out with her steward and the Show Chairman of the Susque-Nango Kennel Club, which was the host club for the Thursday show. Carrying the Best In Show booty, the three walked to center ring and turned to face the seven exhibitors awaiting the judge's decision. They were no sooner in place when Mrs. Thackeray pointed to Cole and announced, "The Newfoundland."

Outside the ring, pandemonium broke out amidst the large crowd. Inside, exhibitors were swarming Emma and Cole to offer congratulations. Emma herself seemed to be a little out of it, but Cole was handling it like it was all in a normal day's work. He stood patiently by until Emma had gathered her wits. Once she was back in control of her faculties, he jumped up and lovingly mauled her. Between the face licks and the nuzzling, Cole was all over her and Emma had to hold on to him for dear life, afraid he'd knock her down in his exuberance.

Joanie and Sally were making a spectacle of themselves by way of the victory dance they were performing and a three-foot radius had been cleared around them. It seems that nobody wanted to be too close to the action lest they be mistakenly identified as being part of it. At one point Joanie tried to execute a moonwalk and failed miserably; instead she looked like she was going to go into a full neurological seizure. Thankfully Sally knew better than to even try it. She was content to do a dance that looked like a cross between the Twist and the Mashed Potato. But whatever it was it came out ugly.

After all the hubbub inside the ring wrapped up, Emma and Cole approached her two friends who were for once uncommonly quiet and standing still, their so-called dancing having run its natural course. They were, however, visibly vibrating with excitement. Uh-oh! Suspiciously cautious, Emma stopped about three feet in front of them. She thought she was prepared for whatever they were going to do, but as usual they surprised the hell out of her. Before she knew what was happening, they catapulted themselves toward her without any warning and captured her body between the two of theirs. In the split-second she had before they made contact, Emma tensed every muscle she could voluntarily control and braced for impact. They were practically hanging off both her front and back while screaming their congratulations. Emma was bowing under the strain, not to mention choking from the death grips they had around her throat. As her life passed before her eyes, Emma wondered if they stayed up into the wee hours of the night scripting these moves.

"Em, Em, what a way to come back! Hallelujah! Yahooeeeee!"

"Fabulous! Absolutely fabulous! Way to go!"

"C-can you let... go?" Emma squeaked out. "I...can't breathe."

At Emma's strangled request Joanie and Sally both stopped their excited chirping and looked at her questioningly. Next they looked at each other; then they looked at their arms wrapped tightly around Emma's throat like they didn't know who they belonged to, where they'd come from, or how they'd gotten there.

"Yikes! Sorry about that," Sally said, removing her arms quickly. "I guess we were choking you a little bit."

"A little bit?"

"Well, okay, more than a little bit. You're face *is* kind of red."

"Yeah, so's your throat," Joanie admitted, following Sally's lead and dropping her arms. "In fact, I think you've got a few little marks on it. They look a little like a hickey."

"Oh great, just what I need."

"I think they look kind of cute."

"You would. Now get off me, please."

"Oh, yeah. Sure."

The teammates in celebratory assault gave Emma a little room and Cole gave them each a nudge, which they recognized for what it was. Cole may not have been able to enunciate what he wanted, but he got his point across, which in two words was, "Back off!"

They went back to their set-up and attempted to break down the crates and load the dollies with them and the other paraphernalia they were taking back to the motel. Progress was slow, however, because people were still coming by to chat and offer congratulations. Some of those people stopping to talk were professional handlers and whether they'd gotten their information by interaction with Emma herself, or by witnessing the demonstration that had taken place in September, or by knowledge gained indirectly through the grapevine, they all knew that Cole was off-limits. Not one of them would be handling the young Newfoundland. Nevertheless, that insight did not prevent them from wanting to discover for themselves what made Cole so special, at least structurally. They wanted the opportunity to lay their hands on the dog that moved so consistently true time and time again in the ring.

It was almost quarter to seven when the girls finally left the show grounds and went back to the motel. Upon their arrival, they exercised the dogs and then hauled everything back up to the room. Once equipment and dogs were settled, the girls flung themselves onto the infamous solitary bed, drinks in hand, and debated their dinner choices: go out or take-out, fast-food or leisurely dining, Italian or Chinese, good old American or Greek.

They eventually decided on Chinese and looked to the guest directory to find the nearest place. It appeared there was a restaurant just down the street a ways. Perfect! They finished their drinks, tidied up, and with Sally firmly in place behind the wheel, went to dinner.

# Chapter Fifteen

The next morning found Emma up before the wakeup call splintered the morning stillness. Halfway through the night she'd opted for the comfort or discomfort, depending on how you wanted to look at it, of the bedside chair rather than spend one minute longer in the middle of the bed. After Joanie, deep in sleep and dreaming about God knows what, gave her a not-so-gentle punch in the back, not once but twice, Emma decided she'd rather have a stiff neck than bruised kidneys. Besides, her shin splints had been killing her and if Sally's foot had brushed down the front of her lower leg one more time, she would have screamed. Around 4:30 she'd given up altogether on getting any more sleep and had taken her shower; at least there'd been no rush and she'd been able to indulge in a lengthy one.

Cole was in the ring promptly at 8:30, so the girls had to get to the show grounds no later than 7:30. Since Emma had been dressed and ready before the other two had even gotten out of bed, she took care of the dogs and got breakfast laid out while Fric and Frac took turns in the bathroom and got beautiful. They munched on some more of the peach scones, they each had a banana, and Sally loaded up on coffee while Emma and Joanie got their caffeine jolt with Diet Pepsi.

By 7:20 they were skipping out the door. Well, all right, maybe they weren't skipping loaded down with dogs and equipment as they were, but they *were* moving with speed and purpose. They pulled into the show grounds at 7:28.

Joanie and Sally had let Emma drive over again; they didn't want her to have a guilt trip over not sharing in the driving duties. Yet, they still wanted to live; so driving back and forth between the motel and the show grounds was about the extent of the opportunity they felt they could safely give her to fulfill her so-called driving obligation. The only thing they had to do was make sure that Emma had absolutely no chance of getting herself into a situation where she might have to back up and that included easing the van into a parking space. They needed a wide-open area, preferably one twice the size of the van, to accommodate her driving technique. It was to that end that they directed her to a spot on a near-deserted lane where she had about fifty feet in all directions to play with. Emma managed to bring them in for a safe landing, although she stopped and then inched the van forward three times before she felt it was parked straight enough.

Once they had all their gear in the building and set up, Emma concentrated solely on getting Cole groomed and ready for showing. The whole crew, including Tank and Kirby, arrived at Ring Five promptly at 8:30 where a good-sized crowd had already gathered. Emma hadn't expected that, not at that hour. But the people were there, waiting to see if Cole was going to do it again.

He didn't disappoint them and took the win with his trademark style that was quickly becoming well-known throughout the dog world. He took Best of Breed with a flourish and an unmistakable joy in showing. He lit up the ring with his presence and delighted bystanders with his obvious will-to-please attitude toward Emma. His performance time and again was testament to the devotion he reserved only for her.

Joanie and Sally's customary congratulatory escapade was sufficiently watered down this time so that Emma didn't have to fear bodily harm. Perhaps primitive survival instincts buried deep in her subconscious were why she'd suggested that Tank and Kirby accompany them to the ring. With their hands full of dog, the girls couldn't go berserk with jubilation and put Emma's very life in jeopardy. Pleased with the way things had turned out, Emma thought she just might have to employ this divert-their-attention tactic again in the future.

They weren't back at their set-up more than two minutes when the Newfie bitch that had won Best of Winners both days and her owners came calling. For whatever reason, Cole's reaction to the other dog didn't register with Emma at first. Cole had become instantly alert and was quivering with excitement; he'd pulled himself up so that he looked like he'd grown several inches in height and his tail was wagging furiously. He seemed to have been completely mesmerized by the other Newfoundland. Emma had never seen him react to another dog this way, whether it was male or female, and she became intrigued by Cole's reaction. She looked from one dog to the other. Surprisingly, it appeared that the bitch was just as enthralled as Cole. Finally, the subsequent light bulb clicked on. Well, well, thought Emma, could it be? Was her boy coming into his own and experiencing the first of his mating instincts? Cole stepped forward and gently kissed the object of his fascination. She gave him a lick back. He nuzzled her neck; she leaned into him. Yep, Emma thought as she closely watched the two canines, they were definitely making googily eyes at each other.

"Hi. Mrs. Rogers?"

Emma tore her gaze away from Cole and focused on the woman who was addressing her. "Yes?"

"My name is Beverly Miller and this is my husband, Peter. I hope we're not intruding?"

"No, not at all. It's nice to meet you." Gesturing to the girls, Emma said, "These are my friends, Joanie Davis and Sally Higgins."

Greetings and handshakes were exchanged all around; then, pointing to the Newfoundland bitch, Emma asked, "And who is this lovely creature?"

"You mean the one who's acting like a shameful hussy? That's Molly," Bev replied, a smile in her voice.

"Well, Miss Molly's certainly gotten Cole's attention."

"I think she's been plotting how to use her feminine wiles on him ever since she saw him in the ring yesterday," Bev laughed.

"By the looks of it, I think she succeeded," Emma said. Cole's attention was still riveted on the other Newfoundland.

"Cripe, you can say that again. Is she in heat?" Joanie asked.

"No, although she's acting like it, isn't she? Molly isn't due to come in season until the middle of February."

"Hell, she'll probably lay him out flat then."

"Joanie..." Emma gave her friend a look designed to shut her up.

"What?"

Emma leaned over and whispered in her outspoken friend's ear, "Cool it, will you. These people don't know us. I don't want you to scare 'em off."

Joanie, a disbelieving expression on her face, whispered back, "You're kidding, right? How would I do that?"

Emma rolled her eyes. "As if you didn't know."

Joanie shrugged and moved off to stand with Sally. She turned back toward Emma with what could only be called a "porky" look on her face, and pantomimed zipping her lips.

Emma shot her a quelling stare and mouthed a "good" right back at her.

Glancing over at Joanie for a moment and not quite sure what to make of her, Bev went on to tell Emma that she and her husband had thoughts of breeding Molly to Cole when the time came. They were hopeful that Emma wouldn't have any objections and would agree to the match.

"Well," Emma began, "to tell you the truth, I hadn't even thought about breeding Cole yet. He won't be two years old until the 4th of January and will have to be OFA'd. I've had preliminary x-rays done and the results were excellent, but of course nothing's official until the films are taken at two and then there's all the other testing that needs to be done. I think Molly's an absolutely beautiful bitch though; my friends and I were admiring her yesterday in the ring. I really like her movement and top line. She seems to have a wonderful personality. How old is she?"

"She'll be two December 29th."

"Do you mind if I go over her?"

"No, go right ahead."

Bev set Molly up in a stack and Emma went over her from top to bottom looking for bone structure and correct angulations in shoulder, stifle, and hock. She examined her head, teeth, eyes, ear set, back, rib spring, height, the tightness of her feet, the depth of her chest, and her coat. Emma was very pleased with what she'd found.

"She's nice, very nice. Tell you what," Emma said. "Get me a copy of her pedigree so I can study it and we'll see how the bloodlines compare. I don't mind telling you that on the surface it looks like it would be a very good match both conformation and movement wise."

"Yeah, we kind of thought so too," Peter said. "Although we'd only heard about Cole previously to seeing him at this show, everything we'd heard pointed to him being an excellent choice of stud for Molly."

"Really? Wow! Okay, well, why don't we investigate further then? Let me go over the pedigrees and see if things look good. I'll call you after I've compared the two bloodlines. Is that all right?"

"Sure. Let me give you our phone number." Bev handed Peter a notepad and pen from her purse. He wrote down their name and number on a sheet of paper and ripped it off the pad. He handed the paper to Emma, which she folded and put in her pocket.

"You're over in Marilla, right? On Four Rod Road?"

"Yes, we only moved into the area a few months ago. I was transferred here because of my job. We're originally from Chicago," Peter explained.

"You're not too far from where we live, maybe a 30-35 minute drive."

"Is that all? I wasn't sure. We haven't had much time to explore the area yet; we've been so busy settling in with the house and kids and all that. This is our first show since we moved."

"What does Molly need to finish?"

"With today's win, she only needs one more point."

"That's great! I'm sure she won't have any trouble picking up the last one. You've got an excellent chance of finishing her this weekend."

"It would be wonderful if it worked out that way," Bev said, starting to inch away. "Well, listen, we won't keep you any longer. It was very nice meeting you all and hopefully we'll be talking in the near future. I'll get a copy of the pedigree to you right away, Emma. You're address is in the show catalog, right?"

"Yes, it should be. Good luck with the rest of the show. I'm sure we'll be seeing you at ringside."

"I'm sure," Bev said, waving as she turned to leave.

Peter gave Molly's leash a little tug and she looked at him with eyes that asked, "Do we really have to go now?"

Cole gave her a nudge and licked her face. Molly whimpered softly and turned to go with her people. Cole watched his new friend until the crowd swallowed her up.

Joanie was about ready to burst. It had been a real strain to keep her mouth shut for that amount of time. So what if it had only been for five minutes? For Joanie that was a lifetime. "Can I talk now?" she asked.

"Can we stop you?"

"No way in hell."

"All right. Get on with it. I can hardly wait to hear what's going to come out of your mouth," Emma said, giving Sally a resigned look.

"It's another act of divine intervention."

"Oh, damn, not again," Sally said, rolling her eyes.

"Why am I not surprised?" Emma blew out a breath.

"Maybe because you know me? But it is. I know it is."

"And why would you think that?" Emma asked, knowing she was going to hate herself for asking.

"Because."

"*Because*? Because why?"

"Because of all the Newfoundlands in the world Cole and Molly found each other and were instantly attracted to one another."

Emma rubbed her temples, she could feel a headache coming on, a Joanie-size headache. "You make it sound like they've been on a quest to find the ideal mate."

"Well, what's life all about, especially for a dog?"

"Oh, God, here we go."

"What do you mean by that?"

"You know what I mean. Have you been taking lessons on the side from Tammy?"

"*Nooo*. I'm telling you, Cole's her man and she's his woman. It's their destiny. They've been brought together by a Higher Being."

"Joanie, look over here. You see this big pile of black fur with four legs, a tail, and a wet nose? It's a *dog.* A D-O-G. A dog."

"Doesn't matter. They were made for each other. I think he loves her."

Emma looked to Sally for help, but wasn't getting so much as a glimmer of a response from her. Sally didn't even look like she comprehended what was being said; there was a definite blankness to her features. She looked like she was mentally out to lunch. Great, Emma thought, she wouldn't be getting any support from her.

"You think Cole loves Molly," she said.

"Yep," Joanie replied. "He's made Molly his own. She's his, all right."

"And just how did he do that?"

"Body language."

"Body language... Right. It all makes perfect sense now. Body language, of course. How stupid of me not to realize," Emma said, shaking her head.

"Well, yeah. It was obvious."

"Joanie?"

"Yeah?"

"Lord help me, but I think I might have to perform a mercy killing," Emma admitted as she closed the distance between them.

"A mercy killing?"

"Yeah, by getting rid of you, Sally and I will have been mercifully saved from your nutso logic."

"Whoa! Hold up a minute here," Joanie said, backing up a little. "I don't know why you can't see it. He did it right here. Of course, *I* was watching Cole since *I* had nothing better to do while you were busy yapping. It wasn't like *I* could talk, now was it... I must say he did a fine job for never having done it before. He was quite the gentleman."

"Well, I hate to tell you but you're quite the ass."

"*Phhh*, there was never any doubt about *that*. So what? That's old news. Doesn't change what I saw and I saw Cole make Molly his."

"Fine, whatever you say. I'm not up to arguing with you. Congratulations on your great observation skills." Emma waved the conversation away and reached into her purse for some aspirin, mumbling the whole time about what an idiot her friend was and how ludicrous it was for Joanie to think that Tammy was the weird one. They were two birds of the same feather! Well, maybe they had different plumage, but they were in the same species. "Don't we have to get somebody ready for the ring?"

"Yeah, isn't Tank supposed to be in soon?" Sally asked, emerging from what Emma suspected had been a self-imposed and convenient coma while Joanie had been dispensing her convoluted words of wisdom. Sally had probably been operating under the misguided notion that she could protect her mental capabilities from short-circuiting trying to follow Joanie's reasoning; hence the near-comatose trance she'd put herself into. Sally ought to know by now that nothing she did was going to save her sanity from being tested by her twisted friend.

"Tank isn't going in the ring today," Joanie stated emphatically. She gave the terrier a hard look.

Somehow Tank knew the conversation had shifted over to him and he looked out from his crate with an oh-well attitude. He snuffed once, laid his head down, and got comfortable. He appeared not to have a care in the world. At least that's what he'd like you to think. Joanie knew better; that little dog's brain never stopped plotting.

Emma and Sally stared at Joanie, their eyes asking if they'd heard her correctly.

"He's not going in."

"Why?" Emma and Sally asked in unison obviously surprised.

"'Cause I'm not giving him another chance to make an ass out of me, that's why. At least, not this soon anyway."

"But, Joanie, he does such a nice job." Her friends couldn't help it; they had to hassle her.

"Yeah, you could say he's perfected it to a new art form," Emma laughed, then washed the aspirin down her throat with some Diet Pepsi.

"You two are a big help."

"Aren't we though?"

"Yeah, well, I decided he needed a day off."

"*Who* needed a day off?"

"All right, me, I needed a day off. I admit it. The little shithead did me in yesterday."

"He *was* brutal," Sally acquiesced.

"Brutal? He was downright vicious. Let's not mince words, guys; he could have passed for the devil himself."

"I wouldn't go that far," Emma said.

"You weren't in the ring with him. You can afford to be generous. Not me."

"So, what? Are you pulling him for the rest of the weekend?"

"No, hopefully just today. I need to regroup and he needs a big time-out. He needs to think about his many sins."

"Like he's going to do that. Get real, Joanie."

"Let me have my fantasies, okay, guys? I need to hang onto something. I'm going to have to draw on every bit of courage I have to get back in the ring with that little schemer tomorrow."

"You're right about that. I don't think I could do it. Once would be enough for me," Sally said.

"It'd be a shame if he didn't finish this weekend. This is our last show for the year." Emma shifted her gaze over to Tank. He looked like he was sleeping.

"Yeah, I know, but what will be, will be. I—"

" 'Que Sera, Sera'."

"What?"

" 'Que Sera, Sera'. 'Whatever will be, will be'."

"What the hell are you talking about?"

"From the Doris Day movie, *The Man Who Knew Too Much.* You know, the one with Jimmy Stewart. That's the song."

"What song?"

" 'Que Sera, Sera'." Emma proceeded to sing the refrain to the melody right then and there and Joanie looked at her like she'd gone around the bend.

"I hate it when you do this."

"Do what?"

"Throw old movie stuff at me."

"Can't help it; it just comes out."

"Well, try a little harder to keep a lid on it, will ya?"

"I'll try."

"And I want you to promise me something."

"What?"

"Promise me that you will never, ever sing, and I use that term loosely, in public again."

"That bad?"

"That bad."

Emma looked to Sally for her opinion, hoping she'd find support. No luck.

"Sorry, Em, but that was worse than bad."

"Well, I know I'm not great, but—"

"Em, you stink. Promise—not ever again in public," Joanie demanded.

Emma looked thoughtful. "How about humming?"

"Only in the shop and I'll allow it there only because you own half the place. Nowhere else."

"I already do it there."

"Yeah, and if you want to continue to do it, you'll make with the promise."

Sally indicated that she went along with Joanie when Emma again looked to her for support. No dice. Those two were sticking together.

"All right, all ready," Emma griped. Just how bad could her singing be? Emma wondered. For sure it wasn't as bad as their dancing. *Nothing* was as bad as that. "Now, if we could put what you two term my lack of singing talent aside, do you think we could get back to the Tank issue?"

"There's nothing more to discuss. I need a day off from the little conniver, therefore I am not stepping foot in the ring today."

"What's your plan? Do you even have a plan?"

"Well, yeah, sort of… Maybe I can have a talk with him later."

"That's it? That's the plan? A talk?"

"Yeah…that's all I've got."

"Oh, brother," Sally groaned. Joanie was definitely in deep shit.

"Do you think it'll help?" Emma asked.

"Well, it couldn't hurt. Every once in a while he seems to get the message. You know the talk I mean, the one where I threaten to make his life a living hell, removing each and every one of his favorite things and condemning him to sleeping in the basement. That one?"

"Yeah, I remember hearing that talk a few times. You're right, every once in a while he seems to get the message."

"I'll have to see if I can put it to use one more time, although I think I may have to break out the wine a little early to get myself prepared."

"Ya think?"

"Yeah."

"How early?"

"Oh, kind of early. Like maybe after lunch."

"That early, huh?"

"Yeah. I think the situation calls for special fortification, don't you?"

"In this instance, I can't argue with you," Emma said.

"Yeah, I have to be at the top of my game for this confrontation so a little false courage is called for."

The discussion was cut short when friends stopped by to chat, the girls turning their attention to their visitors. Tank opened his eyes and unbeknownst to Joanie gave her a look that said, "Oh, you poor sap." He closed his eyes; the corners of his mouth turned up in a sick grin and he drifted off for a quick nap.

*　*　*　*

After the girls had dined once again on gigantic sandwiches and Joanie was halfway through her second glass of wine, they got Kirby ready for her afternoon rendezvous with destiny.

Sally and group got to Ring Six with plenty of time to spare. The judge, Mrs. Lillian Spothkin from New York, New York was still judging Flat-Coated Retrievers and the girls had the opportunity to observe her ring technique, which was always a good thing to acquaint yourself with before stepping into a particular judge's ring. An exhibitor could lose points quickly with a judge if the exhibitor failed to follow directions or was ignorant of what the judge expected in her ring. As far as Mrs. Spothkin went, it looked pretty straightforward.

The Flatties finished up and judging for Labradors began. Sally was going to have a long wait till Kirby's class was called; there were twenty dogs and twenty-two bitches in competition that day. The spoils for the winners in both sexes would be two points. Kirby's class was one of the last to be judged, so the girls used the time to renew acquaintances, watch the proceedings, and attend to all the last minute fussing that seemed to go on at every ring at every dog show.

Kirby's class was finally called into the ring. Mrs. Spothkin immediately sent the six bitches and their handlers around. Sally and Kirby were third in line and waited anxiously for their turn to be up for inspection. When it came, they moved to the head of the line and Sally stacked Kirby in a perfect show pose. The judge approached and after viewing Kirby from a short distance, moved in for the exam.

Sally sensed a perfunctory attitude as Mrs. Spothkin went over Kirby and flashed Emma and Sally a here-we-go-again look while the judge was supposedly busy. Her inspection over, the judge straightened away from Kirby, and asked Sally to do the down and back. She complied and led Kirby off, the two trotting down the mat in perfect form. Sally pulled Kirby up for the free stand, which she executed with a liberal dose of panache. Mrs. Spothkin seemed to be immune and as they moved into the go around, Sally noted that the judge barely even gave them a look. Chalk up another swoop, Sally thought as she brought Kirby to a stop back at the end of the line.

Sure enough, they stayed right where they'd started; they took a third when the placements were handed out. Sally snorted in disgust and left the ring. She didn't mind losing when she'd been given an equal chance, but this she suspected had been a foregone conclusion for the bitch that had taken the win. She was justified in her thinking when the same bitch went on to take Winners.

Of course, Joanie had no intention of taking this affront lying down. She was ready to tear the hide off the judge and Emma had to literally grab hold of her so she wouldn't go storming into the ring to avenge her friend.

"Emma! Let me go!"

"Not on your life, you maniac. You want to get barred from AKC events or what?"

"Right now I don't really care."

"Well, you will later on, so chill out."

Sally grabbed hold of Joanie's other arm with her free hand and added her strength in restraining her hell-bent friend. "Joanie, cool it. Nothing you do or say is going to make any difference. The dye has been cast. You'll only make trouble for yourself."

"Well, hell. The bitch did wrong and I don't mean the dog."

"That's the way it goes sometimes and you know it. So while I appreciate your gesture, just drop it. We'll try again tomorrow."

"Are you sure? I could probably embarrass the shit out of her or get in a quick pop before they hauled me away."

"I'm sure, and I don't want to see you get hauled away. It would give me nightmares for a year. Let's go back."

"Don't you want to wait and see who takes Breed?"

"No, I think I've seen enough already."

"Yeah, me too. Let's go. Emma, you coming?"

"I'm right with you."

They'd started to walk away when Joanie pulled herself out of their grasp, a mischievous glint in her eyes. Before Emma and Sally could recover and regain their hold on her, Joanie was back at the ring standing as close as she could without being inside it. There was no way to get her back without causing a scene, so Emma and Sally stayed where they were and hoped for the best. The Best of Breed and subsequent other wins were awarded and the ring eventually emptied. With the judge momentarily free, Joanie called her name and gestured for the woman to come over. Mrs. Spothkin walked over to where Joanie stood, the ring fencing between them. Joanie leaned slightly forward, bringing her mouth near the judge's right ear in an attempt to keep their conversation private.

After Joanie had talked for only a moment or two, Emma and Sally saw rather than heard the judge thank Joanie and at the same time observed Mrs. Spothkin touching her chin. Joanie raised her hand to ward off any thanks, then turned away and rejoined her friends.

"What in heaven's name did you say to her?" Sally demanded.

"Not much." Joanie's grin, which had magically appeared after she'd turned around, couldn't have gotten any bigger if she'd tried.

"Well, what was it? And are you going to be banned from AKC events from now 'til doomsday?"

"Hardly. I merely pointed out what every woman our age would want to know if they were unaware of its existence."

"What are you talking about?"

"I told her she had a chin hair."

Both Emma and Sally's mouth fell open. Emma recovered first. "You didn't."

"Yep. I told her it was quite noticeable in this light." Joanie's look of innocence was almost convincing. "I told her that I thought she'd want to know. She was very appreciative that I'd bothered to inform her."

"Oh, my God! I don't believe you did that."

"Hey, you have to seize the opportunity for payback when you can and this one was too good to pass up."

"Joanie," Emma was starting to giggle now, "You are such an ass."

"Yeah, no shit."

"Tell me this," Sally said, not able to suppress the laughter in her voice. "Did you really see a hair?"

"Nope, not a one, and I looked."

"Joanie, you *are* evil."

"I know. She's going to drive herself nuts trying to find it. Consider yourself avenged, Sally."

"Oh, I do, believe me." Sally gave Joanie a quick hug. "Thanks."

"No problem."

"Okay," Emma said, "but that's it. No more wine, Joanie. We're cutting you off until we're done for the day. You drink any more now, there's no telling what you'd do at the Group Ring if things don't go our way."

"Truly, you wound me, Emma."

"Tough. No more wine."

"All right, if you insist."

"I do. Let's go."

The band of three left ringside and went back to their set-up, overhearing on the way other disgruntled exhibitors. Joanie wasn't alone in her desire to give the judge her just desserts.

# Chapter Sixteen

The call for the Working Group came before they knew it. Cole was eager to get in the ring and do his thing; he'd practically danced all the way over. Could it be he wanted to show off for his new lady friend? Whatever the reason, he was raring to go; Emma meant to accommodate him.

All twenty-four breeds filed in while the crowd at ringside grew even larger. The main topic of conversation among the bystanders seemed to center around Cole and whether he would continue on with his winning ways and take the Group again. From the looks of it, Joanie and Sally thought it was a definite possibility. They hadn't thought he could be anymore "on" than he normally was, but they were wrong. He was absolutely dazzling as Emma walked him to his place in the lineup.

The judge, Mr. Jonas Tremont from Indianapolis, Indiana entered the ring and all attention shifted to him. He took his place at center ring and gave the dogs an initial look; then he gestured for the go around. Emma and Cole were stationed about a third of the way down the line. The front dogs moved out, setting the pace, with the dogs behind them stepping into motion when it was their turn. Emma and Cole had just settled into their rhythm when there was a disruptive commotion behind them. Three dogs back, a heavyset handler had snagged her heel on the side of the matting and had fallen down. Dog and handler were sprawled on the floor and the forward momentum of some of the handlers behind her was enough that they were unable to avoid the crash as it were and tumbled down when they got caught up in it. It was kind of like watching a chain reaction car accident, the end result being that the tangle of bodies and dogs looked like a multi-car pile-up on the highway. There were downed handlers and dogs everywhere. Exactly how many was hard to tell at first because there were arms and legs going every which way. Luckily, the dogs at the end of the line had been able to avoid being part of the disaster. Their handlers though, were standing transfixed, dumbfounded as to what they should do. The front group had come to a complete standstill, unsure of their role.

What followed next could be considered controlled chaos. Once the consequential paralysis generated by the incident was broken, people rushed in from all fronts to assist the downed exhibitors. Dogs were calmed, leashes untangled, and people righted. Amazingly, no injuries were sustained by either handlers or dogs.

The last person down, the one on the bottom of the pile was, of course, the poor heavyset woman who had started the whole thing. She was on her back and Joanie couldn't help but think she looked like an upended turtle. So much for Joanie's sympathetic feelings!

It took several men to get the woman back on her feet. Her dog seemed fine, but she was shaky and rather than risk another downward spiral, the men assisted her to a chair that was just inside the ring. She fell into it heavily and tried to catch her breath, which appeared to be in short supply by the way she was huffing and puffing. Someone brought her a cup of water and slowly the bright red color of her face subsided to a more normal hue.

While she recuperated, the judge allowed the other exhibitors to break formation and loosen their dogs up. It was another five minutes before judging could resume, the traumatized woman and her dog, a gorgeous Saint Bernard, opting to discontinue competing. They left the ring amid a round of applause for their recovery.

The remaining dogs were once again sent around the ring and thankfully this time there were no mishaps. Everyone returned to his or her original position safely and the individual inspections began. Cole appeared to be unaffected by the delay as he played tug-of-war with the drool towel that Emma wrestled him for while they waited their turn.

When they were within two dogs of going up, Emma guided Cole into a stack and kept him in it until it was their time to be presented front and center. Walking Cole out to the middle of the ring, Emma noticed he had an even more pronounced lilt in his step. She guided him into his stack and he locked on and held position; Emma didn't think there was a lax muscle in his body.

Mr. Tremont moved in to examine the young champion and Cole stood like he'd been hewn from rock. Emma had to wonder if he was even breathing, he was so still. It was amazing the affect a little feminine fluff was having. Maybe Joanie was right, Emma thought, Cole sure was acting like he was smitten. God forbid she should have to admit her friend had been right though; there was nothing worse than seeing Joanie gloat. Emma decided right then and there to keep her mouth shut.

Having been asked to do the down and back, Emma gathered the lead and moved Cole into his rhythmic, powerful gait as they flew over the rubber mat. They made their turn and came back toward the judge. When they were within eight feet of Mr. Tremont, Emma drifted to the right and Cole nimbly executed his patented free stand, turning all his attention to the one person he cared most for. His expression left nothing to doubt.

Released from the stack by the judge's signal, Emma and Cole went around the ring and back to their place in line. Mr. Tremont worked his way through the rest of the lineup and then it was time for him to make his first cut. He pulled out eight dogs and excused the remainder of the Group. He'd picked a beautiful Alaskan Malamute, a muscular Bullmastiff, a Giant Schnauzer that was black as night, a regal Great Pyrenees, a powerful-looking Rottweiler, a smiling Samoyed, a blue-eyed Siberian Husky, and the ever-impressive Cole.

The handlers were still stacking their dogs when the judge pointed for Cole to move to the number one position. He quickly placed the Rottweiler, then the Great Pyrenees, and lastly the Siberian Husky in the second, third and fourth positions, respectively. He gave the go-ahead for the go around and handlers and dogs moved out. Mr. Tremont called out the placements as they stood and Cole had himself another Group One.

Response from the crowd was swift and loud. The cacophony of shouts, cheers and whistles drowned out any congratulations that were being given to Emma from the other competitors. She could barely hear herself think. Even Cole, who was prancing at her side, was giving voice to an occasional bark; Emma wasn't sure, but she thought she heard an answering bark coming from the outside of the ring. Cole barked again and she strained her ears to hear. Sure enough, there it was. Focusing her attention on Cole, she looked in the direction where Cole's concentration seemed to be fixed. It didn't take her long to spot Molly and her owners; they were standing not too far from where Joanie and Sally were busy doing one of their outrageously awful dances. She hoped and prayed the Millers wouldn't look to their left; they might never get over the shock.

After Emma left the ring and picture-taking was finished in the area set aside for it, she joined her friends, approaching them with due caution. They appeared to be calm; they were talking to each other, their attention at the moment not focused on her. Breathing a little easier, Emma strode up and stopped with maybe a foot between them. If they decided to attack, how much leverage could they get from that distance?

Enough it seemed. As soon as they became aware of her presence, they were like runners exploding out of their blocks. They were on top of her before she knew what hit her. One of these days they were going to kill her; she just knew it. Cole came to her rescue and persisted until he was wedged between Emma and the two crazies, forcing them to release their grip on her.

"Geez, guys, lighten up, will you?" Emma rubbed her neck, trying to get some feeling back in it. "You about took my skin off."

"Sorry, Em. I guess we get carried away," Sally apologized. "We just get so excited."

"No shit."

"Hey, we're entitled," Joanie said.

"What makes you think so?"

"You're our friend, that gives us the right."

"That sounds perfectly logical, Joanie." Emma rolled her eyes. "I'm sure that reasoning will go over really big once you finally do kill me."

"Hey, it works for me. Besides, Sally will back me up."

"I will?"

"Of course you will."

"I don't know, Joanie. I think you'd better leave me out of this one."

"No can do. You're in it up to your neck."

"Well, I'm opting out."

"Turncoat."

"Joanie…"

"Yeah, yeah, I know. I'm an ass."

"Yeah, a really big one."

"Ya think? Okay. Well, how about this?" She flipped them both the bird and grabbed Cole's lead. "Come on, big boy, let's leave these two weenies and get you ready for Best In Show."

Emma and Sally followed and, laughing while they did it, discreetly shot the one-finger salute right back at her.

\* \* \* \*

During the interim between competitions, Emma used the time to relax Cole and then get him ready for their final time in the ring. Joanie and Sally took Tank and Kirby outside for some exercise and venting of energy. They first walked the dogs around the perimeter of the building and then let them wrestle on the grass, their leads inevitably becoming a tangled mess. The girls had their hands full keeping the dogs free from the restraints of the snarled leather and were happy when the two canines tired of the horseplay.

Sally made to go in, but Joanie held back.

"Aren't you coming?" Sally asked.

"No, I'm going to stay outside a minute and have a one-on-one with Tank here."

"Uh-oh. Is this it?"

"Yeah. It's time for us to have a little talk. I want his undivided attention."

"Should I stay to referee?"

"Uh-uh."

"How about medical personnel? Should I have them on standby?"

"I really don't think that'll be necessary. I'm only going to talk to him for cripe's sake. Tank will be fine."

"I wasn't worried about him."

"Very funny. Go on. We'll be in in a minute."

"All right, if you're sure. Tank?" The terrier looked over to Sally. "Don't be too hard on her." Tank barked and Joanie rolled her eyes.

Sally departed with a laugh that Joanie thought was entirely misplaced; she turned her attention to Tank and narrowed her eyes to mere slits. "Let's go somewhere private."

They walked around one side of the building where a covered dumpster was standing. Joanie scooped Tank up and put him on top of the dumpster so that he'd be at eye level with her. Tank sat down immediately as if he knew what was coming and wanted to get comfortable. You could almost see the wheels turning in that diabolical brain of his. From past experience he knew this could take a while, depending on how caught up she got in it. His mouth quirked up into that maddening grin; Joanie was already at a disadvantage, but he wasn't about to tip his hand, not just yet anyway.

"Now listen, Tank," Joanie began. "You've been a little devil, you know. What you did in the ring this last time was really too much." Tank cocked his head, giving every appearance of being innocent of the crime. "No, don't give me that look. You know I'm right. Hell, if your goal was to embarrass me you succeeded with flying colors, you little shit." Tank cocked his head the other way. "Quit with the innocent act. It isn't going to work. I know how you operate, mister." Tank lay down and put his head on his paws, giving Joanie the full effect of a wide-eyed stare. "You're good. I'll give you that, you little bugger. But I'm better." Tank snuffed, Joanie knew it was his version of a laugh. "Listen, wise guy, why don't we forget about past sins and concentrate on the future, huh?" Tank just continued to stare. "What do you say we call a truce? Let's get this last leg for your obedience title out of the way. Okay?" Tank's eyes were starting to look sleepy, his eyelids drooping. "Tank, I have the feeling I'm losing you here…Hey, don't you dare

211

go to sleep on me. Come on, get those eyes open. Tank? So help me...." Tank's eyes were fully closed. "Tank? Are you asleep or are you faking it? God knows you're fully capable of it. Can you hear me? Give me a sign." Tank let out a little snore. "Well, shit. A lot of good this did me; I don't know why I even bother."

Joanie carefully lifted Tank off the dumpster and cradled him in her arms; she walked back to the building's entrance and went inside. Tank cracked open one eye, grinned, and snuggled closer.

\* \* \* \*

It was time for Best In Show. The seven competitors were in the ring awaiting the entrance of the judge. Cole was second in line after the German Shepherd Dog from the Herding Group. Behind Cole was the Scottish Deerhound from the Hound Group, an English Springer Spaniel from Sporting, the same Norfolk Terrier from yesterday representing the Terrier Group, a Boston Terrier from Non-Sporting, and a Pekingese from the Toy Group.

The buzzing crowd around the ring was larger than the one that had assembled the day before. More and more people were anxious to see if the Newfoundland could win it all again.

Judge Anne Phillips from Milford, Connecticut strode briskly into the arena and cast her eyes upon the Group winners. She took her time and gave them each a thorough going over from her spot in the center of the ring. She signaled for the go around and the competitors moved out. The Shepherd moved out like a bat out of hell, leaving Cole and the rest of the dogs a fair distance behind. Emma was always amazed at the speed these dogs were moved at in order to show their gait advantageously. It seemed to Emma that the handler didn't appear to be in control; he looked like he was totally off balance. Cripe, if he tripped at the speed he was going, he was likely to break his fool neck. If it was Emma at the end of that lead, it would be a foregone conclusion.

Individual inspections were done and Cole not only performed with his usual perfection, but with Emma's guidance added a little zip at the end. After he'd stuck his free stand at the end of the down and back, the judge sent them on the go around back to their place in line. When Emma and Cole neared their spot, the two added a flourish by duplicating Cole's simultaneous-four-foot-down free stand; with a sign from Emma, Cole then gave the move emphasis by finishing with a single bark. The crowd loved it and Emma snuck Cole a discreet thumbs-up. The twinkle in Cole's eyes confirmed he understood that he'd pulled off a good one. If he'd had any doubts, hearing Joanie and Sally woo-hooing loud enough to shake the rafters would have dispelled them.

Miss Phillips went down the line for the last time, scrutinizing each dog in preparation for her final decision. When she got to Cole, his posture was so positively regal, she felt sure there should have been a crown sitting upon his noble head. After completing her inspection of the last dog, she moved briskly to the table to mark her book.

When she came back out, her steward and the Show Chairman of the host club, which was the Chenango Valley Kennel Club, accompanied her. They came out to center ring armed with the spoils of the Best In Show win. With broad smiles on their faces, the three stood there for a second or two before the judge announced, "The Newfoundland."

Emma looked at Cole; he looked at her. The next thing anybody knew, he was up on his hind legs with his front paws on her shoulders, licking her face and nuzzling his big head into her neck. Anybody could see that Emma was straining to keep her footing, but only those closest to them, if they listened really hard, would have been able to hear Emma softly exclaiming, "Son of a bitch, we did it again!"

After all the hoopla of congratulations and awarding of prizes had been done with, and the other competitors had left the ring, Miss Phillips held up the photographer when he was about to set up his equipment. He backed out of the ring while the judge spoke quietly to Emma.

No one had moved from ringside and questions about what was going on were circulating through the wondering crowd. Exhibitors who had been present at the show in September were whispering excitedly, hoping they were about to see a repeat performance. Their hopes were realized within seconds.

Without a word being spoken in explanation, Emma handed back the prizes she'd been balancing in her hands to the judge, who in turn gave them to the steward. The crowd had quieted immediately, sensing something was about to happen that wasn't on the normal agenda. Miss Phillips moved to the end of the ring with Emma and Cole, then placed herself off to the sidelines so she wouldn't be in the way. Emma went down on her haunches in front of Cole and spoke so softly to the big dog that only he could hear what she was about to say.

"Well, Cole, my boy, guess what? The judge has asked if we'd consent to putting on a demonstration for her and all these lovely people. What do you think? Are you up for it?" Cole woofed. "I thought you'd say that. Okay, let's give 'em one they won't forget." Emma ruffled his ears and stood up. She might have misgivings about doing it because it sure wasn't going to take them out of the limelight, but how do you refuse a judge? Cole gave her another woof and pranced a few steps around her. Despite her reluctance, she brought him back to her side and took off his lead. Cole's attention was centered completely on Emma. The crowd gasped in delight; any doubts they might have had as to what was going to happen were dispersed now.

Emma gave Cole the proper hand signal and he was off, flying around the ring in superb form. You could have heard a pin drop around the ring; people seemed to be absolutely mesmerized. Cole came back to Emma and when he was within striking distance, she gave him another signal and he came down in his now-famous free stand. He never moved a muscle until she released him and then he bounded to her side.

After lavishing her devoted friend with hugs and kisses, she walked him into position for the down and back, and sent him out. Cole strode down the mat in cadenced stride, turned, and came back the same way he'd gone down—perfectly. He did his free stand the second Emma gave him the cue. There was still no sound to be heard around the ring; bystanders appeared to be completely entranced.

Next, Emma directed Cole to execute the triangular figuration and he did so without missing a beat. Finally the silence around the ring was broken by one voice. A loud "woo-hoo" was heard reverberating in the vast building. Emma knew who it was without even looking; it was Joanie, of course. She must have broken the spell that had gripped the captivated audience because the air was suddenly filled with the booming noise of cheers and clapping.

Emma sent Cole out around the ring one more time amid the deafening applause. She moved out to center ring and he met her there after completing his circuit. She signaled and he went into his low bow; Emma bowed back. They turned to face the judge, Emma signaled, and they both bowed at the same time. With a look to his mistress, Cole sprang up and placed his front paws on her shoulders, tucking his head into her neck. Emma wrapped her arms around his big body and whispered loving words in his ear. She gave him a kiss and he licked her face. With a pat to his side, Cole got down on all four feet and after Emma exchanged a handshake with a very impressed judge, the photographer finally got the go-ahead to set up for pictures.

Joanie and Sally were waiting at the ring entrance when Emma and Cole finally left the judging area and Emma quickly shoved the Best In Show prizes into their hands. They couldn't do much damage if their hands were full, could they? It had worked fairly well when they'd had Tank and Kirby at the ring. Forget it; they were still dangerous, she thought a second later as the sharp edge of the silver-plated bowl dug into her ribs when Joanie hugged her. Sally wasn't any better; she'd come within a hair's width of cold-cocking her with the plaque that she'd been holding. Maybe the best thing Emma could do before she competed would be to heavily lace any refreshment the girls were drinking with strong tranquilizers. You know, give them enough to take down a horse. *Then* she might be safe. It was worth thinking about.

Much the same as yesterday, it took the girls forever to leave the building what with exhibitors wanting to talk and get a closer look at Cole. The three friends had to be almost rude in order to break camp and depart, although Joanie seemed to embrace her role with more gusto than was needed. She could be heard more than once shouting, "Move your butts, people. Get out of the way."

Once they were back in their room, there was no way in hell they were leaving other than to take the dogs out to the bathroom. They found a pizza place that delivered, got in their jammies, broke out the booze, and spent the night watching movies on HBO.

\* \* \* \*

While the girls were decompressing, the woman who meant to pursue her vengeful mission the next day was busy preparing for the trip. She'd already packed an overnight bag with necessities and was now in her lab, which was housed in the basement of her Tudor-style home.

There was nighttime blackness beyond the block-glass windows, which were set high in the wall. Moira had had them installed to allow for some measure of natural daytime lighting, yet their translucency protected her privacy.

The lab, which encompassed half of the underground space, was blindingly bright; everything had been painted a glaring white—walls, ceiling, wooden cabinets. The counter tops were white Formica. The floor was tiled in tan-speckled white squares. The fluorescent lighting was almost eye-achingly brilliant. The environment was pristine—pure. It suited her purpose perfectly.

Donning a pair of latex gloves, she opened the small white refrigerator and took out a covered beaker of clear, odorless liquid and placed it deliberately on the counter. The vial she'd take to the show tomorrow was already there, waiting to be filled. She uncovered the beaker, then unscrewed the top of the small vial. She placed a tiny funnel in the vial and with great care poured the contents of the beaker into the little receptacle until it was full. With painstaking movements she set the beaker down and recovered it. She took the funnel out of the vial, placed it immediately into the porcelain sink, and then screwed the top back on the vial. She placed both the beaker and vial back in the refrigerator. She turned to the sink and quickly washed the funnel with an industrial-strength detergent and hot water; then she rinsed until the soapsuds disappeared. That done, she stripped off her gloves and deposited them in the trash.

With a sigh that bespoke exhaustion, Moira leaned back against the counter and tiredly went through her "to do" list, mentally checking off the preparations that were complete. As far as she could tell, everything was ready. All she had to do in the morning was shower, dress, grab her bag, retrieve the vial, and put it in her purse. She'd be out the door by 6:15 and at ringside by 8:30.

As for the remainder of the night, she needed to spend it getting some uninterrupted, revitalizing sleep. The excitement that had been building within her for days had prevented restorative rest, although it had kept the nightmares at bay. But now she was tired to the bone and needed to simply sleep.

She went up the stairs to the first floor, turning off lights as she wandered through the house. She climbed the stairs to the second floor, her footsteps heavy, and entered her bedroom. She turned the bed down and changed into her nightgown. Carrying her discarded clothes, she went into the adjoining bathroom and threw the clothing into the hamper. She washed the makeup off her face and brushed her teeth. Then she reached into the medicine chest for the sleeping pills that would tranquilize her excitement, ensure a sleep deep enough to rejuvenate her tired body, and hold off any terrors lurking in the dark recesses of her mind.

# Chapter Seventeen

When the girls awoke the next morning, Sally had dutifully fulfilled her obligation and had put in a full night at her position in the middle if the bed, giving a good impression of the "L" in a BLT sandwich. It was an experience she didn't want to repeat any time soon; maybe in another thirty or forty years she'd be able to tolerate it again. The wakeup call had come as a blessed relief, this from someone who normally had difficulty leaving the warmth of her bed in the morning. This particular morning she sprang out of bed on the first ring of the telephone like her pants were on fire.

Her bedmates hadn't been quite as tired as they'd been the night of their arrival, giving rise to even more movement and shifting of body parts while slumbering in close quarters to one another. Unfortunately for Sally, a lot of that activity had been directed toward the center of the bed where she just happened to be lying. Enough was enough; she was out of there!

She called first dibs on the bathroom and darted in before the other two had their eyes fully open. Emma and Joanie roused themselves and saw to the dogs needs first, the fresh air chasing away any lingering cobwebs. It did Joanie's heart good to see Mr. Rottweiler Man dutifully cleaning up after his dog, especially when it looked like the effort was killing him.

Sally had finished with her shower when they returned and Emma took her turn in the bathroom. Joanie gave the dogs fresh water and biscuits, then let them make themselves at home on the bed. She got involved with getting breakfast ready and Sally, finished with makeup and hair, was putting her toiletries away. Nobody was paying any attention to the dogs and they took advantage of it. In the mischief that was to follow, Cole was the undisputed ringleader.

Keeping a wary eye on the unsuspecting duo, the dogs, one by one, snuck over to the closed bathroom door. Cole took the doorknob in his mouth and carefully turned it. With Tank and Kirby anxiously watching, the door opened. The shower curtain was drawn, the sound of running water filling the room. The three dogs crept forward. Once they were inside, Cole quietly closed the door. They looked at one another; then they looked at the shower curtain. They looked back at each other; then they moved toward the tub.

Cole silently nudged the curtain aside just far enough so he could see inside. Emma had her back to them, rinsing her hair. Cole's eyes lit up when he saw all that water falling from the showerhead. It was beckoning to him and his sidekicks like a mermaid to a sailor. It was much too powerful a call to ignore. They took the plunge—literally. All three dogs jumped into the tub, knocking Emma off her feet in their recklessness. She went down with a crash and a shriek. Before she knew what had hit her, all three dogs were entangled and water was spraying everywhere. A very emphatic "son of a bitch" rang out loud enough to wake the dead.

Emma's shriek and expletive brought Joanie and Sally running and they were presently standing on the other side of the door asking if she was okay.

"Yeah, I'm just great," Emma said between clenched teeth. She'd made it to her feet and was clutching the handrail lest she go down again amid three dogs that were themselves trying to gain a foothold on the slippery surface.

"What happened?" Joanie asked through the closed door.

"Wouldn't you like to know," Emma shot back, struggling desperately to shut the water off.

"Well, yeah, that's why I asked."

"Joanie, if you know what's good for you, don't get smart with me right now."

"Why? What'd I do?"

"Obviously, nothing."

"What's that mean? And what's all that noise in there?"

Emma ignored the question and asked one of her own. "You guys missing anything out there?" Emma was trying without much success to get the dogs to stand still before they took her legs out from under her again.

"Missing anything? What would we be missing?"

"You tell me. Look around. What isn't out there?"

Sally and Joanie gave each other a confused look, shrugged their shoulders, and then checked the room. These two were definitely falling beneath rocket science level at the moment; in fact, they were going blond fast. Mumbling under their breaths about what the hell Emma could be talking about, it wasn't until they saw the empty, open crates that they remembered the dogs had been on the bed. The operative words being "had been". They weren't there now. They weren't anywhere in the room which meant only one thing. They could only be in one place. Uh-oh! They were in the bathroom—with Emma—with water. They scrambled back to the door.

"Are the dogs in there?" Sally asked.

At this point that question had to be about the dumbest one Emma had ever heard and she gave her head a couple of quick hits with the palm of her hand to make sure she was processing it right. "Did you just ask me if the dogs were in here?" There was a look of incredulous amazement on her face.

"Umm, yeaah." Sally instinctively backed up a step from the door. There was something in Emma's voice that was not conducive to warm, fuzzy feelings.

"What do you think?" Emma called back as she managed to step out of the tub and grab a towel, wrapping it around herself.

"Um, I think they might be in there," Joanie said, "'cause they aren't out here."

"Really? You're deductive powers astound me. Well, guess what? You're right; they are in here. Now if you would be so kind (there was definite underlying hostility in those words), get your asses in here!"

With some trepidation, the girls opened the door.

"Get in here and shut the door. God help us if they get out."

Joanie shoved Sally inside and quickly shut the door. They both stayed where they were, with their backs hugging the only means of escape if it became necessary, and surveyed the scene in front of them. Holy shit! What a mess!

Emma, although wrapped in a towel, was still dripping and standing in a puddle of water. The shower curtain, which had been whipped to the side, had obviously been displaced to the outside of the tub during the melee and was now instrumental in depositing pooling water on the tiles beneath it. The mirror on the wall opposite the tub was covered in droplets of water, which were slowing leaving wet trails as they slid down the surface. And finally, there were the dogs. God help them, they looked like three drowned rats! Three very happy, contented drowned rats! The girls' first impulse was to wring their little waterlogged necks!

Without another word and managing as best they could within the confines of the crowded room, all three grabbed towels and the appropriate dog and went to work. Thank God, nobody was in the ring until 9:00. They had a chance of pulling this off—barely!

When the worst of the water had been sopped from their coats and there wasn't a dry towel to be had, the hair dryers went into action. Cole and Kirby were escorted to their crates while Sally started on Tank. Joanie called housekeeping and got more towels. She cleaned up the bathroom as best she could, then took her shower. Emma got dressed and made-up; as soon as she was finished she grabbed another hair dryer and attacked Kirby's wet coat. Sally wrapped it up with Tank (thank God for short-haired dogs) and joined Emma, turning her efforts to helping with the Lab. By the time Joanie was dressed and had her face on, Emma and Sally were ready for Cole. This was going to take a little time, something they didn't have all that much of.

They put the two hair dryers to work and hoped that Lady Luck would be with them. The last thing they needed was for the dryers to overheat or blow a fuse. God, Cole had coat! And Sally and Emma's arms were getting tired. Joanie was stuffing her face, but when she finished, she relieved Sally who ate her breakfast while on the run packing up their gear.

They got Cole to the point where he was just damp and Emma quit long enough to shove some food in her mouth. Joanie kept at it and started brushing him out while Emma and Sally took everything down to the van.

Everything was loaded except the dogs, two of which were lounging on the bed, and the paraphernalia the girls were using on Cole. Emma picked up another brush and added her energies to Joanie's while Sally debunked Kirby and Tank and took them out to the bathroom. She was back in the room within five minutes, minus the dogs; they were safely ensconced in their crates in the van.

Joanie and Emma worked for another ten minutes with Sally lending a hand manning the hair dryer while the other two brushed out sections of coat for her to dry. All of this was done on the floor with Cole either standing or lying on his side. The grooming tables had been left at the show so the only place they had to work was a cramped area in the middle of the room.

The girls were on their knees, bending and twisting every which way to get him groomed. When he was finally finished, they naturally saw absolutely no reason to stay on the floor another minute and made to get up. Easier said than done! Those old bones were not cooperating. They looked like a bunch of 80-year olds as the struggled to their feet and straightened backs and knees that were protesting in earnest. It was easiest for Sally; she'd been down the shortest amount of time, although her ascent certainly couldn't be called graceful. Emma needed to brace herself on Cole to gain her feet and it took her a minute to unbend, letting out a groan as she straightened her back. Her first couple of steps weren't any too steady. Then there was Joanie. She was the youngest of the group, but she'd been on the floor the longest. And she wasn't making any attempt to get up. She was on all fours and kind of scrunched up.

"Joanie, come on. We have to go."

"I can't get up. Everything seems to be locked in this position."

"Hang on. Come on, Sally, help me." Between the two of them, Emma and Sally managed to straighten Joanie up from the floor and lift her off her knees. They had her hanging by her arms before she was able to uncurl her legs and get her feet back on the floor. They kept hold of her until she showed signs of being able to move on her own.

"Damn! It's a bitch getting old, isn't it?"

"Sure is. Nothing works right anymore."

"Want some aspirin?"

"I think I need a double dose."

"I'll give you some on the way. Come on. We've got to get moving." Emma checked the time. "Cripe! We've got about five minutes before I'm supposed to be in the ring."

They moved as fast as their stiff joints would allow and piled into the van. Emma and Cole slid into the back seat—forget the crate. Joanie jumped into the front passenger seat and Sally shot behind the wheel with no argument from Emma this time. There was no time for dillydallying and absolutely none for trying to find a parking space big enough for Emma to deal with. Besides, she had to be ready to make a run for it.

Sally pulled into the first spot she found and threw the van into Park. Emma grabbed Cole and ran as fast as she could, which at her age wasn't particularly graceful, into the building. She arrived at Ring Three at the same time the Open Class for dogs was going in. She claimed her armband and quickly put it on, the whole while trying to get her heart rate down and her breathing back to normal. She probably looked like a candidate for having a heart attack at any moment. She kind of felt like one too; she knew her face was red from running and she was huffing and puffing like a locomotive. Thankfully, there were still a few minutes to complete the metamorphosis from impending cardiac arrest victim to a calm, in-charge, unruffled exhibitor. *Yeah, right!* Not after the morning they'd had! Emma closed her eyes and concentrated on bringing her heart rate down and slowing her breathing. She took a page out of dippy Tammy's book, and willed herself to go to her happy place, wherever the hell that was. Well, cripe, she figured it was worth a shot.

\* \* \* \*

225

She'd arrived at the Fairgrounds at 8:25 and was hanging around the rings by 8:29. Her timing had been perfect as was all her planning. She'd had to quell a rising tide of terror as she'd driven toward Syracuse, but succeeded in gaining control over her fear by the time she'd parked her car. It had even been a little easier than the last time.

Now as she meandered through the building, she watched and listened while carefully skirting around any dogs that passed by. At all times she tried to keep a safe distance between herself and them, maneuvering carefully so as not to draw undue attention. At the same time she concentrated on blocking out the incessant barking so she could keep herself centered and eavesdrop on conversations. She was in essence, reconnoitering her hunting ground.

As Moira advanced in her circuit of the building, pausing now and then at the different rings and booths, a definite buzz of excitement seemed to prevail. People were talking in excited tones about something that had happened yesterday. She couldn't get the whole drift of it, but it was apparent these people believed that one of the dogs had done something quite remarkable. She doubted that whatever it was was noteworthy, but she wanted to know more. Her need for gathering any and all information that might affect either directly or indirectly the success of her endeavor could be likened to that of a military general planning his assault on the enemy.

She decided to head over to the grooming area where she could possibly glean that very information while checking out potential targets. She touched the side of her leather purse, which was hanging off her shoulder, her fingers feeling for the vial that was safely hidden inside.

* * * *

One good thing about the morning's disaster at the motel was that Emma and Cole were in and out of the ring with the

Best of Breed win before Joanie and Sally had a chance to get there. Thank God for small favors, Emma thought. For once she hadn't had to endure a revolting celebration dance or slaps on the back that could send her into next week. There is a reason for everything, she thought and for once it had worked in her favor. The powers that be must have known she needed a break from the disco duo.

She'd even had a chance to congratulate the Millers on Molly's win, which gave the dog her championship without having to battle her friends to stay upright and conscious.

She was on the way back to where they'd set up when Joanie and Sally, with Kirby in tow, met her and raced on by somewhat frantically.

"Hey, where're you going?" Emma called out.

"Kirby's due in the ring."

"*Whaaat*?" A look of total confusion crossed Emma's face.

"We've got to get to the ring."

"But—"

"She's in now, Em."

"She is?"

"Yeah, right now. We read the schedule wrong."

"We did?"

"Yeah. We've got to go. Labs are already going in."

"How'd we do that?"

"Hell if I know."

"Damn. What ring?"

"Seven."

"I'll meet you there in a minute."

"Okay."

All this was said on the run, their voices getting louder the further away they got from each other. Emma turned back and walked quickly to their set-up. She put Cole in his crate and gave him some water, wondering the whole time how all three of them had managed to misread the schedule.

Well, no real mystery there, they were who they were, after all, and all three were subject to "senior moments". They must have all had one at the same time.

She checked on Tank and then set out for Ring Seven. By the time she got there, the American Bred class for dogs was already in. Emma found the girls and Kirby waiting about fifteen feet from the entrance to the ring.

"Hey. So, do I need to ask? Did you take Best of Breed?" Joanie asked.

"Yep, Cole was right on the money again."

"When isn't he?" Sally interjected while she ran a brush over Kirby's coat, which already looked perfect. The action was purely reflexive, part of the ringside fussing that went on continuously.

"Never."

"You've got that right."

"How's the judging going? Any surprises?"

"No, Mrs. Markham seems to be doing her usual good job. We've been agreeing with most of her choices."

"Good, then Kirby should be in the running."

"Let's hope so."

The chatter continued as the judging progressed through the classes. Finally it was time for Sally and Kirby to do their thing, which that day they did with even more precision and style than normal. The harried pace of the morning must have gotten their adrenalin pumping. At any rate, they won their class and after waiting for the Open Bitch, Chocolate winner to be decided, they were now back in the ring competing for Winners Bitch.

Emma and Joanie were holding their breaths and crossing their fingers. A win today would not only complete Kirby's championship, but it would mean that she finished with three majors. Today's win was worth three points and, Lord, if anybody deserved it, Sally and Kirby did. The girls shot a little prayer heavenward.

Mrs. Markham looked over the entrants from the center of the ring; the dogs were stacked in the usual manner. Sally and Kirby were second in line and doing their best to impress the judge. Mrs. Markham walked over to the first dog and asked the handler to execute the down and back, finishing the exercise with the free stack. She proceeded in like manner down the line, each exhibitor in turn doing as she requested. Mrs. Markham strode back to the first dog and then waltzed down the line taking another look at each one individually. By the time she'd gotten to the last exhibitor Sally was about ready to come out of her skin. Just get this freakin' thing over with, she thought.

The judge, in no apparent hurry, signaled nonchalantly for the go around. Hopefully, this was it; she'd made her decision. The group started out, dogs and handlers moving around the ring. Mrs. Markham waited until they were three quarters of the way around before she waved them on and kept them moving for another circuit. What the hell, was this never to end? They were close to starting another lap when the judge finally raised her arm, pointed to Sally and Kirby, and called out, "Winners."

Well, holy shit!

Sally couldn't contain herself and let a big "Yahooee!" rip from her mouth. She slipped immediately into performing one of her not-so-pretty dances and sad to say Joanie was matching her step for step on the outside of the ring. People couldn't decide which one was the worse of the two as their eyes darted back and forth between them pretty much like they were following the ball in a tennis match. Overall it was a scene that many didn't want to see repeated. After Joanie had soundly thumped Emma on the back, enough to make her stagger headfirst into the person standing in front of her, Emma had retreated to a safe distance. She was showing her congratulatory response in the customary, time-honored way by clapping and cheering. She even gave a few exuberant "woo-hoos" accompanied by the ensuing raised arm, but she would not under any circumstances join in the demented frenzy that her friends grossly mislabeled as dance. It was just too sick!

Sally was finally calm enough to accept congratulations from the other exhibitors and receive the Winners ribbon from the judge. Upon exiting the ring while judging for Reserve went on, Sally quickly sought out Emma and Joanie.

"Hot damn! You did it, Sal." Joanie threw an arm around her neck, squeezing her until Sally couldn't breathe.

Emma noticed, her experience with all too-forceful-congrats alerting her to Sally's discomfort. She loosened Joanie's arm. "Joan, take it easy. She still has to go in for Best of Breed. She needs to be alive to do that."

"What? Oh, oh, sure. Sorry about that. I'm just so damned excited for you."

"No shit," Sally said, rubbing her neck. "Hey, we did it! Kirby's a champion! Hallelujah!"

"I told you, didn't I? I said you'd finish her by Christmas." Emma reached down and gave the Lab a couple of quick pats on the side.

"Yeah, you sure did. We finally swept. No more swooping."

"Don't start that bullshit again," Joanie said. "It makes me dizzy. Hey, heads up. They're going in. Give 'em hell, kiddo."

"Yeah, knock 'em dead, Sal."

Sally and Kirby reentered the ring for Best of Breed competition. They were at the very end of the twelve-dog lineup. Mrs. Markham had them do a go around. God, this could get tiring! At this point, however, Sally wasn't noticing; she was on the veritable cloud nine. Individual inspections of the Specials began, and Sally and the handler with the Winners Dog relaxed their animals. Kirby was only too happy to play tug-of-war with a small plush squirrel that Sally had pulled out of her pocket.

By the time Mrs. Markham reached the Winners Dog, both he and Kirby were back in their stack. She instructed them each to do a down and back and then had them travel around the ring together. She next moved Kirby up behind one of the male Specials and had them go around the ring together. Sally at this point was so tired of running around the ring that she just wanted out. She was beyond comprehending what the significance of her moving up to her present position was.

When both dogs were back in place, the judge moved Kirby in front of the Special and gave everyone one last look before sending the entire group around the ring. Sally was still clueless. In what was to be a huge upset, Mrs. Markham awarded Best of Breed and Best of Winners to none other than Kirby. The gorgeous male Special took Best of Opposite.

Talk about going out in a blaze of glory! Damn!

What had happened finally hit home and Sally was in a word, thunderstruck. In fact, she looked like she was on the verge of passing out. All color had leeched from her face and she wasn't moving. She had stopped dead in her tracks, which thankfully had put her in a spot not too far from the awards area. But she was just standing there with her mouth open and her eyes glazed. Kirby was attempting to get her attention by jumping straight up into her face, but Sally wasn't responding. She was transfixed; nobody was home. She didn't even respond when the judge came over to give her the ribbons. Mrs. Markham in somewhat of a quandary, took hold of Sally's right hand, put the ribbons in it, and closed her fingers around them. Then she looked around imploringly for some help. What was she to do with this near catatonic woman? Emma and Joanie rushed to the rescue.

As they approached their friend, Sally gave no indication that she was aware of their presence. She was still rooted to the same spot acting like a prime candidate for the loony bin.

"Hey, Sal." Emma snapped her fingers within an inch of Sally's face. "Yoo-hoo, Sal. Anybody in there?"

"Sal, get with the program. Come on, let's get it together." Joanie waved her hands back and forth in front of her friend's eyes.

"We're not getting any response here, Joanie."

"Yeah, I know," Joanie agreed. "Sal, come on, you're making an ass out of yourself."

"Oh, like that's going to help," Emma chided.

"Hell, it was worth a shot. Thought maybe I could get a rise out of her."

"Well, what are we going to do?" Emma had taken charge of Kirby who was looking at her mistress with bewildered eyes.

"Well, other than slapping her upside the head, there's only one thing to do."

"What?"

"This." Joanie promptly reached around to Sally's backside and goosed her with probably a little more enthusiasm than was absolutely necessary.

"Ow!" Sally shrieked. "What the hell?" Sally sprang alive, indignation spewing forth.

"That certainly worked," Emma said.

"Told you."

"What the hell was that for?" Sally demanded, rubbing her butt.

"I'll tell you what it was for," Joanie stated emphatically. "It was because you were standing there like the village idiot and nobody could get you to move. That's what it was for."

"Oh."

232

"We needed to take desperate measures. You weren't responding to normal stimuli… like the judge."

"Oh, crap. Really?"

"Yep, you were a goner."

"I guess I must have really been out of it."

"That's an understatement if ever I heard one." Emma murmured, raising her eyebrows.

"It was the shock of the thing. Shit. I took Breed!"

"Yeah, we know. So does everybody else who's been watching you for the last five minutes while you've been in another world."

"Oh, boy." Sally looked around self-consciously. Yep, people were certainly watching her.

"Now do think you can pull yourself together long enough to get a picture? I would imagine you do want a picture, don't you?"

"Of course I want a picture. Don't be stupid."

"Right. Well, let's get the damn thing then. They might want to use this ring for other judging, don't you think?" The judge was giving the girls an expectant look; there was a schedule that had to be adhered to after all.

"Oh, yeah, sure. Sorry… Emma?"

"Yeah, Sal?"

"We sure did sweep, didn't we?" Sally's face was radiant with a huge smile.

"You sure did. Congratulations." Emma gave her happy friend a heartfelt hug. "Now go get your damn picture." As she watched Sally walk over to where the judge and photographer waited, Emma knew without a single doubt that the manhattans would be flowing that night and deservedly so.

# Chapter Eighteen

While the girls had been busy at Ring Seven, the young woman who was so intent on revenge had been roaming the grooming area, talking to different exhibitors here and there, getting the full story on yesterday's excitement. She now knew about the dog that had taken Best In Show for the second time in as many days and who had put on a thrilling exhibition after competition had been over. She was suitably impressed, but strictly for her own reasons. The dog was a Newfoundland; they were black. She had learned in her research that there were black and white ones called Landseers and also browns and even grays, but she knew from what she'd learned that this particular one was a solid black. And he fit right in with her plans.

She continued her meandering, forever the interested bystander. Her potential victims were rising in number; there could be quite a few this time. She had over 2,500 dogs to choose from.

*   *   *   *

It was close to 11:15 when the girls got back to their daytime home away from home, namely their set-up in the grooming area. They each collapsed on whatever bare surface they could find and rested for a minute. That's all they had, a minute. They cracked open the Diet Pepsi and toasted Sally's success. They'd get to the hard stuff later.

The restful lull was nearly over before it started—if it could have even been considered to have existed at all; Tank was due in the Obedience Ring at 11:30 and they had to walk over to the Pepsi Pavilion.

"We'd better get our butts in gear, guys," Emma said. "We've got a ways to walk."

"Joanie, get Tank on the table. He probably needs some sprucing up," Sally said, reaching for a brush.

Joanie continued to drink her soda, a pained expression flitting across her face.

"What's the matter?" asked Emma. "Come on, we've got to get a move on."

"I'm thinking I won't put him in today."

"What? Why not?"

"I'm not ready to go back in the ring with him."

"That's bullshit and you know it."

"No, it's fact. I'm scared of what he's going to do next. He's getting deadly."

"Tough. You're going in," Sally said, grabbing Tank out of his crate and swinging him up to the table. She ran a brush over his coat and declared him good to go.

"Let's move."

Sally tucked Tank under her arm and both Emma and Sally latched on to Joanie and hustled her out of the building. She protested the whole time and tried to make excuses why they couldn't compete, including the one that Tank hadn't relieved himself yet and he was sure to do it in the ring. Sally gave her an exasperated look, put Tank down, and commanded him in no uncertain terms to do his business. Miracle upon miracle, he did.

Accepting that she had no way out, Joanie and entourage entered the Pavilion. Emma retrieved Joanie's armband and put it on her arm. Then Emma positioned herself behind her jittery friend so she couldn't bolt. Sally, who continued to be in charge of Tank, stood close to Emma so as to reinforce the flight-preventative barricade.

Tank sat at attention, unusually subdued; somehow he'd gotten the message that now was not the time to screw around. Maybe it had been Sally's almost constant scowl that she'd been directing his way ever since they'd left the Center. That could certainly do it, not to mention the no-bullshit-or-else threat she was telegraphing through the lead that went from her hand to his collar. If nothing else, Tank was not a stupid dog!

Several minutes had passed while they waited for Joanie and Tank's turn. It was relatively quiet at ringside, so when they heard a rather disgusting noise, Emma and Sally knew right away from whom it was originating—Joanie. It was a distinctive sound, something between a spit and a blown raspberry. What the hell was she doing?

Emma tapped Joanie on the shoulder and she turned her head back toward her friend. "What are you doing?"

"I don't have any spit," she said, continuing to work her mouth in the quest for some form of lubrication. "Tank's got me so nerved up my mouth's dry as toast. I don't have any saliva."

"Here." Sally dug into the bottom of her purse. "Have a stick of gum. It'll get your saliva flowing."

"Thanks." Joanie put the gum in her mouth and started chewing for all she was worth. She kind of looked like a cow chewing its cud—not aesthetically pleasing. Nobody said anything though. Now was not the time to be worried about etiquette, which would have disavowed the chewing of gum to begin with. So who cared what Joanie looked like as long as she got her salivary glands working?

Any exhibitor knew there was no way you could possibly go into the ring without spit in your mouth. It had to be there in the beginning because how else were you going to know when it dried up due to nervous tension during the course of the competition. No, spit was as necessary as your dog when you stepped into the ring. Leave it to Emma to be the exception to the rule with her nerves decreasing the longer she was in the ring. It's a wonder she didn't need a drool towel herself by the time she walked out.

Just before it was time for the battling duo to enter the ring, Sally had a little *tête-à-tête* with Tank just in case the message she'd been sending was a bit muddled yet. She impressed a few truths on him—like if he wanted to live out the day he'd better behave and not give Joanie any grief in the ring. And in case he thought that was a bluff (and of course, he did), Sally told him that if he screwed up today he was to be forever banned from the shop. Now that threat he could believe. Sally thought he looked like he was taking it to heart, but who knew what was really going on behind that attentive expression.

It was time to go in. Joanie was still chewing hard enough to give herself TMJ problems, but at least the much sought-after spit was now practically dripping out of her mouth. Sally handed Tank over, but not before she gave him one last meaningful look. The next few minutes would tell if her efforts had any affect.

They got through the Heel on Leash and Figure-8 without incident. Joanie held her breath until she was close to turning blue while the Stand For Examination was being performed, but Tank was good as gold. However, instead of beginning to feel like she could relax a little bit, Joanie was getting even more uptight. When, she wondered, is he going to deliver the deathblow?

They continued on with the Heel off Leash and although Tank slipped her a look that she didn't at all trust, he got the job done without causing Joanie any embarrassment. It was now on to the Recall. Oh, this could be nasty! Outside the ring, Emma and Sally were on pins and needles waiting for Tank to do his dirty work.

Joanie put Tank into a sit and after the judge, Mr. Kenneth Strong from Albany, New York gave her the command to "Leave your dog", Joanie walked to the opposite side of the ring, half expecting Tank to be trotting right along behind her. When she turned to face him, it was almost a shock to see him over where he was supposed to be. Mr. Strong told her to "Call your dog". Joanie did and closed her eyes. Whatever Tank was going to do, she didn't want to see it until it was absolutely necessary.

When Joanie figured enough time had elapsed for whatever was going to happen to have happened, she cracked open one eye. To her disbelief, she found Tank sitting in front of her not more than five inches away. The little bugger was in perfect position. She was still gawking at him when the judge told her to "Finish". She gave Tank the command and, lo and behold, didn't he do just that and with an extra little spin to boot. Joanie really didn't trust him now; whatever spit she'd had was no longer in abundance; her mouth had gone bone dry. He was going to get her and get her good; she knew it with every fiber of her being.

The wait for Long Sits and Downs was excruciating. Joanie couldn't even look at Tank; she was afraid of the evil she might find lurking in his eyes. In fact, she'd given him back to Sally the minute she'd left the ring. Maybe it was better to put a little distance between them. God knows it wouldn't take much to send Joanie running for the hills right about now. Tank seemed to be very complacent, at least outwardly. They all knew it could be a complete scam. He was, after all, sometimes known to be spawn of the devil.

After what was way too short a time for Joanie, the call for the Long Sit went out. Resigned once again to the fate that awaited her, Joanie took Tank's lead from Sally and entered the ring. They lined up with the other exhibitors and on commands from the judge, Joanie sat Tank, gave the signal to "Stay", left him, and walked to the other side of the ring. When she turned around, she was surprised once more that Tank was where she'd left him. This was pure torture; she wished he'd just get it over with. Whatever he was going to do, she wanted him to just bring it on. He was proving to be even more demonic than she'd ever thought him capable of being. Damn his little black-souled hide!

Tank completed the Long Sit with nary a hint of mischief. This had to be it, Joanie thought, he's going to get me big time on the Long Down. The exhibitors were preparing to leave their dogs. The dogs were already in the down position and Mr. Strong instructed them to leave their dogs. The handlers again walked across the ring to the opposite side and turned to face their canine counterparts. Joanie did so almost fearfully; this was it. Whatever Tank was going to do, he was going to do it now. The judge started the stopwatch. Joanie looked at Tank; Tank looked back—and smiled. Oh, shit! This was truly it!

Joanie tried to prepare herself for what was to come: the humiliation, the embarrassment, the urge to strangle that little piece of insolent dog flesh. She closed her eyes and gathered her inner strength. She could do this, she could. She slowly opened her eyes, expecting to see Tank in some form of wicked misbehavior. Instead, she found that he was still down right where he was supposed to be, but he was still grinning. What was that all about? What did it mean? Was he going to wait till the last few ticks of the second hand to spring his trap? Joanie's tension level was flying off the charts.

She was so intent on Tank that she barely heard the command, "Return to your dogs". She looked at the people moving out on either side of her like she'd didn't quite believe what she'd thought she'd heard, but sure enough they were going back to their dogs. She hurried to catch up, still dazed with what had happened, or more correctly, what hadn't happened. Tank hadn't brought her down! He hadn't humiliated her! No wait, he could still do it. The dogs hadn't been released yet; he could still blow it. Oh, God, please, have mercy, Joanie prayed as she neared the bane of her existence.

To her utter astonishment, Tank remained where he was until the release was given. It took her a minute, but then it clicked. Son of a bitch! They had the third leg! He'd gotten his obedience title; she could put a CD after his name! And they were both still alive! Holy shit!

Joanie scooped Tank up and literally danced out of the ring. It was one of her better performances. Emma and Sally were ecstatic; they were hugging each other and jumping up and down, rotating in a small circle as they did so. One would have thought it was their dog in there. Well, in a way he was; they were all part of a family of close friends. So Joanie and Tank's success was theirs to share too. It had been a long hard road for everybody. Thank God it was over!

When Joanie got close enough, the girls pulled her into their group hug and continued revolving. Tank looked like he was enjoying it, although bystanders had drifted away, giving wide berth to the human carousel.

The three goofs had to put the brakes on when the competitors were called back into the ring for the official results. But it was now fact; Tank had his CD. Bless his little black heart!

Joanie was walking out of the ring talking to another exhibitor when she suddenly broke out into raucous laughter. She was laughing so hard she was practically bent in half and tears were streaming down her face. The woman whom she'd been talking to gave her an incredulous look and moved away from her so fast she almost tripped on the matting. Joanie slowly made her way back to Emma and Sally, hampered in her efforts by sidesplitting laughter.

"What's so funny?" Emma asked, offering Joanie a tissue to wipe her tears.

Joanie couldn't answer; every time she opened her mouth nothing but another horselaugh came out.

"Geez, it must be a good one," Sally said, taking the leash out of Joanie's limp hand and gathering Tank in her arms. She gave him a resounding kiss on the nose and scratched his ears. Emma leaned over and lavished her own affectionate gestures on the victorious terrier.

Joanie nodded vigorously; she was totally incapable of speech and if she kept this up much longer she was going to be in dire danger of peeing her pants. Emma and Sally looked around nonchalantly, waiting for their friend to gain control. They noticed there was nobody within a ten to twelve foot radius of them now. The girls couldn't blame them; Joanie was acting like a lunatic. There was even a kind of wild, crazy look in her eyes. Hopefully, it wouldn't be too much longer before she was acting normally again, which for her wasn't saying much.

She finally calmed enough to speak. "You won't believe what Janice asked me."

"Well, from your reaction it had to be pretty good."

"She wanted to know…" Joanie started to laugh again. "Crap…I don't know if I …can get this out."

Emma noticed that Joanie's eyes were retaining that wild look. She wondered what in the world Janice could have asked her.

"She wanted to know if…Oh, God…She wanted to know if I was going to go—"

"What? Go what?" Sally interrupted, her need to know greater than any semblance of politeness.

"—for Tank's CDX!" Joanie covered her mouth with both hands, but they couldn't contain her almost hysterical laughter.

A CDX, or Companion Dog Excellent, was the next title in line to be won in the AKC obedience system. It followed the same rules for CD in that it had to be won under three different judges at three separate licensed AKC trials, but there was a bit more to it. First, the competitors had to compete from the Open class and there had to be a minimum of six dogs in the trial in order to win a leg. Then, the heeling and all other exercises were done off leash. The exercises to be performed also differed from those of a CD. In addition to the Heel Free, there was the Drop on Recall, the Retrieve on the Flat, the Retrieve over High Jump, and a Broad Jump. The Long Sits and Downs were done with the handler out of sight of the dog and the duration of the exercises was longer. The Sit was for three minutes and the Down was for five.

It didn't take a genius to figure out that for Joanie to attempt to compete in this arena with Tank was tantamount to leading the proverbial lamb to slaughter and in this case she would most definitely be featured as the poor dumb-ass lamb.

Emma and Sally stared at her, immediately grasping the true horror of the question. That wild look in Joanie's eyes had been put there from sheer terror, not out-of-control laughter, which was in truth close to hysteria caused by pure, unadulterated panic. Without even realizing they'd done it, Emma and Sally took a reflexive step back, not wanting any part of that prospective adventure.

"You're not thinking about doing it, are you?" Emma asked, her face a study in downright fear.

Joanie sobered so fast it was like someone had thrown a bucket of cold water in her face. "Are you out of you're freakin' mind. Of course I'm not."

"Thank God! I didn't think so, but I had to ask to make sure."

"I don't think I'd live through the trials of getting a CDX."

243

"None of us would, so don't go changing your mind."
Emma shuddered at the very thought.

"Don't worry, I won't. This was as close to death as I
ever want to get for the sake of a title."

"Amen to that."

"It's written in stone, guys. No way, no how am I going
for his CDX. Close of chapter, end of story, however you
want to put it. It ain't gonna happen. Nope, never, never,
never. Okay?"

"Okay."

"I'm going to hold you to it," Sally promised.

"Go ahead, not a problem… So listen, why don't we go
back and have some lunch. I'm starving. It's been a hell of a
morning. My reserves are on empty. I need to refuel."

"Yeah, me too," Emma said, "especially after that scare.
The very thought of having to get Tank through a CDX sent
my blood-sugar levels so far down they don't exist."

"Hey, I'm with you two." Sally still had Tank tucked
under her arm and gave him a wary look. "Joanie, I gotta tell
ya, if you ever put Tank in for his CDX, I'll run for the hills.
I'm not that strong, and I don't care who knows it."

"Listen, if I ever even start to *think* about doing it, you
have my permission to haul out TFG and shoot me where
I stand."

"Don't think we won't."

"If I'm ever that stupid, don't hesitate, just blast away.
I'd deserve it. But, honest, guys, I swear, I'll never try to
get his CDX," Joanie assured the girls. "Now let's head out,
I've got to eat."

So with an ironclad promise that sounded like it had
been forged in steel ringing in their ears, the three walked
back to the Cargill Center to feed their faces.

\* \* \* \*

244

There was no way to tell which Newfoundland was the one she was searching for. They were all either in their crates, on grooming tables, or walking with their handlers in the building or outside. She couldn't very well make inquiries about each one without drawing attention to herself. She supposed she could ask someone to point out which one he was, but she didn't want anyone to remember talking to her. She'd have to wait till the Group judging. She'd heard he'd won Best of Breed, so she knew he'd be in the Group Ring later. Once she was able to identify him and his handler there'd still be time to do what she wanted.

Meanwhile, she'd had time to pick out several other potential victims and in one case she'd removed the "potential" and made him a real victim. It had been too easy to pass up. The bait had been right out there in the open; the handler had been practicing with the dog and her attention had been focused entirely on what she was doing. A quick flick of her wrist over the bait container and it had been done. The next piece of bait the handler took was all that was necessary to see her plan come to immediate fruition. She'd grabbed one of the pieces that had been poisoned and the dog had taken it greedily.

She thought the handler said the dog was a Flat-Coated Retriever. She'd never heard of one before, but that was neither here nor there. He'd be dead by morning.

# Chapter Nineteen

After a relaxing lunch, during which the three ravenous friends made gluttonous pigs of themselves over sandwiches made this time of tuna fish (Joanie had thought of everything including small packets of mayo that she'd collected from who knows where and for how long so they didn't have to worry about spoilage and salmonella poisoning), tomatoes, lettuce, and sweet pickles on big crusty rolls. They had Fritos as a side dish and for dessert, Twinkies, of all things. They each ate a twin-pack of those. Their next order of business was getting Kirby ready for the Group Ring.

The Sporting Group was being judged before Working, so Kirby's needs came first. Emma and Joanie took over the grooming duties since Sally was a resigned-to-lose lump of nerves just thinking about going into the Group Ring. She was about as useful as a bump on a log, so the other two unceremoniously plunked her down on one of the other tables so she'd be out of their way. They let her vegetate while they got down to business.

Kirby was finished and had been replaced by Cole on the table before Sally gathered herself enough to check her watch and announce that it was time to head for the ring. There was another Group in between Sporting and Working so Emma would have plenty of time to finish Cole's grooming when they got back. She shooed him into his crate and they headed off to the ring with the Lab.

There were twenty-four entrants in the Sporting Group and a less than enthusiastic Sally took her place. If she'd had her way she would have skipped this part, but Emma and Joanie had insisted she take her rightful place. Sally thought she probably wouldn't even make the first cut. But, oh well, whatever.

Then, prodded by a guilty conscience, she had a change of heart. Looking down into Kirby's trusting eyes, Sally knew there was no way she could let her best friend down. Her bad attitude wasn't fair to Kirby who deserved nothing less than her very best effort. After all the work it had taken to get this far, there was no way she could give a lackluster performance. Kirby had always given her 110% every time out no matter what. Sally could do no less.

So with that in mind, she readjusted her attitude and her posture, shaking off any nerves that still lingered. She bent down to stack Kirby and when her mouth neared Kirby's ear, she whispered, "We're going to do the best we can, ol' girl. Hell, screw 'em. They probably think we're nothing to worry about. Let's show 'em what we've got and maybe we'll throw a monkey wrench into the outcome."

Cripe, now she'd gone into warrior/attack mode!

Kirby gave her a lick and a look that said, "Count me in!" She tightened her stack until she was giving a perfect imitation of Cole and when the judge, Mr. Charles Westerly from Richmond, Virginia looked down the line she was just as, if not more, impressive than the rest of the Group.

Mr. Westerly signaled for the go around and when it came time for Kirby to move out, she flew around the ring with her tail up and wagging. Damn! If nothing else, she was going to have a good time and make the judge notice her!

Everyone returned to his or her original position and the individual inspections began. Sally and Kirby, now fully in tune with the proceedings, acted like this was nothing out of the ordinary for them and nonchalantly played another game of tug-of-war with the little toy squirrel while they waited their turn. When it came right down to it, what did they have to lose? Not a darn thing. It wasn't like Sally was going to special Kirby. This was a one-time deal. Might as well go for broke!

Sally stacked her up when it was their turn at center stage and Kirby locked into position. The judge approached and gave her a look from a short distance away. Then he moved in for the hands-on. Kirby held her pose and Sally adeptly handled her loyal friend. Mr. Westerly moved back, looked, then gave the signal for the down and back. Sally and Kirby moved out, their stride perfectly coordinated. On the return, Sally halted Kirby for the free stand and Kirby stepped into an ideal position, her attention fixed on Sally. The judge took note and had them execute the go around. Back in line, they relaxed and awaited the rest of the group's performance.

When the judge made his first cut Sally and Kirby were included in the chosen nine. Sally, although she looked a little shell-shocked, was beaming and Emma and Joanie gave her encouragement from the sidelines.

The judge went down the line of the remaining exhibitors and pulled out the German Wirehaired Pointer and moved him to the first spot. Next came the Brittany; then he moved the Vizsla into the third slot. The fourth spot was filled when Mr. Westerly crooked his finger at Sally and had her move Kirby up in place. He gave the signal for the go around and that's how they finished, one, two, three, and four, with the fourth spot being filled with an ecstatic Sally and an exuberant Kirby. Don't think that dogs don't know when they've done well. They know—oh, yeah, do they ever! It was all right there in Kirby's shining eyes, wiggling body, and furiously wagging tail. The same could be said for Sally, all but the wagging tail, of course; but then again, at the moment, her jiggling butt did kind of look like the mirror image of Kirby's backend.

They were pounced upon as soon as they left the ring and Sally literally dragged Emma and Joanie with her to another ring for pictures. The excitement didn't abate until the girls were seriously into the preparations for Cole's competition in Group.

* * * *

Moira was standing outside the ring watching the Newfoundland win the Working Group. She thought she'd spotted him while he was being groomed but waited to be sure she had the right dog. Now she was.

She made mental notes about him and the woman who was handling him. She looked his number up in the catalog and found out what the woman's name was and where she lived. It said they lived in Glenwood; she thought that was somewhere near Buffalo, maybe a little south.

There could be a problem though. She'd seen the woman put a piece of bait in her pocket before they left the grooming area, but she hadn't seen her use it in the ring. Had she somehow missed it? She wondered about that or had the bait never left her pocket? She needed to find out; it was crucial.

* * * *

Emma and Cole came out of the ring and were immediately caught up in the now all too familiar celebratory antics of her friends. Emma didn't know how long she was going to hold up under their continual assaults; she'd swear the physically demonstrative celebrations were taking years off her life. She was always at least a little sore and sometimes bruised afterwards. Man, with friends like these two, who needed enemies? Lately she'd been giving considerable consideration to resorting to restraints, of the straightjacket kind, to corral the dynamic duo's exuberant activity. They could be strapped in before she went in the ring. Emma doubted she'd have any trouble getting someone to help her if they put up a fuss. Plus, if they had those things on they wouldn't be so prone to dance either. Cripe, she'd probably have a waiting list of people willing to help out if they knew that. Yep, she could see restraints becoming mandatory show equipment, especially if the heavy drugs she had previously thought to use didn't pan out.

"Hey, Em, another damn good job," Joanie cheered.

"Our boy looked fantastic once again," Sally said, stooping to give Cole's head a friendly shake, who in turn gave her a slurp with a very wet tongue.

"We're on a serious roll here, guys."

"No shit."

"You can say that again," Sally declared, giving Emma another bruising hug.

"No shit."

"No, not that, you idiot."

"What?" Joanie protested

"That Emma and Cole are on a serious roll."

"Oh...well, shit yeah!"

"I give up," Sally groaned.

Joanie gave her a puzzled look, then shrugged her shoulders and moved off. She certainly didn't know what the problem was. Emma and Sally just rolled their eyes and followed with Cole. Time to get ready for Best In Show.

\* \* \* \*

She hovered on the perimeter of where the girls were set up. She already had the vial containing the poison in her hand, which was shoved inside her front pants pocket.

It would take her only a second to flick her wrist over the bait.

The dog was on the grooming table and all three women were fussing over him. She started walking slowly, taking her time, not wanting anyone to notice her movements, but steadily getting nearer to where they were. She took her hand out of her pocket with the vial concealed in her palm and let her arm hang loosely at her side. She pretended interest in other dogs, smiling at their owners, asking what the owners must have thought were inane questions here and there. Questions whose answers she could have cared two shits about, but she acted interested, nevertheless. In reality, her mind was totally focused on the goings on where the Newfoundland was being attended.

She gradually wove her way through the close quarters of the myriad tables and crates until she was within easy reach of the girls' set-up. Her hand containing the vial was still down at her side, her closed fingers brushing against her leg as she walked.

She quickly swept the area with a searching look only to discover that there was no bait container on the vacant table she was closest to or in the open tack boxes that were on the floor. Her hand tightened reflexively around the vial. Did the Rogers woman still have the same bait in her pocket? Had the dog never gotten it? Or was it gone and she just hadn't gotten more yet? She needed to get closer yet to see when and if the container came out. She had to be much closer to poison the bait before the woman took it and put it in her pocket. She moved toward them.

\* \* \* \*

"You ready, Em? It's about time."

"Yeah, I'd say we're about as good as we're going to get." Emma slipped Cole's show collar on and moved him off the table. She adjusted her armband and unconsciously patted her pocket, feeling the piece of bait that resided there in case she needed it. She had never needed it to date and doubted she ever would, but carried it strictly in readiness for any eventuality. Emma gathered her lead and grabbed the drool towel, slipping her brush into the other pocket of her jacket.

"Let's head on over then," Sally said while she finished putting the grooming spray, scissors, and comb back in the tack box.

Joanie and Sally gave a pat on the head to Kirby and Tank who were lounging in their respective crates with Joanie adding a you-be-good look for Tank. He smiled devilishly back at her. Joanie snorted.

They started for the ring.

\* \* \* \*

Moira backpedaled automatically when the girls started to leave the area. She'd been ready—God, so ready!—but the bait had never come out. Realization slammed into her—she wasn't going to be able to get to this one. She clenched the vial so hard, the thin metal spout jabbed sharply into her hand. The pain jarred her and before she could stop herself she'd brought her hand up and opened her fist. For a second she could only look dumbly at what was in her hand, nothing registered. Just as quickly, she snapped out of it and shoved her hand and what was in it into her pants pocket. Her attention then shifted back to the woman and dog; they were fast disappearing from view. She continued to stare in their direction.

At last count, she'd been able to poison the bait of eleven dogs at the show, but she'd wanted one more. She hated odd numbers and she wanted the Newfoundland to be the one to make it even. But it was more than the number thing; she'd wanted him, specifically him and there was no way she was going to get him, at least not this time.

Her disappointment was crushing. It blocked out everything she had accomplished. Her resolve and fervor immediately weakened. Control began to slip away. She knew that horror hovered just beyond her conscious thoughts.

The room started to spin and she closed her eyes to steady herself while reaching out to grab hold of a table that she remembered was to her left. She held on and forced her eyes open, praying she could stay ahead of the impending terror that was threatening to break through. Sweat broke out on her forehead and her upper lip. Her underarms grew moist and her back was instantly covered in a thin sheen of perspiration. She was so hot she could feel her face getting red. Her body was trembling and she could feel her stomach starting to rebel. The noise was suddenly overwhelming and her head began to pound with an intensifying pressure. The images of that long-ago day started to cut across her vision.

She knew she wasn't going to beat it and she looked quickly to where the restrooms were. She had to get over there before she dumped the contents of her stomach in the middle of the floor. She wanted to flat-out run, but knew she couldn't. That would be remembered; so she walked in a manner someone would use if they were late getting to the ring and needed to hurry. She hit the outside doors of the bathroom, her hand at her mouth and lost no time getting into a stall where the inevitable happened.

*  *  *  *

Emma shivered, but kept walking toward the ring. Cole looked up at her expectantly as the quiver had gone right down the lead. She gave him a reassuring pat on the head.

"What was that?" The eagle-eyed Joanie asked.

"What?"

"That little wiggle you just did."

"Nothing. I just felt a chill go down my spine."

"A chill?"

"Yeah, a little chill." Emma knew something wasn't quite right; she didn't get these feelings for nothing.

"Why?" Joanie asked, suddenly tense and completely focused on her friend.

"How do I know? I just felt a chill. It was like somebody walked over my grave."

"Well, nobody did, so just forget it."

"You know...when you think about it, that's kind of a stupid saying, don't you think?"

"What? The somebody-walking-over-your-grave thing?"

"Yeah, I mean how would you know how it feels to have somebody walk over your grave if you're dead? You wouldn't have a grave unless you were dead, right? So how would you know what it felt like? And if you're alive, you wouldn't have a grave *sooo* what gives?"

"Jesus, Em, who the hell knows?"

"Exactly. If you're dead, you feel nothing and if you're alive you don't have a grave, so it really doesn't make any sense... I wonder who thought that one up?"

"Don't know, don't care, Em. But what does matter is that nothing weird happened. Right?"

"I guess so. Geez, Joanie, I don't want to argue about it. I just felt a chill go down my spine, that's all."

"No, you didn't."

"Sorry, but I did."

"I'm telling you, you didn't."

"Yeah, I did."

"Em, listen to me now, I'm not kidding. There'll be none of those hinky feelings of yours. We had enough of them a few months ago. Remember? We're having no problems? None. Nada. Got it?"

"Yeah, if you say so," Emma said. No problems, huh? What about that friggin' bed? she wondered. In her mind that *had* to qualify as a problem. "Quit worrying. I just felt a little weird there for a minute."

"Well, ditch the feeling right now. You were probably in a draft or something. You know how these big buildings are with the doors constantly opening and closing."

"Yeah, you're probably right."

"Of course, I am. Now get your mind on the ring. They're ready to call you in."

A few seconds later, Emma and Cole were in the ring with the six other exhibitors who were representing their individual Groups. Moon, the German Wirehaired Pointer, was back from Sporting, the Afghan Hound, Chloe, was there with Nancy Bullis from the Hound Group, the Border Terrier, an upset winner, represented the Terrier Group, the Toys had a Pug in, Non-Sporting, a Dalmatian, and there was a Bearded Collie from Herding.

While Emma was setting Cole up, Joanie was bending Sally's ear. "We are *not* doing this again."

"Doing what?" Sally asked as she watched the dogs move out on the first go around.

"Getting into shit again."

"Joanie, what are you talking about?"

"Emma. She thinks she felt something."

"She shivered. I don't think it was any big deal."

"Yeah, well, I do. You know how she is. She's not fooling me. She doesn't get those feelings for nothing. She's going to think it means something. I shut her down for now, but she's going to come back to it. I know that for sure and then we'll be right back in it."

"Maybe not. Maybe it was just a draft."

"Man, I hope so. But I don't think she thought so. She was just shutting me up."

"Ya think? Well, good for her, at least she knows how."

"Hey!"

"I wish I had the knack."

"Sal, I could take offense to that, you know."

"Geez, I wish you would, then maybe we'd have some peace and quiet around here."

"Yeah…well…"

"Uh-huh, that's what I thought."

"Yeah, but I'm tellin' ya, that little shiver is going to mean problems. Big ones."

"Well, if you're right, at least we've been forewarned. So…we'll be prepared."

"Yeah, but we're supposed to be done with all that stuff. No more problems for us. We're supposed to be free and clear. I declared it. Remember?"

"I remember. I just don't think you can control what happens."

"No? Why not?"

"It might have something to do with the forces of nature."

"And *I'm* not one of those forces? *Pfff*…Give me a break."

"I stand corrected, oh mighty one."

"You damn well should be, smart-ass. I'm a definite force to be reckoned with."

"Don't I know it," Sally mumbled. "The force of idiocy."

"What'd you say?"

"Nothing, not a thing."

Joanie nudged Sally with her elbow. "Let's pay attention. Cole's up for inspection."

"Gladly."

Cole was in his stack in the center of the ring and Emma was standing back, waiting for the judge to do her thing. Mrs. Sarah Piedmont from Savannah, Georgia, the Best In Show judge, stayed back for a minute and simply gazed at the overall picture that Cole made. It was as impressive as judges before her had found. He was a shining example of the breed and a consummate showman.

Then she approached Cole and did her exam. When she was finished, she called for the down and back, which Emma and Cole performed flawlessly, their individual strides completely harmonious with each other's. Cole went into the free stand like he was shooting for a perfect ten score and the image he made was enough to take your breath away. If he had been being scored he would have earned a twelve! There was no doubt about it; he just kept getting better and better.

After Mrs. Piedmont gave Cole a good long look, she signaled for the go around and as Emma and Cole slipped around the ring every eye at ringside was watching. Cole didn't disappoint; he appeared to glide back to his spot in line and finished his performance off with a stack that looked like his feet were riveted to the floor. Emma bent down and gave him a kiss on his nose. He licked her face and pure joy shone in his eyes.

The remainder of the dogs went through their exams and then once again they were all back in line for the final look and the decision that would follow. Mrs. Piedmont took her stroll, then went back to mark her book.

It was but a minute before she was back at center ring with her steward and the Show Chairman of the Del-Otse-Nango Kennel Club. The crowd was hushed as they waited for the announcement. A smile that couldn't get any bigger if it was painted on with clown's paint broke out on the judge's face as she lifted her arm, pointed, and said, "The Newfoundland."

There was an immediate rush by the other exhibitors to congratulate Emma and Cole and they found themselves surrounded by their colleagues. Cole decided to get vocal and voiced his apparent happiness with short little barks while butting his wiggling body into Emma's. While Emma shook hands, she very wisely braced her feet and locked her knees so that she'd stay upright and not go down in a heap. It was bad enough her goofy friends always put her in danger of falling on her ass; she wasn't about to let her dog do the same thing. A girl had to know where to draw the line! Besides, she could control Cole a lot better than Joanie and Sally.

*  *  *  *

She could hear the muted cheering and clapping from inside the bathroom where she was now leaning against a sink, one of the many positioned along the mirrored wall. In the aftermath of getting sick, she was in the process of trying to regroup.

She was facing away from the wall and its traitorous reflections, her face and neck still slightly damp from the water she'd splashed over them. She was looking up at the ceiling, but her gaze was vacant. Her breathing was becoming slower and less labored. Her skin tone was returning to normal, having paled to a sickly white after the initial heated red flush. Mentally, she was almost back on an even keel.

She didn't move for a minute or two, but let her body recover and her mind wander aimlessly. It was so blissfully peaceful when she didn't have to think or remember. It sometimes made her yearn for the complete solitude of a drug-induced stupor provided in a protected environment of padded walls where nothing but her own reality existed. There she could be free from all her nightmares and demons.

She shifted her body away from the sink, the movement splintering her idyllic musings. It was time to concentrate on her plan, to look at her options, but not here. She needed the isolation and quietude of her hotel room to think clearly. It was imperative that she figure out how to get to the Newfoundland. She was certain that it was important that he be one of the casualties of her private war. She had to eliminate him and if she couldn't do it with the poison, then she'd have to find another way.

Without any conscious effort, she fluffed her hair and straightened her clothes. Her immediate concern turned to pulling herself together enough so that she looked as undisturbed and normal as anyone else. Adjusting the strap of her handbag on her shoulder, she darted a quick glance in the mirror to check her appearance. Satisfied that her mask was firmly in place, she left the restroom and the building.

\* \* \* \*

Damn if it wasn't time to rock and roll! Kirby had finished with a Breed win, plus gotten herself a Group Four; Cole had racked up another Best In Show, and Tank, dear sweet lovable the-devil-made-me-do-it Tank, had gotten his CD. Lord love a duck! If that alone wasn't cause for celebration than nothing was. Hell, that was reason enough to get completely shit-faced! And after eating dinner out at a local restaurant where the girls stuffed themselves with grilled salmon, Fettuccini Alfredo, Filet Mignon, and all that came with it, they went back to their room and did precisely that.

They partied hearty into the late hours of the night, toasting everything from Cole's shiny coat, to Kirby's wet nose, to Tank's brown spot over his eye, to Emma's shin splints, to Sally's new skirt, to Joanie's making the reservations, to Joanie's screwing up the reservations, to the good weather, to adequate parking spaces, to great food, to ring success, to Cole's new friend, Molly, to the judges who gave them the win, to enough hot water for them all to take a shower, to clean underwear, and even to THE BED! You name it; they toasted it. When they were close to finishing off the last of their booze they made one final toast, which capped things off in a style that was uniquely theirs.

The final toast made went to Joanie's world-class ass! God, they'd covered everything!

When they at last gave in to their exhaustion, Joanie was too far-gone to realize she was once again in the unenviable position of being in the middle of the bed. Actually, she could have been laid out on a bed of nails or stretched out on a rack and she wouldn't have been any the wiser. Sally and Emma had to help her into her jammies, which was another comedy of errors because they didn't have all their wits about them either. It's a wonder she didn't end up with the top where the bottom should have been and visa versa.

As a smiling Joanie snuggled into the comfort of the sheets, she kept mumbling over and over, "He's done, he's all done, the little shithead's all done." After a few minutes she quieted and finally gave in to sleep, which is to say, she passed out.

Mission accomplished, Sally and Emma congratulated themselves on a job well done and got themselves ready for bed as best they could. It wasn't a pretty sight, but it was hilarious. Why there were no injuries incurred while they were changing into their pajamas is anybody's guess. At least once, Emma was in danger of knocking herself out and Sally had a close call in the bathroom, which would have seen her with at the very least a major bruise on her ass and upper thighs. It's funny how those damn toilets seem to weave all over the place when you've had too much to drink.

Eventually, the two remaining semi-functioning friends got into bed, one on either side of the out-cold Joanie. It didn't take them long once their heads hit the pillows to drift off and lapse into a drink-induced coma. Good thing—morning was going to come all too soon.

# Chapter Twenty

The shrill ringing of the telephone that served as the motel's alarm clock brought  moans and groans from all three of the revelers that rivaled any and all of the day-after complaints that have ever escaped the lips of erstwhile partiers throughout the ages. While the girls enjoyed their wine and manhattans on a regular basis, they were not as a rule in the habit of getting falling-down drunk. So this little walk on the wild side was going to cost them. How much? Plenty, but only time would tell for sure. First, they had to get out of bed! That alone could kill them.

Blinking sleep from eyes that felt as if there were razor blades in them, they tried to stretch limbs that weren't cooperating one little bit. Somehow the message wasn't getting from their brains to the body part that they wanted to move. Maybe it would be better to lie still for a minute or two. See what happened, if anything.

After a short time had passed, their heads cleared enough to take stock—they were still breathing. That must mean they were still alive. Well, that was something, anyway. They had to get points for that!

Slowly, ever so slowly, the wayward three started to move. Emma draped a leg over the side of the bed and felt the floor with her bare foot. It seemed solid. While remaining in a prone position, she swiveled her body on the bed with great care until she was able to place her other foot alongside the one that was already down on the floor. The earth held firm; Emma rested.

Sally was performing an almost identical maneuver on her side of the bed, but only managed to plant one foot on the rug before she felt compelled to take a break and gather not only strength, but courage too.

And then there was Joanie, the slug in the middle of that infamous bed. God help her; she was toast! Her eyes were open, but there was nobody home. She hadn't moved a muscle. She hadn't even tried; she'd faked it. You're pretty damn good when you can fool even yourself. But other than that redeeming quality, she had about as much going for her as road kill. Even breathing, which was the extent of her movement if you could call it that, required extraordinary effort. She wasn't going to make it; death had to be lurking nearby.

"Emma, remember your promise." It took a superhuman effort for Joanie to get those few words out.

"What promise?" Emma asked, her voice not much above a whisper.

"The one about me dying. You have to throw Tank in with me when I get buried."

"Oh, yeah. That promise. Don't give it another thought. I'll heave him in right on top of you."

"Thanks... Today might be the day."

"Ya think? You're that close?"

"Yeah, life seems to be a bit too painful right now. I think death would feel really good."

"No argument there."

"You can help send me on my way if you want. Just put the pillow over my face."

"Don't tempt me."

"No, really, feel free."

"I think I'll pass; it would take too much effort. If you're going to go, you'll have to do it on your own."

"Well, all right. It would have been too easy anyway. But I want my affairs to be in order, just in case."

"Say no more. Where you go, Tank follows."

"Thanks, you're a real friend."

"Don't mention it."

"I can die in peace now."

"Go right ahead. I'll probably join you."

"You can't. You have to throw Tank in."

"All right. I'll wait and do it after that."

"Okay, thanks for everything. Bye, Sal; it's been a pleasure knowing you."

Sally, very carefully, turned her head in the direction of her two friends and gave them an "*oh, puhleeze*" look. She would have rolled her eyes, but it hurt too much. "Cram it, you guys. We've got to get rolling; there's no time for anybody to die. Besides, it's too messy. Joanie, I don't want all your body fluids to let loose while I'm still in the same bed with you. If you know what's good for you, you'll direct all your energies to staying alive and getting up."

"You're asking the impossible."

"Listen, sister. If I can do it, you can do it."

"Yeah? Well, I don't see you doing it."

"Look real close. See, I'm moving." Sally had managed to slide her other foot off the bed and onto the floor.

"Yeah, you're a regular gazelle."

"I'm doing better than you are."

"Maybe, but I've got further to go. I'm in the middle."

"All the more reason for you to start moving. Start inching down to the foot of the bed."

"Oh, God, do I have to?"

"If you want a ride back home you do."

"God, you're a sadistic beast."

"One does what one has to."

"I'm not going to comment on that right now. I'll save it for later."

"I'm sure you will."

Through all the banter, there had been no progress made in getting themselves off the bed. Emma and Sally seemed to be stuck in their present contorted positions and Joanie was still flat on her back.

"Guys," Emma suggested, "maybe if we concentrate and give it the big push we can do it."

"It hurts too much to concentrate," Joanie whined. "I have to engage my brain for that."

"Well, do what you can. Are you ready?"

"Yeah."

"I guess."

"All right. Here we go. On the count of three: One… Two…Three."

Emma and Sally managed to lift themselves off the bed a couple of inches before they collapsed back onto the mattress, and Joanie had scooted down maybe half a foot before she groaned and gave it up.

It took them four more tries before they were vertical and then they were holding onto anything that was nearby to ensure they stayed that way. It was a very slow process to get them cleaned up and dressed.

As if sensing the girls' distress, the dogs were undemanding and content to stay in their crates until one of their errant mistresses realized they needed to get outside to go to the bathroom. It was Emma who finally became aware that the dogs' needs hadn't been met. Joanie was still in the shower, had been for a long time, but a knock on the door had brought a grunt in response so they knew she was still alive at least. Emma grabbed Sally and in a joint effort the two managed to put the dogs on lead and take them outside, their descent down the two flights of stairs jarring the headaches they were nursing. The cold air that met them when they opened the double doors, however, was like a slap in the face and instrumental in clearing the stupor that had enveloped their brains.

The morning sky was diffused with soft light, the way it looks when sunshine filters through high clouds. This was kind of eerie though; a slightly greenish tinge colored the atmosphere as the hidden sun sent shafts of light through gray clouds, a phenomenon more closely associated with the advent of a severe summer thunderstorm. The wind whipped up, scattering discarded papers through the parking lot and playing havoc with the girls' hair. As they walked the dogs over to the grass, Emma looked to the far western horizon where the sky seemed to be much darker. Does it just look darker because it's far away? Emma wondered, or is that a bank of storm clouds?

"Sal, what was the weather forecast for today?"

"I don't know. Last one I paid attention to was the one I heard before we left."

"That was four days ago. God knows it could have changed by now."

"Yeah, well, we've been a little busy."

"What was it when we left?"

"I think it was the same as what we've been having. Temps in the high thirties, low forties, cloudy, chance of flurries."

"I wonder if it might have changed."

"Why?"

"Look over there." Emma pointed to the west.

Sally turned and looked. "Ohhh boy, that could be trouble."

"Yep."

"If those are storm clouds, the snow they're carrying is definitely not the flurry kind."

"No kidding."

"We might be in for a hard time getting home."

"To say the least."

Sally gave Emma a speculative look. "Wanna drive?"

"Not on your life, wise guy."

The dogs finished up and they headed back upstairs. Joanie was out of the shower, made up, and partially dressed. Emma and Sally lit a fire under her butt and hurried her along. They had to get everything packed and loaded, get checked out of the motel, and buzz over to the show grounds. Cole was in at 10:00, Kirby at 11:15. She was competing as a class dog even though she was now a champion so the major wouldn't be broken. Tank was officially retired, never to darken the inside of an obedience ring again. He'd get to be a spectator.

Sally called the local Weatherline in Buffalo on her cell phone while packing. The forecast had changed from flurries to light snow with accumulations of one to two inches accompanied by brisk winds between 25 and 35 mph. Even with the change in the forecast, they shouldn't have a problem. Of course, that depended on the weatherman being correct and everybody knew how often that happened. So, figuring the odds at 50/50 (they were being generous), the girls knew the trip home could turn out to be quite the adventure.

Reinforced with liberal doses of aspirin, Tylenol, or Advil, depending on their personal preference, the day-after celebrants went into a watered-down version of their usual efficient mode of operation. The well-oiled machine wasn't quite what it usually was. In fact there were a few breakdowns, but forty-five minutes later they were on their way to the show.

\* \* \* \*

As soon as they stepped inside the doors of the Cargill Center, the girls knew that something was terribly wrong. It was quiet. At a dog show? That didn't happen. But the noise that usually abounded in limitless volume and duration was missing. There wasn't any underlying chatter and spookiest of all was the lack of barking. The girls did a quick perusal and the dogs they could see, whether they were in the ring, or in their crates, or on the table, were silent. You could have heard the proverbial pin drop. The only sound that breached the stillness was the muted cadence of paws and feet on rubber mats as exhibitors went through their paces in the ring.

Passing rings that were all in use as they walked to where their set-up was, the girls saw that judging was being conducted, but activity around the rings was far from normal. People weren't talking, dogs weren't being played with, and even last-minute grooming had been abandoned. People and dogs were just standing there like statues waiting their turn to compete. Inside the ring, judges were making their choices and handing out awards, but if there were any smiles to be seen, they were small and quick to vanish. What was going on?

The girls dumped their stuff, settled the dogs, and went in search of somebody they knew. They found Alice Smalley outside Ring Eight where Rhodesian Ridgebacks were waiting to go in.

Joanie didn't even bother with the pleasantries. "Alice, what's going on?" she asked as soon as they got close.

"You haven't heard?"

"Heard what? We just got here."

"Nine dogs are dead," Alice informed them in hushed tones.

"What?" the trio chorused in shocked disbelief.

Heads turned in their direction since theirs were the only voices that permeated the eerie silence. The girls ducked their heads in reaction to the disapproving looks aimed their way.

"Their owners discovered them this morning," Alice continued. "They were all dead in their crates."

That earned a big "holy shit" from all three, but at least they whispered it.

"What happened?" Emma asked, reeling with the impossible news.

"They don't know. There's no outward sings of trauma in any of them from what I understand. They're just dead. Like they died in their sleep."

"Are any of them dogs we know?" Joanie asked, even though she was afraid to voice the question and hoping with everything she had that they wouldn't know any of the dogs or the people who owned them.

"Yeah, two of them."

"Shit," Emma breathed, closing her eyes, wanting to shut out what she was about to hear.

"Who are they?" Sally whispered.

"One is Nancy Bullis' Chloe—"

"Oh, God, no!" Emma interrupted, her breath sucked in sharply in shock. "Not Chloe! Oh, poor Nancy!" Nancy Bullis was a professional handler the girls were friends with and who had helped in the search for Cole that past summer.

"Yeah, I'm afraid so. Nancy was one of the first to report it."

"Who else?" Joanie asked, her dread building.

"Diane Baker's Axel."

"Oh, damn." The words were barely audible, the girls almost frozen in utter dismay.

For a minute or two nobody said a word, shock having robbed them of their power of speech. The girls looked at each other in disbelief with eyes that were blinking back tears. Small unconscious gestures communicated their distress—Emma's hand had moved to cover her mouth; Joanie's arms had wrapped themselves around her waist, and Sally's head kept shaking in denial. The paralysis slowly ebbed away.

"Chloe and Axel were black," Emma mumbled more to herself than to anyone in particular.

"What, Em?"

"The dogs, they were black." Chloe had been a gorgeous black Afghan Hound and was ranked #1 in her breed. She'd been a multiple Best In Show winner. Axel, a young black and tan smooth-coated Dachshund had just been starting his show career. "Alice, do you know which other dogs died?"

"Umm…let me think…I believe there was a Flattie, a Scottie, a Giant Schnauzer, two Labs, I think…How many dogs does that make?"

Joanie counted them up in her head. "Seven."

"I'm not positive, but I think the other two might have been a Rottie and maybe a Puli."

"They're all black, or could be," Emma said.

"Looks like it, if those are the breeds that died."

"Just like at Back Mountain."

"What do you mean, Emma?" Alice asked.

"Don't you know? Four dogs and a handler died at the Back Mountain show. All the dogs were black."

"Geez! I didn't know that."

"It happened about a week ago."

"Do they know what caused the deaths?"

"We haven't heard."

"Do you think this is related?"

"It has to be. Stuff like this doesn't just happen, not a week apart anyway. No way can these deaths and those at Back Mountain be a coincidence." Emma shivered and hoped nobody noticed.

No such luck—Joanie spotted it out of the corner of her eye and swore under her breath. Damn, she thought, they were in it again!

Alice's class was called into the ring and the girls stayed to watch until she was finished. She took a second place and was done for the day. When Alice came out of the ring, they promised to stay in touch and a very solemn trio went back to their set-up.

\* \* \* \*

She'd positioned herself early that morning so that she'd have an unobstructed view of the main doors. There she'd waited, somewhat impatiently, for Emma Rogers and her friends to arrive and once they had, she'd never let them out of sight.

While she'd waited, she'd listened to the quiet whisperings and shocked gasps as people learned of the dogs' deaths. There had been nine, they said. Tell me something I don't know, she'd wordlessly mocked. The other two must not have taken the lethal bait yet. But they would, sooner or later. She felt satisfaction and it should have been enough, but it wasn't. She hadn't gotten number twelve and it tainted everything.

The women were back at their grooming area now, getting the big Newfie ready for the ring. Maybe she could still have a shot at him and if not him, perhaps his owner. She moved closer, her hand going into her shoulder bag to retrieve the vial.

# Chapter Twenty-One

Emma took a couple big gulps of her soda and set the can down on the grooming table behind her. God, she was thirsty. Well, what did she expect after last night's celebration? She'd be pouring liquid down her throat all day. Of course, Joanie and Sally weren't in any better shape than she was, so she'd take solace in that. Actually, Joanie was probably in worse shape. That thought caused a big grin to appear momentarily on Emma's face. There was always a bright side!

She continued getting Cole ready, although in all honesty, she didn't feel much like doing this today. The hangover certainly wasn't helping, of course, but the deaths of so many dogs had put a definite pall over the goings on. How were you supposed to get excited about showing when there was so much sorrow surrounding the event now? The competition hardly seemed important and the quiescence of the dogs put a creepy melancholy over the whole building. The tragedy and sorrow of their owners had certainly been telegraphed to their canine charges and they had reacted with near-total silence.

It reminded Emma of the time her bloodhound had died. The beloved dog had been at the vet's recuperating from surgery necessitated by her bloating and torsion. It was three days after the operation when Emma got the call that Scarlet had just dropped dead from heart failure. Devastated, Emma had numbly hung up the phone and moved to look out the dining room window in the house where she was living at the time. The other dogs that she'd owned then were out in the kennels about 100 yards away from the house. One or two seconds after Emma had appeared in the window, every last one of them had started to howl and wouldn't stop. They'd carried on for over an hour and in that time, Emma had neither moved nor spoken a word. The dogs had somehow known that Scarlet had died; she wasn't coming back. Emma's overwhelming sorrow had been transmitted over those 100 yards to each and every one of them.

So it was at this show. The only difference was in how the dogs had reacted to their owners' grief and heartache. They'd gone silent.

Joanie and Sally were mulling over the same type of insights as they helped with Cole, their usual chatter kept to a minimum. Cole, for his part, stood still, patiently submitting to the grooming routine. Kirby and Tank, meanwhile, rested quietly in their crates. All three dogs had tuned in to the overall sobriety that had taken over the arena, their innate instincts keyed in to the horrific tragedy that had occurred.

Nevertheless, it was time to get to Ring Five. Emma put Cole's show lead on and had him get down off the table. She grabbed a brush and towel, patted her jacket pocket feeling for the bait that was still there from yesterday, took one more gulp of Diet Pepsi, and headed out. Sally and Joanie followed, both of them finishing off their sodas and dropping the cans in a trash bin on the way.

\* \* \* \*

She'd been watching close by, the vial in her hand. But something she had hoped would happen didn't. The bait container never came out. The bitch was wearing the same jacket as she had the day before and must have still had some doggy treats in her pocket. Damn her! And now they were leaving.

Moira stayed where she was until they were out of sight. Disappointment and frustration raged once again. She was about to leave when she spied the soda can that had been left on the table and her heart rate jumped. Glancing around the surrounding area quickly, she saw that no one was paying any attention to her. She strolled over to the table as nonchalantly as she could under the circumstances; her blood was pounding. The fury that had consumed her just moments before had been quickly replaced by almost uncontainable excitement. She placed her body between the people who were set-up to the left and the can. She checked a second time to see if anyone was taking notice of her movements. No one was other than the two dogs that were in crates along the wall. She lifted the can and swirled it. It was about half full. She carefully put the can back down where it had been and taking her right hand out of her pants pocket, flicked her wrist over the can making sure the nozzle fit into the opening. She quickly returned her hand to her pocket and checked a final time to see if she was being observed. The only scrutiny she was under was from the two crated dogs. Unconcerned, she turned from the table and walked away, thinking that if she couldn't get the dog, she'd at least get the owner.

* * * *

Cole won the Breed without any trouble and, for once, Joanie and Sally were subdued in their congratulations, being respectful of the prevailing somber atmosphere that hung over the entire building.

They ran into Nancy Bullis on the way back and offered their condolences. Nancy was heartbroken; the evidence clearly displayed on her tear-stained face.

"Nancy, I am so sorry," Emma said, giving the woman a gentle hug.

"I can't believe she's gone," Nancy whispered, her eyes filling with fresh tears.

"Do you know what happened?" Joanie asked, her own eyes tearing up.

"I don't have a clue. She was absolutely fine yesterday, showed her heart out. There was nothing to even hint there was a problem. She ate well, drank the usual amount of water. She played with the other dogs before they went to bed; there was nothing wrong. Then this morning, she was dead." A sob broke from her throat and the tears that had been gathering in her eyes spilled down her cheeks.

"Oh, God, Nancy. Here, take this." Sally pushed tissues into her hand, while the three friends formed a protective circle around the distraught woman.

Emma made small, comforting circles on her back while Nancy got her emotions under control. "Is there anything we can do?"

"God, if only there was. But, no, there's nothing. I've got to call Chloe's owners. I just haven't been able to face that yet. They're going to be so devastated... I don't know how I'm going to get through it." Nancy sniffed, then straightened her shoulders and took a deep breath. "And I've got to get myself pulled together; I've got dogs to show, although it's the very last thing I want to do right now."

"Do you want us to help get the dogs ready? Take some in the ring?"

"No, but thanks for the offer. I've got my two assistants to help even though they're nearly hysterical... I'd better get going; my Tibetan is in pretty soon."

"Okay, but if you need anything, let us know."

"I will, I promise."

The girls each gave Nancy another hug before they let her go. The girls stood where they were for a minute, contemplating the huge loss to Nancy, Chloe's owners, the world of dog showing, and the breed. She was going to be sorely missed.

The three friends, walking back to where they were set up, were noisily heralded by Tank and Kirby well before they reached them. Both dogs, having spied them amongst the crowd, had sprung to their feet and started barking excitedly, giving every indication they'd been waiting anxiously for the girls to return.

"Guess they have to go," Joanie said. "I'll take 'em." She walked over to Tank's crate and opened it, but before she could grab him, he shot out and ran toward the table where the can of soda sat. He jumped to get on top of it, but fell a little short because his legs weren't quite long enough. He did, however, land with his front paws on the near set of legs that supported the table and jostled it hard enough to topple the can. Soda spilled all over the table and dripped off the side.

"Hey! Somebody grab him!" Joanie shouted.

Sally was closest, so she hauled him into her arms. "What the hell was that?" she asked.

"Damned if I know. Cripe, he was like a friggin' tornado coming out of there."

"Tank, stop squirming," Sally reprimanded as Tank continued to fight her.

"What got into him?" Emma asked.

"Beats me. And what's with Kirby? She never barks like that."

"I don't know," Sally said. "Kirby! Hush!"

"Look at that mess. Shit. Kirby, quiet!" Joanie said, opening her crate. Kirby lunged to get out. "Whoa, Kirby!"

"What's *with* her?" Sally asked. "She never tries to bolt out of her crate like that."

"I don't know," Joanie answered, making a grab for the dog. "Maybe she really has to go."

"Go ahead and get 'em out," Emma said. "I'll clean up." She was already unrolling a string of paper towels.

"Sally, you'd better come with me. I'll never be able to handle the both of them; they're too wound up."

"Okay. But here, let's switch. Give me Kirby."

"Oh, great, I get the Tasmanian devil."

"He is your dog."

"Yeah, don't remind me."

They made the exchange, but not before Kirby gave Tank a friendly lick for a job well done. Unaware that Tank had probably saved her from certain death, Emma cleaned up the mess.

\* \* \* \*

Watching from a safe distance, Moira was furious, almost to the point of being out of control. Son of a bitch! That fucking little dog had spoiled everything! She could have at least killed the woman except for that stupid mutt! God, she couldn't believe it. Now what? Swallowing her frustration and anger, she knew she needed to get out of there before she totally lost her composure , which at the moment she was holding on to by a mere thread. Having been thwarted in executing her plan, her focus had shattered and she could feel her control rapidly slipping. Turning on her heel, she lost no time making for the exit. She tried to console herself with the nine dogs she had already disposed of and the two that would soon follow. But somehow it wasn't enough. Her victory had been ruined with her failure to get the last dog. She needed, yes, *needed*, number twelve *and* his owner, especially his damn owner. She just needed a little time, that's all, a little time to figure out how she was going to get them.

\* \* \* \*

278

Kirby took Reserve Winners Bitch in the Labrador judging. Not bad for a competitor that had gone in the ring only to preserve the sanctity of the major, especially when Sally had handled her with less than her usual proficiency. Kirby already had her championship, so why not stack the deck a little in someone else's favor? Couldn't hurt!

Afterwards, the girls went in search of Diane Baker and offered their condolences on the death of Axel. She wasn't in very good shape and being an owner-handler, had pulled the rest of her dogs from competition. Professionals didn't have that luxury; they were being paid to show their clients' dogs. Diane hadn't left the grounds yet simply because she was still too distraught to drive.

After doing what they could, which was tantamount to nothing except to be there for her, the girls went back to their set-up and conjured up lunch although the effort was half-hearted and half-assed. Lost in their individual thoughts, which all centered on the same thing, they ate robotically, the food tasting like cardboard.

"I think we should go home," Emma said, tossing her half-eaten sandwich in the trash.

"Now?" Joanie asked, Emma's statement catching her up short.

"Yeah."

"What about Group?" Sally queried, not really surprised by Emma's wish to leave.

"What about it?"

"Don't you want to stay and compete?"

"Nah. My heart's not in it today, not after what's happened here."

"You're sure?"

"Yeah."

"It's up to you, Em, but I kind of feel the same way. I wouldn't mind leaving early. All the fun's gone out of it today."

279

"I'm with you guys," Sally said. "I don't feel much like being here myself."

"Then why don't we pack it in and go," Emma said.

"Sounds like the thing to do," Sally agreed.

"Let's get started then," Joanie said. "No sense hanging around any longer."

As it was, by the time they packed everything, loaded the van, walked the dogs, made a pit stop themselves, said their goodbyes, and gassed the van it was almost two hours later.

It was closing in on three o'clock when they hit the tollbooth for the westbound Thruway with Joanie at the wheel. Sally was in the front passenger seat and Emma was in the back. The dogs were nestled in their crates, already snoozing. Seasoned travelers that they were, it only took the motion of the moving van to lull them to sleep.

The sky above them was a washed-out gray, but the clouds that still hung in the western sky looked ominous. It wasn't snowing where they were, but the girls knew they were heading into it. Whether it would be light snow or more was anybody's guess. They had to hope the weatherman was correct in his prediction. They mentally crossed their fingers.

By the time they reached the exit for Waterloo, it was flurrying and the sky was definitely darker, which was sure to bring on the semblance of nighttime that much sooner. The roads were wet, but clear of snow so the van was still doing a steady 65 mph.

When they got to Exit 45, the first of the Rochester exits, the snow was coming down steadily and was accumulating on the roadway. Traffic had slowed to 45 mph, except of course for the idiots who were flying by in the passing lane at well over the speed limit.

The weather, as they passed the Batavia exit, deteriorated dramatically with the wind whipping the now fast-falling snow into blizzard-like conditions. Traffic was crawling along. The girls recognized two of the cars that were in the ditch on the left-hand side of the road as those that had passed them going at breakneck speeds earlier.

"Serves the assholes right," Joanie muttered, tooting her horn in sarcastic salute as the van rolled by the accident scene.

It took them an hour to get past the Pembroke exit, the weather worsening with every mile they drove. Whiteouts were frequent and Joanie sometimes couldn't see the taillights of the car ahead of her, which was probably no more than a distance of fifteen feet away. The weatherman had definitely blown it.

They inched along with repeated stops that were becoming more and more frequent. After about half an hour at this maddening pace, traffic traveling east and west came to a complete and final stop in both lanes, although the girls didn't realize it yet. All they knew was that nothing was moving ahead of them. Due to the swirling snow that had obscured all landmarks and even the large road signs, the girls had no idea where they were exactly. The only thing they did know was that they were at a dead stop. Joanie looked in her rearview mirror and was able to make out the headlights of the car behind her, and vaguely the two behind him. That was as far as the snow permitted her to see. Up ahead, she saw the taillights of two cars before the curtain of white blocked off everything else.

Dead in the water as they were, they sat and waited while the wind and snow continued to buffet the van.

"Geez, I wonder what the holdup is?" Joanie asked, turning the windshield wipers up all the way.

Emma and Sally looked at her like she'd just sprouted horns. "Joanie?" Emma probed.

"Yeah?"

"Did Sally and I miss something? Are we wrong in thinking that we've been driving through a storm with near zero visibility for the last several hours?"

"*Nooo….*"

"Then why the hell do you think we're at a standstill, you dork?"

"Oh…" Had the light finally dawned? "It's 'cause of the storm?"

"Give the girl a gold star."

The enlightenment was short-lived. "Yeah, but do you think it's actually because of the weather? Maybe it's because of an accident or something that's holding things up."

"She still doesn't get it," Emma said, shaking her head

Joanie looked at her in the rearview mirror with a blank look on her face.

"To repeat—just in case you missed it the first time, numb nuts, we're in the middle of a friggin' blizzard!" Sally shouted beside her.

"Well, yeah, I know that. That part I get. But I wonder why we're not moving?"

Sometimes, certain correlations between cause and effect were slow to form in Joanie's brain. Like now. Must be all that wine she drinks.

"Forget it," Sally said. "I'm not in the mood to try and explain it to you. Just take my word for it, okay? Accept the fact that we're not moving for whatever reason and I think we might be stuck here for a while."

"You really think so?"

"I'd say the chances are good."

"Well, hell. But why—"

"Joanie, shut your mouth. Use it only to breathe. I don't want to hear another word. Whatever the reason, we're stuck here."

With a mutinous glare, Joanie clamped her mouth shut and slid down in her seat, folding her arms over her chest.

Uh-oh, this could mean war! Except for the rumble of the motor, the swish of the wiper blades, and the hum of the heater, there was silence. Emma checked her watch to see how long it would last. She'd give it maybe five minutes. Sure enough, not even four minutes later, Joanie was chirping again.

"*Sooo*, how long you think we're going to be here?"

"Haven't a clue."

"Think they'll get us moving."

"Don't know."

"Hope so."

"Yep, me too."

This time the silence that descended was because they'd run out of things to say about the situation. So, they all just kind of sat there looking straight ahead, hoping to see some movement. They didn't see any. Instead what they did see were taillights blinking out as drivers turned their cars off to conserve gas. The girls followed suit. It looked like they were going to be there for quite some time.

\* \* \* \*

Moira was lying on the couch, one arm draped over closed eyes behind which a monumental headache was pounding unmercifully. The drone of the television in the background filtered sporadically through her pain. The newscaster was talking about the unexpected storm and the havoc it was wreaking on the roads. She'd been lucky to make it home before the Thruway was closed. She wondered briefly if Emma Rogers and her dog were sitting somewhere, stranded on the toll road. She hoped they were, but pushed the thought away. She didn't want to think about them at all right now. Her head hurt too much and they were the cause.

She hadn't been able to turn her mind away from the problem the entire ride home and between that and the stress of trying to stay on the road and avoiding an accident, the mother of all headaches had been born. She'd no sooner entered her house than she went in search of some Tylenol and water. She'd downed four of the pills and was still waiting for relief from the hammering pain. The last thing she wanted to think about was how she had failed to add the two of them to her victim's list. She needed to empty her mind for a while and just *be*.

The newscaster prattled on, his voice receding further and further into the distance as she started to relax and drift toward sleep. The medication had finally kicked in and the jarring pain in her head had been reduced to a dull throb. Her mind achieved a temporary peace and she fell into a deep sleep. She'd face her problems and demons tomorrow.

# Chapter Twenty-Two

It was two hours later and they hadn't moved so much as an inch. It wasn't looking good. What it did look like was this—they were probably going to spend the entire freaking night on the New York State Thruway in the luxurious accommodations of one packed-to-the gills Chevy van. Shit and double shit!

The girls had taken turns calling home—Joanie to Sam, Sally to Richard, her boyfriend of ten years, and the restaurant, Emma to Mandie (she had a habit of worrying when she didn't know where her mother was. God knows she had good reason to) and Ben. They got the same report from everyone. The Thruway was shut down from Rochester to Erie, Pennsylvania. For how long? Nobody knew, but snow was falling at a rate of 2-3″ per hour everywhere. The entire region was under siege. So much for the freakin' weather report!

At the moment, Emma (she'd been elected since she was in the back seat) was busy crawling over and around the loaded gear to get her hands on the coolers and bags holding their leftover food supply. Good thing she'd changed into jeans before they'd hit the road because the positions she was contorting her body into to get to the food were none too pretty. If she'd still had a skirt on, she'd definitely be shooting a beaver and the many variations thereof.

As far as the food went, once Emma got her hands on it and dragged it back to her seat, there wasn't all that much of it. The girls weren't known for their small appetites. Put food in front of them, any amount, and it was usually gone. So what did they have? There were four cans of Diet Pepsi, one package of Twinkies, maybe a quarter bag of chips, which were in all likelihood mostly crumbs, one stale roll, two rather limp-looking pieces of cheese, and a few pickles. A feast it was not; in fact it was pretty slim pickin's.

They were delving into what was left of the chips when a rap on the window by Joanie's head just about sent her into orbit. They all turned to see who or what it was, squinting through the fogged window. Joanie brushed her hand over the pane to remove the condensation and they saw a huddled figure standing next to the van. At least they thought the person was huddled. Fact of it was, the person, a male person as it turned out, was just short—very, very short. He was maybe a couple of inches over five feet tall.

Joanie rolled the window down and cold air and snow swirled into the van. "Can we help you?" she gulped as the cold air hit her hard.

"Yes, ma'am. I hope so. I'm in the van next to you."

Everybody's attention swung to the van sitting next to them. The girls took it in, then swiveled their gaze back to the man.

"What can we do for you, sir?" Joanie asked.

"Well, ma'am, the storm has kinda caught me in a tight spot."

"Yeah? How's that?"

"Well, ya see, ma'am," the man scratched his forehead, lifting his hat a little on one side when he did, "I was transporting a body from the hospital to the mortuary when the storm hit and so…well… I didn't get there yet. To the mortuary, I mean."

"*Yeaaah…?*"

"Well, it's still in the van."

"What's still in the van?"

"The body."

"The body?"

"Yes, ma'am. The body."

"A real body?"

"Yes, ma'am."

"Like in… a dead body?"

"Yes, ma'am."

"You're kidding, right?"

"No ma'am, I'm not."

"You've really got a dead body in there?"

"Yes, ma'am, I do."

Joanie stared at the man for a minute while she tried to come to grips with what the guy was telling her. After two false starts where she took on the appearance of a gasping fish, she could finally put her thoughts into words. "Let me make sure we're on the same page here, mister. You're telling us that you've got an-honest-to-God-dead, not-breathing, gone-from-this-world body in that van. The one that's sitting right next to us."

"Yes, ma'am."

"You're sure?"

"Yes, ma'am."

"You're not shittin' us?"

"No ma'am."

"Damn."

"Yes, ma'am."

Joanie turned away from the man and looked at Sally and Emma, her expression saying exactly what Sally and Emma were thinking. *Son of a bitch, it could only happen to us!* Nobody but them could be stranded on the Thruway in a blizzard and of all the cars that were in the same boat, they'd be the ones next to a van that had a dead body in it. Shit, nobody could make this stuff up even if they tried!

Joanie turned back to the little man, one eyebrow elevating to new heights. "Soooo, what do you want us to do?"

"Well, ma'am, if it wouldn't be too much trouble, do you think I could stay in your vehicle with you until we get moving again? It's kind of creepy being in mine with only a dead body to keep me company."

Joanie stared at the little guy. "You want to stay with us."

"Yes, ma'am, if that would be all right."

"In our van."

"Yes, ma'am."

Well, shit! Rack up another one! The weird and wacky certainly seemed to be the distinguishing characteristics required for revolving in the threesome's orbit. How lucky could they get? But hell, it wasn't like they could refuse the guy, could they? Or could they? No, probably not. Dammit! This definitely called for a conference.

"Can you give us a minute here? My friends and I need to discuss this."

"Oh, sure, sure. I'll go back to my van and wait 'til you're through. Let me know what you decide."

The little man turned away to go back to his vehicle and Joanie rolled up her window, turning in her seat to face her two buddies. "Well, fuck a duck. Do you believe this shit?"

"Why not? We're friggin' magnets for this kind of crap," Sally said.

Emma didn't have to say a word, her expression and body language spoke volumes.

"Well, what do you think, guys?" Sally asked.

"I don't know," Joanie pondered, not willing to give the guy unquestioned believability. "How do we know this guy's telling the truth?"

"We don't, but there's one way to find out."

"How?"

"We go take a look in his van."

"Yeah, right. We go take a look in his van."

"Do you have a better idea?"

"Well, *nooo*."

"How about you, Emma?"

"None that I can think of at the moment."

"Well, then that's the plan."

"Just what I want to do, go take a look at a dead guy... Is it a dead guy?"

"What do you mean, 'is it a dead guy'?"

"You know, is it a guy?"

"As opposed to...?"

"A girl."

"Well, shit. I don't know. He just said it was a dead body, didn't he? What difference does it make?"

"None, I guess. I don't suppose it matters."

"No, I don't suppose it does."

"As long as it's dead."

"Yeah, as long as it's dead."

"What if it isn't dead?"

"Don't even go there."

"But what if it's alive and just drugged or something."

"Well, cripe, I told you not to go there."

"It just kind of followed. I can't help it; that's the way my mind works."

"Heaven help us."

"Never mind that. What's going to happen if it's not dead?"

"Then I think we'd have a problem."

"Yeah, a big one."

"We'd be in deep shit."

"Really deep."

"He could have another motive, you know."

"What are you talking about, Joanie?"

"To get in our van."

"Why would he want to get in here other than to get away from a dead body?"

"He might want us."

"Want us?"

"Yeah, you know, 'cause we're hot."

Emma and Sally both bowed their heads and closed their eyes. "I don't believe it," Emma moaned.

"We have to consider it," Joanie argued.

"I'm gonna consider throwing you out of the van and letting you fend for yourself."

"Emma, that's not very nice. You may not want to acknowledge our sexual power, but I can't ignore it."

"You can't ignore this either," Sally said and flipped her the bird. "Look at us, you ass. We're so bundled up even Superman couldn't see what's under all these clothes."

"He doesn't have to see, we radiate."

"Oh, damn."

"It's our 'it' factor."

"Well, factor this—shut up!"

"But—"

"No buts. There will be nothing more said about this crap." Joanie opened her mouth to protest and Sally threw her a look that would have withered Hercules himself. "Now, about the dead guy…"

"We have to find out," Emma said, stating the obvious.

"Yeah, we have to," Joanie agreed, even though she still felt the guy might have an ulterior motive, namely getting his hands on their bods.

"Who's gonna do it?"

"One of you two," Sally said. "I'm gonna make sure we're ready in case there's a problem."

"How're you going to do that?"

"How do you think? Emma, slide out our backup."

"Our what?"

"Our backup," Sally said. Emma and Joanie continued to give her a puzzled look. "Jesus, you two are about as slow as a constipated turtle. Give me the gun, Emma. The one we brought in case there *was* a problem. You know, our old friend, TFG, formerly known as *the fucking gun*."

"Geez, do you really think that's necessary?"

"Yep, we're not taking any chances. Hand it up here."

Emma reached under the blanket and slid the gun out from behind Cole's crate. She passed it up to Sally who'd already taken the bullets out of the glove compartment. She quickly loaded a shell into each chamber and snapped the barrels shut. She swung the barrels up and held the gun across her chest. She looked like she was ready for anything that came their way. Emma almost started laughing at the picture she made. Put a Stetson on her head, a cheroot between her teeth, and a pair of well-worn boots on her feet and she could pass for an outlaw keeping watch on top of a bluff in the Old West.

"Okay, which one of you two is going over to see if there is a dead body?" Sally asked.

"Why don't you go?" Joanie retorted. "You've got the gun."

"'Cause I'm defending the home front."

"What home front?"

"This," Sally gestured, her arm sweeping in an arc, "home front."

"What a crock."

"Maybe, but it's my crock."

"That still isn't any excuse."

"It's the only one I've got and the only one you're going to get."

"Shit."

"You betcha, Toots."

"All right, Joanie. Which one of us is going?" Emma asked, knowing full well there would be no budging Sally.

"Why don't we both go?"

"No," Sally said. "If he's not on the up and up that would give him two hostages."

"Hostages? Where are you getting this shit from?"

"Just trying to cover all the bases."

"Well, cut it out. You're making me nervous. Cripe!"

"I'll go," Emma volunteered. "You've still got kids at home, Joanie."

"Oh, for pete's sake, cut the crap. I'm going. Listen to yourselves—and you think I'm nuts 'cause I think he might want sexual favors from our incredible selves? Give me a break. I'm going over there and seeing what's what."

"Well, if that's the way you feel, don't let us stop you," Emma said, a glint of victory shining in her eyes.

It took Joanie a beat to realize she'd been had, as usual. Christ, she thought, they were getting really good at this. She had to admire them for it. She'd get even, but she'd give them credit. At any rate, she was up to the challenge; she could do this blindfolded. "All right, I'm going," she said, pulling her gloves on. "I'll be the one sacrificed for the good of all. Just remember to mourn me. Make sure there's plenty of flowers." She certainly wasn't above laying on the guilt though.

Sally rolled her eyes. "Now listen," she instructed, "if he tries anything, just knee 'im. You're good at that and it'll give you time to get away. I'll have the gun trained on 'im the whole time."

Joanie gave her an incredulous look. "What the hell are you talking about?"

"You know; if he tries to grab ya, knee the sucker."

"Yeah, but you might have to bend down a little 'cause he's so short," Emma added.

"You two are really out there."

"Remember, hit him hard."

"Oh, brother! I'm going. I can't listen to any more of this." She opened her door, then turned back to Sally and Emma for a farewell wave. "Don't worry. If I knee the bastard he won't be getting off the ground for at least a week."

"That's our girl! It's a good thing you're on our side, Joanie."

"Don't I know it."

"Any last words?" Sally asked.

"Yeah. Just to cover all the bases, if I don't make it, tell Sam and the kids I love 'em… And Emma, remember to throw Tank into my grave." She had to throw in a parting shot of guilt.

Emma saluted her departing friend and Joanie headed toward the little man's van. Sally brought the gun up and aimed it in that direction. Deadeye was on the job.

Joanie rapped on the driver's window. The little man rolled it down. Forsaking all polite preliminaries, Joanie asked, "Can I see the body?"

"You want to see the body?" he asked, dumbfounded by the request.

"Yeah, if you wouldn't mind."

"Honest?"

"Yeah, we want to know there's really a body back there."

"Why?"

"So we'll know if you're on the up and up."

The little man shook his head. He was speechless and just stared at her like she was from outer space.

Joanie stared right back at him and shrugged her shoulders. "Hey, you can never be too careful."

"Right. You're sure you want to do this?"

"Yep." Shit, she could fake out the best of them.

"All right. Let's go around to the back doors."

"Okay, but let's get there by going around the front of the vehicle."

"All right, but do you mind if I ask why?"

"'Cause my friend has a shotgun aimed this way just in case and I don't want her to lose sight of us."

"You're kidding, right?"

"Nope. Take a look." The little man's eyes darted over to where Sally sat with the shotgun leveled right at him. "Don't worry; she won't shoot unless you piss her off. Then she'll blast ya. Believe me, you won't feel a thing. It'll be over before you even have time to register you've been hit." God, was she good or what?!

The little man got out of the van and went around the front of the vehicle with Joanie walking a short distance behind. The little man kept his gaze intent upon the shotgun he could barely make out behind the fogged windows of the girls' van. Joanie had a stupid grin on her face and gave Sally a thumbs-up as she passed by. Emma kept tract of their progress, wiping off condensation as was needed to keep her view unobstructed. Sally swiveled the gun in line with her prey as dictated by Emma's actions.

With the snow and wind whipping around them, Joanie and the little man reached the back doors of his van. He took out keys and unlocked the doors. With an effort, he pulled them open, struggling against the raging wind. Inside, strapped on a collapsible gurney that was anchored to the floor was a black body bag. From where she stood, Joanie could see there was something in it big enough to be a dead person. If the bag was zipped, the person had to be dead, right? There wasn't any air in those bags. Call her chicken, but she didn't need to see anymore. Her curiosity was satisfied—in spades!

"That's okay," she said as the man reached to unzip the bag. "I believe you."

"You're sure? If you want to take a little peek…"

"No, no, that's fine. We're all set here. I'll tell my friend she can lower the gun. You get your stuff and come on over."

"Okay. I'll just lock everything up then. Thanks."

"Don't mention it. Oh, one more thing."

"Yeah?"

"You don't have any ideas about, well, you know… with us, do ya?" The little man looked at her blankly. Joanie raised her eyebrow.

"Uh, uh, no," the man stammered when he realized the implication.

"Just checking. We'd have to blow you away if you did. Get your stuff." Joanie scurried over to her own vehicle and slid in. "God, it's cold out there."

"No shit," Sally said impatiently. "Is there a body in there?"

"I'd say so. It's in a body bag."

"Did he open it?"

"No. I told him it wasn't necessary."

"Not necessary? He could have rocks in that thing for all we know."

"Give me a break, will you? If you want to see the damn thing, then you go take a look. I'm done and put that damn gun down. I'm telling you, the guy's okay."

"He'd better be."

"I even made sure he wasn't out to make a move on us."

"A move?"

"Yeah, sexually."

"Jesus!"

"Relax, Sally, everything's fine. But if it'll make you feel better, keep TFG within easy reach."

"I fully intend to."

"Well, at least slide it down a little, okay? I think the little guy's scared shitless as it is."

"And I intend to help him stay that way."

"God help us, she's turned into a cross between Annie Oakley and Rambo."

"I'd prefer a cross between Angie Dickinson's Policewoman and Magnum."

"I don't think either one of them ever used a shotgun."

"Doesn't matter. They're the ones I want."

"Whatever."

"Besides, Angie Dickinson is a hell of a lot cuter than Annie Oakley."

"How do you know?"

"I think I remember seeing a picture of her once. I don't think she had much in the looks department. And of course Tom Sellack has it all over Sylvester Stallone."

"Yeah, I think so too. He's quite the stud."

"He gets my juices flowing. Gotta love that moustache."

"Oh, yeah, the moustache. Is it sexy or what?"

"I could do 'im."

"Me too."

"Me three."

"Fine, all three of us'll go for a roll in the hay with Mr. Sellack if we ever get the chance. Meanwhile, we'll let Sally have her cross between Angie and Tom."

"Good, I'm happy with that."

"You don't know how glad that makes me," Joanie said, her words heavy with sarcasm. "But any way you cut it, Sal, you've still gone over the top."

They watched the little man come around the front of their van, his head bent against the fury of the storm. He opened the side door and slipped in beside Emma.

"Thank you, ladies. I appreciate it," he said, giving Sally a wary look. The barrel of the gun wasn't visible above the front seat, but the little man had a sneaking suspicion it was still up there. The bottom of the stock was actually sitting in the footwell next to Sally's feet, the barrels resting up against her leg. She could have it up and aimed in a flash.

He was a swarthy-looking little guy probably somewhere in his late fifties. When he took his hat off, salt and pepper hair that didn't look any too clean was plastered to his head. Bushy eyebrows that were still black as coal arched over brown eyes that appeared somewhat bloodshot and were framed by thin silver-rimmed glasses. Wrinkles crisscrossed his face and an unkempt, black and silver moustache that desperately needed trimming decorated his upper lip. It didn't look any too clean either. The girls didn't want to speculate as to what gave it it's untidy appearance. Five o'clock shadow darkened his cheeks, or maybe it was dirt. Emma, the closest one to him, couldn't tell. But the black under his nails and in the creases of his hands was definitely dirt and it looked like it could have been there for a very long time.

Under his gray (?) heavy winter coat, he wore a red plaid flannel shirt over what might have originally been white long underwear. The color right now would be considered grayish yellow. Yuck! His workpants were a dark blue—maybe. Streaks of something grayish brownish made it hard to tell. His work boots were brown with stains of God knows what on them. The girls refused to look at his socks.

"Your welcome, Mr.—"

"Kowalski. Stanley Kowalski."

"Nice to meet you, Stan," Joanie said. "I'm Joanie," then pointing to Sally, continued with, "and this is Sally. Sitting next to you is Emma."

"Nice to meet you, ladies."

"Yeah, you too," Emma said, a whiff of something unpleasant reaching her nose. Stan and her two friends launched into a conversation about the crappy weather while Emma tried to get a fix on the strange odor that was beginning to make her eyes water. It had to be coming from Stan and if she could smell it, it had to be bad. God knows her olfactory sense wasn't what it used to be.

The dogs, of course, had picked up on the strange scent the minute Stan had opened the door. With their heightened sense of smell, the push the unpleasant aroma received from the gusty wind swirling around the man hadn't been at all necessary for it to reach their sensitive nostrils. It *had,* however, succeeded in hurling the pungency full force at the three canines and they reacted immediately. Sneezing and snuffing had erupted from each of them with their front paws rubbing their noses trying to dislodge the offending stink.

The odor had caught up with Sally too. Emma could tell the exact moment it hit her because she gagged. Covering her mouth and working hard to keep the contents of her stomach where they belonged, Sally threw her a questioning glance. Emma shrugged. She'd be dipped if she knew what it was. Wait till it smacked Joanie in the face; all they could do was keep their fingers crossed that she'd be diplomatic. *Yeah, right!*

Their wait was almost non-existent.

"What the hell is that smell?" Joanie asked, her nose wrinkling in distaste.

So much for diplomacy.

Emma and Sally squirmed in their seats, shooting looks that clearly stated to anybody who knew them—and Joanie certainly did—that she was to shut the hell up. But, heaven help them, she was on a roll.

"Can't you guys smell that? It's awful."

"I don't smell anything. Do you, Emma?" Sally quickly jumped into the fray, trying to cover Joanie's major faux pas.

"Come on, you don't smell that stench?"

Oh, God, this was going from bad to worse.

"No, I don't smell a thing," Emma said, trying to tell Joanie with her eyes to put a lid on it.

"Well, you I believe, Emma. You don't smell anything. But Sally, you have got to smell that. There's no way in hell you don't smell that. And listen to the dogs. They certainly smell it."

Emma darted a cautious look over to Stan to see what his reaction was. He looked like he was totally oblivious. Sure, he was probably so used to his own smell that he didn't even notice it anymore. Damn their luck! It was bad enough they had a dead guy in the van next to them, but they had to go and have a guy who smelled half dead himself in the car with them.

"Umm, you know what, Joanie? I think it's passing. I don't smell it so much any more," Sally said, reaching across the console and giving Joanie's fingers a hard squeeze.

"Hey, what the hell was that for?" Joanie asked, snatching her fingers back. "Geez, that hurt."

At least they'd gotten her attention—finally. "Nope, I don't smell it anymore. Do you?" Sally asked, giving Joanie a look that only a blind man could fail to interpret.

"Uh...uh, no. I don't smell it anymore," Joanie said, still puzzled, but following Sally's lead.

"So, Stan, how long have you been doing this sort of work?" Emma asked before anyone else could put their foot in their mouth.

Stan launched into his full work history and was talking non-stop when there was another knock on the window. This time it was Sally's turn to jump a foot.

"Jesus," she muttered, "these people are going to give all of us a heart attack."

She rolled down her window and before her stood a young woman who was carrying something wrapped in a blanket. "Can you help me?" the girl asked.

"What do you need, hon?" Sally inquired.

"Could we stay in your van?"

"We?"

"My baby and me."

"That bundle is a baby?"

"Yeah."

"Well, get the hell in here, girl."

There was no need for a discussion this time. Emma and Stan moved over and the girl hurried into the back seat. Joanie, meanwhile, was mumbling something under her breath about being the friggin' Red Cross. As soon as she was settled, the girl opened the blanket and there staring out at all of them was the sweetest little face any of them had seen in a long time. Even Stan was oohing and aahing. Suddenly, the baby wrinkled up her nose and let out with a wail. Uh-oh, she must have just gotten a whiff. The girl shushed her and put her over her shoulder. The baby quieted. Must be she wasn't in the line of fire with the odor from hell any more.

"What's your name, hon?" Sally asked.

"Melissa. Melissa Lang."

Melissa Lang was twenty-two years old and stood 5'5″ in her bare feet. She had long, shining dark brown hair that had chestnut highlights. Her big brown eyes were set in a very pretty oval face that lit up when she smiled and her peaches and cream complexion was flawless. She was wearing a wintergreen sweater and black corduroy pants, black boots, and a pastel blue ski jacket

"Nice to meet you, Melissa. I'm Sally. Next to me is Joanie, then there's Emma and next to you is Stan, someone else we've rescued."

"Nice to meet all of you," Melissa said, making eye contact with everyone. Her eyes widened slightly when she took in a sniff of Stan, but she was too well-mannered to say anything. She could give Joanie a few lessons; on second thought, no, it was way too late for that.

"What's your little girl's name? With a face like that the baby has to be a girl." It was easy to see whom the baby took after.

"Yep, she's a girl, all right. Her name's Sarah."

"Oh, what a pretty name. It suits her, don't you think, Emma, Joanie?"

"Yep, it's perfect," Emma agreed

"How old is she?"

"Six months."

"She's darling."

"Thank you."

"Well, what in the world are you two doing out on a night like this?" Joanie asked, her curiosity getting the better of her.

"We were on our way home. I was visiting a friend of mine over the weekend. If I'd known there was going to be a storm I wouldn't have made the trip. My old car isn't all that reliable. I had half a tank of gas when we started out today, but if I have to keep running it to stay warm, I'm going to run out. Besides that, the heater isn't all that great. Sometimes it works and sometimes it doesn't. I was worried about keeping Sarah warm."

"Well, you don't have to worry about that any more," Sally said. "You can stay with us. We had a full tank when we started out from Syracuse, so I don't think we'll be running out. Besides, there's enough body heat in here anyway what with everybody jammed in the way they are."

301

"And if you get tired of holding Sarah, there's plenty of arms ready to take up the slack. We even have a special babysitter if you'd care to use him," Emma offered.

"You can't go wrong there. He's one in a million," Joanie said.

At Melissa's baffled look, Sally spoke up. "Melissa, they're talking about Cole."

"Who's Cole?" Melissa asked.

"He's Emma's Newfoundland. He's in the back with Kirby and Tank, our other dogs."

Melissa turned around to get a look, but wasn't able to see much. "Why is he the special babysitter?"

"'Cause he loves children and in this particular case with his heavy coat and big size, he'd be almost like a heating blanket for the baby. If I know Cole, he'll wrap himself right around Sarah."

"Oh, I don't know. Are you sure he wouldn't hurt her?"

"Who, Cole? Not in this lifetime. He's gentle as a lamb with children."

"Well… maybe," she said hesitantly. "I'll have to think about it."

"No problem. He's here if you want a break. Not that we'd mind holding Sarah, it's just that Cole might be able to keep her warmer. He's like a little furnace."

"You're sure it would be all right?"

"Absolutely."

"I don't want her to catch cold," she said, thinking it over for a bit. "Okay, maybe later."

"Fine. Just let me know when you want him to take over. Cole will do the rest."

"Do you think one of you could hold her now while I get what I'll need from my car. I didn't want to bring anything with me before I found out if we could stay."

302

"Sure," Emma volunteered, "hand her over." Melissa passed Sarah to Emma, who settled nicely in her arms.

"I'll go with you," Joanie said, zipping up her jacket and pulling her hat on her head.

"Thanks, that'd be a big help."

They were scrambling for Melissa's car a minute later, the wind and stinging snow trying to drive them back. After a few minutes they returned with the necessary items, which among other things included bottles and diapers. When the doors were opened to allow them inside, a fresh gust of wind accompanied them and stirred the air that was in the van. Needless to say, the fetid odor surrounding Stan was brought to new life and the four women (poor Melissa had to be included now; she wasn't any more immune than the other three) had to struggle not to react. Luckily, little Sarah was still happily content and asleep in Emma's arms, although her little nose did twitch a time or two.

They passed the time by telling stories from their varied pasts in between eating what was left of the girls' food and the few snacks that Melissa had brought. Stan had slipped out to his van and brought back his contribution, which was a flask of Black Velvet whiskey. Everybody took their turn at taking a hit, the girls rationalizing that any germs that most assuredly resided on the opening were neutralized by the alcohol. They weren't normally straight whiskey drinkers, but the occasion seemed to call for it.

Sarah had been given into the care of Cole while they ate and she was as snug as a bug in a rug. After her initial trepidation had been proven groundless, Melissa became fascinated in the manner with which Cole cared for his young charge.

Lying on a crate pad that kept both the dog and the baby off the chill of the metal floor, Cole curled his body into a semicircle completely surrounding Sarah on three sides. Once she was braced comfortably against his body, he placed his great head gently across her blanketed legs so that she was completely cocooned by his warmth. She looked like she was wearing a luxurious black fur coat, one that would keep her safe even at the risk of his own life.

One of the wacky stories to make the rounds once the alcohol had loosened their tongues involved who else but Joanie.

One day when Sam was still with the FBI and attached to the Buffalo office, Joanie went shopping at one of the local Valu stores. She'd pulled into a parking slot and had just gotten out of her car and locked the door when she fumbled the keys and dropped them down the storm sewer that she'd had the misfortune of parking next to. While anxious mothers scrambled to remove their children from within hearing distance, a very vocally pissed off Joanie went to find a phone. She got hold of Sam, told him where she was and what had happened. He said he'd be there in half an hour. Joanie went back to her car to wait, grumbling the whole time.

It was only twenty minutes later that the parking lot exploded with sirens and flashing lights coming in from all directions and converged on one astounded Joanie Davis. Seems that Sam thought it would be a good joke to play on his wife so he coordinated a "raid" with a few of his buddies who temporarily must not have had anything better to do. Must have been a slow crime day! At any rate, six FBI issued Crown Vics raced in and surrounded Joanie and her car. The agents all braked their cars to a stop, slammed them into Park, and exited their vehicles on the run. You would have thought she was on the Ten Most Wanted List and that's exactly the effect they were striving for. It's a wonder they didn't come out with guns blazing! Talk about a spectacle! It made a lot of people's day to be so close to the action. Too bad Joanie really wasn't a criminal. Gawking bystanders would have loved to watch her being hauled away.

When all the hullabaloo had died down, the agents did indeed have a tool to rescue Joanie's keys and they were quickly retrieved. Any embarrassment Joanie might have suffered from the actions of her husband was quickly replaced with an I'll-get-you-for-this attitude. As Emma recalled, Joanie made Sam suffer for something like two weeks. How she did that was never specifically spelled out, but knowing Joanie, one could safely assume that poor Sam didn't reap any of the physical benefits of being married. As Joanie had put it, "The gates of hell are closed!"

You had to love the way she referred to having sex. God only knows what it meant, but it had to have had a special meaning for her. Emma and Sally had never gathered enough courage to ask for an explanation and they never would. Some doors were best kept firmly closed.

# Chapter Twenty-Three

It must have been around ten o'clock that night when Emma could avoid it no longer and uttered the fatal words. "I have to go to the bathroom."

"No, you don't," Joanie shot back quickly.

"Yes, I do."

"No, you don't."

"Yeah, I do."

"And I'm telling you, you don't."

"I don't care what you're telling me, I have to go."

"No, you don't."

"Jesus, Joanie, come on. I've been holding it for hours; I can't wait any longer."

"Yes, you can."

"I have to go too," Sally admitted.

"No, you don't."

"I do so."

"Stop talking about it."

"That isn't going to change anything, Joanie."

"Yes, it is. Don't think about it. Get your mind on something else."

"It won't do any good."

"I have to go to the bathroom too," Melissa piped up.

"Oh, for pete's sake," Joanie grumbled.

"Now that you mention it, I could stand to take a leak myself," Stan said.

"Don't you people having any holding power?" Joanie asked, obviously put out by this latest development.

"We've *been* holding it since we got stuck here for cripe's sake."

"Yeah, well, you could go a bit longer."

"Says who?"

"Says me. Look, I'm fine. I don't have to go yet."

"How come she doesn't have to go?" Stan wondered.

"'Cause she's like a friggin' camel when it comes to pee," supplied Sally.

"Sal, shut up."

"It's one of her many talents," Emma said. "She's known for it. But it has its down side too. If she laughs too hard, she pees; if she coughs too hard, she pees; if she gets excited at a football game and jumps up and down, she pees. But if you think you'll ever get her to admit it's because her bladder's so damn full it has to let a little trickle go every so often to relieve the pressure, forget it; she never will."

"That's enough, Emma."

No way was Emma stopping now. "You know what would probably happen right now if we got her on a laughing jag? She'd pee her pants. It'd probably be a real soaker."

"Emma…"

"It'd probably run right down her leg into her shoe."

"Emma, if you know what's good for you…"

Sally nimbly stepped in and took up the tale. "Yeah, whenever we go on a trip we practically have to force her to go to the bathroom before we leave. She says peeing is a waste of time; she's got other, more important things to do. Like it takes a lot of time to go to the bathroom."

"It *is* a waste of time," Joanie declared emphatically.

"That's weird." Melissa gave Joanie a look that reinforced her feelings on the subject.

"It's also not healthy, but try telling her that."

"Okay, you guys. Enough. They get the point." Joanie was determined to put a halt to this conversation. "When I drop over dead because I held my pee too long, you can say, 'I told you so'. Until then, shut the hell up."

"Fine. But I still have to go," Emma said.

The air was filled with a demanding chorus of "me too's".

"*All right...* You guys aren't going to give this up, are you?"

"Nope. Gotta go, Joan."

"Okay... but we're only going to do this once. Got it?"

"Got it."

"I'm not going out in this weather more than once for a pee break."

"Understood, oh, humped-back one."

"Real cute, Em... All right... let's get organized... Melissa, put the baby back with Cole. Emma, hop in the back and get something to defend ourselves with out of the tack boxes. Sally, get the flashlight. Stan, get ready to plow a path."

"Wait, wait, wait. Hold up a minute there, everybody," Sally directed. "What's Emma supposed to get?"

"Something to defend ourselves with."

"For what?"

"For anything that might be out there waiting to get us."

"Like what?"

"Bad guys, villains, coyotes, bears."

"Bears?"

"Whatever. We need weapons."

"Like what?"

"I don't know, but I do know that we can't go traipsing around out there with a shotgun to go to the bathroom."

"I suppose not," Sally conceded.

From the back, where Emma had already been rummaging through the tack boxes while Joanie and Sally debated the finer points of the operation, came a mystified question. "What the hell should I get?"

"Something sharp, like scissors."

"Oh, all right. How about a stripping knife? Would that work?"

"Em, what are you going to do with that? Strip the guy's hair to death?"

"Hmm. Wouldn't work, huh? How about a hemostat?"

"Em, you're not quite getting it, are ya? What do you think you're going to do with a hemostat? Pull out all the guy's nose or ear hair? Do you really think you want to get that intimate with an attacker? And what if there's a coyote? You gonna pluck out some fur?" Joanie gave Emma a look that said she ought to know better. "That'll really stop 'em."

"Okay, I see your point. Well, then all we have is scissors for weapons."

"How about some hair spray? We've got some of that, don't we?"

"Oh, yeah. Yeah, that's good. Here's some right here."

"What are we going to do with hair spray?" Melissa asked.

"Spray it in their faces. It'll hurt like hell if it gets in their eyes. Blinds 'em too."

"I never would have thought of that," Melissa said.

"Leave it to us, we're old hands at this stuff."

"You are? How come?"

"Joanie's husband is retired FBI. He taught her all the moves," Emma informed Melissa.

"Really?"

"Yeah, we're fully prepared to handle just about anything," Joanie boasted.

"In your dreams," Emma muttered, which Joanie heard and retaliated by shooting her friend a dark look. Emma ignored her.

"I still think we should just take the damn gun," Sally groused.

"You know we can't, so drop it. We've got enough scissors so everybody can have a pair. Emma, hand 'em out. Put 'em in your jacket pocket, everybody. How many cans of hairspray do we have, Em?"

"I found two."

"Okay. You keep one and give me the other. We'll space ourselves out among the troops."

"Jesus, we aren't going into battle, Joanie."

"Yes, we are. We have to be ready for anything. Who knows what's out there. Could be anything."

"We've already listed our possible foes and none sounds too viable to me," Sally said. "But what are *you* going for, Joanie? What stalking evil is in that twisted mind of yours? A deranged killer? A rabid raccoon? A rogue elephant?"

"Maybe all three, smart-ass. Stranger things have been known to happen." Both Emma and Sally gave her the eye. Exasperated, Joanie asked, "Need I remind you two that we're talking about us?"

Emma and Sally gave each other a sideways look, acknowledgement in their expressions. "Say no more," Sally acquiesced. "Let's get crackin', people."

After Emma had done her part to ensure that everyone was armed and dangerous, she resettled herself in the back seat. Melissa then handed Sarah to Emma so she could slip over. Once she was in the back, Emma handed the sleeping baby to her and Melissa settled her in with Cole. Satisfied that Sarah was content, Melissa crawled back over the seat.

"You're sure she'll be all right while we're gone?"

"I'm sure," Emma answered. "Don't worry. Cole will keep her safe. We aren't going to be gone that long anyway. She probably won't even wake up."

"You'll lock the car though, won't you?"

"Absolutely," Joanie said.

"We should take Tank and Kirby with us," Sally said, preparing to face the elements. "That way they can get done with their business and they'll add an extra measure of protection."

"Good thinking, Sal. We'll get Cole out when we get back."

"Okay, sounds like a plan," Emma said, pulling on her gloves. "Everybody ready? Let's get this show on the road. I'll be peeing *my* pants if we don't get a move on."

So with pint-sized stinky Stan leading the way, the five of them left the van and trudged through the snow, hoping to find a spot that offered some degree of privacy, although with the snow coming down as hard as it was there really wasn't any danger of anybody seeing them. Nevertheless, they were in luck. After hiking about fifteen or twenty yards, they literally walked into trees. Well, Stan did anyway. He'd had his head down, fighting the snow and the wind and had run smack into a tree. The impact almost knocked the little guy out. Joanie was next in line and she quickly steadied him before he went face first into the snow.

Once they'd made certain he was all right (which meant he hadn't passed out, his head wasn't cracked open, and he wasn't talking gibberish), the group proceeded deeper into the woods. Stan had the flashlight and directed the beam in a 360-degree arc. Looked like a good spot to tend to business.

It didn't take long for Tank and Kirby to do their thing, although Tank had a little bit of trouble lifting his leg in the deep snow. He was also in danger of being lost in the mounting snowdrifts. Good thing he was on a leash; Joanie saw it as his lifeline. If his adventurous soul led him into trouble, Joanie had the option of pulling him out, or not, depending on how she felt about him at the time. Since the little terrier hadn't pissed her off in a while she kept hauling him out.

Stan went first. He walked a short distance away from the girls and did his thing. They'd turned their backs to him the second he'd stepped away and kept up a line of chatter so any sounds he made were drowned out. The girls didn't want any recollections of this particular episode lodged in their memory banks.

Stan was done in no time—another case of men having the advantage. It's so damn easy for them to tend to their needs no matter where they are. Lucky bastards! For women it's another whole ball game. Undoubtedly one of the many curses women have had to put up with since that whole Adam and Eve thing.

Anyway, Stan returned to the group when he was finished, the flashlight bouncing over the terrain.

"Okay, Stan. Our turn. You stay here and face that way. We're going to find a spot a little further in and relieve our bladders. Give me the flashlight," Joanie said.

Stan handed over the flashlight; the girls started to walk away.

"And, Stan."

"Yeah?"

"If you turn around and look, I'll have to kill you."

Stan nodded, but didn't dare turn around. The girls continued to walk deeper into the copse of trees, each armed with a few papers towels they'd scavenged from the van.

"I've held myself back, but I can't any longer," Joanie said.

"About what?"

"Well, what do you think? That man's stench, of course."

"Joanie…"

"Oh, come on. You know he stinks as well as I do."

"Well, yeah, but—"

"Never mind being polite. That man stinks to high heaven and you know it. It's a wonder we haven't all dropped dead from the fumes."

"Jesus…" Sally moaned.

"I haven't figured out why it's so bad, but there's something besides the smell of cigarettes and body odor that's mixing in there."

"All right, if we're going to forget about being polite, I'll have to agree with you," Emma said, resigned to clear the air so to speak. "I noticed it too. There is some other odor that puts his smell right over the top."

"Okay, you guys, you dragged it out of me. I noticed it too," Sally confessed. "It's kind of a sickly sweet smell."

"I didn't want to say anything," Melissa added, "what with you all being kind enough to let Sarah and me stay in your car, but Stan does smell awful."

"I know I've smelled something like it before. If only I could place it…Oh, shit."

"What, oh, shit?"

"It just came to me. I know what it smells like."

"Well, what?"

"You know that smell you get in the house when a mouse has died in one of your walls…"

"Oh, shit."

"Yeah, exactly. I think we're smelling eau de dead guy."

There was an immediate chorus of "eeeuw!" punctuating the night air and looks of disgust contorting each of their faces. The girls walked the rest of the way in silence, each deep in thought, which no doubt conjured up images of the dead guy.

"This spot is as good as any," Sally said. "Might as well make use of it."

Joanie moved the beam of the flashlight around making sure the spot was up to her standards. "Yeah, might as well."

The four of them selected a spot, each removed a little distance from the others and proceeded to drop their pants, which was no easy feat for Sally and Joanie who were both holding leads attached to their dogs. Joanie had the additional impediment of the flashlight that was still on, although at the moment its beam was moving crazily up, down, and over as Joanie tried to unfasten her pants and hold on to it and the leash at the same time.

She'd almost succeeded in lowering her pants, but while doing so had inadvertently brought the flashlight to rest on Emma who was across the way from her.

"Ya wanna turn that thing off, Joan. I really don't want to give the whole world a show right now."

"Oh, geez, sorry. I didn't realize I was flashing ya." Joanie clicked off the flashlight.

Now, as any girl or woman knows that when one has to relieve oneself in the wild, it behooves that female to pull her pants down as far as she can, squat as low as she can and, as an additional measure of safety, pull her lowered clothing as far away from her body as she possibly can. Being that the female stream of urine is notoriously unreliable as to its force or the direction it will take, these precautions must be taken in order to avoid clothing or shoes from getting sprayed. There's nothing quite like that hot stream hitting the side of your leg and soaking into your sock.

So with that in mind, the girls assumed the position. It was a little tricky avoiding having their bare asses make contact with the cold snow, but they managed for the most part. Kirby was being her usual obedient self and was standing quietly while Sally tended to business. Tank, on the other hand, was in danger if being left in a snowdrift.

While the other girls had done their thing and were putting themselves back together, Joanie was still in a deep squat and Tank was dancing around her, the leash getting a little too taut for comfort at times.

"Joanie, aren't you done yet?" Emma asked.

"Yeah, I'm done."

"Well, come on then."

"I would if I could."

"What does that mean?"

"It *means* I can't get up."

"And *why* can't you get up?" Emma asked, already laughing.

"My knees are doing their thing; they've locked up... Quit laughing, you ass."

"I can't help it," Emma giggled. Joanie shot her a murderous look. "Okay, okay, I'll try." Forget it; she couldn't stop. "Sal, you'd better get over here. We've got a situation."

"Jesus, it never ends," Sally muttered, rolling her eyes. She walked closer to where Joanie was. "What's the problem?" she called.

"Joanie's stuck."

"Again? Didn't we do this once already this weekend?"

"Yeah, but it looks like we've got to do it again."

"Hell's bells. All right, let's get to it."

As if that was the cue he'd been waiting for, Tank, a dangerous gleam in his eye, ceased all movement and went into what could be considered a great show stack. Joanie, instantly alerted by the sudden stillness of the dog, gave her full attention to the devilish terrier and it wasn't because she was admiring his pose. Their eyes locked and if Joanie hadn't been cold before, she sure as hell was now as shivers of dread rolled down her back. Uh-oh, she thought, this was not going to be good.

"Tank, don't do it. Whatever you're planning, don't do it."

Tank didn't move, but he cocked his head to the side and a smile that foretold that nothing good was about to happen stretched from ear to ear.

"Damn, I'm dead where I squat," Joanie groaned.

Before anyone could react and get to her in time, Tank leapt into the air and hurled himself toward Joanie. She reflexively put her arms out to catch him, the impact sending her plopping backwards into the snow, bare ass and all.

*"Shiiit!"* she shrieked, her feet flying up in the air, hobbled as she was with her pants down around her ankles. "Holy shit! Christ, that's cold! Don't just stand there, you guys, get me out of here!"

Emma and Sally rushed to her side, not even trying to hide the fact that they were laughing themselves silly. There was no way they couldn't laugh. Hell, who in their right mind would have been able to keep a straight face? This scene made for one of the all-time greats—a totally ridiculous picture snapped forever into their memory banks.

Sally grabbed Tank's leash, hauled him off Joanie, and handed him off to Melissa who'd come over when she'd heard the shriek. The flashlight had long since been discarded into the snow; Emma picked it up and shoved it into her pocket. Then Sally and Emma both grabbed an arm and pulled Joanie up off the wet, cold ground. They got her on her feet, but she was still bent at the knees, her bare ass covered in snow.

"Pull me up, will ya? I gotta get my knees to unlock."

The girls slowly straightened her up, her knees finally unlocking. And there she stood—her pants down around her ankles, snow hanging off her cold, bare ass. Yet another chapter in their ongoing legacy!

317

"Does anybody have an extra paper towel? I've got to wipe the snow off my butt. I'm freezing."

"Here, Joanie." Melissa passed her a section.

"Thanks."

"I bet you're going to be chapped," Emma said.

"No shit."

"It seems a shame."

"What's a shame?"

"Getting that famous ass chapped."

"Tell me about it. It's world renowned, you know."

"Yeah, so you've told us on numerous occasions."

"It's documented."

"Yeah? By who?"

"Sam."

"He doesn't count."

"Oh, yes, he does."

"No, he doesn't; he's married to you."

"Who better than him to know my ass?"

"Oh, boy…"

"He's the uncontested authority on my ass."

"Okay! Stop! No need to go any further."

"Maybe it'd be better if we didn't."

"Works for me." Emma breathed a mental "phew!", knowing she been on the precipice of *too much information*. But she had to get in one more lick. "Too bad Sam's going to have to see your so-called world-class ass all chapped. It's bound to take some of the shine off it for him."

"I wouldn't bet on that and there's nothing 'so-called' about it."

"Give it a break, you two," Sally interjected, rolling her eyes. Then mumbling to herself, "What choice does poor Sam have? He lives with her; he has to think her butt is world-class or he'd be dead meat." Back to Joan, "Pull your pants up, you bare-assed beauty. We've got to get going."

They hooked up with Stan who, believe it or not, was still in the same spot they'd left him in. He must have taken Joanie's threat seriously—smart of the little guy. As a matter of fact, it didn't look like he'd budged so much as an inch. Could be he figured he might turn into a pillar of salt if he transgressed.

Joanie stopped dead in her tracks when she drew up alongside the man. With enough steel in her voice to fell a California redwood, she curtly spit out, "Did you see that?"

"See what?" Stan asked, visibly startled by her tone.

"Right answer," she growled. "You get to live another day. Let's go to the car."

Stan hesitated a few seconds, clearly taken aback. The girls were a few steps beyond him before he started to move. You could tell he wasn't quite sure if Joanie was serious or not and her two compatriots weren't about to confirm his suspicions one way or the other. Let the little guy keep wondering; it'd keep him honest. The girls had to hand it to Joanie; whenever she put the fear of God into somebody, she did a damn good job!

When they got back to the van, Emma removed Sarah, who was still sleeping, from Cole's care and brought him outside while everybody else piled into the vehicle. She led him only a few feet away from the highway before she stopped and Cole relieved himself. Much to Emma's relief, he didn't pussyfoot around in this kind of weather. It was the little things like this that always meant so much! Very shortly the two of them were back in with the others.

The snow was piling up and the wind was still whipping it into blizzard-like conditions while shaking the van with its intensity. There were times when they couldn't even see the back of Melissa's car, which was only two or three feet in front of them. Everybody took a turn on the cell phones and made their last calls of the night to the appropriate people.

Joanie was still in the driver's seat, so it was up to her to run the car when it cooled off a little too much for comfort. Everybody else tried to get comfortable and catch a few winks, although the insipid chill that invaded the van at seemingly regular intervals constantly broke up their sleep. Only Sarah seemed to be oblivious to the discomfort, snuggly cocooned as she was within Cole's warmth.

So the night passed for the stranded travelers. There was a bit of grumbling and a little swearing, but then things wouldn't have been normal if there hadn't been. The girls never had been ones to keep their feelings to themselves, although they did tone it down some for Sarah's sake. She couldn't understand what was said, of course, but it was the principle of the thing. They were mothers themselves after all. It was, however, taxing to be on their best behavior on top of everything else and they prayed that morning would hurry up and get there. It goes without saying that included in that prayer was the plea for clear skies and plowed roads.

# Chapter Twenty-Four

It was finally here; morning had at long last arrived. Grateful to all the forces of the universe and then some, the longest night of their lives had ended and they were still alive to bitch about it!

The van was facing west, but the rising sun—yes, the sun—that all too often gone-missing golden orb was indeed cresting the horizon in the east and light was shining through the back windows of the van, even if they were frosted over. And if the sun was visible that meant that the ugly dark clouds had taken a powder and whisked away with them the dratted snow, aided, no doubt, by the powerful force of the now-depleted winds. Hallelujah!

"Rise and shine, guys," Joanie called, giving Sally a poke to hasten the process. "Looks like the storm's over."

There was a lot of stretching, rubbing of eyes, and yawning before there was any verbal response to Joanie's announcement.

"Hey, it stopped snowing," Sally said, swiveling in her seat and looking out all the windows. Like what? It might not be snowing out the windshield, but maybe it was out the side windows. Duh!

"Damn, you're quick," Joanie teased.

"Like a bunny."

"Dream on, you old fart."

"Geez, the snow's not even blowing around," Emma noticed. "The wind must have died down too."

"And, lo and behold, the sun's actually shining."

"Cripe, if we had any more booze, I'd celebrate."

"What a difference a day makes, huh, guys?"

Sarah chose that moment to make her presence known, letting everybody know in no uncertain terms that she was awake and hungry and probably in need of a diaper change as well. Melissa hurried to rectify her various complaints.

Stan was fully awake himself now and in dire need of a cigarette. How many hours had it been since his last one? Way too many. "I'm gonna step out and have a smoke, ladies. Think I'll check on things in my van."

"Okay, Stan. Take your time."

He was pulling his pack out even before he was out the door.

"What's he going to check on? See if the guy came back to life?"

"Who knows? Maybe he just needs to get away from us for a few minutes."

"Why would he want to do that? We're great company."

"Some people might not fully appreciate us, Joanie."

"Like that could happen."

"It's sad, but true. I would imagine there are any number of people who we might rub the wrong way."

"You really think so?" she asked, quite incredulous that the possibility could even exist, much less be true.

"Yeah. I know it's a blow, but one we'll have to live with." Sally was getting sarcastically philosophical.

"Not me. Screw 'em." And she flipped them, whoever they were, the bird. She kept it low so Sarah couldn't see from where she was in the back seat just so there'd be no danger later in life of a repressed memory surfacing in Sarah's mind of being corrupted by an obscene gesture in her formative years.

"Well, that says it all, I guess," Emma observed wryly.

"It does for me," Joanie stated emphatically.

Stan opened the side door just then and stuck his head in. "Look up ahead. I think cars are starting to move."

Everybody swung her head forward and looked out the windshield. Sure enough, cars were moving in the distance. The girls let loose with a big "yahoo" and in doing so, scared the daylights out of Sarah who jumped in Melissa's arms and started to wail. While Melissa tried to shush her, the girls fell all over themselves apologizing and Stan backed up, looking relieved that the ordeal was over. He must have felt it was the perfect time to make his exit, so he thanked the girls for their hospitality and then left to go to his own vehicle.

Melissa got the baby quieted down and gathered their things in preparation for her departure. Their goodbyes took a bit longer than they had with Stan, and the girls made Melissa promise to come out and see them sometime in the near future. Sally helped her carry their belongings back to the car and stayed with Melissa until the baby and all the gear were safely stowed, and the car running.

One by one the cars ahead of them started to move until it was Melissa's turn and then the girls'. Stan's vehicle began moving at the same time theirs did and they rode side by side until Stan's lane increased in speed and he was pulling away from them. He gave a farewell toot on the horn and motored away. Joanie returned the gesture and they saw that he saluted Melissa in the same fashion as he passed her.

Traffic started to move at speeds that were well below normal, but at least it was moving and it made the girls wonder just what the hell the holdup had been in the first place. What had started the whole backup thing? What had made traffic come to a standstill? Could it be totally blamed on the storm? Had there been a major accident? The plows certainly hadn't been through where they'd been stranded so how come the road was passable? Had it always been? Was it a case of some nincompoop doing something stupid that had caused the whole tie-up? What? The girls decided it was probably going to turn out to be one of those mysteries of life that can never be solved and worse yet, never make any sense.

Be that as it may, the girls discovered they'd been a lot closer to the Williamsville toll booths than they would have thought. It's funny (well, maybe not) how during a snowstorm you lose all perspective of where you are even in the most familiar settings. At least that's the way it was for Emma, but then everyone knew she'd be lost within fifty feet of her house if she was behind the wheel during a blizzard. And maybe Joanie really had known exactly where they were and just didn't want to let on. No way. If she had, you can be sure she would *not* have been quiet about it. Gloating was one of her best talents.

Anyway, they paid the toll, you know, the one that was supposed to be done away with years ago—well, that one, and continued on their way. Melissa, who was still ahead of them, turned off at the Walden Avenue West exit. She gave a toot of the horn and a wave, which the girls returned when they sped past. The mainline continued to be clear as they pushed past the 400 exit and on to the 219 extension. Somehow the road crew had done a wonderful job of clearing the snow that had shut down the roadways the night before.

The girls got off at the Armor Duells exit and made their way down Route 240 where there was far more evidence of last night's storm than what they'd already encountered. The road had been plowed, but there was still a coating of snow the consistency and color of brown sugar covering the asphalt. Naturally, it looked like their area had gotten twice as much as anywhere else they'd been, but that was par for the course as Emma was quick to point out, even though it wasn't necessary. Joanie and Sally were well acquainted with Emma's hostile views on snow and cold and weren't surprised when a disgusted "shit" reached their ears. Emma continued to grumble the rest of the way home.

At last they pulled into the parking lot at the Hearthmoor. It felt like they'd been gone for a year. Even the dogs seemed relieved to be back home and the first thing the girls did was to get their furry friends out of the confining crates. They put them in the exercise area and the three canines lost no time going a little crazy with each other and with what some consider God's perfect natural toy. Of course, for Emma, it would never be anything more than that damn snow! But the dogs loved it! They romped and tumbled, ran and slid, and pounced and escaped. Before long they were coated with the white stuff and looked like walking snowballs of various sizes. They were happy dogs!

Tank was his usual bad-boy self and Cole and Kirby had to put him in his place a few times. Nothing serious, mind you, but they felt the need to swat him a couple of times and sent him tumbling backwards through the snow. Of course, the devil dog actually liked it and came back for more. Never let it be said that Cole and Kirby wouldn't oblige him and so the battle was on. God, what fun they had!

Meanwhile, their human counterparts were busy unloading, reloading, and carrying. Within three quarters of an hour, everything was where it should have been and Emma and Joanie were ready to take off. Getting home was the only thing on each of their minds. That thought alone filled their equally weary gray matter. It's a wonder they still had the faculties to drive a car.

Joanie did have a few reservations as to Emma's ability, so to her credit she had the presence of mind to let Emma pull out first once they were ready to get on the road. She wasn't taking any chances. There was no way she was going to put herself in front, thereby placing herself in Emma's direct line of fire. If Emma was going to go out of control, Joanie wanted to be well behind the action. She stayed back a good thirty feet and watched Emma's vehicle like a hawk. She loved her friend with all her heart and would do anything for her, but there was snow on the ground so all bets were off. It was a matter of survival.

Emma turned off at the shop's parking lot and gave Joanie a wave. Joanie tooted and waved back, then continued on home. All Emma had to do was get herself up the hill. Joanie thought she should be able to manage that without wrapping herself around a tree, but she'd call her when she got home just in case.

* * * *

That evening, Ben came over and wanted to know everything about the three bosom buddies' latest adventure. Emma and Cole, rested and fed, were ready to tell the tale.

After Emma had unloaded and put their gear away, she and Cole had both collapsed and slept for roughly three hours, sleep deprivation from the night before catching up with them. Dinner had been an easy matter of whisking some clam chowder from the freezer and heating it up in the microwave oven. Emma whipped up some baking powder biscuits from scratch, threw a salad together, and within half an hour had a great meal. Cole had been happy to sink his teeth into kibble generously dribbled with the savory chowder.

Now as they sat in Emma's comfortable living room, a fire blazing in the fireplace, she was giving Ben all the gory details. Throughout Emma's recitation, Cole sat at attention and listened to every word. He punctuated the story with amazing intuitiveness at several junctures by voicing a confirming "woof".

"Geez, Em, what an experience," Ben said when Emma had finished narrating her saga. At tale's end, she'd sunk back into the couch's deep cushions, looking like it had taken a lot out of her to relive the experience. Cole's body posture seemed to echo the same sentiment. He'd liquefied into a puddle at Emma's feet. "Do you guys ever do anything that's normal? Crazy stuff seems to happen to you all the time."

"Yeah, I know. "

"Is this pretty much how it always goes?"

"Yeah, I'd have to say pretty much. We seem to be magnets for attracting the screwy and loony," Emma answered, laughing. Cole blew air out through his nose; it definitely sounded like a snort.

"Never a dull moment, huh?"

"Not with us it seems."

"Lord, woman! What exactly have I gotten myself into?"

Emma blinked and drew back. "I don't know. I guess that's for you to decide."

"Yeah, I guess it is, isn't it?" Ben's voice had turned smoky and soft.

"Yeah," Emma said, her breath hitching and her heart stopping at the expression on Ben's face.

Like quicksilver, the atmosphere had changed from playful to serious. Uh-oh, Emma thought, what just happened? What'd she say? Why was Ben looking at her like that? Ohhh, boy!

"Em?"

"Yeah," Emma answered hesitantly, not knowing what was coming next, not even sure she wanted to *know* what was coming next. She was suddenly so tense she could hardly breathe.

"Em, I…"

The discordant ringing of the telephone broke the spell and dissolved the tension-laden atmosphere. Emma sprang up from the couch like someone who'd been given a reprieve from death's door and hurried to answer it. She didn't look back at Ben, but kept her attention focused on the phone. Cole had moved to Emma's side, aware that something was unsettling her; he could feel the nervous energy pulsating all around her. He'd have had to be in a coma to miss it; she'd all but jumped out of her skin when the phone rang.

It was Mandie, calling to get the whole, unabridged, give-me-every-detail scoop on the trip. This could take hours! Thank God! Emma looked over to Ben and mouthed an apology, even though she was actually overjoyed at the postponement from whatever declaration Ben had been going to make and she was sure he'd been going to make one.

As for Ben, he was smart enough to know the moment and the evening were over once the caller had been identified and had already gotten up and was putting on his jacket.

"Mandie, hold on a minute," Emma said, then crushed the receiver to her chest. "Ben, you don't have to leave." She was praying he would.

"That's okay, Em."

"I'm sorry about this," Emma said, indicating the phone. "You didn't finish what you were going to say." Emma thought it polite to mention it, but in all honesty she really didn't think she wanted to know what Ben had been about to say. In fact, she knew she didn't want to know.

"It'll keep. I'll talk to you tomorrow." He smiled and gave her a kiss, so tender she wanted to melt. His eyes on hers, he pulled back. "Don't keep Mandie waiting; she'll be complaining to Mack I monopolize all your time."

Emma rolled her eyes and leaned in to give him a quick kiss on his cheek. Ben turned slightly just in time to capture her mouth with his. He wasn't going to have any of this cheek business; when they kissed, he wanted both of them to know it had been a KISS!

Emma, a little wobbly now from the impact of his kiss, watched Ben as he went out the door before getting back to her daughter. She was both relieved and maybe a little disappointed that the pregnant moment had been cut short. Who knows what would have happened or what Ben might have said? But old fears resurfaced and Emma's insecurities taunted her. She knew in her heart she was better off not knowing, because she was just plain scared of what she feared he might have been going to say.

A muffled, "Mom? Mom? Are you there?" broke into her thoughts and Emma's attention snapped back to the phone in her hand.

"Yeah, Mand, I'm here."

"Where'd you go?"

"I was saying goodbye to Ben."

"Must have been some goodbye. Are you finished now? Do you have time for your daughter?"

"Don't be a wise-ass."

"Who? Me?"

"Yeah, you."

"Can't help it. I've learned from the best."

"Give me a break," Emma laughed.

"Okay, if you insist. But we both know what a good teacher you are."

"Mandie…"

"Oh, all right. Tell me about your weekend."

It was two hours later when Emma finally got off the phone. In addition to telling her story, Emma had to be filled in on the latest in Mandie's family's life and the most current escapades of little Miss Sydney who at the grand old age of three was starting to assert her personality and test the parental waters. The age-old battle was on and the time-out chair was seeing its fair share of Syd's little butt.

Emma hoped she wouldn't have to repeat the story again, but common sense told her that she'd be doing it at least two more times—once to her other daughter, Tracy and again to her son, Mack. Their calls should be coming in within the next few days, but for now she had a respite and wanted only to get into her big, comfortable bed and stay there, preferably unconscious, till morning. Cole was welcome to join her, which he did as soon as Emma put her pajamas on. He was, in fact, a bed hog and she had to push him over so she could even get in. Once sleeping positions were established, it took no more than five minutes for both of them to succumb to a deep, gonna-take-a-bomb-to-wake-them-up slumber.

\* \* \* \*

Meanwhile, Moira sat in bed, enveloped in darkness, propped up by a half dozen pillows. She was stewing, obviously upset and agitated to the point of being on the verge of leaping out of bed and pacing. She couldn't get the Newfie or its owner out of her mind. Her failure with them was driving her crazy. She was unraveling and couldn't seem to stop it. She had yet to come up with an alternative plan and it was becoming hard to concentrate on anything else. Everything she'd worked for for so long was in jeopardy because of her obsession with the pair. But she couldn't seem to help herself. She wanted to find out more about them, where they lived, how they lived. She wanted to know everything so she could see to their destruction. With her fractured mind churning furiously, she made plans to find some answers that weekend.

# Chapter Twenty-Five

Tuesday through Friday, business at the shop saw the usual crazy, almost-out-of-control yearly frenzy caused by holiday shoppers frantic in their desire to get ahead of the game. Emma and Joanie were hard pressed to keep up with it and the end of each day found them exhausted, a little out of sorts, and ready for an early bedtime. For them and most store owners it was a huge relief when Christmas was finally over.

However, on Tuesday, which had been their first day back after being gone for four days, the girls' normal sense of well-being had taken a dramatic turn downward. Shortly after opening the shop, Emma and Joanie, standing across from each other on opposite sides of the counter, had been scanning the sale receipts that had accumulated while they were away. Flipping through the slips from Thursday and Friday when Aunt Agnes and Mrs. Foster had covered, they noticed a few stick figures and what at first appeared to be mindless doodles mixed in with the product numbers and descriptions. At first it didn't register, but then realization slammed home with a terrifying foreboding. Both their heads snapped up and with wide knowing eyes the girls locked gazes. The same terrible sense of doom was reflected in their twin pained expressions.

Joanie broke the taut silence first. "Emma?"

"Yeah, Joanie…"

"You do see what I see, don't you?"

"Oh, yeah. I really wish I didn't, but unfortunately I do."

"Emma… how did this happen?"

"I don't have any idea."

"Are you sure?"

"Honest, I don't have a clue."

"We have to do something."

"I know."

"Right away,"

"It goes without saying."

"You're going to have to—"

"You don't have to say it. I'll have a talk with her."

"You'd better."

"I will."

"And quick, Em."

"I know."

"Real quick."

"Like the speed of light."

"Don't get cute with me, Em. If you don't, *I* will."

"Ohhh, no! Simmer down, Joan. I'll do it. I promise." A sit-down with her aunt was obviously in order. There were no two ways about it and the sooner the better. Emma had to wonder exactly who had taken whom under their wing. Was it Aunt Agnes or was it Tammy? Emma was a little afraid to find out, but she did know one thing. She had to keep Joanie out of it, or her dear sweet aunt could end up traumatized for the rest of her life!

"So, when?" Joanie persisited.

"Soon."

"How soon?"

"Very soon."

"How soon is very soon?" Joanie was like a woman possessed. The thought of having to deal with anything that even resembled a Tammy-influenced sales receipt was sending her beyond the normal parameters of logic and common sense.

"This week."

'When?"

"I don't know."

"Give me a day. I need a day."

"I don't know...Thursday. How's Thursday sound?"

"Thursday sounds good."

"Okay. Thursday's the day."

"Are you sure?"

"Yeah... I'll do it Thursday."

"You won't forget?"

"No, I won't forget."

"You promise?"

"Yeah, I promise."

"Okay... make sure you don't forget."

"I won't ...How's this? I'll tie a string around my finger, just in case."

Joanie narrowed her eyes and gave Emma a look that only a true friend could forgive. "Don't be a wise-ass."

"Not me."

"Yeah, right. Be serious, Em. This is important."

"I know and I swear I'll get it straightened out with Aunt Agnes."

"Okay," Joanie sighed. "I feel a little better now."

"Good. I'm glad to hear it."

Joanie's sense of well-being lasted all of about one second. "Wait!"

"Now what?"

"I just had a terrible thought."

"What?... Or on second thought, maybe I don't want to know."

"Oh, yes you do. Have you looked at any of Jackie's slips yet?"

"No, but what—"

"We'd better check them too, don't you think?"

"You don't think—"

"God, I hope not."

"All right, we'd better make sure I suppose, but I don't think we have anything to worry about."

"Right."

The girls quickly searched through the stack of receipts until they found those from Saturday and Sunday. They frantically pawed through each and every one of them. There were no drawings to be found, just plain-as-the-nose-on-your-face boring product numbers.

"Whew! Good old Jackie!. Thank God she hasn't been corrupted."

"I didn't really think she would be," Emma said.

"Yeah, well, you never know. This is like a friggin' virus. It could infect anybody. We have to nip it in the bud, Emma. Right now."

"I'm going to take care of it, Joanie."

"You have to do it, Em."

"I will."

"You'd better or so help me—"

"Yeah, yeah, I know. You'll quit. Like I believe you."

"Won't you be surprised when I don't show up one day."

"Promises, promises. Don't worry, I'll take care of it. I swear."

"If you don't you might as well cart me off to the nearest mental institution or set me up with Alcoholics Anonymous because I'll be drinking myself stupid."

"Although those two options might give me some sense of satisfaction, I don't think they'll be necessary. I'll take care of it."

"Bless you, Em. Just remember, my life is in your hands."

"Oh, goody."

The girls passed the rest of the day in peaceful accord since they were far too busy to give much additional thought to their pressing problem. Anything that distracted Joanie from what she considered a crisis in the making was a godsend for which Emma was eternally thankful.

\* \* \* \*

Emma did indeed have her little powwow with Aunt Agnes on Thursday. She'd gone over to her aunt and uncle's house on Lower East Hill Road in Colden after work; actually, she'd left a little early, squeezing her visit in before class started that night. After Cole had been fussed over and given a treat, Emma had gotten right to the heart of the matter.

"Um, Aunt Agnes, I noticed something a little different about the sales slips this time."

"Oh? What would that be, dear?"

"There was little drawings and doodles on some of them."

"There were? My, I don't seem to remember those."

"Yeah, as a matter of fact they were on quite a few of the receipts."

"Really."

"And they were only on the ones from the days you and Mrs. Foster were in the shop."

"Are you sure?"

"Uh-huh. What's going on?"

"Why, nothing, dear. Would you like something to eat?"

"No, thank you…Was Tammy in the shop with you?"

"Why would you ask, Emma?"

"Oh, no reason in particular, except that she likes to draw pictures on her receipts."

"She does? Now isn't that interesting. Would you care for something to drink? Soda? Water?"

"No, nothing, thank you. It is interesting, isn't it? Kind of a coincidence, don't you think?"

"It would seem so, yes. How's Ben, Emma?"

"He's fine."

"That's nice. You two getting along all right?"

"Yes, Aunt Agnes, we're doing just great. Now about those slips."

"I think you make a lovely couple. I'm so glad everything's going well."

"Aunt Agnes…"

"Do you think Cole would like another biscuit? He looks a little hungry."

Emma gave her aunt a look that told her she'd run out of wiggle room and it was time to 'fess up. In other words—no more bullshit. "What's going on, Aunt Agnes?"

Looking a little like she'd been caught with her hand in the cookie jar, her aunt confessed, "Tammy was in the shop."

"Yeah, I figured."

"But I didn't let her near the register."

"No, just the receipts. I don't have a problem with her at the register, Aunt Agnes. The money is always right. It's those damn sales slips."

"Don't swear, dear. Actually, Tammy didn't do the drawings; she just showed us how. She has a real talent for it, don't you think?"

"Yeah, she's got a real talent all right."

"But Mrs. Foster and I did all the drawings."

"Should I even bother to ask why?"

"Well, if you'd like, dear."

"All right. Why'd you feel you needed artwork on the receipts?"

"Well, it's simple, really. They just look so much cuter."

"Cuter?"

"Well, yes, you know, not so drab and businesslike."

"Oh, heaven forbid they should look businesslike."

"Now, Emma, don't be sarcastic." Emma rolled her eyes. "We still put all the stock numbers down, but it was ever so much fun to do the drawings. It really livened up the day."

"Well, thank God you put the numbers down too. I think Joanie would have committed suicide if you hadn't."

"Oh, Emma, don't be silly."

"I'm not, believe me."

"Well, if that's true, dear, then Joanie needs to chill out."

"Aw, geez."

"She tends to be a little too serious sometimes, don't you think?"

"Joanie? Are we talking about my partner, Joanie?"

"Well, who else, dear?" Emma just shook her head, trying to clear it. "She's a lovely person, don't get me wrong, but sometimes a little too intense. Why, the air fairly crackles around her."

"I'll agree with that one, she does crackle the air." If you only knew the half of it, Emma thought.

"Well, not to worry. You can set Joanie's mind at ease. We just decorated the slips up a bit."

"Make sure that's all you do, Aunt Agnes."

"Of course, dear."

"I'm serious, Aunt Agnes. Don't mess with those numbers."

"Never fear, sweetie. 'All's well that ends well'."

"Uh-huh." Emma didn't think Shakespeare would appreciate Aunt Agnes quoting him in this instance. She knew she didn't.

When Emma left she was far from convinced that she and Aunt Agnes were on the same page, but she'd take her aunt at her word, at least for now. Aunt Agnes's acquiescence in any given situation was historically unpredictable, so who knew if Emma's lecture had really gotten through. And if it had, would her aunt heed her warning or put her own interpretation on the mandate? They'd probably find out soon enough.

However, as far as Joanie was concerned, everything was shipshape, no problem, everything had been worked out. Emma was not about to tell her anything differently. It was best to keep Joanie in the dark about any niggling suspicions Emma might have had, letting peace reign for however long it would last.

\* \* \* \*

One of the bright spots of the week came on Friday when Emma received Molly's pedigree from the Millers. She'd picked up her mail at the post office before she'd ventured into the shop, so she'd barely had a chance to look it over before Joanie arrived.

"What's that?" Joanie had asked even before she'd taken her coat off.

"Molly's pedigree."

"How's it look?"

"I haven't really had a chance to do more than glance at it, but it looks like it'll be a good match. They've got some lines in common. They both have some great dogs behind them."

"Great! Now we can have a wedding!"

"A wedding?"

"Well, sure. I told you they were in love."

"Let's not get into that again. Remember, Joan, they're dogs."

"Yeah, yeah, whatever. We need to do something special for them."

"How about some extra treats?"

"No way! We need to do something romantic… maybe some flowers, a few scented candles burning, soft mus—" Joanie narrowed her eyes at Emma. "Wait a minute."

"What?"

"You are going to let them do this the old-fashioned way, aren't you?"

"I don't know."

"Oh, come on. Where's your sense of romance? We're talking about your boy becoming a man. We're talking about your boy doing it for the first time. Em, his first time! You cannot *not* let him know what it's all about."

"Joanie, we're talking about a dog, not a son and if it were a son I wouldn't be talking about it at all. I wouldn't even be thinking about it."

"Well, hell, I hope not. Geez! But let's get back to Cole. You can't have Cole's first time at stud ruined by doing it with AI. You just can't."

"You know it's the way a lot of breeding is done now. It's considered to be safer for both the bitch and the dog." AI or artificial insemination was indeed the preferred method of impregnating the bitch for many breeders in today's dog world.

"You said a lot. That doesn't mean all."

"I know what it means."

"Sooo… we're in the part that's not a lot. That means we should let Cole do it the natural way."

"We'll see."

"You have to let 'em, Em. They're both virgins; they'll have had all the tests to make sure they're healthy. Why not let 'em have a little fun and romance? It's un-American to deny them one of life's great pleasures."

"Un-American? They're dogs!"

"Doesn't make any difference. They live in America, so they're entitled."

"That's a unique argument even for you."

"What can I tell ya. I'm pulling out all the stops. Cole deserves it."

"I'll have to see what the Millers want to do."

Joanie, sensing Emma was weakening, saw only victory ahead. "Hell, don't worry about them. I'll make sure they make the right choice."

"Joanie, leave the Millers alone."

"No way. This is for our boy and the love of his life."

"Oh, Lord."

"Don't worry, I'll kill 'em with kindness. You'll see; I'm up to the job. I won't let you down. You can count on me."

Joanie's boastful reassurance did nothing to bolster Emma's peace of mind. Lord only knows what tactics she intended to use under the guise of kindness to make good on her claim and once Joanie set her course, there was no turning her back. With the sort of "help" she was offering, there might never be a breeding, regardless of the method chosen to facilitate it.

So, with that festering little problem newly wedged in the back of their minds, plus the stress of an extremely busy week, not to mention the Aunt Agnes fiasco, by the time Saturday rolled around, neither Emma nor Joanie (they both worked the weekends during the holiday rush) was in the mood to deal with a new customer who was proving to be a cantankerous, ill-tempered, demanding harridan. To put it in terms of the vernacular, the woman was a total bitch—and not in the doggy sense of the word.

She'd bulldozed her way into the shop like a battleship plowing through rough water on the high seas. She even

340

looked the part. She was big and she was gray! Physically, she was both tall (she had to go at least six foot) and wide (the girls guessed she must have weighed in at an easy 300 lbs.). Yikes! We're talking mucho big! To put it bluntly she was built like a brick shithouse!

Add to the immenseness of the woman the fact that she was entirely gray from her gun-metal gray hair, which was pulled back so severely into a tightly wound bun that her eyes were slanted, to her size-twelve feet housed in light gray shoes. All of her clothing, coat, sweater, blouse, and pants were some shade of gray. Even her purse and glasses' frames were gray. Not a living soul on this earth could ever accuse the woman of dressing flamboyantly. Of course, no one would ever live long enough to get the comment entirely out of their mouth if she was within hearing distance.

Unlike the "Gray Ghost" of the dog world, this woman was ponderous and heavy on her feet; merchandise was shaking on the shelves as she walked by. She had the agility and gracefulness of a Sherman tank and that was saying a lot.

Instinctively, the girls had tried to give her a wide berth the minute they'd spotted her cruising down an aisle. She'd looked like she could and would roll over anything and anyone that got in her way. Not wanting to be counted among the floating wreckage, the girls had taken cover behind the checkout counter. The ploy hadn't worked, however. The woman had steered a straight course right for them and the girls were now in danger of being swamped in her wake as she demanded personalized service as if it were her due. Damn! It looked like they'd been successfully shanghaied.

*　*　*　*

She couldn't find the house! She'd been up and down the damn road for miles going on five times now and she still couldn't find it.

She'd started out early—about 8:00. It'd taken her a little over an hour and a half to get in the area and she'd wasted another forty minutes or so trying to find the blasted house. The directions she'd taken off the computer map site hadn't been any help since there was no house where the map indicated there should be one. The only thing standing in the spot where the house was supposed to be was a big pine tree. On top of that, she knew she wouldn't be able to get directions from anyone at the post office she kept passing because of that stupid Privacy Act that was now law. Not wanting to waste any more time on this so-far-fruitless search, she realized the only sensible thing for her to do was to stop at some local place of business and ask for help.

Easier said than done. There weren't any gas stations around, the pizza place didn't look like it was open yet, and the bar down the road was certainly closed. It became apparent she was going to have to go back to the one place she knew had to be open judging from the lighted windows and the cars in the lot—the shop next door to the post office. Lord knows it wouldn't have been her first choice, too public, too many people inside who might remember seeing her. But what choice did she have? She was running out of options. She certainly couldn't go knocking on doors, nor could she just keep driving around for God knows how long and still not find Rogers' house.

She pulled into the next driveway she came to and turned around, heading back to the store.

\* \* \* \*

The battleship-Sherman tank-brick shithouse woman was demanding the girls' total attention and Joanie was ready to blow. After the first few shouted questions and resulting commands to go fetch this or that, the girls had thought it might be in their best interest if they followed her around rather than listen to her bellow across the room.

The only problem was, this put Joanie in close proximity to the woman. Way too close for comfort to Emma's way of thinking. Emma herself had retreated a few steps behind Joanie due in part to the fact that the woman reminded her a little too much of her bunion-bestowing grandmother and childhood defense mechanisms sprang to the forefront. Best to keep some distance just in case.

Nevertheless, Emma needed to watch Joanie like a hawk. Joanie had already given the woman's back the one-finger salute and Emma had had to slap her hand down before the woman noticed. Joanie had retaliated by sticking her tongue out, first at Emma and then the battleship. She'd barely gotten her tongue back in her mouth when the woman had turned around to bark out a question. Christ! It was like baby-sitting a two-year old! Thank God there weren't many other customers in the shop. Those who were there were regulars and while they commiserated with the girls' predicament on one level, they were finding the whole situation vastly amusing on another. Turncoats, Emma thought; wait till they see how funny it is when their wine's been cut off.

They made steady progress down one aisle and up the next, the Gray Mountain making demands at nearly every display. She had yet to buy anything though and Joanie's patience was hurtling downward at breakneck speed. She had in fact, graduated—well, maybe "regressed" is a better word—to making devil's horns behind the woman's head every chance she got. Emma was seriously considering laying a bitch-slap on her.

And what were the girls' devoted, loyal, steadfast, love-you-till-I-die four-footed friends doing while all this was going on? Well, they were sitting on their butts, watching the whole spectacle and grinning from ear to ear. Cole, as usual, was being a gentleman about it. He might be enjoying Emma's predicament, but he wasn't going to gloat. It was enough that Emma knew he found it amusing. Tank, on the other hand... well, that was another story.

Tank's smile might appear to be innocent to someone who was unacquainted with the little dog, but to those who knew him, they recognized the devilish satisfaction behind it. The looks he directed toward Joanie had a clear message—let's see you get out of this one 'cause I'm not going to help you. He wasn't going to lift a paw and Joanie knew it right down to her toes, so she shot him a look that told Tank she didn't need his help and he could just stuff it.

Not to be outdone, Tank gave Joanie a raised eyebrow in return, which told Joanie he was giving her a "heh, heh, heh," and probably "the finger" to boot. She narrowed her eyes at him, but would have to take her revenge later. Right now she had enough on her hands dealing with the Gray Whale and warding off Emma's slaps.

\* \* \* \*

Moira Spenser had entered the shop with every intention of going straight to the checkout counter, getting the information she needed, and beating a hasty retreat, but she pulled up short and ducked down the next aisle when she saw who was following a rather large woman down the same aisle she had just been in. It was her, Emma Rogers, the very person whose house she was trying to find, and in front of her was the same friend who'd been with her at the show. What were they doing here? Her initial shock gave way to near panic before she forced herself to calm down. She couldn't let them see her on the off chance they might remember her from the dog show, but she had to find out what was going on.

She kept carefully hidden behind displays while she observed the three women. It was obvious one of them was a customer and from the looks of it she was driving the other two a little nuts. That must mean that Emma and her friend either worked there or owned the place.

She was so intent on observing the threesome she didn't see another woman moving in the same aisle that she had gone to and ended up running into her.

"Oh, I'm so sorry. Please excuse me. I wasn't looking where I was going," she apologized, keeping her voice lowered.

"Oh, no problem. Neither was I. I was so focused on what was going on with Emma and Joanie that I wasn't paying any attention to what I was doing," the customer laughed.

"Emma and Joanie?" she questioned.

"Yeah, the owners. They've got one doozy of a problem on their hands."

"Oh, you mean the other woman with them. Is she a customer?"

"Afraid so. And I bet they hope she never comes back."

"That bad, huh?"

"Yep. You can bet they'll be hitting the wine once she leaves."

"From what I've seen, I don't blame them."

"Yeah, neither do I."

The two women separated, the regular customer going one way, Moira going the other. She stayed at a safe distance and continued to observe for a few more minutes. She hadn't found out where Emma lived, but she knew where she worked and even that she owned the place. That would be enough.

She was about to turn and leave the building when the big Newfoundland came into view. He was sitting with another dog. Damn if it wasn't that son of a bitch that had tipped the soda can over! God, they were all right here! Her mind hurtled over the possibilities that now presented themselves. This discovery was almost too good to be true.

A loud crash brought her back to the reality of where she was, making her jump in surprise. A large painted tin watering can had fallen from its perch on top of a hutch when the bothersome customer had tried to take it down. She would have liked to stay and watch what would happen next, but it was definitely time to go. She didn't want to risk being seen. Not now.

She stepped back and turned around, strolling nonchalantly toward the exit, feigning mild interest in the merchandise she passed by. She slipped out, closing the door quietly behind her. Breathing in the cold, crisp air, she allowed herself a moment of triumph and went to her car.

# Chapter Twenty-Six

Joanie and Emma never noticed the quiet retreat of the slender, pretty woman who'd slipped unnoticed out the door. They never even knew she'd been there. They were oblivious to anything that was going on in the shop other than the clamoring of their obnoxious customer who loomed over them like a giant gray thundercloud and whose roaring, grating voice had certainly come straight from the depths of Hades. Emma was sure she'd be hearing it in her sleep for the next month.

After the watering can had come crashing down, Joanie had been ready to tell the woman off in terms that would have shocked most of their friends (well, maybe not), but Emma had clamped a hand over her mouth before the vile words could be spewed forth. All Emma wanted to do now was get the woman out of the shop and keep Joanie from landing them in the middle of a lawsuit or worse, like jail.

She succeeded in doing what seemed to be nearly impossible about an hour later. The woman who was still alive and healthy (a miracle in itself) was gone, having purchased a grand total of $11.35 worth of merchandise. The police were no nearer their doorstep than they had been before the hulking woman from hell had darkened their store and the girls were in no danger of becoming jail bait. All in all it had been a successful coup on Emma's part.

At the moment, Joanie was slouched in a chair behind the counter, her posture proclaiming that she'd gone boneless. "I'm wiped out, Em. That battle-ax did me in. Thank the powers that rule the universe she's gone. Not that they were any help."

"Yeah, really. Where the hell are they when you need 'em?"

"Not anywhere near us, that's for damn sure."

"Geez, I didn't think she was ever going to leave."

"Me either. Let's hope she *never* comes back."

"Amen to that!"

"Think about it. We had to take all that crap for a lousy $11.35. Forget it; no way was it worth it. I'm blackballing her. She's never to be allowed back in this store."

"And how're you going to accomplish that?"

"I'm not quite sure yet, but give me a little time. I'll come up with something."

"I have no doubt, but will it be legal?"

"Who knows and who cares. Don't concern yourself. I just know that I am never, ever going to deal with that woman again… I need some wine."

"I've been waiting for that announcement," Emma said, giving Joanie a raised eyebrow.

"Don't be giving me that eyebrow thing, Miss Emma Smarty-pants. If I know you and I do, you'll want some too."

"I can see there's no fooling you," Emma said tongue-in-cheek. "Bring it on. I'll order lunch. We deserve a treat after the morning we've had."

The girls had their lunch in front of them twenty minutes later and had started on their second glass of wine. The first one had gone down like water. Trauma like they'd been through that morning was bound to make them thirsty. They were savoring the second glass with their meal, which was one of their favorites, a potato pizza.

Now that bit of culinary magic may sound a bit strange, but it was by far one of the best taste treats around. A thin coating of olive oil was spread across a thick crust of dough and then slices of fresh tomatoes, chunks of cooked potato, sliced mushrooms, Italian herbs and spices, and coarsely-grated parmesan cheese were placed on top and baked to perfection. Mmm, Mmm, Mmm!

The two piggies ate every last crumb and it was no small pizza! They got even with the dogs for their lack of help by not giving them a single bite. From Cole and Tank's point of view, sometimes the girls' payback was akin to cruel and unusual punishment. This was one of those times and if there had been anyone around to assist them, they would have filed a complaint with the local chapter of the ASPCA. However, they were far from powerless, especially Tank, and of course, as far as he was concerned this was far from over. Determined little devil that he was, he'd get the last payback in yet and probably when Joanie least expected it.

The remainder of the day was busy, but normal with nothing else occurring to upset the precarious balance of two women who were a little tipsy from their earlier dip into the soothing nectar of the fermented grape. It had taken the consumption of three somewhat large glasses of the golden ambrosia before they'd felt themselves soothed enough to continue with the rest of the day and by the time they closed up and went home they were still mellow and in good spirits.

The only downside to drinking *that* early in the day that the girls could see was that it made them really tired. Why the hell that happened was anybody's guess, but that's the way it was. Why alcohol didn't affect them in a like manner in late afternoon or evening had been reason for serious contemplation at one time in their lives (naturally, they'd been drinking when the rumination had taken hold). But since the answer had eluded them (in the condition they were in at the time, a herd of elephants would have eluded them) they gave it up as one of the many mysteries of life that was bound to drive you stark raving mad if you thought about it long enough. So it was best to accept things the way they were and not get themselves in an uproar over something they really didn't want an answer to anyway. If there was any scientific reasoning behind it, they could have cared less. It suited their purposes much more to delve into the mystical side of things when it applied to their wine and had therefore concluded that it was not their place to question, but rather to accept and enjoy the benefits of drink no matter the time of day it was consumed and to stoically suffer any adverse consequences brought on by their imbibing. What a crock! But they could feed you a really good line, couldn't they?

Anyway, it was no surprise to Emma that after dinner she caught herself falling asleep. The book she'd been reading slipped from her fingers and landed on the broad back of her faithful dog that was lying next to the couch she was stretched out on. Cole only opened one eye in response to the thud on his body and then drifted back into a light doze.

\* \* \* \*

They didn't have any plans for the evening, but Ben needed to see Emma. They'd only talked on the phone twice since Monday and their conversations had been rather short and impersonal. He had a feeling that Emma was pulling back, putting a little distance between them after what had happened, or not happened Monday night.

He'd been aware of the panic in her eyes and the rigidity of her body in the moments before the phone rang. She'd been afraid of what he'd been going to say. It was obvious to him that she wasn't ready to hear that he loved her and wanted her for his own.

He knew how badly Emma had been hurt by her husband's unfaithfulness. The emotional devastation she'd suffered from the subsequent divorce had been painful and long-lived. And even though she'd never admitted it to him, he knew she was afraid to let herself love again. During the time they'd spent together over the past six months, it had become clear to Ben that when Emma loved, she loved with her whole being and in so doing left herself wide open for heartache should her love and trust be misplaced. He also knew it would be extremely difficult for her to accept love from someone because of her insecurities and fear of betrayal. To place herself in such a vulnerable position would be almost impossible for her to do at this point. But he was determined to show her that she could trust him; he loved her and wanted to spend the rest of his life with her.

His own protective walls had come tumbling down almost from the instant he'd first been introduced to her that day in May when he'd gone into the shop to buy his niece a birthday gift. There had just been something about her that had gone straight to his heart and even though he'd been surprised and mystified by his reaction to her, he hadn't fought it. Their sexual attraction had been instantaneous and their relationship these past months had only served to intensify his feelings for her. He loved everything about Emma and if he had to clamp down on his feelings and not declare himself just yet so she wouldn't be scared off, then that's what he'd do.

But right now he was going over to see the lady he loved, whether or not she wanted to see him.

*   *   *   *

Cole heard the now familiar rumble of Ben's car motor coming up the hill. With ears pricked, he sat up quickly and looked at Emma. She was still sleeping. He got up and paced to the door; Ben had parked the Jeep and was walking

351

toward the house. Cole looked at Emma again; she hadn't stirred. Not wanting the peal of the doorbell to awaken her, Cole opened the door just as Ben stepped onto the porch.

Ben spied the sleeping Emma as soon as he looked through the open doorway. Ruffling Cole's ears in greeting with one hand and bringing the index finger of the other hand to his lips, he shushed the big Newfie to be quiet. Cole gave him a look that said, "Oh, brother! What do you think I've been trying to get across to *you*?" Disgusted, Cole gave a muffled snort and went into the kitchen for a drink of water.

\* \* \* \*

Emma was having the most delicious dream about Ben. It seemed so real. She thought she could actually feel his body heat hovering over her and could smell the scent of his cologne in the air. When she felt his lips upon her own she whimpered and reached reflexively for more. It took full body contact before her eyes fluttered open and she realized that the man of her dreams was indeed there in the flesh. And was he ever!

"Mmm. What are you doing here?" Emma asked, putting her arms around Ben.

"What does it look like?" He shifted his weight and snuggled his body closer to Emma's.

"It looks like you're trying to take advantage of an unconscious woman."

"Does it now?" Ben moved his hips, gently forcing Emma's legs apart so he could settle into the V her body had created.

"Yes, it does," she smiled, her arousal going from a simmer to a full boil.

"Hmmm. Well, you're not unconscious now."

"No, I'm not, am I?"

"Nope."

"Then I think you should have your wicked way with me."

"No need to say more."

Ben captured her mouth in a scorching kiss and the world instantly floated away. The two lovers missed the amused look that Cole gave them before he ambled into the mudroom and went into his crate. Flopping down on the comfortable crate mat, he puffed out a long-suffering sigh; it looked like it was going to be a while before he got any attention from his beloved mistress.

\* \* \* \*

Later that same night, all four windows on the front of the store were smashed and the tableau on the decorated porch viciously vandalized.

# Chapter Twenty-Seven

"What the hell happened here?" Joanie screeched. "Jesus! It looks like a bomb went off."

It was quarter to ten on Sunday morning. Two hours before the shop would normally open on a Sunday. Joanie had just gotten there and was shocked at the damage done to the store. Emma had arrived about fifteen minutes before her partner, alerted to the problem by one of their regular customers who'd seen the destruction while driving by on her way to church and had called Emma on her cell phone. Emma had had a bit more time to pull herself together than Joanie and was focused now on the practicalities of what needed to be done.

"I've already called the sheriff's department. They'll be here any minute," Emma said. "Don't touch anything."

"I'm calling Sam. I don't believe this shit. Who would have done this?"

"I don't know, but they sure did a good job. Every window's broken and the stuff on the porch, well, most of it's ruined."

"What a friggin' mess. Look at the poor trees. They had to wreck the trees? What assholes!"

"Ben'll be here in a few minutes. I called him as soon as I saw the damage. He's going to take care of the windows. I guess he'll have to board 'em up 'til we can get a window guy in here."

Joanie started dialing the phone. "Son of a bitch! When I get my hands— Yeah, Sam. Come down to the shop right away, will you? We've got a big problem… What's wrong? I'll tell you what's wrong. Some asshole broke all our windows and wrecked everything on the porch… Yeah, really…Okay, see ya in a few."

"Sam's on his way?"

"Yeah… Look at this glass; it's all over everything."

"I know; it must have sprayed back a good fifteen, twenty feet."

"We'll be cleaning it up forever, probably into June."

"And then we'll still miss some."

"Damn… Hey, where's the big guy?" Joanie asked, looking around.

"Who? You mean Cole? He's in the back room and probably none too happy about it."

"I would imagine."

"After I saw there was glass all over the porch, I came in through the back door. I thought it would be best to keep him in the back room until I saw how bad it was in here. I'm glad I did; there's glass all over the place."

"You're not kidding. I didn't look real close on the way in, but I hope it's not as bad out there as it is in here."

"There's not as much, but it's bad enough."

"Crap. I wish we could get started on the cleanup. I hate just standing around."

"Me too, but we have to wait 'til the sheriffs get finished."

"Lord only knows how long that's going to take."

"I know, but we don't have much choice, Joanie. We have to let them do their job if we hope to find out who did this."

"I know; you're right. It's just that I need to do something."

"Believe me, I know how you feel." Preoccupied as she was, it took Emma till then to realize they were missing one four-footed friend. "Umm… hey, Joanie. Should I ask?"

"Ask what?"

"Where your bosom buddy is."

"Bosom buddy? Who would you be talking about? Surely not the dog I live with. No. The creature that resides in the same house as I do is none other than the devil incarnate himself, wreaking havoc and disaster at will."

"*O-kaaay*, I'll go along with that, but where is he?"

"Home. He may never see the light of day again."

"How come?"

"He's being punished."

"For what? What'd he do?"

"For being smarter than I am, goddammit."

"And how'd he prove that?"

Joanie gave her a long look. "You're a real friend."

"I know."

"I'm being sarcastic."

"Really? I would've never guessed…Come on, spit it out. I'm dying of curiosity. How'd he best you this time?"

"You're just asking for it, aren't you?"

Emma gave a little sideways bob of her head, which along with the infamous raised eyebrow said, "Whatever."

"All right. Look at me. What don't you see?"

"Where am I supposed to be looking?"

Joanie closed her eyes in frustration. "At me! Look at me! Look at my body. What don't you see?"

Emma gave Joanie the once-over and then she did it a second time. "I don't know. What don't I see?"

"Cripe, you're as bad as Sam… If you'll look closely, oh, blind one, you will notice that I am not—and I repeat, not—wearing my favorite bracelet. You know, the one I *love*, the one I wear *everyday*, the one *Sam* gave me for my fortieth birthday."

"Oh, that one."

"Yeah, that one."

"It's gone?"

"Yeah, and that, my dense friend, is the problem."

"Ohhh."

"Yeah, ohhh. The little shithead hid it, dammit all."

"You can't find it?"

"Am I not getting through to you? Are you suddenly not able to understand English? Of course I can't find it. What do you think? I'm mad 'cause I did find it."

"Well, no."

"You're damn right 'no'. I searched every nook and cranny in that flippin' house and I still can't find it. But that's not the worst part."

"What could be worse than losing the bracelet?"

"The fact that the little weasel actually rubbed my nose in it. You know what he did? Do you want to know what he did?"

"I'm not sure that I do, but I'll bet there's no way of stopping you from telling me."

"*Pfff*, get real… You know where I keep the bracelet when I take it off, don't you?"

"Yeah, on top of your dresser in that little china dish. The one that's got the purple thistles painted on it… I always liked that dish."

"Yeah, yeah, me too, that's why I have it. Well, like always, that's where I put my bracelet last night when I was getting ready for bed. But when I came out of the bathroom, it was gone and Tank, my supposedly devoted—"

"Yeah, devoted to mayhem," Emma interrupted.

"—canine friend was sitting on top of my dresser with his paw plunked right in the middle of the dish with that goddamn shit-eating grin on his face."

"Oh, brother." Emma put her hand to her head and closed her eyes. These two were going to be the deaths of each other yet, she thought. "So what'd you do?"

"To Tank?"

"Mmm, yeah, that would be who I was asking about."

"Not a whole hell of a lot. What was I going to do other than rant and rave and make a complete ass of myself. He was just waiting for me to do that, you know. But I wasn't going to give him the satisfaction. I kept my mouth shut, and believe me, it was really hard. In fact, I bit my cheek; it's still sore. Anyway, I simply scooped him off the dresser and put him in his crate. Let me tell you, he didn't like that one little bit."

"Oh, I bet he didn't," Emma agreed sarcastically. "Whew! What a payback! It boggles the mind. Joanie, what can I say, you rule."

Joanie squinted her eyes at Emma, not quite sure how she should take her friend's comments. "You wouldn't be making fun of me, would you?"

"Perish the thought," Emma said, rolling her eyes. No wonder Tank comes out on top nine out of ten times, Emma mused. "So what'd you do then, tear your house apart searching for the bracelet?"

"Yeah, for hours."

"And had no luck finding it."

"Nope. I don't where he hid it, but it's a damn good spot."

"It'll turn up."

"Yeah, when Mr. Wicked Dog decides to give it back."

"Exactly."

Joanie looked at her friend and then slumped. "Em?"

"Yeah?"

"He did it again, didn't he?"

"Afraid so."

"Made a fool out of me, huh?"

"Yep."

"Even though I didn't scream at him, right?"

"Right."

"Where'd I go wrong?"

"Don't you know?"

"Nope."

"You never should have looked for the bracelet, you dope."

"Damn! I knew it. I knew I shouldn't have looked. I knew I should have listened to that little voice in my head that kept telling me, 'Don't look, don't look'."

"Yeah, you should have listened."

"I know, but I couldn't help myself. The urge was too great. It blocked out reason and everything else. I was a maniac."

"I have no trouble believing that."

"Yeah, well, it's not like I wasn't provoked."

"Per usual."

"So now what?"

"He'll give it back when he's ready."

"Let's hope… Em, I was so close, so close to beating him at his own game." Joanie glanced hopefully at her friend for a sign of confirmation. "I was, wasn't I?"

"No, you weren't, you poor deluded creature," Emma scoffed. "Quit kidding yourself."

"Not even a little close?"

"No."

Joanie puffed out a big breath. "Let me pretend, all right? It's all I have."

"You've got that part right."

Any further journey into Joanie's fantasy world was cut short by the simultaneous arrival of Sam and Erie County

Deputy Sheriff Tim O'Connor. The two men were shaking hands as they stepped through the front door.

"Joanie, Emma, good to see you again," the sheriff said in greeting. "Too bad it's under unpleasant circumstances."

"Hi, Tim. Thanks for coming," Joanie said, then crossed over to Sam and gave him a kiss. "Hi, hon. What a mess, huh?"

"Yeah, big time."

"It was like this when you came in this morning?" O'Connor asked, looking around.

"Yeah, we've been careful not to touch anything."

"'Preciate it. Let me get the unit in here and they can do their thing. We'll dust for finger prints, but I doubt we'll find anything. Whoever did it probably had gloves on if for no other reason than it was cold last night. Can you tell if anything was stolen?"

"We haven't looked really close yet, but I don't think so, sheriff," Emma said. "It looks like whoever did it just wanted to smash stuff up."

"All right. After we get through, I'll have you do a thorough inspection. I'll get started now, so if you'll excuse me…" The sheriff turned toward the door and spoke over his shoulder. "If you haven't already done so, you might want to call your insurance agent."

"We will sheriff and thank you."

"Thanks, Tim," Sam said. "Let me walk you out." Both men went out to the squad car where they huddled in conversation for a few minutes. Then the sheriff got on his radio and Sam came back inside.

"So? What'd you two come up with?" Joanie asked her husband.

"We just discussed the possibilities."

"Of what?"

"Who might have done this."

"And…"

"At first glance, it looks like kids."

"Yeah, but we've never had any trouble before."

"I know, but still. It looks like criminal mischief. You know, it's the same old story. Kids get bored, they do a little underage drinking, they look for some thrills and presto, they cause some kind of trouble."

"Does Tim have anybody in mind?"

"O'Connor says he knows a couple of teenage boys in the area who get into trouble quite frequently. They'll be at the top of his list."

Just then Ben hurried in, said hello to Sam and Joanie, and gave Emma a hug. After getting the full story, he took a quick look at the shattered windows and figured out what he needed to secure the front of the building. Next thing the girls knew, both men were piling into Sam's truck to go to the local lumber yard down on Route 16.

"Well that was fast."

"They didn't waste any time, did they?"

"Nope. They're on a mission."

"Too bad I can't get Sam to move that fast all the time," Joanie complained.

"What fun would that be? You wouldn't have anything to bitch about."

"Oh, ye of little faith, shame on you. I can always find something to bitch about."

"Hell, don't I know it… Listen, I'm going to take Cole up to the house before I do anything else. He's miserable being locked in the back room. He'll be happier at home. I'll be back in a few minutes."

"Take your time. It's not like we can do anything for a while. I'll call our insurance agent while you're gone. I probably won't get anybody since it's Sunday, but I'll leave a message."

"All right, I'll be back soon." Emma went to the back room and rescued the big Newfie. He was overjoyed to be let out of his "prison" so to speak, no matter how many toys were in there. The back room didn't hold quite the same appeal when there was no Tank to play with and the door was closed. He didn't like having a barrier between himself and Emma.

Emma took her time walking up the hill. Joanie was right; there wasn't anything they could do yet except sit around and go a little crazy with frustration. So she enjoyed the brisk air and the golden sunlight that filtered through the now denuded trees. The sky was crystalline blue with only a trace of clouds forming scalloped lines here and there and the wind, a mere whisper of movement that Emma could feel brushing her cheeks occasionally. Snow from the previous storm had almost all melted, but where it still remained it glittered like diamonds in the bright sunshine.

When they reached the house, Emma led Cole out back and they had a game of "keep away" before she took him inside. In the mudroom, Emma toweled Cole off, concentrating on those big, webbed feet, then gave him a couple treats. He accepted them eagerly, the chewing and swallowing taking no longer than a second or two.

Intending to put Cole in his crate, she opened the door and motioned him in. Cole took one look and sat down, sending Emma a direct message that was impossible to misinterpret. He wasn't having any of it; no way was he going in that crate. Hadn't he just been released from a closed room? A room he could have gotten out of if he'd had a mind to. But he hadn't opened that door simply because Emma hadn't him wanted to. Now, however, he wasn't about to get shut into another confined space. Not right now, anyway. He was staying with Emma.

Emma tried to get him up—no dice. She tried to sweet talk him; he didn't fall for that either. She tempted him with more treats; he locked his jaw. Exasperated, she gave it up. "I'm not going to get you in there, am I?

363

Cole only cocked his head and looked Emma square in the eye.

"Yeah, I didn't think so. All right, come on. But you have to stay where I put you at the shop. I don't want you getting hurt. Understand?"

Cole woofed and sprang up onto all fours, quickly heading for the door. Emma caught up and the two of them headed back down to the store.

Joanie didn't seem at all surprised to see the returning Cole. "Wouldn't stay home without you, would he?"

"Nope."

"I could have told you he wouldn't."

"Then why didn't you?"

"It was more fun this way."

"Fun for whom?"

"For me, of course."

"Right, I should have known that," Emma said acerbically. "You mind telling me why it was so much fun for you?"

"Nope, not at all, but you might not appreciate it as much as I do."

"Try me."

"Okay... but remember who we are as individuals and who we live with."

"All right..."

"Well, if you keep those things in mind, you should be able to understand how really great it was for me to see someone other than myself go down in defeat in the battle of wits."

Emma thought about that for a minute. "I'm glad I could make your day."

"You did, believe me. Thank you very much."

"Anytime. I live to serve."

"It's deeply appreciated."

It was close to one-thirty before the sheriff's department cleared out and the girls could start cleaning up. Upon closer inspection they could discern that nothing had been stolen and had relayed that information to Deputy O'Connor. Sam and Ben were back with the needed plywood and were busy nailing it up. The lack of windows on the front of the building was going to make the shop really dark and gloomy. Hopefully, they could get the windows replaced this week, but with Thanksgiving on Thursday, they might not be able to. The girls planned on calling the glazier first thing Monday morning.

While Emma had been at the house, Joanie had wisely made and put up a large sign declaring the shop temporarily closed on the side of the building facing the parking lot, but people had still been pulling in and had to be turned away at the door. The girls told everyone the shop would be open as usual on Tuesday morning at 10:00. Wouldn't you know it, one of the customers that had to be turned away was none other than Angie Newmann. Damn! They couldn't get a break! They knew all too well she'd be back on Tuesday, probably waiting at the front door hours before they opened. The black cloud was definitely hovering.

Emma and Joanie cleaned up inside and out for the rest of the day, salvaging what they could from the destruction on the porch. The men worked right alongside the girls and Ben volunteered to get more trees the next day to replace the ones that had been so cruelly uprooted and damaged beyond saving. By the time they called it quits it was 6:30 and they'd done all they could. Somebody suggested having dinner at the Hearthmoor; it didn't take any longer than five minutes for the shop to be closed and for everybody, including Cole, to be in their cars and on the way.

\* \* \* \*

Moira was going to bed early tonight, the exertion and late hours of the night before catching up with her. She could hardly keep her eyes open, and it was only 7:00. But it had been worth it; she'd accomplished a great deal. After she ate a light meal, which she was busy preparing now, she'd take a relaxing bath and go straight to bed. She'd probably only need one sleeping pill she was so tired. Her eyes fluttered shut for a moment and she sighed. Between her exhaustion and the capsule of white powder she would take, she was assured a peaceful night.

# Chapter Twenty-Eight

Monday was anything but a day off, starting with the many phone calls the girls had to make first thing in the morning. The call to their insurance agent was rather straightforward; he'd be out on Tuesday to file the claim and take a look at the police report. The search to find a glazier, well that took a little more doing and a lot more phone calls. The girls finally found one who would commit himself to replacing the windows that week and they scheduled him for Wednesday.

Ben was at the shop by ten, fully armed with six new Douglas firs. He helped the girls put the smaller trees in baskets and the two larger ones in the copper boilers, which had gotten a little banged up in the Saturday night carnage.

Joanie had flown via her speeding truck to the Wal-Mart in Springville earlier that morning and picked up more lights and waxed apples. The rusted ornaments had survived the onslaught for the most part and were ready to be put back on the trees.

The pine boughs and silk baby's breath from the window boxes had been scattered amidst the debris, but were otherwise unharmed. The pinecones had either been thrown around the parking lot or ground into pieces so the girls had gone into Emma's woods and found new ones. Along with the new apples, they were able to put the window boxes back together quite easily.

Most of the wooden figures that had stood on the porch were broken, however, and the girls were going to have to make new ones. Some of the baskets had been crushed, so the girls replaced them with ones they'd had in the back room.

The large balsam wreath had been snatched off the door and flung over by the creek that ran alongside the post office side of the building. It only took a little dusting off for it to look good as new. The garland that had been wrapped around the railing, however, was a complete loss and the girls thought they'd just give it a quick burial and forego replacing it.

The lighted wire deer were mangled beyond repair and Sam had been sent on the hunt for new ones, which he'd be lucky to find this late in the season. His other job was to get new flag poles. All six had been snapped in half. He was going to have to travel all the way into Depew to a flag store at Transit and Broadway to buy them. The girls didn't expect to see him until late afternoon if then. It was within the realm of possibility that Sam's quest could take him far longer—like into the evening or even the next day. In all likelihood he was not going to be a happy man by the time he finally did get home.

Of notable absence throughout the day was one adorable (?) little terrier who at times went by certain names that should not be repeated in the presence of children. It would appear that the little hellion had not as yet revealed the location of one missing bracelet and until he did, his banishment was to continue. The question now was, who was going to hold out longer? Joanie, who was trying to be a hard-ass, or Tank, who had on numerous occasions already proven he was smarter than she was. Common sense said to put your money on Tank.

Despite the war of the worlds being played out behind the scenes, at day's end pretty much everything was back as it had been with the exception of the wooden figures and their replacements were now in the drying stage on the floor of the back room. Tomorrow the girls would assemble and decorate the Santas and snowmen, and put them in their place on the porch.

Sam had been successful in his hunt for deer, although it had taken seven hours and ten different stores to accomplish his mission; the woodland creatures were now lit and posed amongst the trees. Sam had let it be known with a look that in no way could be misconstrued that he expected compensation for his trouble at home that night; Emma thought Joanie had better be prepared to open the gates of hell.

Lastly, the flags had been put on their new poles and were once again flapping in the gentle breeze that was blowing through the valley. All in all, the porch looked pretty damn good.

\* \* \* \*

The late nights were getting to Moira. She was ready to drop. It was almost 2:30 in the morning and she was only now going up to bed. She wondered fleetingly if she had what it took to finish what she'd started. Trudging slowly up the stairs to her bedroom, she was almost too tired to care.

Entering the room, she fell on the bed and crawled under the blankets. Tonight she didn't have the energy to even bother changing into her nightgown. Snuggling into her pillow she closed her eyes, but in the next instant they flew open as an image danced across her consciousness.

It was the big Newfoundland, the one she couldn't seem to get to. In her warped mind, he'd become the embodiment of the evil that had robbed her of everything. Instead of visualizing the benign countenance common to the breed, her twisted brain had transformed his gentle face into the snarling, snapping, vicious jaws of her attackers. She cried out and sat up quickly, shaking her head vigorously to chase the effigy away.

She swallowed hard and leaned back against the headboard. She had to get hold of herself. Everything was going just as she'd planned and the end result was very close at hand now. She had to hold it together for a little while longer. It would be a struggle getting through the next few days, but with success so near, she had to do it. She couldn't fail now.

She rubbed her burning eyes. She was so tired. The dark smudges under her eyes seemed to be permanent fixtures. She slid down until her head was once again cradled by the pillow. She tentatively lowered her eyelids and held herself very still. Nothing happened. She gradually relaxed by small increments and after what seemed an eternity, fell into a light sleep. She stayed that way until morning.

# Chapter Twenty-Nine

Tuesday brought another unwelcome surprise. Busy with getting the wood figures assembled and answering the questions of their inquisitive customers, Emma and Joanie didn't at first notice that the phone was unusually quiet, especially for the time of year it was. They didn't realize anything was wrong until about 11:30 when Emma tried to put a call through to the insurance agent because he hadn't shown up yet. That was when they found out the phone was deader than a doornail. And if the phone was dead it not only meant they couldn't make or receive calls, it also meant they couldn't process any sales purchased with credit cards. Up to that point, they'd lucked out and all sales had either been paid for in cash or with a check, but it was obvious a charged sale had to be lurking right around the corner.

"This is great! Just friggin' great!" Joanie complained, totally pissed off.

"Calm down, Joanie. Let me think."

"What's next? The roof gonna fall in?"

"Bite your tongue. Let's not borrow trouble, okay?"

"I guess."

"Now be quiet so I can think."

"What for? We're dead in the water."

"No... No, we're not. Give me a minute."

"Think all you want, it won't do any good."

"Joanie, put a lid on it, will ya? I'm trying to think."

A few seconds passed while Emma tried to figure out what to do. Joanie wasn't any help; she just looked on skeptically, drumming her fingers on the counter, not even attempting to come up with a solution.

"Stop doing that. I can't concentrate."

Joanie stilled her fingers. "As though it matters. It's not like you're going to come up with anything."

"You are so wrong. I'll come up with something."

"Right," Joanie said, rolling he eyes.

Another few seconds went by and then. "Ah-ha!"

"What ah-ha?"

"I know what we're going to do."

"You do? You mind telling me?"

"Go in the back room and get the manual slide machine. You know, the one we use at craft shows. We'll use that until the phone's working again and then punch the charges in by hand on the key pad."

Comprehension came to Joanie like a punch to the gut. "Oh, you wonderful person, you. I love ya, I love ya, I love ya. Come here; let me plant a big one on ya."

"Let's not go overboard," Emma said, taking a few steps back. "Just go get the machine."

"I'm on my way... See, this is why we're such a good team."

"What is?"

"This. What just happened."

"I'm not following. Explain."

"It's because you're so smart. You figure stuff out."

"It wasn't that big a deal, Joanie."

"Yeah, it was. See, you stay calm and work your way through the problem."

"Okay, I'll accept that. Now, what's your part in our team?"

"I'm the one who recognizes you're so smart."

Emma blinked, looked away, brought her gaze back to Joanie, and blinked again. "That's it? That's your whole part?"

"Yeah, but I'm also the one who encourages you and then brings up the rear."

*Encourages her? It didn't sound like encouragement a minute ago.* Emma stared at her friend for a minute, trying to follow her line of reasoning. She couldn't and would be way better off if she didn't attempt to. Shaking her head slightly to throw off the confusing thoughts Joanie's insights always conjured up, Emma told her friend, "You're right and you do a damn fine job of it. Now go to the rear of the shop and get the machine. Bring one of our cell phones up here too."

Smiling broadly, Joanie went to do Emma's bidding.

\* \* \* \*

It was late afternoon and the girls were taking a break. The shop was blessedly empty of shoppers for the moment and they had a chance to sit down and rest their tired legs. A glass of wine would unquestionably help to ease away the aches and pains.

Relaxing in chairs behind the counter, the girls reflected on what had so far made up their day. They'd finally gotten hold of the insurance agent and he'd been there and gone, promising a quick settlement. The wooden figures were all assembled and sitting in their rightful place on the front porch. They'd waited on what seemed like a thousand customers and had been able to conduct business without a problem with the portable charge machine. Most importantly, the conspicuous absence of Tank was testament to the ongoing contest still being battled between woman and dog. It appeared to be at a stalemate, which at least meant that

Joanie hadn't lost—yet. To top it off, the phone company truck was at that very instant pulling into the parking lot, a sure indication that very soon their phone problems would be a thing of the past.

So if the aches-and-pains excuse didn't quite cut it, they could always fall back on the "reasons to celebrate" pretext of why a glass of wine was appropriate. Right? It didn't really matter. Either way, they had their glass of wine.

The repairman was outside checking things out for only a few minutes before he came in. In fact, he'd taken more time getting out of his truck and getting his gear together than he had determining what the problem was. The girls sensed that could be a bad sign.

The repairman identified himself as he walked toward the counter and once there he gave the girls the bad news. "I'm afraid the reason you don't have any phone service is because your lines have been cut."

"What?" Both girls asked, not sure they'd heard correctly.

"Somebody cut your phone wires, ladies."

"Well, son of a bitch, " Joanie stated incredulously.

"If that don't take the cake," Emma said.

Joanie turned to face Emma and gave her an I-don't-believe-you said-that look while mouthing, "Don't take the cake?" Joanie shook her head and then said aloud, "Where'd you pull that one out of? Your a—"

"Don't say it," Emma interrupted quickly.

"Geez, you come up with some good ones," Joanie laughed.

"Ladies, about your phone lines…"

"Yeah, what?" Both girls snapped back to the immediate problem.

"You might want to notify the police."

"Oh cripe. Yeah, I guess we'd better call Tim," Joanie said. "Give me the cell, I'll do it."

While Joanie made the call, Emma explained to the repairman about the vandalism they'd had over the weekend.

"Looks like somebody's got it out for you."

"It's sure starting to look that way."

"Tim wasn't on duty yet, but they're sending another sheriff over," Joanie explained, ending the call. "He'll be here in a few minutes."

"I'll wait for him outside then," the repairmen said. "As soon as he's finished with whatever he has to do, I'll replace the wires."

"Thanks, we'd appreciate it."

"No problem, ladies."

True to their word, a sheriff's car pulled into the lot within ten minutes. The fact that the Colden substation was a mere three miles down the road was clearly an advantage. The girls watched as the repairman took the sheriff over to the "scene of the crime" as it were. The sheriff did his thing, but just what that thing was the girls didn't exactly know other than he looked at the cut wires and spoke to the repairman. They couldn't hear the discussion, but once the officer gave a quick nod, the repairman started to do *his* thing. That looked promising; maybe matters would get back to normal and the girls would be free to do *their* thing! Hope, at any rate, springs eternal!

After the sheriff had gotten whatever information he could from Emma and Joanie, which amounted to nothing, he left to file a report. The girls were just starting to restock the shelves when didn't Angie "the-mouth" Neumann stroll in.

Joanie expressed both their sentiments quite succinctly with a resignedly hissed, "Son of a bitch."

Emma couldn't do anything more than hang her head, fighting the urge to flee while she still had the chance; their nemesis hadn't seen them yet. Maybe she could sneak out and leave Joanie to wage the war of words…. She eyed the distance to the back door longingly. No, she'd never make it; Joanie was sure to tackle her before she got two feet away. So much for escape…

"Emma, Joanie, are you here?"

Joanie slapped her hand across Emma's mouth. "Don't answer her," Joanie whispered. "Maybe she'll go away."

Emma pulled her partner's hand away. "Yeah, right. What planet are you living on?"

"The one dedicated to self-preservation."

"It doesn't exist."

"Don't I know it."

"Emma? Joanie?" The dreaded voice and the person who owned it weren't going to go away.

"Damn, we might as well get it over with."

The girls came out from behind the display unit that had hidden them from view with forced smiles on their faces. Cole, who'd been lounging nearby, beat a speedy exit to the back room, closing the door once he got inside. For this he'd be separated from Emma! Emma looked enviously after him. What she wouldn't give…

"There you are. You must have not have heard me come in," Angie said.

"No…we, ah… didn't hear you. We were busy restocking," Joanie lied.

"We get so caught up, we kind of blank out everything else," Emma said, reinforcing Joanie's claim.

"Well, you know, that's not a particularly good thing to do."

Why she was going to travel down this road Joanie had no idea, but she asked the question anyway. "And why is that?"

"You know."

Oh, God, it was starting. It certainly hadn't taken long.

"No, I don't. Why don't you tell me?" Please, Lord, Joanie prayed, let whatever she's going to say be brief and to the point no matter how screwed up it is.

"Because of your customers."

"What about 'em?"

"They need to be happy."

"They do?"

"Well, of course."

"All the time?"

"Maybe not all the time."

"Then when?"

"When they're here."

"I think they are."

"Are you sure?"

"Why wouldn't they be?" Emma couldn't stay on the sidelines any longer. What was it, maybe a minute into the game? She felt compelled to wade into the midst of it.

"'Cause you weren't paying attention."

"To what?"

"No, you mean, to whom?"

"All right. To whom?"

"The customers."

"When weren't we paying attention to the customers?"

"Before."

"Before when?"

"When I came in."

"Oh, well, that's different."

"Why?"

"'Cause it was you."

"Why's it different? I'm a customer."

"Yeah, but we consider you a friend."

Angie looked a little stumped. Score one for the girls. "I don't get it."

"You don't."

"No."

"We thought it was obvious."

"You'd better explain it to me."

"It's simple; you're a friend."

Angie's forehead furrowed in concentration. "I'm not getting it. Maybe you'd better explain it again."

"You're more than a customer."

Angie's gaze traveled from Emma to Joanie and back again. The two friends smiling affectionately at the woman who drove them nuts, although it caused them a great deal of physical pain. This time they would win. They could smell victory!

"Ohhhh…yeah… okay."

That was it! They had her!

However, the next words out of her mouth had them ready to launch missiles, really big ones, directly at the woman in front of them.

"But what about when I'm just a customer?"

It was all downhill from there. Not only did the girls have to reiterate the entire conversation just passed, but they had to explain about the vandalism to the shop and the presence of the telephone repairman. It was not only a gargantuan task, but a painful one. No wonder the wine bottle had reappeared and was being constantly tipped and with increasing speed. The girls weren't even using glasses any more. They were taking their fortitude directly from the bottle.

By the time Angie was satisfied, Emma and Joanie didn't actually give a good goddamn whether she was or not. At that point, they didn't really give a shit about anything. They were pleasantly tipsy!

After they'd scooted the scourge of their existence out the door and dealt with the repairman after he'd finished the repair job, the girls managed to close the shop, although by the following morning they would have no recollection of doing so. Somebody, they never would remember which one, had had enough sense to call Sam and let him know that Joanie was going to need a ride home. More than likely it had been Emma, but nobody could swear to it.

Cole had released himself from his self-imposed prison as soon as he'd heard Angie leave, but when he saw the state the girls were in he almost re-imprisoned himself. However, loyalty and duty quickly reaffirmed themselves as Cole watched the bumbling duo's efforts that finally did get the store shut down in spite of the fact they had to do everything two or three times before they got it right. It simply wasn't in his nature to forsake such pathetic creatures. Call it breeding, call it good genes, call it character, call it whatever you wanted to. He simply could not leave those two wayward females to their own devices. Besides, Emma was going to need some help getting up to the house; she'd never make it under her own power.

Thank God they'd cancelled class for the week because of the holiday.

# Chapter Thirty

It was Thursday, Thanksgiving, and it was snowing like a bitch! This time the white stuff had been forecast, but Emma had hoped against hope that the weatherman would be wrong like he was so much of the time. But no, today of all days he had to be right on the money, dammit!

Emma was supposed to spend the day with Mandie and her family, topping it off with a traditional turkey dinner. Tracy and Mack were staying in Connecticut, opting to come home for Christmas instead. Tracy and family planned on traveling to Mack and Lindsay's home in Milford to celebrate the day.

Mandie had invited Ben to spend Thanksgiving with them and thank God, he'd accepted. If not for the fact that Ben had offered to drive, Emma would have stayed home, even if it was a holiday. She had no desire to end up in a ditch or worse yet, an accident. There was no room for harboring false illusions about her driving abilities under these conditions. With the wind blowing and the snow coming down, her grade point average, if she was lucky, was *maybe* a 1.0.

Joanie would be staying home with Sam and their two boys since the cooking chores for the family gathering had fallen to her this year. The Davis clan was expecting to play host to Sam's brother and his family, his parents, and Joanie's sister and her brood. With sixteen people present, there was going to be a lot of food laid out on the festive table.

Sally and Richard were spending the day with Sally's son and his family, her out-of-state daughter being unable to make it this year. Sally routinely closed the restaurant on Thanksgiving so her employees could enjoy the holiday with their families. It was quite a remarkable gesture on Sally's part when you considered that Thanksgiving was a very profitable day in the food industry. Perhaps that was one of the reasons her staff was so devoted to her.

As far as the dogs were concerned, Cole, of course, was traveling to Mandie's where he was sure to be supplied with lots of dropped food in the vicinity of Sydney's chair. Tank was staying at home, but had already mapped out his strategy for being so damn irresistible that nobody, except for maybe Joanie, would be able to deny him anything. Kirby, on the other hand, upon arriving at Sally's son's home would ingratiate herself with the children and lay her plans for swiping tasty morsels from their often times unattended plates.

It was about ten in the morning when Ben came to pick up Emma and Cole. The snow was already deep enough so that he'd had to put the Jeep into four-wheel drive to get up the hill. When he stepped out of the car and hiked to Emma's front door, he was wading through five inches of the white stuff.

It took Emma no longer than fifteen minutes to get everything, including a 10-inch double-crusted apple pie, collected and ready to go. In addition to the usual necessities that went with them for the day, she'd packed an emergency bag for both Cole and herself just in case the storm got bad enough that they wouldn't make it home that night. Ben had wisely taken the same precaution himself.

Emma was wearing chocolate brown corduroy slacks, a white turtle neck and a teal blue ribbed sweater. She'd gone for comfort; no way was she going to suffer the agonies of pantyhose just because it was a holiday. Uh-uh! There was enough room in those pants to accommodate a whole lot of food.

Now Cole, on the other hand, was going for glamour. He'd been gussied up with a Thanksgiving-themed kerchief tied around his neck and showboat that he was, he was strutting his stuff. He was stylin'!

Emma thought Ben looked especially sexy in the outfit he was wearing. He had on a pair of moss green chinos, a sage/cream checked cotton shirt, and a khaki cotton sweater. To top it off he was wearing a brown leather bomber jacket and had a pair of brown Gore-Tex boots on his feet. His head was hatless, and the remnants of snowflakes sparkled in his black hair. Emma had a wild thought for a moment of forgetting about Thanksgiving and just staying home with Ben all day.

But being the grandmother that she was, she couldn't disappoint Sydney, so she pulled her boots on and got her coat. Ben helped her into it and taking advantage of Emma's closeness, he wrapped his arm around her waist and pulled her back against his chest. Dipping his head, he trailed tiny kisses along her neck and stroked her arm with his free hand.

"God, you smell good," Ben whispered.

"Mmmm, you feel good," Emma answered, her arms covering Ben's at her waist.

"Wanna stay home?" Ben asked, his voice huskier as he continued to nuzzle her neck.

"Don't tempt me because I would love to."

"Well…"

"Ben, you're terrible," Emma laughed. "I can't disappoint Mandie and Syd and you know it."

"Yeah, I know, but I thought it was worth a shot."

Emma moved out of his arms and he let her go. She turned and faced him, a smile on her lips. "We'll have our own celebration when we get back tonight, okay?"

"You promise?"

"What do you think?" Emma moved in close and reached up and pulled his head down to hers, taking his mouth in a kiss that promised pleasurable delights later on.

"I think we'd better leave now or we'll never make it out the door."

"My thoughts exactly," Emma said, nudging him away. "Cole, come on. Let's go."

Once they piled into the Jeep with Cole safely stowed in the back, they headed down to Route 240. It was plowed, but the going was slow with the wind making visibility low at times. Even though she wasn't driving, Emma couldn't relax. It wasn't that Ben wasn't an excellent driver; it was just that storms like this made her extremely nervous. The fast-falling snow completely disoriented her and she had no perception as to where she was, which is why she often times found herself on the wrong side of the road when she was the one driving under similar conditions. Being a passenger hadn't alleviated the problem, so it was no surprise to her that her heart was beating like a jackhammer and her eyes were tearing from the strain of trying to see clearly through the white curtain of snow.

It took them nearly twice as long as usual to get to the 219 Expressway and the going there was just as bad as it had been on Route 240, only here the blowing snow was worse because of the openness of the area. Visibility at times was down to zero, their speed down to a crawl.

When they finally hit the mainline Thruway, the snow started to let up just a bit and by the time the Jeep was getting onto the 290, there wasn't a flake in the air. There wasn't even a coating on the ground. Such was the idiosyncrasy of Lake Effect Snow, commonly known as "LES". While the southtowns of Erie County and the ski areas south of Buffalo could be inundated with blizzard-like conditions, the city and areas north could be under sunny skies. Of course, "LES" could also work in reverse and with many variations in between. If there was a slight shift in the wind over Lake Erie, an area that had been under clear skies an hour ago could all of a sudden find itself deluged with heavy snowfall. The fickle wavering of "LES" certainly made for unpredictable conditions when traveling from one area to another in Western New York during the winter months. Lord only knew what you'd run into.

Ben, Emma, and Cole finally arrived at Mandie's home in Wheatfield and were immediately pounced upon by one over-excited toddler as soon as Emma opened the front door. Sydney launched herself at her Grammy who swept her up into her arms and gave her a hug and kiss. Sydney stayed there long enough to return the embrace, then demanded to be put down so she could give her own welcome to her buddy, Cole. She attached her little arms around his big neck and gave him a smacking kiss on the nose. Cole washed her face thoroughly in response.

Rob and Mandie took their turns welcoming their guests and eventually coats were discarded and hung up, and Ben was relieved of the pie he'd been balancing in his hand. Syd and Cole disappeared upstairs, no doubt going to her bedroom to play. The adults adjourned to the living room and since it was after noon *and* Thanksgiving, they all soon had either a beer or a glass of wine in their hand.

Kick-off for the ever-present football game was just about to take place when Rob's parents and aunt and uncle along with their two daughters showed up. There was another round of greetings and commotion with Syd flying down the stairs, accompanied by the big Newfie who now had a flowered hat perched on top of his head, to take part in the noisy welcome.

Things settled down quickly and again Syd and Cole disappeared upstairs, this time taking the two new arrivals with them. The adults congregated around the center island in the kitchen, which was open to the living room. It was, in fact, one large room with the working area of the kitchen at one end, the eating area in the middle, and the living room at the other. The layout was especially nice for entertaining in that the hostess was never isolated from her guests while preparing the food.

Speaking of which, it was high time for the appetizers to be put out. Mandie had made a scrumptious artichoke dip, the recipe for which had originally come from Joanie. Piping hot, she placed it on the island and surrounded it with a selection of crackers for dipping. Then there was the taco dip with crunchy tortilla chips, which was out of this world. There was a vegetable platter with ranch dip and hot, savory spinach balls that Rob's mother had contributed. A server heaped with cubes of cheddar, Monterey Jack with jalapenos, and Swiss was also offered. And knowing her mother loved it, Mandie had prepared a huge platter piled high with cold shrimp and cocktail sauce. Lastly, and included mainly to appeal to the children's appetites, there were bowls of potato chips, pretzels, and peanuts.

This time when the entourage from upstairs came down, Cole was minus the hat and in its stead was a small blanket tied around his neck serving as a cape. He looked like he was quite proud of it. Super dog to the rescue?

Needless to say, as the food was being eaten, there was enough of it falling from small hands in addition to that which was being snuck directly to the big dog that Cole was in no danger of going without.

The afternoon passed pleasantly between the men watching the game and the women catching up on what was new since the last time they'd been together. There was also the replenishment of refreshments that certainly added to the conviviality of the day.

Five o'clock saw the main event on the table with everyone anxious to dig in. Mandie had outdone herself; it was a virtual feast and Emma couldn't have been prouder of her. From her table settings, to the autumnal floral centerpiece, to the tapers burning in their candlesticks, to the delicious food—everything was perfect.

Cole was so intoxicated by the smells assaulting his nose that he had long ropes of saliva hanging from his jowls. That wasn't just drool, uh-uh; that was proof his salivary glands were going into overdrive. And why wouldn't they? The abundance of food laid out in front of him was enough to bring a dog to his knees.

There was, of course, the heaping platter of juicy roasted turkey, the huge bowl of sour cream mashed potatoes, a boat of rich brown gravy, the oversized dish of bread and sausage stuffing that had been sweetened with bits of apple and raisins, the crock of whole cranberry sauce, the casserole of cauliflower au gratin, the dish of buttered and brown sugared acorn squash, the basket of homemade crescent rolls, and the salad of romaine lettuce, dried cherries, blue cheese, cucumber, and carrots dressed with balsamic vinaigrette. People and dog alike were going to be stuffed after this meal.

And then there was dessert. Ready to be dished up was not only the apple pie that Emma had made to be eaten plain or a la mode, but Rob's aunt had baked two additional pies, one a spicy pumpkin and the other a rich double chocolate with plenty of real whipped cream to be heaped on top.

No question about it—once this banquet was finished, belts were going to have to be loosened and buttons undone and within half an hour there was probably going to be some snoozing going on. Cole couldn't take part in the belt loosening or the button popping, but he sure was right there with the rest of the men when it came to the after- dinner snoozing.

Along about 7:00, Mack and Tracy called the house to exchange holiday greetings with their mom and sister. Syd had to have her turn on the phone and then generously held it out to Cole so he could say hello. He gave it a solid "woof".

Next, Emma gave Joanie a call to see what the weather was like in their neck of the woods. She reported the snow had stopped and the wind had died down so she didn't think there should be any trouble for them getting back home. That was certainly good news.

The party broke up shortly thereafter and Ben, Emma, and Cole were soon on their way home after the usual tearful farewell with Sydney. Emma promised that she could come and visit soon and have a sleep-over. That seemed to pacify her somewhat, but of course she wanted to know when. Emma threw the ball back in Mandie's court by telling her granddaughter that it was up to her mother. Now *she* could be pestered endlessly. Oh, the benefits of being a grandmother!

The ride home went much smoother than the trip up, so it was only about ten minutes longer than usual before the Jeep was pulling into the shop parking lot, which along with Emma's road had already been plowed.

They were just passing the back of the shop when Emma turned to check on Cole and saw an orange glow out of the corner of her eye. Twisting her head more in that direction, she gave a startled gasp.

"What?" Ben asked, braking hard.

"The shop! I think it's on fire!"

"What the—" Ben swiveled his head around and at the same time threw the Jeep into Park. "Emma, call 911!" With that, he was out the car door and running toward the shop.

Emma fumbled in her purse, her hands suddenly clumsy. The phone slipped out of her hands twice before she got a good grip on it and pulled it out. Feeling like her fingers weren't getting the right signals from her brain, she carefully punched in the emergency number. After she gave the dispatcher the necessary information, she left Cole in the Jeep and ran to where Ben was throwing handfuls of snow on the flames. The fire was creeping up the back wall, but hadn't caught the roof yet. Ben was throwing the snow above the flames, trying to keep it contained. Once Emma grasped his strategy, she joined him in the fight.

In a matter of minutes, sirens could be heard approaching the store from both the north and the south. As it was a holiday, the call would have gone out to two volunteer fire companies to assure that enough men would be available to fight the fire. In this case, both the Colden and Concord companies had been called into service. With lights flashing, the big fire trucks wheeled into the lot along with two sheriff's department cruisers and four private vehicles owned by the chief and assistant chief of both volunteer departments.

Instantly, controlled pandemonium took over with men scurrying about, fire hoses being unrolled from the pumper truck and hooked up to the tanker, instructions being shouted out, equipment being unloaded, and traffic control being set up. Emma and Ben were quickly removed from the area and in no time at all, a wall of water was being sprayed on the back of the store. The fire was quickly put out and the stench of burned clapboard siding filled the air. The firemen completely drenched the roof and the surrounding area to make sure there wasn't a hidden spark smoldering somewhere waiting to ignite into flame.

Now that it was over, Emma's nerves got the better of her and she started to shake and couldn't stop. If it hadn't been for Ben moving in to support her, her knees would have given out. He led her over to the Jeep and sat her down in the passenger seat. The Jeep was still running, so it was warm inside. Ben stripped off her soaked gloves and put her hands between his and rubbed them vigorously. Once he had them warmed, he pulled a blanket out of the back and wrapped her in it.

"Stay here, Em. I'll bring the sheriff over here if he wants to talk to you."

Emma could only nod; she was shivering so hard, she couldn't talk. Cole whined from the back seat and laid his head on her shoulder. Ben gave her a quick kiss, then left to find out what he could.

It was obvious to everyone at the scene that the cause of the fire was arson once an empty gasoline can and a pack of matches were found in the nearby shrubbery. When daylight broke the arson investigator would be brought in to sift through the debris looking for a point of origin and other incriminating evidence. A thorough investigation would just be getting started.

One of the sheriffs who'd responded to the call was the same one who'd come to check out the cut phone lines. His name was Kevin Martolli and he'd been on the job for five years. He was young and eager and didn't personally know the girls, Sam, or Ben like Deputy Sheriff O'Connor did. However, when he came over to the Jeep to talk to Emma his manner was again not only professional and efficient, but friendly and concerned. Having already spoken with Ben, Sheriff Martolli quickly took Emma's statement. Then aware of the physical toll the shock of the fire was having on her, Martolli allowed Ben to take Emma up to the house. He would follow them up when he was finished at the scene.

Only when Ben had Emma snugly cocooned in a down comforter with a cup of hot chocolate in her hands and Cole sticking close, did he call Sam. Stunned—was the only word to describe Sam's reaction, but he assured Ben that once he broke the news to Joanie, they'd be over within minutes. It was bound to be a very long night and one not spent the way it had originally been planned.

# Chapter Thirty-One

The faintest glimmer of light was beginning to show in the eastern sky and Moira was still up; she had yet to crawl into bed. The previous night had been unbearably long, but she was filled with an overwhelming sense of fulfillment and vindication, despite her mind-numbing fatigue.

She shuffled into the kitchen, intent on making something to eat; the last meal she'd eaten had been lunch the day before. Standing at the counter, she opened the cupboard doors one after the other and studied her choices. Nothing appealed to her; she moved to the refrigerator, hoping there would be something there that would make her mouth water. But after scanning the contents, the well-stocked fridge held nothing in the way of enticement. She was just too damn tired. Running her hands through her short tousled hair, she turned and left the kitchen, making her way over to the stairs that led to her bedroom.

Upon reaching her room, she stumbled over to the bed, collapsing facedown across it. Taking the time only to turn her head to one side, she instantly fell asleep. The oblivion she fell into was so complete there was no need for the sleeping pill she was too tired to take and no room for the terrifying nightmares from her childhood to disturb her rest and invade her mind.

\*   \*   \*   \*

Cole was doing a really good impression of a fallen log as he lay stretched out on top of Emma. The only thing moving as he exhaled through his nose was his breath, which tickled Emma's nose since the two were only about an inch apart. Emma slit one eye open and found herself looking straight into two of the most soulful brown eyes God had ever created. And she would tell Him that too if she could draw a decent breath into her lungs.

"Cole," she croaked, "you've got to move."

He didn't move.

"Cole, I'm awake, honest."

He didn't move.

"Look, my other eye's open."

He still didn't move.

"I'd pet you if I could… but you've got my arms pinned down."

Cole cocked his head, but he didn't get up.

"Cole, it's getting really hard to breathe."

He cocked his head the other way, but stayed where he was.

"All right… you win. Get it over with before I pass out from lack of oxygen."

Now he moved, forward, but just his head, and gave Emma's face a washing that left no spot untouched. Such was the joy of being kissed by a Newfoundland. When he was quite finished, and it took a while, Cole eased back but still didn't get up.

Emma, whose face was thoroughly wet, not to mention a little blue, could only gasp, "Move!"

Finally, Cole did, his upward push sending Emma sinking into the mattress with an exhaled groan. Cole jumped to the floor; Emma stayed where she was, gazing at the ceiling, breathing in life-supporting air. Cole watched her for a minute, then placed his head on her arm, which was laying listlessly at her side. Emma took the gesture for what it was, a warning, "Get up, or I'll be right back on top of you."

Emma turned her head and gave Cole direct eye to eye contact. "One of these days, Cole, you're going to put me in an iron lung."

He woofed and started to prance.

"I'm coming... honest. I'm just moving like I feel... about a hundred years old." Emma got out of bed and threw on her clothes; it was bound to be cold out there. With her luck, it had probably snowed another foot or two while she'd slept, not that she'd gotten much sleep. Joanie and Sam had been there until almost one in the morning and Ben had stayed till nearly two. When she'd finally gotten to bed, it'd taken Emma another hour to fall asleep and now it was 5:00 and she was getting up. No wonder Cole had had to resort to drastic measures in order to get her out of bed.

Walking to the mudroom, Emma stopped dead in her tracks and moaned, remembering what day it was. Black Friday! The busiest shopping day of the year! And she had to face it with all of two hours sleep. Wonderful! Things couldn't get much worse. Whoops! I'm not even going there, Emma thought; things could always get worse and most of the time did.

Only the most necessary of the usual routine got done that morning with Emma opting to forego her exercise and Cole's roading. Missing one day wasn't going to kill them; in fact, just the opposite could be true under the current conditions. With Emma as tired as she was, only injury or death was sure to be waiting. It would be much safer to be a slow-moving, indolent slug for a day.

To Emma's great relief, no more snow had fallen during the night. At least she had that to be thankful for. Whether the store being allowed to open was a blessing or not was still to be decided. Since the fire had been limited to the back outside wall and no entry had been made into the store itself, the investigation didn't require that the store be kept closed. However, the area around the back of the store had been roped off and was not to be transgressed.

Upon arriving at the shop, Emma and Cole were delighted to find that Tank was there and raring to go. His appearance must mean the impasse had been solved one way or the other. Joanie was only too happy to tell Emma which way the wind had blown.

"I won."

Emma didn't say anything, just gave her a disbelieving look.

"I did. He brought the bracelet back."

"Uh-huh."

"No, he did. Tank brought it back this morning, honest."

"Yeah."

"He did, honest to God."

"Oh, I believe you. I'm sure he brought it back."

"Then what's the matter?"

"Nothing, but I don't think you're the winner."

"Don't be stupid. Of course, I am. He gave the bracelet back."

"Yeah, but on whose terms?"

"What…?"

"Joanie, don't kid yourself."

"I'm not."

"Oh, yes, you are."

"No, I'm not."

"Joanie, I'm not the one being stupid here."

"Hey!…Okay, explain that."

"Why do you think he brought it back after, what, how many days has it been? Five? Why did he bring it back now?"

"'Cause he knew I was going to win this time?"

"God, you're in worse shape than I thought."

"What's that supposed to mean?"

"It means, you dumb-ass, that Tank always has a reason for everything he does, or haven't you figured that out yet?"

"Yeah, yeah, I figured it out."

"Well, hurray for that small insight. So all right, while you're patting yourself on the back, think about why Tank would suddenly decide to give the bracelet back."

Joanie looked thoughtful for a moment. "Ah...It's not 'cause he loves me, is it?"

"Sorry, but I doubt it."

"And probably not because he felt sorry for me, huh?"

"*Pfff*, get real," Emma said, rolling her eyes.

"To get back in my good graces?"

"You dreamer, you."

Joanie looked over to where Tank was playing with Cole in the back room. The two of them were having the time of their lives. Every toy they had was scattered on the floor and they were playing tug-of-war with a Frisbee. "I'm a friggin' idiot."

"You won't be getting any argument from me."

"I'm a complete ass."

"No truer words were ever spoken."

"I am so dumb."

"My thoughts exactly."

"I should be drawn and quartered."

"That's a little extreme."

"What would you suggest?"

"Maybe a good slap upside the head."

"That could do it. Go ahead. Do me."

"I don't think that's necessary....Oh, what the hell." Emma gave her a slap to the back of her head.

"Geez! I didn't think you'd really do it," Joanie complained, rubbing her head.

"It was too good an opportunity to pass up."

"Yeah, well, don't do it again."

"I won't, at least not until next time."

"There won't be a next time."

"Yeah, right."

"There won't. I'm smart to him now."

"You really are an idiot." The size of which varies with the occasion, Emma thought. "Just shut up or I'll have to do more than slap your head."

"Like what?"

"You don't want to know."

"Yeah, you're right. I don't. Let's get down to business. I've got a feeling it's going to be a hell of a day."

"You and me both."

The day turned out as predicted; the shop was a madhouse. Customers were streaming in all day, buying everything that wasn't nailed down. On top of that, the fire investigator came in a few times to ask questions and even Deputy Sheriff Martolli stopped in. By the end of the day, the girls were wrung out and ready for a little fun and relaxation.

They would find it up at the Hearthmoor. The foursome plus two arrived for dinner a little after seven-thirty. While it was still busy, the big rush was over and Sally could turn the bar over to Hank. She and Richard joined their friends at a fireside table. The dogs were all upstairs having a gay old time under the watchful eye of one of the busboys. Talk about cushy duty!

They all decided on the fish, whether it was battered and deep-fried, or baked with peppercorns and lemon. The table was evenly split on French fries and rice; no need to figure out which sex got which; it was fairly obvious. Creamy coleslaw and tartar sauce also accompanied each meal. The basket holding a double order of garlic bread was empty within minutes and had to be replenished, the occupants of the table resembling a lean, mean eating machine!

Conversation centered first on the fire and the ongoing problems at the shop. Both men and women agreed it sounded like the work of delinquent teenagers. Sam told the rest of them that Sheriff O'Connor was leaning on the boys he had tagged as possible suspects, but so far nothing much had turned up.

Then remembering she had big news, Sally revealed that she'd gotten a call from Stu Berger just before the others had shown up.

"What's up?" Joanie asked in between bites of flaky, moist fish.

"You know the dogs that died at Back Mountain?"

"How could we forget?"

"Well, Stu said they don't have all the findings in yet, but the results from the necropsies that have been reported all have one thing in common."

"What?" Emma and Joanie chorused, their forks poised half-way to the mouths.

"There was some unknown chemical substance found in each dog's blood."

"Shit," Joanie breathed.

"That has to mean they were poisoned," Emma said.

"I would think so," Sally agreed.

"How were they poisoned? Do they know?" Joanie asked.

"They think it was ingested. None of the dogs' bodies had any injection sites."

"What about the handler that died?" Joanie asked.

"I don't know. Stu didn't say anything about him. He must not have had any information."

"I bet ya any money, it's going to be the same thing that happened in Syracuse."

"God, I hope not."

"It has to be, Sally. There's no way it can't be related."

"Yeah, but that means there's somebody out there purposely poisoning dogs and maybe people...Oh, yeah, that's another thing, somebody told Stu that two more dogs died that were at Syracuse."

"Really?"

"Yeah, he said one died on Monday and the other on Tuesday."

"Did he say what breeds they were?" Emma asked, knowing all along they were going to be black in coloring.

"Yeah, one was a Black Russian Terrier and the other was a Min Pin."

"Damn, I knew it."

"I know what you're thinking, that they're black too."

"Yep."

"Who would do such a terrible thing?" Joanie asked, completely bewildered. She might rant and rave about Tank and threaten to end his miserable life, but she would never, ever harm so much as a hair on his bedeviled little head.

"Somebody who's crazy, that's who."

"Or somebody who hates dogs."

"Yeah, or maybe it's somebody who wants to get even for God knows what reason," Sam offered.

"They do seem to be targeting certain dogs," Ben added.

"Yeah, but it's not limited to one breed. Color seems to be the deciding factor. "

"I wonder what color has to do with it."

"It has to be a revenge thing."

"Well, whoever's doing it and for whatever reason," Joanie said, "they're twisted right out of their mind."

"That's for damn sure."

"We have to hope they catch whoever's responsible fast. This can't keep happening. It's too devastating."

"Amen to that."

The party broke up shortly afterwards. Tank and Cole were collected and the two couples went their separate ways, with Ben ending up at Emma's house for the night.

# Chapter Thirty-Two

A little over a week later on the following Saturday, while Emma and Joanie were working at the shop and Sally was attending to business at the restaurant, Ben, Sam, and Richard went out to get everybody's Christmas tree. Originally, the entire group was supposed to go, but two things changed the initial plan.

First, it was 21 degrees out and snowing heavily. That put Emma right off. There was no way she was going out in that kind of weather no matter who tried to cajole her into compliance. See... the thing was, every year that Emma did go, she found a tree she liked almost right away. She'd be happy to cut it down and go home. Mission accomplished in about 10-15 minutes. But no matter whom she went with, the others always wanted to look further. She couldn't tell you the number of times she'd heard, "Let's look over there; maybe you'll find a better one," or "Let's keep looking; you don't want to settle for that one right away," or "It's nice, but maybe there's a nicer one over there," or "Let's go down this path; there might be something that'll catch your eye." Well, sorry, but one already caught my eye! Let's cut it and go home! As fate would have it, she was always outvoted and forced to go on, trudging through the sometimes knee-deep snow. Hey, Emma would think, I've got a news flash for you people, this is NOT fun!

No, she'd stay right where she was, thank you very much. Whatever they brought back was fine with her. She didn't care if the damned thing had been in a forest fire. However, her refusal to go and trudge through the woods in a snowstorm touched off a domino effect. If Emma wasn't going, then Joanie wasn't going, and if Emma and Joanie weren't going, then Sally wasn't going. So, there!

Nevertheless, there was something even more potent than Emma not going to make Joanie reconsider going on the outing. Specifically, it was thing number two. When Joanie was unavoidably faced with the probability that Tammy would be called in to cover the shop, she suddenly found herself desperately wanting to stay within the warm confines of the store and forego the pleasures of traipsing through the snow in search of the perfect tree. Actually, if the Tammy threat hadn't existed she would have enjoyed going. The idea of whipping snowballs at Sam held great appeal. But the thought of even one of those dreaded sales receipts crossing her path sent her stomach spinning and she knew her decision was made. She'd stay and tend to business, Christmas trees be damned.

So it was men only when the tree hunters left the shop and piled into Sam's truck. They were going over to a tree farm on Vermont Hill Road in Holland and would have to battle the elements up on Center Road at the top of the hill until their descent on Holland Glenwood Road took them into the town where the weather would be pretty much what it was in their valley. But first they were going to have to face what was probably low visibility and stiff winds up on Center. Good luck, boys!

Sam had the truck in four-wheel drive all the way up the hill on the Glenwood side of Holland Glenwood Road. They crested the top and it was a world of white. The only thing they could see was snow. It was everywhere, blowing, swirling, and landing. Sam had the windshield wipers on high, trying to keep up with it. They couldn't see much at all and followed vague tire tracks on what they assumed was the road. Sam made the turn onto Center and then found where he was supposed to turn right onto the Holland side of Holland Glenwood Road. The going was slow obviously, but the longer they crept down the hill, the more the weather improved. When they neared the entrance of the Speedway, visibility was remarkably better and the road was down to barely-covered blacktop. The weather was actually better here than over at the shop. They crossed Route 16 and went up Vermont Street until they spotted Vermont Hill Road and made a left. The snow had begun to fall in earnest again as they climbed to the higher elevation. They found the tree farm, parked the vehicle, bundled up in their winter gear, and went out to hunt down the elusive perfect Christmas tree times five.

*   *   *   *

While the men were out doing their interpretation of a lumberjack, Emma and Joanie were swamped with customers at the store. The clock was ticking and the holiday shoppers were even more desperate to find that perfect gift before the big day was upon them.

Around noon, an elderly gentleman came into the shop, obviously shopping for a gift intended either for his wife or a lady friend. Problem was, he had absolutely no idea what to get her. After wandering the aisles aimlessly for several minutes and accomplishing nothing, he approached the girls at the counter. He revealed that he'd been married to the same woman for over forty-five years and he still hadn't a clue as to what she liked. One could only speculate as to the reason why. His fault or hers? Pity her or him? Didn't much matter; it was the girls' problem now.

Every question the girls asked the man to help determine his wife's taste was answered with either, "I don't really know", or "I couldn't tell you". He wasn't offering a lot of help. While Joanie was complaining, deservedly or not, about the guy being a typical man, Emma moved to the other side of the counter and decided to take the gentleman in hand before her partner did. She thought it prudent to take some kind of preventive measure, namely stepping in, before Joanie stomped on, over, and down.

Emma escorted the man around the shop pointing out various merchandise. In the first few seconds of their meanderings, the man disclosed that his name was Andrew Wittenger and he was sorry to be such a bother. With the subsequent small talk that followed, Emma took an instant liking to the man and determined that the wife must be the one at fault. She intensified her efforts to help the old dear and if he showed even a smidgen of interest in anything she offered for his consideration, she scooped it up and continued on. By the time they'd made a complete circuit, Emma's arms were bulging with products. She deposited everything on the counter and stood to the side, waiting Mr. Wittenger's decision.

Well, she waited and waited, and then she waited some more. Hell, she was growing roots. Meanwhile, customers were lining up to get checked out. Only they couldn't because the husband of the fortunate and undeserving Mrs. Wittenger couldn't make up his mind. It was almost painful to watch. And since it was apparent there was no hope of a momentary decision, Emma grabbed Mr. Wittenger's preliminary choices off the counter and herded him into the back room.

She plunked the baskets, pictures, Christmas linens, angels, Santas, tart burners, and candles down on the long work table and spread them out. When Emma was finished arranging the objects to her satisfaction she told

Mr. Wittenger to have at it. He was welcome to take all the time he needed, just let her know when he'd made his choice and she'd gift wrap it for him. He nodded his head once and Emma excused herself, saying she had to get back on the floor, before he could ask her opinion. She did *not* want to go there. If Mr. Wittenger took her advice and his wife didn't like the gift, Emma would undoubtedly be blamed. Nope, better he dig his own hole, no matter how much she liked the old guy.

Now, the dogs had been enjoying one of their many games of tug-of-war and this time a plush squeaky toy in the shape of a ladybug was the fought-after prize. Cole was the indisputable winner since Tank's feet couldn't get any traction on the floor against the force of Cole's strength and he was being dragged just about anywhere Cole wanted to take him. But the little guy was tenacious; he wouldn't let go. Unfortunately, the ladybug while squeaking in protest was ripping at the seams and was not long for this world. Mercifully, the toy's agonizing torture was unceremoniously halted when Emma and Mr. Wittenger came into the room. The toy was given up by both parties simultaneously and allowed to drop to the floor in favor of inspecting the newcomer who'd invaded their sacrosanct domain. Cole and Tank cautiously approached the elderly man and sniffed and snuffed until they were satisfied he was A-OK. He'd be allowed to stay.

Well, Mr. Wittenger hemmed and hawed, and waffled and wavered until the dogs grew tired of watching him. Boredom was setting in really fast. Exactly how hard could it be? It looked simple enough to them. Cole and Tank decided to take matters into their own hands, or paws, as the case may be. Besides, they'd wasted enough time already; they had places to go, things to do, toys to rip apart!

Tank moved away from the table and trotted over to the far wall, giving himself some running room. Cole positioned himself and braced; they had this maneuver down pat thanks to Tank's favorite game, namely him banking off Cole's back and leaping into a box full of Styrofoam peanuts.

Tank flew into action. Running at full tilt, he used Cole as a springboard and catapulted himself onto the table, nimbly avoiding landing on any of the objects that had become Mr. Wittenger's personal hell. Cole, for his part, abandoned his stationary position, covered the distance to the table in two steps and rested his big head on top of it so he could have a bird's eye view.

Mr. Wittenger, who'd been startled at first by Tank's surprise landing, gazed at the two dogs with tired eyes. His narrow shoulders were slumped in defeat. The decision was beyond him; he needed help. "You guys got any suggestions?" he asked the two canines in desperation.

Little did he know that help was but a paw away! Tank carefully wound himself around the merchandise, placing his feet catlike on the wooden surface. He'd stop occasionally as if considering the object, giving a glance toward Cole to see what he thought. Their silent communication continued in like fashion until all of the merchandise they deemed relevant had been inspected. Then they made their choice. With Cole's concurrence, Tank sidled over to where their selection was and placed his paw on top of it. The winner was going to be the punched tin tart burner and the pile of fragrant wafer candles sitting next to it.

An expression of pure relief and gratitude crossed the old gentleman's face. He gave Tank a pat on the head and then Cole's. "Thank you, boys. I couldn't have done it without you."

"No shit," was the immediate telepathic message sent out by both dogs. But they too liked the old guy and were glad they could help him out. Cole went out to get Emma.

"Have you decided, Mr. Wittenger?" she asked hopefully when she returned to the back room.

"Yes, I believe I have," he replied, giving the dogs a conspiratorial wink. "I'll take the burner and these little candles."

"Terrific, that'll make a great gift! I'll wrap them up for you."

"That would be wonderful. What kind of paper do you have?"

Oh, no! Emma was *not* falling into that trap! No choices! "We're using this for the holidays," she said, pulling out a length of paper from the cutter.

"That'll be fine, just fine."

"Good. Let me write this up and you can go and pay at the register while I get your gift boxed and wrapped."

"Thank you. You've been very kind."

"My pleasure. Thank *you* for shopping at our store."

"Thanks again, guys," the old gentleman said, giving Tank and Cole a two-finger salute.

The dogs woofed once and Mr. Wittenger turned and walked out to the counter to pay for his purchase. Emma gave Cole and Tank a questioning look; they gave her a look of pure innocence. She wouldn't have thought anything of it if it had only been Cole, but Tank—innocent? Not in a million years!

Emma decided that for the time being it was probably better if she didn't know what had transpired in her absence. Later on she'd figure out if she had to worry about whatever they'd done coming back to bite her in the ass. Right now the shop was way too busy for her to give it much thought.

\* \* \* \*

It was close to five o'clock when the great white hunters appeared on the shop's doorstep. "Mission accomplished," they crowed. "We've got some beauts."

The hunting party was minus Richard because he'd stayed at the restaurant with Sally. Naturally, after their trek into the woodlands of Western New York, their battle with the elements, and their exhaustive search, the hungry men had needed sustenance. Where else would they go but to the Hearthmoor for some hardy food and drink? In fact, they'd needed it so badly—they'd been there for hours! They were very happy men.

Supposedly they'd found five of the most perfect trees God had ever created, two of which were already in Sally's and Richard's possession. That remained to be seen—the perfection of the trees, that is. The girls had heard that line before and on more than one occasion. What they considered perfect and what the men considered perfect could be so totally different that you wondered if they were talking about the same thing. Besides, in years past Sam and Richard's judgment had been known to be a little off. Although the trees were generally nearly perfectly shaped, except for that one year when the trees all had big, gaping bare spots on them, the trunks somehow never quite measured up. What the men perceived as a straight trunk, invariably listed to either one side or the other when the tree was secured in its stand. Many a Christmas found the so-called perfect trees wired to the wall in everybody's house so they wouldn't fall over. Perhaps this year things would be different with Ben added to the mix. Maybe he could look at shape *and* trunk. The girls would try to keep an open mind, but they couldn't help being a tad skeptical. Well, they'd find out soon enough; the spoils of the day were right outside in the bed of Sam's truck.

And Emma and Joanie weren't waiting till closing time to check the trees out either; they grabbed their coats and hustled out the door. Sam and Ben were right behind them. Joanie hoisted herself onto the rear bumper and slipped over the tailgate. Emma was content to stay on the bumper while Joanie picked up the first of the three remaining trees.

"What do you think, Em?"

"Well, from what I can see it looks all right, but then again it's dark out here so I really can't see anything. And besides, they're all covered with snow."

"Hey, guys!" Joanie yelled to the men. "How're we supposed to tell if these are okay?"

"Don't worry about it. I'm telling ya they're real beauties," Sam said.

"Yeah?"

"Yeah."

"I want to see for myself," Joanie said, suspicion raising it's ugly head.

"You do?"

"Yeah."

"Why?"

"Why not, Sam?" Joanie asked, her voice lowering to a dangerous level.

"Oh, no reason."

"Good, help me get this one down. We'll take it into the shop."

"Do you really think that's necessary?"

"Yeah, don't you?"

"Nah, I mean, what difference does it make now? The trees are cut, they're paid for and they're here."

Both Emma and Joanie gave the men the full impact of identically raised left eyebrows. No words were needed when those babies were raised almost to their hairlines.

"Now, girls…"

"Don't 'now, girls' us, Sam Davis. Tell me, is this another year for disaster trees?"

"I don't know."

"You don't know?"

"Not for sure, I don't."

"And why is that?" Joanie asked, resigned already to having another tree from hell.

Sam remained quiet. Ben hadn't so much as even opened his mouth so far and he wasn't about to do it now.

"Why don't you know, Sam?" Joanie asked in a voice that was much too sweet for comfort.

Sam glanced over to the front of the shop. "Hey! Look at the dogs; aren't they cute?"

Well, yeah, they were. Cole and Tank were standing side by side with their noses pressed up against the window, looking out at their people with wistful expressions. It was the stuff that Hallmark cards were made of, but it didn't deter Joanie.

"Nice try, Sam. Answer the question. Why don't you know how the trees look?"

After a few more minutes of procrastination, Sam was forced to come clean. "Because we couldn't get a good look at 'em either. It was snowing too damn hard."

Hands on her hips, Joanie rolled her eyes and blew out her breath. "Oh, brother."

"I'm sure they'll be fine, Joanie." Emma didn't believe it for a minute, but felt she had to say something positive.

"Yeah, right."

Emma turned to Ben. "Aren't you glad you joined this merry group?"

"Wouldn't have missed it for the world."

"I think your viewpoint may have been compromised by a few bottles of Christmas cheer."

"Maybe, but I've had a lot of fun today and this..." he gestured between Joanie and Sam, "...is downright entertaining."

"Ben, you need to go home and think seriously about what you consider fun."

"I'll do that after we unload the trees. Promise. Which one do you want, Em?"

"I don't know, Ben. It probably doesn't make any difference. They're probably all going to need help one way or the other. You guys decide."

"Really?"

"Yeah, that way whatever challenge awaits me this year will be a big surprise."

"Okay... if you're sure."

"Yep, surprise the hell out of me."

"Joanie? Want to get out of the truck now?" Sam asked sheepishly.

"Sure, why not. It's not like I can do anything about these prize winners, is there?"

"No, but if you really like it up there, we could give you a ride."

Joanie shot Sam a withering glare that told everybody he was pushing his luck. Ben gave Sam what he thought was a discreet elbow to the ribs and whispered some prudent advice. "It might be a good idea for you to keep your mouth shut right about now."

Not discreet enough, Joanie picked right up on it. "You're a very wise man, Ben. Sam, you'd be really smart to do as he says." She gave Sam one more telling look and scrambled down from the truck.

Emma was already on the ground and heading for the front door of the shop. "Deliver your trees, boys. Ben, I'll see you tomorrow. Sam, *adiós*."

"*Adiós*, Em. Joanie, I'll see you at home."

"If you're lucky. See ya, Ben."

"Bye, Joanie." Ben, a big grin on his face, grabbed Emma by the arm and whirled her into his arms just as she was about to pass him by. "I love you," he whispered and gave her a quick kiss before he took off for the truck.

"W-what?" Emma looked like she'd been struck by lightning. She couldn't move and her eyes were huge. "What did you s-say?" she stammered weakly.

411

But Ben was already in the truck and Sam was pulling out.

Joanie was at the door, set to go in. "Come on, Em. What are you waiting for?"

"D-did you hear… what he said?" Emma asked in a tiny voice.

"What who said?"

"B-Ben."

"No, I didn't hear anything. What'd he say?"

"He said… he said he l-loves me."

"Yeah? Holy shit!"

"Y-yeah. Holy shit." Emma repeated dazedly.

"This is great!"

"Yeah, great."

"Em?" Joanie asked, walking back to her friend who still hadn't moved a muscle. "What the hell's wrong?"

"I'm… I'm not ready for this."

"Sure you are."

"No… no, I'm not."

"Why not?"

"'Cause I'm not."

"Em, I hate to say it, but you're being dumb."

"Well, I-I don't care. I can't do this."

"Do what for cripe's sake?"

"This…this love thing."

"What's to do? He said he loves you. You should be happy."

"I'm not ready for this yet."

"Well, cripe. When will you be ready?"

"I don't know. Maybe never."

"Maybe never?" Joanie gave her friend a little shake. "Are you nuts? That hunk of a man just said he loves you. You ought to be on top of the world."

Suddenly, Emma's mouth thinned to a taut line, her eyes narrowed, her expression deadened. She propelled herself out of Joanie's grasp and headed for the door. "He didn't mean it." Her voice had gathered strength and gone hard.

"Why would you say that?"

"Because."

"Not good enough, Em. Why didn't he mean it?"

"Because... because he'd been drinking."

"Not that much. It wasn't like he was drunk. Come on, he was just a little happy."

"But that's why he said it."

"You're not making any sense."

"It's very simple, Joanie. If he hadn't been drinking he wouldn't have said it. It was just something to say,. He doesn't love me."

"That's crazy. All right...so maybe his inhibitions were lowered a little bit. That doesn't mean he doesn't love you; it just means he expressed his inner feelings 'cause his guard was down.. Anybody can see the guy's head over heels in love with you. I just wonder what took him so long to tell you."

Emma staggered back like she'd been slapped. She fumbled for the door knob and opened the door while trying to regain her composure. "Don't say that."

"What? That it's obvious he has deep feelings for you?"

"I don't want to talk about this anymore."

"Em..."

"I mean it, Joanie. The subject's closed. Let's finish up in here and go home."

The door banged shut behind Emma and the dogs could be seen rushing to greet her. She gave each a perfunctory pat and headed for the counter.

Outside, Joanie, hands on hips, still stood in the same place, shaken and dismayed by Emma's reaction. "Shit," she muttered under her breath. Casting her eyes downward with a small shake to her head, she blew out a big sigh and uttered a whispered "damn" at the end of it. Knowing instinctively she'd better tread lightly, Joanie opened the door and entered the shop. One look at her friend and she knew Emma had completely withdrawn. The girls closed up with not another word said between them.

\* \* \* \*

Moira made it a point to get to bed early that night. She had to take a break. Besides, she had a lot to do the next day and needed to be sharp.

For one thing she had to go to a stupid bridal shower for a girl she worked with. She really didn't want to go, but it would look a little odd if she didn't attend. *Everybody* was going to be there! She supposed Sue was nice enough, but she wasn't really chummy with her. She wasn't chummy with anybody. But, she'd go for a little while if only to keep up appearances.

She had work enough to do at home, but she had an errand to run tomorrow too and she had to travel a ways to do it. She liked calling it that—an errand. The very thought made her laugh.

She snuggled deeper into the covers and started to hum softly, the tune as familiar to her as her own name. The sleeping pill she'd taken was starting to take affect and her humming became sporadic. The broken melody of "How Much is That Doggy in the Window" was unrecognizable to anyone but her by the time she fell asleep.

# Chapter Thirty-Three

Ben was busy kicking himself halfway to Arkansas. It was Sunday morning and he was lying in bed reflecting on his stupid, stupid move the day before. He was on his side, the sheet and blankets around his hips, his bare chest dappled with winter sunlight streaming through the window. He closed his eyes and grimaced. Jesus! What had he been thinking to blurt it out that way? But that was the whole point, wasn't it? He hadn't been thinking, not at all. What an idiot! What was the old saying? Loose lips sink ships. Well, he might have just sunk his.

He rolled over to his back and crossed his arms over his eyes and sighed deeply. What a jerk! He could still picture the stunned and, if he was going to be honest, terrified look on Emma's face. Damn if he hadn't blown it big time! Why'd he have to go and blurt it out that way? Because she'd just looked so darn cute perched up on the bumper that way, that's why. The snow had been falling all around her and some of it had settled on her hair, a flake or two even resting momentarily on her cheeks. She'd tried to keep her face composed when Joanie and Sam had been going at it, but the corners of her mouth had quirked up and Ben had known she was fighting to keep a giggle in. And then there was that raised eyebrow thing she did. God, he just loved it when she did that. It was so…so… precious! He just couldn't help himself when she'd gotten near, her scent invading his nostrils just seconds before she reached him, a mixture of cold air, Shalimar and eau de Emma. God, he had it bad! And he'd probably screwed it up royally, him and his big, fat mouth. What an ass!

After several more minutes berating himself for his own stupidity, Ben gave a disgusted snort and threw off the covers. He rolled out of bed and got to his feet. He padded to the bathroom on bare feet and braced his hands on either side of the sink, glaring at the face staring back at him. "You are *sooo* stupid. You'd think you would have learned a thing or two by now… Shit!" He turned away from his reflection, giving it a dismissive wave. Maybe he'd feel better about things after he had a shower.

He stripped off his pajama bottoms and stepped into the tub. Closing the curtain, he turned the water on and opened the shower head. He was immediately blasted by a spray of cold water. No doubt he felt he deserved that.

Ben regulated the temperature of the water and let it fall over his head. Emma was supposed to come over that night and help decorate his tree. The plan was to do hers Monday evening. He wondered if she was going to show. He was too big a chicken to call her and find out. One thing he knew for certain, though. It sure was going to be an excruciating long day.

\* \* \* \*

Emma had been up for hours by the time Ben was in the shower. In fact, she'd been up most of the night, tossing and turning when she was in bed, pacing restlessly through the house when she hadn't been.

Cole had tried to comfort her by snuggling up to her in bed, licking her face, resting his great head in her lap, and keeping pace with her as she endlessly walked the floor, but nothing he did brought her any peace. Disturbed by the apparent discomfiture of his mistress and distressed with his inability to console her, he'd retreated to a corner and just watched, his gaze never leaving his troubled friend.

Finally, about 3:30, Emma had fallen into a fitful sleep on the couch and the faithful Cole had been beside her on the floor, lightly dozing, alert to any movement she made.

When she next surfaced to wakefulness with eyes burning from too little sleep and a mind too groggy to think, she wondered absently what time it was. Cole hadn't woken her, but then she hadn't told him to, had she? She searched out the clock and saw that it was 6:45. It took a minute for that to penetrate her exhausted brain. 6:45? It was that late? Only Emma would consider 6:45 late. She looked around the darkened living room. It should be lighter by now, shouldn't it?

Emma pushed herself up on her elbows and looked out the window, squinting to see what lay outside. She looked, focused again, and then stared. She fell onto her back uttering a heartfelt, "Damn!"

Snow was falling at a rate that made it difficult to see the mature pine trees standing within twenty-five feet of the house. Perfect, she thought, the day can only get worse from here. With that assumption her brief respite from unsettling questions concerning Ben ended.

She was thinking about the "I love you" thing, of course, and what his declaration was going to do to their relationship. Not that she wanted to think about it, but she didn't seem to have any way to shut it down. It kept popping into her head and she'd give just about anything to make it go away. It was the last thing she'd thought about before she'd fallen into a troubled sleep in the wee hours of the morning and it was the first thing that came into her head now that she was awake enough to have a coherent thought, snow not withstanding.

Damn! What was she going to do? Everything was going to change now and she didn't want it to. She wanted things to go on just the way they had been. She didn't want Ben to love her, if that was even true. God, she didn't want it to be! She couldn't afford to ever be caught in that spell again. She couldn't trust him to love her. She couldn't trust love itself. It hurt too much when it fell apart. And fall apart it would. Hadn't the breakup of her marriage taught her that? No, she couldn't allow herself to accept his love. It was safer not to. She had to protect herself. Her heart wouldn't survive another wrenching tear.

And what about your feelings for Ben? she asked herself. With her conscience prickling, she grudgingly had to admit she liked him; in fact, she liked him very much. She cared about him too. But love? She wasn't even going to address the issue. She'd decided a long time ago never to let that emotion hold sway over her again. Love? Never. No, it was… lust…yeah, lust…simple, unadulterated lust. That was what she felt for Ben… with some liking and caring thrown in. But that was it, nothing more. She couldn't and wouldn't let it be anything more.

That settled firmly in her mind, Emma moved on to the next immediate problem. They were supposed to decorate his tree tonight. She didn't want to do it; she didn't want to go over there and be alone with him. Who knew what he'd say next? She needed to stay away from him. How was she going to get out of it?

Maybe she could feign illness. Was that a sniffle she felt coming on? Emma touched her forehead. Wasn't she a little warm? Was it a fever? Who was she trying to kid? He'd never believe it—she was healthy as a horse. She almost never got sick. Joanie would probably rat her out anyway. The traitor!

She wasn't likely to break a limb between the house and the shop either. On the other hand, maybe she could kind of accidentally on purpose fall off the bridge that spanned the creek at the bottom of the hill. Most of the time the creek wasn't very deep. In fact most of the time it was a mere trickle of water, so there was no danger of drowning if she were to fall through the thin layer of ice. The fall, however, could be good for a twisted ankle or a dislocated shoulder. She'd have to think about it, but not too much—physical injury did have its downside.

She'd be in pain, she'd be laid up, she wouldn't be able to road Cole, she couldn't exercise. Joanie would try to mother her and probably half kill her in the attempt. Sally would bury her with food from the restaurant... On second thought, scratch that last one; it would be the one positive thing in the whole mess.

And then there was Ben. He would— Crap! Ben would be over there all the time, making her comfortable, doing things for her, probably spending the night, making love, telling her he loved her...No! Not on your life! There would be absolutely NO physical injury!

Emma righted herself on the sofa and trailed her hand over Cole's back. He'd been watching her ever since she'd awakened, ready to spring to her aid. Now he sat in front of her waiting her next move.

"I'm going to have to gut it out, Cole. There's nothing else I can do," she said, seeking comfort in his steady regard. "Besides," she sighed, "I don't like going back on my word. I said I'd help him with his tree, so I have to do it. What's the point in putting it off anyway? He's supposed to come over here tomorrow night and help me with mine. It would only be delaying the inevitable... unless I break off with him completely... I don't know if I want to do that. What do you think?" Cole twitched his ears. "Should I break up with Ben? Hmm?... Maybe I should...I don't know... How 'bout it, big guy? Gonna help me out?" Cole gave Emma his paw and whined, but other than that he was mute on the subject. "Guess I shouldn't expect you to have any answers if I don't. Okay, before I start rambling again, let's get a move on. Maybe if I start doing something other than lying here thinking, this knot in my stomach will go away." Unfortunately, Emma knew that was nothing more than wishful thinking.

# Chapter Thirty-Four

The day had stretched out endlessly for Ben and had passed only too quickly for Emma. But both had decided during the course of their dissimilar day that the only way to get through the evening ahead was to pretend nothing had happened. Now the question was—could they pull it off? They were about to put it to the test.

Emma, armed with bravado and her loyal dog, rang Ben's doorbell and waited anxiously for him to answer it. She was so nervous her hands were shaking and she knew her telltale ears were beet red. Trying to calm herself, she drew in a deep inhalation of air that unfortunately got stuck in her throat just as the door swung open. She choked and coughed and choked again, her eyes filling with tears.

"Em! What the hell's wrong?"

As if she could speak!

"Water," she croaked.

"Right away. Come in, come in."

Emma continued to cough, unsuccessfully trying to clear her throat. Ben guided her into the living room where she ungracefully sank into the recliner. He ran off to fetch a glass of water and she tried to force some air into her lungs. How embarrassing was this?! Could she somehow just melt into the chair and disappear? If only the fates would be so kind!

Cole was hovering close by, wondering what to do while at the same time shooting disgruntled looks toward Ben whom he undoubtedly felt wasn't doing enough. Anxiety for Emma was making him a bit short-tempered and if Ben didn't hurry up with the water he was going to have to leap into action. Maybe a bite on his butt would make the guy move a little faster.

Unbeknownst to him that his derriere was in jeopardy of being tattooed with teeth marks, Ben rushed back with the water and handed the glass to the Emma. "Don't drink too much, hon. Just take a little."

Emma sipped and swallowed, then tried to clear her throat. She coughed a little more, then took another drink. Clearing her throat again, she breathed and took another drink. "Whew! That seems to have done it. Thanks." Her forehead had broken out in a sweat and tears stained her cheeks.

"Just sit there a minute. Let me get you a wet washcloth." Ben was back in a minute with the warm cloth and handed it to Emma. She wiped her face, knowing she must look a wreck.

"I need to freshen up. I'll be back in a minute," she said not meeting his eyes.

"You're sure you're all right?"

"Yeah, I'm fine. Really." Emma got up and went into the bathroom. Closing the door, she leaned against it heavily and closed her eyes. What an entrance! God! Was she jinxed or what? The last thing she wanted was for Ben to be all concerned about her. She crossed over to the closed toilet and sat down. She had to keep tonight on an even keel, no serious stuff. Just two friends decorating a Christmas tree. Right. She could do this.

Feeling empowered, she got up and moved to the sink. Inspecting herself in the mirror above it, she grimaced. Yikes! After repairing the damage as best she could, she opened the door to find Cole positioned at guard right in front of it. She patted her loyal friend on the head, reassuring him she was okay. They walked into the living room and found Ben pacing the floor. He stopped abruptly when he saw them and opened his mouth to speak, but before he had a chance to say a word, Emma plunged in. "Well, let's get to that tree, all right?"

"Sure, Em. Would you like a glass of wine first?"

"No, thank you."

"Are you sure?"

"Yes, but if you'd like something go right ahead."

"Uh, yeah. I think I will." Ben was a little surprised at Emma's brusqueness, but decided to ignore it. No sense causing any more problems with his big mouth.

While Ben got a beer from the fridge, Emma set her sights on the tree. Now that her attention was focused, she quickly spotted the glaring imperfection in the "perfect" tree. There was a huge bare spot located near the top and no amount of decorating was going to camouflage it. She couldn't believe the men hadn't spotted it even though the branches had been covered in snow. Cripe! There weren't any branches there to be covered *with* snow! Emma didn't bother to wonder how they could have missed it. Lamentably, it was par for the course.

Emma was opening the cartons of decorations when Ben returned with beer in hand and together they unraveled the strings of lights. While Ben put them on the tree, Emma stood by and offered advice on placement. Cole stayed out of the way, happy to watch at a distance. Once the lights had been successfully placed, they started on the garland and then the ornaments. When the last ornament had been hung, they stepped back to admire their handiwork. Cole was sleeping peacefully, having lost interest in the whole project.

"It looks pretty nice, bare spot and all," Ben said.

"Yeah, but…" Emma narrowed her eyes and studied the tree.

"But what?"

"It's missing something."

"It is?" Ben stared at the tree, his eyes searching. "What?"

"The topper! Where's your topper?"

"What topper?"

"Your tree topper. You know, the thing that goes on the top of the tree."

"I don't know if I ever had one."

"Everybody has a tree topper."

"Well, I don't think I do. If I did, it would be in one of these boxes."

"I didn't see one."

"Then I must not have one."

"Let's look again."

So they went through each of the boxes once more. They didn't find a tree topper.

"Guess I was right. I don't have one."

"Well, you *have* to have one."

"Why?"

"'Cause you just do. It completes the tree."

"Oh?"

"Yeah, you see that branch at the top, that's what it's for, to put the topper on."

"Oh. I never knew that."

"Well, now you do. I'm gonna run over to the shop and get a topper."

"You don't have to do that."

"I know, but we've got a couple of different kinds. I'll bring one of each back and you can take your pick."

"Em, it really isn't necessary."

"Don't be silly, of course it is. Every tree needs a topper."

"I don't know about that."

"Well, I do. Besides, if you have a topper it'll draw attention away from the bald spot."

Ben zeroed in on the obvious hole on the left side of the tree. "No need to say more. You sold me."

"Okay, I'll be back in a minute."

Emma grabbed her coat and put it on. Cole, ever alert to her movements even when asleep, got to his feet and stretched. "Lie back down, ya big lug. I'll be right back." Emma sailed out the door, closing it quickly behind her. Glad to be free of the underlying tension in the apartment, she bopped down the stairs and headed outside.

The night was crystal clear, the air cold enough that the snow crunched beneath her boots as she walked across the parking lot. Emma looked up into a sky that was inky black and star-jeweled. A trail of icy wind sliced across her face and she lowered her head, hurrying over to the shop. She reached the porch and dug in her pocket for the keys. Unable to select the right one with her glove on, she snatched it off and found the one she was looking for with fingers that were almost instantly frozen. Fumbling in her attempt to fit the key in the lock, she bent over to try to see better in the murky light. She had just gotten the key in and turned the bolt when out of the corner of her eye she saw a shadow loom over her. Sensing the danger too late, she only had time to raise her arm before the heavy object, which was already in its downward arc, crashed into her head.

\* \* \* \*

Cole was pacing restlessly in front of the door, his agitation growing by the second. At first Ben had chalked it up to nothing more than being upset because Emma hadn't taken him along, but now he wondered if there wasn't more to it. The dog was clearly upset, a lot more than he should have been. Ben looked at his watch; Emma had only been gone for ten minutes. That wasn't too long considering she had to walk over there, get the stuff, and walk back. Ben glanced over at Cole who had started to whine and was scratching at the door. Something wasn't right.

"Hell with it," he mumbled and dashed into his office and opened the safe. He took out his Glock, loaded it, and shoved into his jeans at the small of his back. Slipping his jacket on as he trotted to the living room, he got there just in time to see an impatient Cole opening the door. "Hold on there, big guy, I'm right behind you."

Cole wasn't waiting anymore; he streaked down the stairs only to be stopped at the glass doors at the entrance of the building. But Ben was right behind him and opened the doors without breaking stride. Cole rushed out and flew across the lot to the store, Ben hot on his heels.

They found Emma lying unconscious on the porch.

"Oh, Jesus," Ben breathed, his hand coming away sticky with blood from where he'd gently touched her head.

Cole licked her face and Emma groaned.

"Em, can you hear me?"

Emma slowly opened her eyes, although it felt like the lids were weighted down. "Wh-what happened?"

"Oh, thank God. I—"

The sound of something crashing came from inside the shop. Cole's head whipped around and he growled, the hair on his back standing straight up. Ben shushed him and reached for his gun.

"Em," Ben whispered, "will you be all right if I leave you alone with Cole? Whoever hit you is still in the shop. I need to get in there."

"Go," Emma said through gritted teeth; her head was pounding. "I'll be safe with Cole."

"All right." Ben turned to the Newfoundland. "Cole, I'm counting on you. Take care of her."

Cole moved to place his body between Emma and the direction from which he perceived danger would come from. He was right, Ben thought as he moved stealthily to the door where Emma's keys still hung from the lock. Careful not to make any noise, he opened the door and slipped inside.

Moonlight shone through the windows, but it still took Ben a few seconds for his eyes to adjust and make sense of his surroundings. He'd been in the shop enough to know the general layout and unless the girls had changed their floor plan in the last couple of days he should be able to maneuver down the aisles without giving himself away.

He worked his way cautiously up and down each aisle until he was assured the culprit wasn't hiding out in one of them. He came across a pile of broken jar candles and figured that had been the crash he'd heard. He snuck back around to the sales counter and made sure the area was clear. The only place left to search was the back room.

With both hands on the grip of his gun, Ben held it snugly against his chest, the barrel pointed upward, as he quietly approached the doorway. Sliding to one side along the wall, he peeked around the door jam. Straining to see in the darker room, he was able to make out the shadowy form only enough to see that the person was facing the other direction. On silent feet he moved into the room and lowered the gun until it was pointed at the intruder.

"Hold it right there," he commanded. "Put your hands above your head."

The shadowed figure stiffened and slowly turned. Ben still couldn't see well enough to make out any features and he couldn't remember where the damn light switch was. His other senses had gone into high alert, however, and he picked up the faint odor of gasoline.

"I said, 'Put your hands above your head'."

Instead of complying, the figure hurled itself at Ben, lashing out viciously and striking Ben's arm with a heavy object knocking the gun out of his hand. The intruder's momentum took both of them to the floor where they wrestled for control. Ben's right arm was racked by pain, the blow probably having broken a bone. They continued to struggle, rolling across the floor. Ben was much larger and stronger than the other person, but was hampered by his injury and it took him a while before he was able to land a few well-placed punches that slowed his opponent down. Finally, he drove an uppercut into the other's chin that snapped his assailant's head back. Sensing victory, Ben plowed his fist into his adversary's face and heard the crunch of bone. His attacker went limp.

Ben disentangled himself and slowly got to his feet. Cradling his injured arm against his chest, he felt along the wall for the light switch. Finding it, he flipped it on. Blinking against the sudden light, Ben found his gun and returned it to the small of his back while registering distractedly that the prowler must have been planning to burn the shop down as evidenced by the pile of dirty rags and the full gas can he'd come across during his search for his weapon. He walked quickly over to the cupboards and started opening doors. The girls had to have something here to tie somebody up with. He found what he needed in the last cupboard—packing tape. He grabbed a roll and walked over to the prone figure. It was then he realized he couldn't do this by himself, not with his injured arm, which by now was just about useless. He didn't dare leave the culprit alone while he got Emma. Besides, he didn't want her anywhere near the scum. The thought of what this obvious felon had done to her enraged him all over again and he was tempted to beat the criminal to a bloody pulp. He spotted the phone on the wall and went over to it. He dialed 911, told the operator what had happened and requested some EMTs. Then he dialed Sam's number and told him to get his ass down there.

Joanie and Sam beat the sheriffs and medical personnel to the shop. They must have flown out of the house the minute Sam hung up the phone; Joanie was in her pajamas for pete's sake. They found Emma sitting on the floor of the porch, propped up by the building's wall, her eyes closed. Cole stood directly over her outstretched legs, having changed his position the second the truck pulled into the lot. From his menacing posture, Joanie and Sam knew to approach cautiously.

"Hey, Cole, it's only us. It's okay, boy."

"Joanie? That you?" Emma asked, her eyes remaining closed.

"Yep."

"Oh, good... Cole, it's all right, boy." Cole whined, visibly relaxed, but didn't move. "Is Sam here?"

"Yeah, I'm here, Em."

"You'd better go and see if Ben's okay, Sam. I don't know what's happening in there."

"He called me, Em. He's okay, but I'd better go in and give him a hand." Sam hurried into the shop, leaving Joanie to tend to Emma.

"*Sooo...*" Joanie said, squatting down next to her partner. "What's new?"

"Not much."

"Same old, same old, huh?"

"Yep, just another day," Emma laughed, then grimaced. "Ow! Don't make me laugh."

"Hurt, huh?"

"Yeah."

"What the hell happened?"

"I think I can safely assume somebody bashed me over the head."

"Who would do something like that?"

"I have no idea."

"What'd you get hit with?"

"Something hard."

"I would've never guessed."

"Then I'm one up on ya."

"You wish…Em?"

"Yeah?"

"I'm…Well, I'm beginning to sense you're in a bit of a rut here."

"A rut? What kind of a rut?"

"The kind where you keep getting hurt. Geez! What gives?"

"I'd love to know. Must just be my usual bad luck."

"We're gonna have to do something about that then."

"Like what?"

"I don't know. I'll have to think about it…maybe have an exorcism or something. I bet Tammy could invoke something."

"I asked you not to make me laugh," Emma moaned.

"Sorry…Aren't you ever going to open your eyes?"

"No, not for a while yet."

"Why?"

"'Cause every time I do, or move my head, I feel like I'm gonna throw up."

"Oh…" Joanie paused to mull that one over. "Em?"

"Yeah?"

"Keep 'em shut."

"Don't worry; I plan to."

Meanwhile, Sam had found Ben in the back room and helped him tie up the thwarted arsonist who was just starting to come around.

Deputy Sheriff O'Connor showed up with another officer from the sheriff's department and right behind them was the ambulance carrying the two EMTs from the Concord Fire Company. All of a sudden the night was a whirl of red and blue blinking lights that shone through Emma's closed eyelids and made her groan. Car doors slammed and footsteps approached.

"Ladies, we've got to stop meeting like this," O'Connor quipped when he reached the porch.

"Tell me about it," Joanie replied.

"You guys okay?" he asked, crouching down.

"Em needs some medical attention. She got hit on the head."

"Em, how you doing?"

"Okay, I guess."

"The EMTs are right here. They'll check you out."

"Okay, thanks."

"Where's Ben and Sam?"

"In the shop," Joanie told him.

"Okay, sit tight. I'll see what's going on."

"We're not sitting tight too much longer for cripe's sake; it's freezing out here."

"Just until Em's taken care of."

Joanie muttered something unintelligible under her breath and both sheriffs escaped into the shop. The EMTs moved in to take care of Emma and Joanie took charge of Cole, moving him out of the way, reassuring him as she did that Emma was going to be just fine. He watched the two paramedics like a hawk anyway.

It wasn't long before Sam, Ben, the two sheriffs, and the prisoner walking between them were coming out the front door. Joanie, who'd been standing off to the side, had to strengthen her grip on Cole when he spotted the now-handcuffed figure. A low, menacing growl sounded from his throat and the prisoner immediately drew back against the restraining hands the sheriffs had placed on his upper arms.

"Keep that mutt away from me," the nasally voice demanded.

Joanie perked up her ears and studied the man wedged between the two officers. There was something familiar about him. She came forward and peered into his face which was rather liberally caked with blood. Ben must have broken his nose because it was looking really crooked. She looked beyond the blood to his little beady eyes framed behind ugly, black-rimmed glasses. Her eyes widened in amazement. She quickly took in the rest of his body, then went back to his eyes.

"Holy shit!"

"Hello, bitch."

"It is you! Damn!" The captured man glared at her. "You're the one who's been vandalizing the shop. *You* set the fire!" Joanie tore her gaze away from the cretin in front of her and looked over to Emma. "Em, open your damn eyes. You have got to see this."

"Do I have to?"

"Uh-huh. Believe me, it's going to be worth it even if you puke."

Emma cracked one eye open and then the other, her narrowed vision falling on Joanie who was pointing to the man standing between the two sheriffs. Shifting her gaze to the man, her eyes opened fully in recognition. "Oh, my God! It's…it's the asshole."

"I couldn't have said it better myself."

The man lunged for Joanie since she was the nearer of the two, but his efforts were in vain as he was quickly brought back under control by the sheriffs. Joanie had automatically taken a step back and had unconsciously loosened her grip on Cole. He sprang forward and came within a hair's width of exacting his own punishment. Ben and Sam had reacted reflexively and had moved forward to put themselves between the girls and the perpetrator. High levels of male testosterone were shimmering in the night air.

"Okay, everybody, cool it," O'Connor commanded. "Sam, Ben, back off. Joanie, get Cole under control."

Sam and Ben relaxed their stance, but Cole wasn't as easy to call off as Joanie soon found out. He wasn't going to budge no matter what she did. Emma waved the EMTs away long enough to get Cole's attention and on her request he dropped into a down. He was still in front of the man, but at least he was in a non-threatening position if you could ignore the growl that still rumbled in his throat.

"That's as good as it's going to get, Tim," Joanie said. "Cole's not taking any chance with the fallibility of us humans…Uh, don't take it personally."

"Right." O'Connor rolled his eyes, then shifted his gaze from Joanie to Emma. "I take it you know this guy."

"Do we ever," Joanie said.

"Who is he?"

"George Fleming."

"How do you know him? What is he?"

"He's an asshole."

"Joanie…"

"All right, he's a major asshole."

"Joanie…"

"Well, he is. Ask anybody who knows him."

"Besides that."

"He's a lowdown, scum-sucking son of a bitch."

"Joanie…"

"Well, you asked."

"Joanie, give the man a break, will ya?" Sam asked, giving her a reproachful look.

"Oh, all right… But I could go on and on, ya know. Fleming's a total asshole. He—"

"Joanie, for God's sake, give it a rest. We'll be here all night."

Joanie lifted her left eyebrow and shot her husband a look. It didn't take a genius to figure out he'd be paying for that last remark later. She turned back to O'Connor. "Fleming was a sales rep for Always Perfect Gift, one of the companies we deal with."

"Why would he have a problem with you?"

"Because the last time he was in we had a falling out and we stopped using his company and then other stores stopped ordering from them when word got around about what had happened with us. To make a long story short, the company started an investigation and found out old George here was doing a lot more than calling clients names and he was fired."

"Aaah."

"Yeah, aaah. I guess he blames us for his downfall and wanted a little revenge."

"I think he got more than he bargained for," Ben said, rubbing his bruised knuckles.

"And I believe he's about to get even more," Sam said, looking at Fleming like he was a bug he'd like to crush. "Get him out of here, Tim."

"With pleasure."

Never one to pass up a parting shot, Joanie couldn't resist taunting Fleming with a warning, "Hey, George, don't forget, where you're going—it's not safe to bend over in the shower."

The two sheriffs escorted Fleming, who was hurling vicious invectives at the girls, to the back of one of the squad cars and locked him inside until he could be transported to the hospital for medical attention. O'Connor would follow along in his unit and after Fleming received treatment, would escort him to the Erie County Holding Center where he'd be processed and, Joanie hoped, be thrown into a dark, dank dungeon for the rest of his life. Since that didn't have a snowball's chance in hell of happening, the least she could hope for was an uncomfortable overnight stay in a crowded cell of hardened criminals before he made bail.

The other sheriff was going to be busy securing the scene and taking appropriate measures to get the evidence collected, some of which included the rags, gas can, and the heavy metal flashlight Fleming had wielded as a club.

The EMTs, having diagnosed Emma with a head wound and concussion, were loading her into the ambulance and had already called for two more, one from the Colden Fire Company and the other from West Falls. They arrived shortly thereafter and were soon ready to transport Ben and Fleming to the hospital.

It was a caravan of three ambulances, a squad car, and Ben's Jeep that motored down Route 240 to 39 to Bertrand Chaffee Hospital in Springville, the town about twelve miles south of Glenwood. Ben had handed over the keys when it became apparent that Joanie, Sam, *and* Cole were coming with them. Sam's truck couldn't have accommodated all five of them. Four, yes, but not five. And there was no way Cole was staying behind even if he had to remain in the car when they got there.

Upon their arrival, Emma, Ben, and Fleming were hustled into separate cubicles. O'Connor stuck like glue to Fleming and Joanie and Sam split up; Joanie stayed with Emma and Sam with Ben. Fortunately, it was a slow night in the emergency room and the three patients didn't have to wait long for medical attention.

Emma's head laceration was cleaned and stitched and her concussion diagnosed as slight. She was ordered to take it easy for a few days and to dose herself with Tylenol when she needed it. The doctor explained she was probably going to experience headache (no kidding), possibly a little blurred vision, some nausea (been there), and fatigue. Explaining that her symptoms could linger for three to four days, he recommended rest and cold washcloths on her head along with the medication. Joanie, with a look in Emma's direction that told her she'd sit on her if she had to, assured the doctor Emma would follow his instructions to the letter.

When x-rays confirmed what he already knew, Ben's lower right arm was put in a cast after the simple fracture was set. Armed with medication a little more potent than Tylenol, he was ready to go home.

As they exited the hospital, they saw for themselves the unwavering devotion that characterized Emma's loyal friend. There sat Cole, erect and alert, his eyes fastened on the glass doors leading into the building. Emma knew neither his eyes nor his attention had strayed even once during his vigil. As they approached the Jeep, Cole shifted and came to his feet, his tail wagging furiously in wild response to having a reunion with Emma so near at hand.

Sam got behind the wheel and Ben was pushed into the passenger seat after arguing unsuccessfully that he should ride in the back. Declaring it would be way too crowded, Emma, Cole, and Joanie slid into the back seat with Cole wedged between them. Wedged wasn't quite the right word. He had his massive head tucked into Emma's lap and his rear end plopped in Joanie's. Emma placed a comforting hand on his back, then leaned her aching head back on the head rest and closed her eyes. Joanie snorted her lack of appreciation for which end of the beast she was favored with, then quickly turned her head aside as Cole's swishing tail came very close to smacking her in the face. So it was the entire ride home: Sam intent on his driving, Ben resting, Emma lightly dozing, and Joanie dodging rhythmic swipes of a tail gone mad.

\* \* \* \*

Moira was in her laboratory, sitting on a high stool, her appearance disheveled. It was very late at night, although she was unaware of the hour. Her attention was solidly fixed on the embodiment of her success, which was lying right in front of her. There on the counter next to her notebooks, beakers, pipettes, and deadly chemicals was a vial, a vial full of the poison that would do for her what she had been planning for years. All of her sacrifice, hard work, and seemingly unending, long hours had been worth it to have at her disposal this potent means of revenge. Her eyes widened as she studied it, turning it this way and that in hands that shook slightly. Her eyes had a wild, fevered glassiness and a dull throb hammered at the base of her skull.

She put the vial down and braced her elbows on the counter, pushing her fingers through her hair over and over again until it was sticking up in all directions as she stared at the tiny glass container. She started to laugh and cry at the same time, her laughter soon becoming a hysterical screech. Her beautiful face contorted into an ugly mask of madness. Quieting, she paused a moment, her rigid features relaxing. Then she started to hum. It was a tune that seemed familiar, but one she couldn't quite place. She grabbed the vial and sprang to her feet, spinning in circles until the melody died on her lips and dizziness swept over her. Wobbling, she fell back against the counter, thrusting her hand out to steady herself. She felt something sharp and looked down at her hand. She raised it and saw the knife which lay underneath. The shiny blade gleamed in the glow cast by the overhead lights. It wasn't a very big knife as knives go, but it was big enough. Unconcerned with the blood that covered her palm where the knife had sliced it open, she picked it up and twirled it, watching the light play off the blade. She looked at her other hand, the one that still held the vial, and brought it up alongside the knife. She clicked the two together. She did it again and stared. She did it a third time and once more broke into laughter that soon became maniacal. Holding the two together, she danced crazily around the room until she was sweating and breathless.

She sank onto the stool and placed the vial and knife together on the counter, thinking about how clever she was.

Earlier that day she'd put in the required hour at the dopey bridal shower and made all the appropriate small talk. She'd escaped pleading a headache and been off on her so-called errand. She'd driven to Syracuse and returned to the scene of the crime so to speak. The fairgrounds! Her mind jolted. *Scene of the crime? What did that mean?* She shook her head to chase away the strange questions and continued reliving her cleverness.

The site had been hosting a huge gun show in one of the many buildings on the sprawling grounds. What better place to pick up a weapon and remain a faceless entity in a crowd of thousands. *Not the same building.* Again she ignored the disturbing thought breaking into her reverie.

She'd approached a dealer with a story about wanting to get a Christmas gift for her brother who was an ardent hunter. She'd told him she was looking for a knife to replace the one he'd lost in the woods. She wasn't sure what kind it was, only that it was small enough to put in his pocket. Could he help her? Well, of course he could; he knew exactly what she needed and any hunter worth his salt would recognize the brand and be glad to have it. He'd shown her a 5″ Buck folding lock blade knife and she'd known the minute she saw it that it was perfect for what she intended. She hadn't even quibbled over the price; she'd simply paid the man and quickly left.

She reached for the vial and knife, oblivious to the pain of the wound and the blood still dripping from her hand. Totally mesmerized by what she held in her hands, she walked over to the refrigerator and clumsily opened the door. She bent to put the vial inside and stopped, sucking in a startled breath. Blinking several times, she struggled to make sense of what she saw. *Where had that beaker and another vial come from? Who'd put them in there? She'd only just made the poison, hadn't she?*

She shook her head to clear it and looked from the vial in her hand to what was on the shelf. She looked over to the counter and zeroed in on the notebooks in which she'd kept track of her progress. Her forehead wrinkled in confusion. *Were there two? There should only be one, shouldn't there?* Her gaze shifted to the beaker that was still sitting on the counter full of the poison she had worked so long to perfect. *If it was there, how could there be another one already in the refrigerator?* Her mind whirled, but only disjointed fragments emerged, the dull throb that had been at the back of her head escalating to a painful pounding. She tried to think—Syracuse flashed into her mind. *Had she been there before? At the fairgrounds?... Yes, she was sure she had been, but what had she done while she was there? Think!... Dogs, there had been dogs. Lots of dogs... But there was something else. What was it?... Black dogs...something to do with black dogs...They were important somehow, but why?... And she'd had a vial. At least she thought she had. But how could that be? She'd just perfected the poison, hadn't she? Or had she? She didn't know. She just didn't know!*

The pain in her head was excruciating now and she dropped weakly to her knees onto the hard floor. Unable to look away, she stared at the objects in her hands, desperately willing them to provide answers. None came, only more confusion. An image skirted across her consciousness so fast it might not have been. A dog. Indeed a black dog. An immense black dog. *Why? What did it mean?*

She rubbed the handle of the knife with her fingers, then flicked the blade with her thumb. Blood beaded in the small cut. She stared at the knife. *Why did she have it? What was she supposed to do with it?*

With an anguished cry, she spun back to the refrigerator and shoved the vial and knife inside. Jumping to her feet, she kicked the door closed. She clutched the sides of her head with both hands and closed her eyes against the pain and that which defied explanation.

With eyes only partially open and weaving drunkenly, she struggled up the stairs to the first floor and staggered to the bathroom. Letting go of her head only long enough to swallow some aspirin and a sleeping pill, she careened back into the living room and collapsed on the couch, not having the strength to make it upstairs to her bed. Burrowing into the pillows, she prayed for the black void to overtake her.

# Chapter Thirty-Five

The bright winter sun shining through the window onto her face awakened Moira the next morning. Groggily, she opened her eyes and tried to get her bearings. At first she didn't know where she was, but slowly awareness crept in. She turned onto her back and rubbed her hands across her face, then started when she noticed the dried blood crusted on her palm. She examined the cut and wondered how it had gotten there. She closed her eyes, trying to recall the night before. She had only scraps of memory. She opened her eyes and focused on the clock hanging on the wall opposite to where she was, which read 9:00. It couldn't be! But it was. Oh, my God! She should have been at work two hours ago!

She sprang off the couch and ran up the stairs to her bedroom, stopped long enough to call work and make the excuse she'd had car trouble and would be in as soon as she could, then bolted for the shower, tearing her clothes off on the way.

She showered and dressed, applied the minimum of makeup to be considered presentable, passed the dryer quickly over her short hair, and finger combed it into place. Lastly, she covered the cut on her hand with a Band-Aid, still having no idea how it had gotten there.

She gathered what she needed for the day and flew out the door to her Jetta parked in the attached garage. Once on the street she gunned the motor and sped to work.

\* \* \* \*

Emma spent the day on the couch, not by choice, but by the iron will of one Mrs. Joanie Davis. She'd shown up early, at 6:30 to be exact, let herself into the house using the key Emma had given her many years ago, and had proceeded to take charge. Even Cole hadn't stood a chance of outmaneuvering her. When Joanie was in her "take command" mode, there weren't too many who could dissuade her from her self-appointed task. Sam was about the only one who could deter her and he was nowhere in sight. There was no getting around it; they were stuck with General Joan and 1st Lieutenant, Ms. Sally Higgins, who'd arrived about half an hour after her commanding officer.

They'd fussed over Emma until she thought she'd go out of her mind and Cole had serious thoughts of jumping ship. They'd even forced her to stay flat on her back while *they* put up the Christmas tree. Thank God no one else had been around to witness it. Cole had even been forced to slink off to the basement as a matter of self-preservation. They'd been like two crazy people and would have put any man to shame with the colorful language it took to get the tree upright and stable in its stand. So what if they'd had to wire the damn thing to the wall in four different places to accomplish it. It was up, wasn't it? Granted, it didn't look any too pretty, but it was up!

Thankfully, putting the lights and ornaments on had gone a lot smoother and by the time they were finished the tree was at least passable. Joanie had suggested they hang stockings from the support wires, but Emma had had enough strength left to nix that idea with lightning speed.

Relief from her impossible, but well-intentioned friends came only when she napped and Emma had tried to take as many of those as she could manage, even going so far as faking it a few times. Emma felt a little guilty about leaving Cole in their clutches, but since she was in no position to help herself much less him, he was going to have to fend for himself. At least he could go and hide until he was discovered. It was more than she could do. Emma's thoughts drifted to tomorrow. God, they'd be back! She really didn't think she'd survive another day of their loving attention. Maybe once they left, *if* they left, she'd have time to get the locks changed.

\* \* \* \*

Ben, meanwhile, was convalescing at his apartment. His arm wasn't bothering him overly much and when it did the pain medication took care of any discomfort. He was alone and had been since he'd gotten home last night. Sam had called that morning to check up on him, but other than that his solitude had been undisturbed and for that he was thankful. Not one to seek comfort from others, he'd gone to ground whenever the need for healing had been necessary in the past and the habit held fast now. True, he might have made an exception for one very special person, but since she was unavailable and in need of convalescing herself, he remained comfortable with his self-imposed isolation. It gave him time to think, regroup, and formulate a strategy.

Done with self-recrimination and flagellation over what an ass he'd been in the manner in which he'd declared his love, Ben set his sights on the future. He was determined to make Emma his in every way and that meant getting her to agree to be his wife. He loved her and knew she had feelings for him, deep feelings. He knew he wasn't wrong in that, not the way she looked at him when she thought he wasn't watching, not the way she made love with him, and not the way she said his name when she reached her peak. She had deep feelings all right; she just wasn't ready to accept them or his own. But he was going to give her all the time she needed to accept both. If it killed him he was going to give her that time. He wasn't going to push, but he would strive to make her feel secure, enough so that she might start to trust what was between them. If it took the rest of his life, he'd get it done. He wasn't going to lose her.

\* \* \* \*

Moira crumbled into the recliner the minute she walked through the door of her house. Letting her purse and briefcase slide to the floor, she leaned back and exhaled sharply. She'd messed up at work big time and God only knew what the repercussions were going to be. She still wasn't sure how it had happened, but it had and she was the one responsible.

She was a process development engineer for the Hathaway Food Company in Rochester and her field of work concentrated solely on the breakfast cereals they produced. She was responsible for the formulas that determined the makeup of every piece of cereal that left the plant and the process that made it. Additionally, her job also involved creating new or improved processes used to produce that product. She'd worked hard to improve the current process and today had been the first time it had been put into use. However, by the time she'd arrived at the plant, she'd been looking at total disaster.

The first 15 to 20 minutes of any run is called "run to reject". During this time period the product is tested for such things as density and moisture. If the lab gives its approval, then the operator gives the order to "throw it to the good side" and the cereal is processed at 100 lb/minute. From there it goes to packaging. The lab also tests for vitamin levels, but that result could take an hour to get back. When the findings for this particular run came in, the run had been going for more than an hour and had produced over 6,000 lbs. of cereal.

Somehow she'd skewered the formula and the entire run of cereal, namely Dragon Puffies, had been made without the addition of vitamins. That meant every last 20 oz. box that had been produced before the run was shut down was unacceptable, in other words, garbage. And there were a lot of boxes, thousands of them—4800 to be exact. And that meant there was a lot of money involved in product, packaging, wages, electrical power... God, the list was endless!

Moira lifted herself sluggishly out of the chair and wandered aimlessly around the house. Eventually she made her way down to the basement and her lab. She hit the switch for the overhead lights and blinked at their harshness when they came on. She walked around the lab slowly and stopped when she saw the beaker full of poison sitting on the counter. All thoughts of work vanished. Her forehead furrowed and her eyes narrowed. *What was that doing there?* She picked it up and went to the refrigerator. Her eyes widened when she saw another beaker and two vials inside. She carefully placed the beaker in her hand inside. It was then she noticed the knife. She picked it up and saw there was dried blood on the blade. She turned her hand over and looked at the Band-aid covering the cut she had discovered that morning. *What had happened here last night? And why couldn't she remember?*

With knife in hand, she practically ran from the lab. She went into the kitchen, stopping at the sink where she started to scrub the blood from the blade. She continued to scour the knife long after the blood was gone. Finally, satisfied it was clean, she dried it off. She moved to the kitchen table and sat down heavily in one of the chairs grouped around it. Holding the knife in front of her with both hands she concentrated on remembering. Blocking out everything around her, the hum of the refrigerator, the ticking of the clock, the sound of the furnace coming on, she slowly recalled at least some of the events of the day before.

She remembered going to the idiotic bridal shower, driving to Syracuse, and buying the knife. She remembered coming home, but after that, no matter how much she tried, it remained a blank. No memory would come forth, so instead she contemplated the knife. *Why had she bought it?* There was a reason; she knew there was a reason. Once again the vision of a large, black dog sprinted across her consciousness, but this time it was joined by a brief glimpse of a woman. *Concentrate! Who were they?*

Slowly, so slowly that unnoticed hours slipped by, she put some of the pieces together, at least those that applied to the dog and woman. The effort had exhausted her; she could barely move. Too tired to make dinner, she went up to bed, pulling herself up the stairs with the handrail. She got ready for bed, her movements slumberous. Collapsing into the bed, the knife cradled in her hand, her last coherent thought was a challenge to her nightmares, daring them to invade her sleep.

# Chapter Thirty-Six

The shop remained closed until Wednesday. Yellow police tape had been strung from one support column to the next across the porch for all to see, so since that produced the same result as a red flag being waved in front of a snorting bull, there wasn't a soul in Glenwood who didn't know the whole story by dawn on Wednesday morning. And that meant that word had to have traveled to Angie Newmann. God help us!

Both Emma and Joanie were in the shop, having rid the porch of the yellow tape as soon as they'd come in. Emma appeared to be fully recovered. Maybe she experienced a little headache now and again, but no way in hell was she going to let Joanie know that. She'd had enough of Joanie-style nursing. So as far as Joanie was concerned, Emma was good to go. The only outward sign of her ordeal were the three little stitches high on her forehead closing the cut she'd received when the flashlight had struck her and those would be taken out next week.

Ben was recovering nicely, enough so that when he and Emma had talked on Tuesday all he did was complain about the cast on his arm and the fact that he couldn't wait to get it off. He'd have a little bit of a wait—six weeks worth and then he'd have to have some physical therapy. Oh, happy days!

With the number of days growing ever shorter till Christmas, the shop was a hotbed of activity that day. In fact, the day was so busy, they called Tammy, who was almost always available on short notice, to help. They kept her occupied with restocking and fetching and well away from artwork on the sales pads. For the most part she stayed anchored to the earth, although Emma caught her looking like she'd gone off into who knows where a time or two and if Emma wasn't mistaken the number of watches on her arm had increased by two since the last time she'd seen her.

Mrs. Foster and Aunt Agnes came by for some last-minute stocking stuffers and chatted with the girls for a few minutes, getting all the details about the latest crisis straight from the horse's mouth. They were delighted to see Tammy and struck up a conversation with her that the girls weren't privy to, although Joanie tried her darndest to eavesdrop. All she got for her efforts was an elbow in the ribs from Emma.

It was about 2:30 in the afternoon and the girls were gobbling down roast beef and provolone sandwiches they'd hurriedly tossed together in between customers when the Scourge of Glenwood appeared on their doorstep. Damn! And she wasn't alone!

"Crap!" Emma whispered around the food in her mouth.

"Double crap!" Joanie hissed and promptly choked.

Emma slapped her on the back. "You all right?"

"I'd be better if you'd let me choke to death."

"Hey, if I've gotta be here, you've gotta be here. I'm not facing this alone."

"Chicken shit."

"You better believe it."

"Strength in numbers, right?"

"Right."

"Okay then, let's take her on."

By this time Angie Newmann was just stepping up to the counter and in her arms was Susie, the Cockapoo she thought was a gift from heaven. The girls had collected ample evidence over the years that proved she came straight from the bowels of hell.

"Look who I brought!"

"Yeah, look," Emma singsonged.

"How come you brought her?" Joanie asked, her cadence imitating Emma's

"She came to cheer you up."

"Oh, shit," Emma muttered under her breath in the same monotonous rhythm.

"*She* came to cheer *us* up?" All metered speech abruptly stopped.

"Yeah, she loves to cheer people up." The little bitch was snarling and curling her lip.

"She looks it."

"I know. Isn't she just the sweetest thing?"

The answer the girls gave her was an unintelligible sound that could possibly pass for a grunt if hard pressed.

"Let Susie cheer you up."

"We don't need cheering up."

"Yeah, you look like you need cheering up."

"No, we most definitely don't look like we need cheering up." The girls were working as a tag team as usual.

"Oh, I think you do. After what you've been through, anybody would need cheering up."

Emma figured this could go on for hours and if they ever wanted to get rid of Angie it was probably in their best interest to give in and get themselves cheered up, whether they needed it or not. "Well, have at it then. Cheer us up."

"Oh, good. You're going to love this. Are you ready?"

"As we'll ever be."

And with that Angie stood Susie on top of the counter on her hind legs and launched into her rendition of "I'm a Little Teapot", helping Susie use her front legs to go through the motions every child learned in kindergarten if not pre-school. Emma and Joanie just flat-out gaped, stared, gawked. Whatever you wanted to call it, their mouths hung open in disbelief and... shock? Horror?

Cole and Tank had seen enough from the safety of the back room where they'd taken refuge the minute they knew who had entered the shop. Both of them were embarrassed down to their toe nails at such a display by one of their own species. The last straw came at the finale when Angie tipped Susie over in imitation of a teapot pouring tea. Cole got up and with a mighty swipe of his paw slammed the door shut. Enough was enough!

When Angie and Susie had taken their final bow, and that was another aberration of nature, nobody moved; nobody said a word. The silence was deafening.

"Well, what'd ya think?" Angie asked, her face glowing with maternal pride. When no response was forthcoming, Angie prompted, "Emma? Joanie?"

"I'm...I'm...," Emma babbled, "...speechless."

Angie beamed her delight that their performance had robbed Emma of her normal communication skills.

But by this time, Joanie had sufficiently gathered her wits. "Well, I'm not," she blurted. "Fu—"

"Joanie..." Emma warned over her friend's aborted expletive.

"Hey! You know as well as I do that sometimes it's the only word that covers a particular situation and this is one of them! Hell, this one deserves a double, maybe even a triple!"

"What word?" Angie asked, her innocence so tempting to exploit that Joanie's eyes actually lit up.

"Fabulous," Emma hastily said before Joanie could open her mouth. "That's the word, Angie—fabulous! Yep, Joanie's right on as usual. Susie's performance deserves a double fabulous! Right, Joan?"

"Fabulous?"

"Yeah, fabulous, Joan." Emma gave her a meaningful look.

"Yeah, okay. Sure. Whatever you say," she growled. "Susie was fabulous, freakin' goddamn fabulous."

"I just knew you'd love her. She's got real talent, don't you think?"

"Sure."

"Why don't you give her a kiss? You know, let her know how much you liked her performance."

"Couldn't I just pat her on the head?" Emma asked, knowing full well she could lose a lip if she got that close.

"Well, I guess so, but it wouldn't be the same as giving her a kiss. It shows so much more affection. You know what I mean?"

"Yeah, I know what you mean and I'm not feeling that affectionate," Joanie grumbled. "She's getting a pat on the head, take it or leave it."

"Oh, you guys," Angie scoffed. "Okay, pat her on the head."

Emma and Joanie exchanged a look that asked who was going to be the brave one and when Joanie held her ground, Emma took the bull by the horns and raised her hand to give Susie the required pat on the head. As soon as her hand was within striking distance, sweet little Susie clamped her teeth down on Emma's little finger.

"Ow! Why you little bi—"

"Now, Em, watch what you say 'cause little Susie's fabulous, remember?"

While trying to shake off the biting canine, Emma shot Joanie a look that could have impaled her. Still, it was beyond Joanie's limited abilities not to laugh. She knew she shouldn't, but God help her, the sight of Emma trying to dislodge that bundle of bad-tempered fur was just too funny.

Having opened the door a few seconds after Angie had sung the last note of her little ditty, Cole and Tank were witness to the bite and lurched forward. Emma saw them coming out of the corner of her eye and effectively halted their vengeful intent with a raised hand. Obediently they detoured to where the girls were and although thwarted in their immediate retaliation, they had no intention of letting Susie get away scot-free. She was, in fact, dead meat in their eyes.

Susie finally let go when Emma snapped her in the nose with her finger, a very effective method of discouraging bad behavior. But wouldn't you know it, Susie reacted liked she'd been beaten with a stick, flogged with a whip, or run through with a sword. She cried and yipped and hastily turned to the comforting arms of Angie who was only too glad to croon and soothe her baby.

"Oh, my God! I can't believe you hurt her, Emma."

"I really didn't hurt her, Ang. I surprised her."

"No, you hurt her. Listen to her. She's hurt."

"Ang, she's not hurt. Maybe her nose stung a little, but that's all."

"I don't believe you. Why'd you hurt her?"

Joanie had had enough of both Angie and her spoiled pet. "In case you hadn't noticed, Ang, she was taking a bite out of Emma's finger for cripe's sake."

"It was only a little love bite."

"A little love bite?" Joanie was incredulous. "You need friggin' help."

"Joanie…"

"No, really, Em." Joanie grabbed Emma's hand and shoved it in Angie's face, keeping out of range of Susie's marauding mouth. "Look at her finger, Ang. Susie damn near broke the skin. Those marks are gonna stay there a while and Emma's gonna have a nasty bruise, not to mention it's gonna be sore."

"She didn't mean it," Angie said, looking somewhat put out.

"Don't fool yourself."

"She gives these little love bites all the time. It's her way of showing affection. Nobody else has put up such a fuss."

"I bet."

"Really, you've just blown this all out of proportion."

"Whatever, Ang." It was clear to the girls they weren't getting their point across and probably never would. Had they really thought they'd be able to? Look who they were dealing with for heaven's sake. They must have lost touch with reality for a minute or two. Damn those senior moments!

"I know what it is," she said, cuddling the Cockapoo whose twitching lip was curled over her teeth.

"What?" Joanie's tone barely suppressed the fact that she wanted to be done with the whole mess.

"I know what this boils down to."

"What are you talking about?"

"You think Susie's beneath you because I don't show her."

"Oh, God," Emma breathed, letting her head fall to her chest. "I'm not up to this today."

"Ang, that's one of the stupidest things you've ever said and believe me there's been a bunch of 'em." Joanie's diplomatic skills had flown right out the window and she wasn't expected to get them back any time soon.

"Well, it's true. I know you consider Susie a...a...second class citizen."

Joanie looked at her in amazement. "Where do you get this shit?"

453

"Don't you swear at me, Joanie."

"Ohhh, sweetie, if you think this is swearing…"

"Well, I never, Joanie Davis."

"No shit!"

Emma slapped her hand on the counter, effectively silencing the two combatants. Too late she realized she'd used the one Susie had bitten and the pain from her little finger radiated up her entire arm. "Damn!" she shouted, grabbing her hand and rubbing her finger. Susie must have taken offense because she snarled and let loose with a high-pitched bark. Cole took a step forward and gave Susie a menacing look and in that one steely gaze let her know she was on notice. Susie cowered against Angie.

"Did you hurt yourself, Em? You really should know better than to pound the counter like that."

Joanie clenched her hands into fists and bit her lip to keep her mouth shut.

"I'm fine, Ang," Emma replied in a strained voice.

"You need to be more careful. Stuff's always happening to you."

Emma and Joanie both raised their eyebrow. It was weird, but they both only ever raised their left one.

Meanwhile, Tank, choosing to ignore the aforementioned desist order, had crept to the other side of the counter and was now standing directly behind Angie and her precious bundle. Looking up, he was blessed with an unrestricted view of one canine derriere, tail and all. It was too good to resist, besides it was tit for tat. He lowered his front end, his muscles coiling, ready to spring. And he did—quick as a flash he hit the bull's eye, grabbing a small patch of fur as his prize.

Needless to say, old Susie reacted with a blood-curdling scream and Angie must have jumped three feet off the ground. Tank had already made his escape, hurdling into the back room with strands of white hair hanging from his mouth, leaving Emma and Joanie to deal with the outraged woman.

"He bit my Susie!" Angie spit out in between making baby coos of comfort to her still crying dog.

"He did?" The girls could play dumb with the best of them.

"He most certainly did. Look here, the hair is gone," she said, shoving Susie's back end in their faces.

Upon examination, there did appear to be a very small bare spot on Susie's butt. That's my boy, Joanie thought, beaming with pride.

"Don't see a break in the skin," Emma observed.

"You're right, no break," Joanie agreed. Then with a pointed look at Angie she said, "Must have been a love bite." And both girls smiled big shit-eatin' grins.

"Well!" Angie huffed, then turned on her heel and left, taking her princess of a pooch with her.

"You think we finally got rid of her?" Joanie asked, watching the retreating figure before she stormed out the door.

"Maybe for a month or two."

"Then let's enjoy it while we can. Woo-hoo! Break out the dog biscuits and crank up the stereo. Get that Christmas music off and put something on that's gonna wail."

"Like what?"

"How about the Vaughn Brothers', *Family Style*?"

"That'll do it, but what about the customers?"

"What about 'em?"

"They may not like the selection."

"Listen, everybody I know is tired of hearing "Jingle Bells" and the rest of the holiday songs. They've been on the radio since the week before Thanksgiving for pete's sake. They'll be glad for the change."

"You're right. We owe it to them as concerned shopkeepers."

"You're damn right. Now go crank it up."

"Your wish is my command."

The rest of the afternoon was filled with music that would rock their customers' socks. The volume was loud and the beat designed to insure dancing in the aisles. Leave it to the girls to use their reprieve from Angie as reason for an impromptu party. Of course, when you've got the "Queen of Parties" at your disposal, it's a natural outcome.

# Chapter Thirty-Seven

Christmas Eve was ushered in with some unusual weather. It was in the low 40's and raining! The gusting wind was so fierce the rain was coming down in sheets and the drenched flags on the front porch were being battered to the point where the girls wondered if they should take them down before the poles snapped. If the present weather wasn't bad enough, the forecast for the rest of the day was even worse. Temperatures were supposed to drop through the thirties as the day progressed, the rain turning to snow. But before the snow arrived all that water was sure to change to ice and that meant hazardous driving conditions and probable power outages. Just what Emma needed with a houseful of company and Christmas dinner to get ready.

Mack and Lindsay had arrived late the night before, so at least they were safely there. Tracy, David, and the kids were supposed to arrive that afternoon, so hopefully they'd get in before it got too bad. Mandie, Rob, and Sydney were scheduled to come out early tomorrow morning because they were attending a get-together on Rob's side of the family that evening. It remained to be seen what conditions would be like tomorrow.

But right now, Mack and Lindsay were off visiting Lindsay's relatives in Newfane, which when Emma thought about it, made her realize they weren't safely there after all. They had to get back all the way from Newfane, which was about an hour and a half away. What a day this was going to be, one undoubtedly filled with lots of worry. It was one of those things mothers did best and it never seemed to end no matter how old your kids were.

As far as things at the shop went, it was the day the girls had nicknamed, Last Minute Man Day. Nine out ten customers were some sort of man, whether it was a husband, father, uncle, son, grandson, boyfriend, fiancé, brother, grandfather, or just plain friend. They were all there to do their Christmas shopping at the last minute and not one of them had a clear idea of what they wanted. Emma and Joanie had thought to call in Tammy, but that would only throw fuel on the fire as far as clear thinking was concerned. They weren't about to impose on Aunt Agnes or Mrs. Foster at this late date and Jackie was otherwise committed as any sane person ought to be, so they were struggling through on their own with only their loyal pets there to help out.

Decked out in their holiday finery, Cole and Tank were the picture of cooperation and servitude. Cole had on one of his Christmas bandanas decorated with Santas and elves and as usual he was busy carrying packages and being a goodwill ambassador. Tank was wearing a bandana trimmed in Christmas trees and snowflakes and, maybe because he'd been infected with the holiday spirit, was actually behaving himself. If that in itself wasn't enough to make the girls stop and take notice, the fact that he was being helpful was enough to make them question their eyesight. Not only was he patrolling the aisles judiciously in search of would-be shoplifters, but he was also keeping the smaller children entertained so their fathers could shop. Not once had Joanie had to reprimand him or apologize to someone for some sort of high jinks he'd pulled. Joanie was having her Christmas miracle; she wanted nothing more.

Around about 3:00, who should show up but Mr. Wittenger. As soon as the girls spotted him they groaned. Likable as the old guy was, they didn't have time to personally escort him around the shop. It was too darn busy. They needn't have feared, however, because help came in the form of Sir Cole and Sir Tank, their four-footed knights in shining armor.

Mr. Wittenger hadn't even made it to the sales desk when Cole grabbed one of the baskets they had for shoppers to use and approached the elderly gentleman. Tank came alongside and jumped on his leg. The old man reached down and petted him and then gave Cole a chuck under his chin. "You boys think you might want to help me out?" he asked, a smile in his voice.

Both dogs woofed.

"Do you mind if I borrow the boys?" he asked Emma and Joanie.

"Not at all, go right ahead."

"They did such a good job last time, it'd be a shame not to use their talents again."

"Feel free to put to put 'em to work, Mr. Wittenger."

"Thank you. It's kind of like having my own personal shoppers, isn't it?" he chuckled.

"Well, I don't know if I'd go that far," Emma said, eyeing the two dogs suspiciously, "but if you think they can help take 'em along." She wondered again just what the two wily canines had done the last time the old gentleman had been in.

"You ready to go, boys?" Cole and Tank, both of whom could barely stand still, woofed again. "All right, let's go shopping."

And with that they were off. Cole stayed with Mr. Wittenger while Tank roamed the aisles and made known what objects were to be considered by stopping and either laying a paw on the merchandise or if they were too high for him to reach, barking when Mr. Wittenger touched the right one and put it in the basket. If Cole disagreed with a choice, he'd turn his head away and wouldn't let Mr. Wittenger put it in the basket. Tank would then be forced to reconsider and the object would invariably be returned to the shelf.

"If I wasn't seeing it with my own eyes I wouldn't believe it," Joanie said.

"Me either."

"Kind of makes you wonder what else they can do that we don't know about."

"That could be scary, Joanie."

"Tell me about it."

In between helping other customers, the girls kept their eye on the threesome as they made their way around the store. Twice already they'd had to go to the back room and unload the basket. At one point Mr. Wittenger stumbled and Cole shifted his body so adroitly to steady the elderly gentleman that you never would have realized anything had happened. Only Mr. Wittenger's hand on Cole's strong back and the slight disruption in forward progress gave it away.

After another ten minutes of perusing the aisles and filling the basket, man and dogs made their final trip to the back room. Joanie couldn't stand not knowing what was going on, so she headed back there. She peeked around the corner and saw merchandise laid out on every available bare surface. She closed her eyes and shook her head. She wanted no part of this dilemma. And thankfully, it looked like she wouldn't have to because as she watched, Tank and Cole were systematically sorting through it and narrowing the field. Joanie decided Mr. Wittenger couldn't be in better hands. There was obviously something about the old gentleman the two dogs sympathized with and felt obliged to help him. Whether their, *ahem*, choices in merchandise were correct or not was anybody's guess, but Mr. Wittenger seemed more than willing to place his faith in them and that was all that mattered. If he was happy, the girls were happy.

It took another fifteen minutes, but then the final choice was made. The winner was a Williraye Santa on Skis. Mr. Wittenger thought his wife was going to like it so much she'd probably leave it out year round. Emma did the honors and wrapped it up in holiday paper and a big red bow. After giving each of the dogs a biscuit and a gentle pat on the head, Mr. Wittenger wished the girls a Merry Christmas and headed for the door. Worried about the slippery footing in the worsening weather, Emma and Cole hurried after him and helped him to his car.

Emma was startled when she stepped outside at how much the temperature had dropped. The standing water was beginning to freeze and the parking lot would soon be turned into a skating rink. Snowflakes were interspersed with the rain, but it wouldn't be long until the precipitation changed over to all snow. A plow went by laying down salt and Emma hoped the roads would stay good for a while longer.

No sooner had the thought filled her head than Tracy and family pulled into the lot. Megan and Brandon tumbled out the side doors of the minivan, anxious to be rid of the confines of the vehicle after the seven-hour trip. Tracy and David made a much more graceful exit, but it was clear they too were glad the journey had come to an end. After the usual hugs and kisses, they all went into the shop to get out of the weather. More greetings were exchanged with Joanie and Tank and then the two dogs commandeered the kids, leading them into the back room where all the toys were and therefore all the fun.

While the kids were being entertained and at the same time conversely entertaining, the adults chitchatted and caught up on what was going on in their busy lives. The shop was still bustling, so conversation was fragmented and sporadic while the girls took care of customers. When David wandered away from the counter after a while and strolled down the aisles, Emma had a hunch that maybe all his Christmas shopping wasn't done. It didn't take a genius to figure out she needed to get Tracy out of the shop, so she suggested to her daughter that she take the kids up to the house and get settled. Tracy was about to object when her mother gave her a meaningful look and she acquiesced, noting the whereabouts of her husband. So with another flurry of activity, Tracy and kids bundled up and headed for the van, taking Cole with them. David gave his mother-in-law a grateful smile and took out his credit card.

The shop closed at five, an hour earlier than usual, in deference to the holiday. Joanie gave Emma, David, and all his newly wrapped packages a ride up to the house, then left for her own family's festivities.

The house was decorated from top to bottom and then some for the holidays. The pine trees in the front yard were lit with white lights as was the porch railing where they were wound through the fragrant pine boughs that Emma had fashioned into a garland. There was a huge wreath on the front door and electric candles with white bulbs in every window. Also on the porch spotlighted in white light was a small sleigh filled with colorfully wrapped packages and greenery.

The decorated railing followed the rest of the porch around the side of the house and morphed into the back deck where lighted wire snowmen held court. Emma chose to forego representing deer artificially since she had enough of the real thing living in the woods that surrounded her house. When they came into the clearing in the back yard under moonlit skies they provided their own scene of natural beauty regardless of whether or not it was the holidays.

There was another big wreath on the back door decorated with pinecones and homespun ribbon and a lighted live tree, which would be planted in the spring, stood next to one of the snowmen.

Inside, there was, of course, the infamous Christmas tree. It really didn't look all that bad, considering... Actually, you'd have to consider a lot in order for it to pass muster, but it was there at any rate. Emma had decided to view it as a conversation piece.

The mantle over the fireplace was decorated with pine boughs, lights, and different Santa figurines Emma had collected over the years. Hanging from three wrought iron star-shaped stocking holders were quilted stockings for each of the grandchildren. There were two tall wooden snowmen dressed in knit hats and long scarves standing guard on either side of the hearth and a large, oblong, antique basket filled with greenery, pinecones, and tall white candles was sitting on the coffee table. Real sleigh bells hung from each of the outside doors and the inner doors had small wooden plaques that Emma had painted depicting angels, Santas, or snowmen hanging from their knobs.

There was an antique wooden bowl that had to date back to the 1700's eighteen inches in diameter in the middle of the kitchen table heaped to overflowing with all kinds of fruits and nuts. Standing alongside it was a Steinbach nutcracker just waiting to be put to use. Watching the old German brew master crack the nut shells was one of Syd's favorite things and even Megan still got a kick out of it. Brandon, now a bonafide teenager, had gone on to bigger things.

The hutches were decorated with pine boughs and pinecones and nestled among them were more Santas, snowmen, angels, and reindeer. Throughout the house, including the bathroom, there was Christmas in some shape or form. Even Cole's crate was strung with garland and attached to the door was a wreath heavily decorated in biscuits and rawhide.

Much to Emma's relief, Mack and Lindsay arrived back at the house around seven. The temperature was still dropping and the snow was starting to add up, but the road crews were out in full force salting and clearing the roads, staying ahead of the inclement weather.

With Christmas music playing in the background, the evening was spent telling stories and jokes, and eating so much food everybody thought they would burst. Cole had attached himself to the kids, so sneaky handouts were pretty much the norm.

Sometime during the evening, talk got around to Ben and Emma did her best to sidestep the issue. Her answers to probing questions were vague and she appeared, to Mack at least, to be uncomfortable answering them. He wondered what was going on. He decided he was going to have to have a little sit-down with his mother at some point; the only question was when. There wasn't going to be much privacy afforded anyone with this many people in the house and tomorrow there'd be even more with Mandie, Rob, and Syd coming. But somehow he'd get her alone; they didn't call him "Keeper of the Gate" for nothing.

\* \* \* \*

The Tudor-style house was the only one in the neighborhood not decorated for the holidays. It appeared totally dark now as it had for several days. The house had an abandoned look to it; snow had piled up in the driveway, mail was still in the mailbox, and wet, soggy newspapers half buried in snow littered the front stoop.

Heavy draperies were closed over the windows fronting the street and inside it was dark except for one lamp on in the living room; there was no Christmas music playing, no lighted tree, no decorations, and no family gathered. There was nothing but the near empty bottle of vodka sitting on the table next to the chair where Moira sprawled. She blearily looked around the room; nothing she saw penetrated her drunken stupor. Almost nothing. Her bloodshot eyes fell on the papers she'd hurled across the room a few days ago. They still lay exactly where they'd fallen, her walking papers—official notification of termination of employment. The mistake at work had cost her her job and she hadn't moved out of the house since.

Wearily, she brought the bottle up to her lips and drank. Vodka dribbled down her chin and she wiped it away with her sleeve. Her eyes closed, her fingers loosened, and the bottle fell to the floor as she passed out.

# Chapter Thirty-Eight

Sunshine! Bright, beautiful sunshine welcomed in Christmas morning. Emma had been up for hours getting this, that, and the other thing done, which included making a special breakfast that was a family tradition, and thumbed her nose at the dismal weather forecast that had been predicted. There was no sign of stormy clouds, falling snow, or howling winds. Instead there was dazzling sunshine and blue, cloudless skies. Thank you, Lord!

With so many sleeping people in the house and bodies seemingly everywhere, Emma had tried to be as quiet as possible while she went about her business. Tracy and David had taken the guest room, Mack and Lindsay were in her bedroom, and Brandon and Megan had camped out in sleeping bags on the living room floor with Cole in between them. She'd slept on the couch for the short amount of time she'd been on it.

But some noise was inevitable and Brandon was the first to stir; his sister was next. Cole's lick on her face probably hastened things along, but that was just a guess, educated, but still a guess. Once the kids were up, with whispering an art form they hadn't yet mastered, the adults soon followed.

Showers and dressing had just been completed by the time Mandie, Rob, and Sydney arrived and after the usual hubbub of greetings, they were now getting ready to sit down and eat because the kids had assured anybody who'd listen that they would surely die of hunger if they had to wait any longer. So with that dire pronouncement in mind, they gathered around the table and prepared to dig in. Emma's antique table had been extended as much as it could be, but it still wasn't big enough to accommodate everybody. A few of the adults were going to have to eat in the living room. Mack and Rob said they didn't mind; as long as they had access to the food they didn't care where they ate it. Just keep it coming!

As to the meal, well, it was a small feast. There was orange and cranberry juices, milk, and for those who wanted it, coffee. Tracy had brought her coffee maker and coffee since Emma had neither. Everybody who knew Emma, including her children, knew that if you wanted coffee at her house you brought your own. She could and would supply you with a mug, but that was only because she collected them.

There was a platter of crisp bacon and juicy sausage, a mixed fruit bowl, homemade cinnamon rolls drizzled with frosting that were the size of a salad plate, crunchy, spiced home fries, and an Egg and Cheese Puff that everybody loved. Its ingredients were basic, but oh what a result. It used bread (any kind would do, although Italian or sourdough were best), Monterey Jack cheese, Parmesan cheese, eggs, milk, parsley, and salt and pepper. Once prepared and baked, it was to die for.

Breakfast was over in very short order; the food appeared to have been inhaled. There wasn't much left either, half a roll here, a piece of bacon there. It was a good thing Cole had taken what he could from the kids while there was still food to go around. He knew what he was doing; he'd seen these hungry people at work before. He got while the getting was good.

The table had barely been cleared and the dishes put in the dishwasher before the kids were pleading to open the gifts. Mack took on the task of handing them out and used the kids as helpers. They took their jobs very seriously, especially Syd who was still kind of new to all this. Let's face it, at three she didn't have a whole lot of experience to draw from. Her little eyes got huge every time Mack handed her a gift and told her who it was for. Then, handling the package very carefully in her outstretched hands, she'd bring it to the right person and smile like she'd just delivered Sesame Street's Elmo himself.

When all the presents had been doled out, opened, admired, and thanked for, the mountain of wrapping paper, bows, and ribbons were put in the trash before they were spread all over the house. It was simply amazing how hours of work could be destroyed in but a few minutes. Mothers organized their family's gifts and put them in piles, which the kids kept messing up as they pulled out a new toy, or necklace, or baseball cap to examine one more time.

Cole had his own pile of goodies, which Emma had shoved under the tree. He'd gotten a stocking full of rawhides, two new balls, some dog treats, a rawhide bone that had to be three feet long and from Syd, a new stuffed animal. This time it was a little hedgehog which of course she named "Heggie". Dear, sweet, bedraggled Froggy could now be retired to his final reward, although not when either Syd or Cole was around.

The magical lure of the outdoors soon called to the children and they were bundled up by mothers proficient in doing so, and scooted outside. Cole, in part because of his natural guardianship tendencies, darted out the door with them. The other part that drove him was anticipation of a great good time. And he had one.

Brandon, the oldest, more or less supervised and acted as director of activities. Kindhearted as he was, he helped Megan and Syd build a snowman first and then showed Syd how to make snow angels. He'd die of embarrassment if the guys at school found out, so he'd have to swear Megan to secrecy.

Megan had just turned ten and was getting to be a real expert at torturing her brother as all sisters have throughout time. So it went without saying he had his work cut out for himself. He was going to have to come up with something really, really good to get her to keep her mouth shut. Maybe a little bribery, a little blackmail? He'd figure it out.

The kids started throwing snowballs for Cole to catch and he was doing a fine job of grabbing them out of the air when slowly but surely the snowballs started finding other targets and before you knew it, there was an all-out snowball war with the girls against Brandon. Syd's throws didn't amount to much and Brandon let her off the hook, tossing easy throws he made sure fell short of the mark. She had enough snow on her just from falling down.

The men came out enticed by the whizzing snowballs and plunged into battle. It was every man for himself, but it would be safe to say they all gave as good as they got. The girls retreated to the safety of the porch where they were happy to cheer from the sidelines. Cole, meanwhile, was having a gay old time racing after any snowball that happened to fall his way.

The old sleds were brought out after the battle had died out and the kids had a great time sledding down the hill. The men even took a few runs and by the time they called it quits and went back to the house everybody was snow-covered and hungry.

Anticipating their needs, the women had sandwiches, hot chocolate, coffee, Christmas cookies, and dry clothes ready. Cole was toweled off and headed for the basement so the dryer could do its work when he put the brakes on. No way did he want to miss out on one minute of the fun; he wasn't going down there. Unlike his usual obedient self, he refused to budge and didn't little Syd come to the rescue.

"Come on, Cole," she said, starting for the stairs. "I'll go with you." Emma had to grab her hand before she went down on her own. Looking at her grandmother, she pursed her lips and put her hands on her hips. "I can do it by myself, Grammy."

*Oh, sure you can!* "How about you help me then?" Emma asked, trying to hide a smirk.

"Okay, Grammy, I'll help you. Come on." Syd took Emma's hand and together they went down the stairs. When they reached the bottom, Syd looked up at Cole who was standing at the top watching the two of them. "Cole, you have to come down. *Now.*" And she stamped her little foot!

Well, didn't he come down just like that! Emma coaxed him into his crate and turned the big dryer on. Syd pulled up a little stool and sat down next to his crate. She laced her fingers between the bars so she was touching Cole and, jabbering a mile a minute, waved her grandmother away. Damn, Emma thought, I know when I've been dismissed.

Megan and Brandon went down to the basement when they were finished eating, so they could relieve Syd and she could go up and eat. They promised their little cousin that they would stay with Cole so he wouldn't be alone. But Sydney was adamant and wouldn't leave—not until Cole was dry and allowed upstairs. Only then could she be persuaded to abandon her post and, with Cole in tow, went upstairs to eat. As it turned out, she ended up giving most of her food to her big furry friend anyway.

The afternoon passed with the kids playing with their new toys, the men watching TV, and the women talking while busy in the kitchen. Cole stuck with the kids for the most part, taking an occasional trip to the kitchen to check on Emma and any food that might have fallen on the floor.

It was just after 4:00 when Ben showed up. Mack had been wondering if he was going to show at all. His earlier conversation with his mother had hardly been enlightening and, other than the fact that she had been uncomfortable discussing Ben, he was still in the dark as to what was going on. But something was definitely up; he knew that without a doubt. Maybe he could get Ben to spill the beans.

Mack watched as Ben greeted his mom. He put his good hand on her shoulder, leaned in, and kissed her cheek. Kissed her cheek? What the hell was that? His mother gave a weak smile and avoided looking into Ben's eyes. Oh, boy! They had trouble!

Somebody asked Ben about his arm and the two broke apart. Emma scurried back to the kitchen, claiming she had some last minute things to do, and Ben found a seat in the living room and answered the question.

Soon it was time to sit down to the holiday dinner starting with cheddar broccoli soup, followed by Caesar salad and homemade crescent rolls and honeyed butter. The main course consisted of prime rib, twice baked potatoes, glazed carrots and green beans almandine. Dessert came in the form of from-scratch chocolate chip cheesecake and homemade cream puffs.

Mack's opportunity to talk to Ben came when someone was needed to go down to the basement to retrieve the two trays of cream puffs in the extra refrigerator. Volunteering their services, Mack hustled Ben down the stairs. Not wanting to be overheard, Mack waited to speak until they were in the corner where the fridge stood.

"What's going on, Ben?" Mack wasn't about to beat around the bush.

"Going on?"

"Yeah, with you and my mom."

"Oh… you noticed."

"Yeah, I noticed."

"Did you talk to your mother?"

"Yeah, but she wasn't too forthcoming."

"Oh…well…"

"What's the problem?"

"Mack, I really feel this is between your mother and me."

"Wrong. Anything that involves my mother, involves me too."

"Really." Ben's temper was starting to flare.

"Yeah, really, especially when it has to do with her happiness." The two men eyed one another, each taking the other's measure. After a tension-filled, testosterone-packed minute, Mack looked away and relaxed his stance. "Look, I don't want to argue with you, Ben. Just tell me, maybe I can help."

"I don't know if I should say anything."

"I'm not giving up until I get a straight answer, so you might as well tell me."

Ben hesitated a second or two, then, "We've got a bit of a problem."

"What is it?"

"This is a little awkward."

"Just tell me."

Ben ran his fingers through his hair and blew out a breath. "I made the mistake of telling your mother that I love her."

"You love her?"

"Yeah."

"Well, that's great. Hell, that's terrific…Well… Wait a minute. I don't understand. Why was telling her that you love her a mistake?"

"Because she didn't want to hear it."

"Why?"

Ben gave Emma's son a pointed look. "I should think you'd know better than I would."

Mack's shoulders slumped. "Oh, my father."

"Right."

"Damn."

"Yeah."

"So what are you going to do?"

"There's only one thing I can do. I'm gonna back off."

"You aren't going to break up with her?"

"No, no, of course not. I'm just going to give her a little space, you know, go slow. Let her start to build some trust in what we have."

"That's the thing; she doesn't trust anybody or anything where love's concerned. The family, Joanie, Sally, we're the only ones she lets in. She's built up some pretty high walls; not that I can blame her after what he put her through."

"I know, but I'm going to tear them down if it kills me."

"If it's any encouragement, I think she cares for you a great deal."

"I think she does too. She just has to learn to trust me and her feelings."

Somebody yelled down, "Hey, you guys, what's taking so long? You eatin' 'em all by yourselves?"

"We'd better get up there." Mack handed Ben a tray.

"Yeah... Mack?"

"Hmm?"

"I want you to know I'll never willingly hurt your mother and I'll never leave her unless she wants me to. I swear it."

"I know you won't."

"I wish she did."

"Do like you said. Give her some time."

"I only want her to be happy."

"Me too and if it means anything, you've got my support."

"It does, and thanks; I think I'm going to need it."

Carrying the rich dessert, they went upstairs. A few minutes later, they were distracted from thoughts of their conversation by Sydney, who'd been transformed into a human cream puff. By the looks of her, she couldn't have gotten more than one bite inside her mouth. The rest of it surely had to be on her face and hands. What a mess! And was she ever the happy camper—as was Cole as he licked it off!

*   *   *   *

Moira had sobered up enough to clean herself up. She'd showered, washed her hair, brushed her teeth, and changed her clothes. She wasn't up to fixing her hair or putting on makeup, but it was a big improvement from the way she'd looked the day before.

She'd been shocked when she'd looked in the mirror and saw the scratches on her face. At first, she didn't know how they could have gotten there. She didn't remember doing it, but something had happened to cause the marks. Had she fallen and accidentally scraped her face on something sharp? Staring at her reflection, she'd tentatively placed her fingers on the scratches and drawn them lightly down her face following the red, raised lines. The trail was the same as if she'd raked her nails down her cheeks. Startled, she realized she must have done it herself, but she couldn't remember when or why. No, that was a lie. She knew why she'd done it. When she thought about it, she was surprised she hadn't done it long before this. She hated her face, that beautiful, perfect, unblemished, *fake* face. But last night with the courage found in the bottom of a bottle, she'd finally had the guts to do it, to make that perfect face not quite so perfect, to make it a little ugly. It didn't matter she told herself; drunk or not, she'd actually gone and done it and she felt really good about it.

Wearing her scratches like a badge of honor, she'd drifted through her day without direction. When she happened to look at the calendar and realized it was Christmas Day she gave a dismissive snort and continued with what she was doing, which hadn't been much of anything other than trailing through the house.

Late in the day her mindless wandering took her down to the lab, which she traversed five times before she stopped in front of the refrigerator. She stared at it for a long time before she opened the door. Inside she saw the beakers and vials of poison. She recognized them for what they were, but no longer worried about why there were two of everything instead of one. She couldn't explain it and no longer wanted to. It was easier to accept things the way they were. If she tried to think, her head would start to pound and she wanted to avoid that. The hangover was bad enough. The important thing was there was poison available and the knife was upstairs in her room.

She'd closed the refrigerator, satisfied that all was as it should be. Turning off the light, she'd started up the stairs humming her favorite song. She had remembered one thing—what she was going to do with them.

# Chapter Thirty-Nine

The week between Christmas and New Year's passed quickly. Emma's houseguests left Monday morning and she spent the rest of the day cleaning the house, stripping beds, doing laundry, and all the other things minus the cooking she'd done *before* her company had arrived. Talk about repeating yourself!

Monday was, of course, the 26th, the day after Christmas. It was the day when everything in the world went on sale. It was also the day of the week the shop was normally closed. And that's the way it was going to stay come hell or high water. No way were the girls opening the store on their day off. Tuesday was time enough to deal with the countless bargain hunters who were sure to descend upon them the entire week.

Therefore it followed that Tuesday through Saturday the shop was jam packed with customers from opening to closing. The store was such a bedraggled mess at the end of each day that it took the girls anywhere from an hour to two to straighten it up. It stood to reason then that by the time the shop closed on New Year's Eve they were a little cranky and not in the best frame of mind to celebrate. But give them an hour and they'd rally, especially if they had a glass of wine to help them along.

Ben was picking Emma up at 8:00. They were meeting Joanie and Sam at the Hearthmoor where Sally and Richard would join them. Sally had declared herself officially off duty for the night; her competent crew could handle anything and everything for the entire evening. They'd been given instructions to pretend she wasn't even there, except when it came to service, naturally.

Emma had to rush to be ready on time and she figured that was a good thing because it didn't give her any time to think about Ben or the evening ahead. She hadn't seen him much since Christmas and was relieved that their time together had been limited to quick visits at the shop and a few phone calls. There hadn't been an opportunity for any deep discussions and she wanted to keep it that way.

They hadn't been intimate in a while now and she missed it, but maybe it was better this way after Ben's declaration of love. What he'd said had scared her to death and she didn't want him to repeat it in the throes of passion, which seemed to her to be the most likely time. Best to keep some distance between them, even if she was horny as hell.

Ben arrived on time, looking like the gorgeous stud he was. Dressed in black wool slacks, dazzling white shirt, and green silk tie, he was enough to stop the hearts of women twenty years his junior. What a hunk! Even lacking a suit jacket and with his right sleeve rolled up because of the cast, he looked delicious. Emma almost forgot to breathe, but recovered sufficiently enough to ask him in.

"Hi, Em… You look beautiful." She had on a clingy red dress that showed off all her curves and some strappy little heels. Granted they were low heels, but they were still sexy as hell. Out of necessity, her wardrobe had improved somewhat since their first date. It was only common sense she couldn't keep raiding Joanie and Sally's closets forever, although she'd held out as long as she could before she gave in to the inevitable.

"So do you. I mean, well, not beautiful—handsome."

Ben laughed. "Whatever you mean, thank you. Sorry about looking so informal, but I couldn't get my suit coat's sleeve over the cast."

"It doesn't matter, you look fine." Boy, did he ever!

"The cast comes off in another week, thank God."

"Hmm."

Emma was still looking at him with wide eyes, unable to look away from his handsome face, although she knew it wasn't safe to do so. Ben, strategist that he was, wasn't about to let the opportunity pass. He stepped forward and gently wrapped his big hands around her upper arms and brought her closer. She didn't resist. He lowered his head and brushed her lips with his. She sighed; he deepened the kiss, slanting his head to one side. He licked her bottom lip and her mouth opened. He traced her open mouth with his tongue, but by an act of sheer will, didn't enter. He ended the kiss and drew back. Emma's eyes remained closed for a second or two savoring his taste.

"Are you ready to go?" he asked when Emma opened her eyes, looking a little confused.

"Y-yes… Give me a minute to get my things."

Ben watched as she left to get her purse and coat. He wasn't going to push, but he'd be damned if he was going to give up without a fight. And if he had to fight dirty—so be it.

\* \* \* \*

The Hearthmoor had been transformed into a holiday fantasy starting with the entranceway. Three white spruce trees, each between six and seven feet tall, ablaze with white lights graced the entry. The remaining corner was occupied with a wooden cart decked out in an arrangement of lights, twigs, boughs, and ornaments. Standing alongside was none other than the infamous wooden Santa Sally had made in class. Emma had to admit he looked pretty darn good.

The door into the barroom sported a wreath trimmed in woodland fashion and inside festive white lights were hung everywhere. There was a small decorated tree sitting on one end of the bar and the apple branches suspended above it were now embellished with snowflakes of varying sizes. Electric candles were in every window throughout the restaurant and another, larger tree stood on the floor at one end of the fireplace in the dining room. A large wooden snowman on one end and a primitive angel on the other adorned the raised hearth; the mantle was covered in lights, pine boughs, and glittering snowflakes. Above the mantle, attached to the fieldstone was a huge decorated wreath and in the grate burned a welcoming fire.

Sally, Richard, and the Davises were already seated at a table near the fireplace, so Emma and Ben quickly joined them. It was a night of good friends and great food and before they knew it, it was approaching midnight. Flutes of champagne appeared magically before them, courtesy of Sally, and they toasted in the New Year when the countdown ended.

Placing his left hand against her cheek, Ben tilted Emma's head up and gave her a lingering kiss. Her response was immediate as her mouth softened under his and her hand found its way to his chest. A smile of male satisfaction crossed his face. "Happy New Year, Em."

She replied in like manner, but if someone had asked her, she wouldn't have been able to say for sure what she'd said. Ben knew it and that knowledge allowed him to have very high hopes for the New Year.

\* \* \* \*

In the house at 162 Appler Way in Pittsford, midnight had come and gone without any sort of celebration. Moira was still up, but the significance of the hour and the day was lost on her. It held no meaning for her as she drifted back and forth between sanity and psychosis.

She was in her pajamas, the ones she'd lived in all week. She hadn't bathed since Christmas, much less brushed her teeth or washed her hair. She couldn't remember when she'd eaten last or what it was she'd eaten. She knew she'd drunk some vodka, a lot of it. She'd even had to go to the store yesterday to get more. Was it yesterday? She couldn't remember. It didn't matter anyway. And pills—she'd taken lots of pills. She'd made sure the nightmares couldn't sneak up on her when she finally slept, not that she ever slept more than a few hours at a time.

Right now she was sitting in the pretty flowered chair in her bedroom. She had a hand mirror in one hand and the knife in the other. There was one thing she'd done all week with strict regularity. She'd examined her face and the scratches on it. At the first sign the angry red lines were fading and healing, she'd clawed her face again. It had become a compulsion, this self-mutilation and she took great satisfaction in marring her onetime perfect face. She was going to make sure it was never perfect again.

This time though, she was going to use the knife. She wanted to feel how it felt when it slit the skin on her cheeks. She slowly drew the blade down her face following one of the lines made by her clawing fingers. It was a shallow cut, but the skin separated and blood oozed from the opening. She laughed out loud as she watched the blood run down her face in a narrow stream, impervious to the pain. She made another cut and then another until she had traced every mark on her face. With blood running down her neck, her laughter became hysterical. She looked from the mirror to the knife and slashed the air widely. She sprang to her feet and with a fierce scowl, thrust the knife forward with a straight arm, putting all of her strength behind it. Fighting an imaginary enemy, she kept thrusting the knife over and over until her arm tired and she sank back into the chair, her face covered in blood, her breath short. That's how I'll do it, she thought, exactly like that; that's how I'll get both of them.

# Chapter Forty

It was January 4th and Cole was two years old. It was his birthday and how were they going to celebrate? In addition to a party today, he was going to the vet tomorrow! Oh, lucky boy!

Well, actually he was. Emma had decided to go ahead with the breeding to Molly and tests needed to be done. Results of the testing for both dogs would determine if there would indeed be an actual breeding. So, the sooner the results were in, the better.

Some of the testing recommended for the breed had already been done. After Cole had turned a year old he was tested for heart osculation by a board certified cardiologist and for cystinuria, a kidney disease. Both are inherited problems and could be passed on to the puppies if either Cole or Molly were affected. Neither was.

Examination of the eyes, CERF, was a yearly exam and so far both dogs were fine.

Tomorrow, Cole would be x-rayed for hips, elbow, and patella to get his OFA certification. Even though he'd already had preliminary x-rays done, certification could not be given until after he was two years old. For his hips he'd be ranked poor, fair, good, or excellent and for elbows and patellas he'd be given a normal rating if he passed and no rating if they didn't. It usually took a month to get the findings.

The other test Cole was going to undergo was for his thyroid to make sure it was functioning normally. Again, this one couldn't be done until after he was two years old and it took about a week to get the results.

If Cole or Molly failed to pass any one of these tests they would be considered undesirable for breeding and would be spayed or neutered and that action would succinctly end their show careers.

All together, testing up to this point totaled upwards of $1,000.00. If the dogs passed these tests, then breeding tests were done such as progesterone levels in the bitch, semen evaluation for the dog, microplasm test, vaginal cytology, and brucellosis.

Heaven help the backyard breeder who throws two dogs together and hopes for the best. Breeding quality puppies is a complex, expensive business and there's no room for amateurs. Every breed has health issues that have to be dealt with responsibly to ensure healthy, stable puppies that are the future of any given breed. Was it any wonder that Emma saw red whenever somebody told her about the cute puppies so-and-so just had because she wanted to let her kids experience the birth? That in itself was enough to piss her off royally, much less the fact that so-and-so used the black Lab down the block because she wanted to see what she'd get if he mated with her yellow one. UGH!!!!! What'd so-and-so think she'd get? Yellow puppies with black stripes or black puppies with yellow stripes? Emma knew she'd have to bite her tongue if so-and-so came into the shop. If she went off on her like she'd want to, it'd be really bad for business, not to mention being slapped with a lawsuit for defamation of character. And if Joanie got into it, well, hell, they'd be looking at jail time.

At any rate, the birthday party was scheduled for 4:00. Emma and Joanie had decorated the back room in a doggy theme complete with streamers, balloons, and birthday banners. Emma had baked cookies in the shape of a big dog bone for both humans and dogs, and Joanie had sculpted a dog house made out of cooked ground liver liberally spiced with garlic.

Sally was coming down with Kirby and they should be there any minute. Aunt Agnes, Mrs. Foster, and Tammy were the other invited guests and they too should be arriving at any time.

Cole had his birthday bandana, which sported birthday cakes and balloons, tied around his neck and he knew he was a handsome boy. He'd been parading up and down the aisles all day. Emma couldn't figure out how he'd done it, but there'd been a definite swagger in his step all day. She and Joanie had gone so far as to try to imitate him and if watching that display hadn't been enough to make you drink, nothing was. Sometimes the girls needed a whole lot more to do with their time.

Everybody arrived within minutes of each other and the party got under way. Customers were going to have to fend for themselves. The party hats came out and everybody had to wear one with no exceptions. The dogs looked adorable, Aunt Agnes and Mrs. Foster were cute, Tammy looked... like Tammy, and the girls, well, they looked like idiots. Could have been because of the smart-ass way they were wearing them.

The cookies and liver dog house got laid out along with Sally's contribution of puppy porridge, which was her name for a savory stew she made up from whatever leftovers the restaurant had that would send a dog's salivary glands into overproduction. Aunt Agnes and Mrs. Foster brought boxes of Cole's favorite dog biscuits and Tammy brought...water. That's right, water. She'd brought a six pack of bottled water thinking it would be a real treat from tap water for Cole. Her mind was a scary place.

There was plenty of people food too: chips, pretzels, veggies and dip, pizza, wings, ice cream, and, of course, the omnipresent wine. Emma had even made a cake decorated with what was supposed to be a Newfoundland, but you couldn't prove it by Joanie. She thought it looked more like a big black blob with feet and a tail. So freehand drawing had never been Emma's strong suit. So what? It was the thought that counted. Right? Besides, once Joanie started eating she wouldn't care what it looked like.

After everybody, including the three dogs, had stuffed their faces, Cole took center stage while they sang the birthday song. Tank and Kirby joined in and added their howls to the slightly off-key melody. If the expression on Cole's face was any indication, he was mighty relieved when the last note finally died out.

Gifts came next and didn't Cole pull in the booty. He got two new crate mats, a Booda Bone, a Jollyball, a Cressite Tug-a-War, an official AKC plush toy rabbit, and lastly four different kinds of Newman's Own Organic Treats. Most people only needed one guess to know who gave him that one. Not that they weren't a fine product; it was just that it was a perfect example of how Tammy's mind worked, or didn't as the case may be. Her reasoning was sure to be so convoluted that it was far better to accept the gift at face value rather than wonder how she arrived at the appropriateness of it. Emma and Joanie could almost guarantee it wasn't because the snacks were healthy.

The conversation soon drifted to the upcoming show at the International Agri-Center on the Erie County Fairgrounds in Hamburg. It was a little more than a week away.

"You don't need us on Thursday?" Aunt Agnes asked.

"No, just Friday. I've got a doctor's appointment on Thursday that I've had scheduled for almost a year and I don't want to cancel it."

"What about you girls?" she asked pointing to Joanie and Sally.

"I've got Kirby in as a Special on Saturday and Sunday," Sally answered. "I put her in as a favor to the local club, you know, to get the entry up."

"What about Tank, Joanie?"

"Tank's going as a spectator *if* he behaves himself."

"Aaah, so in other words he might not be going at all."

"You've got it," she said, looking pointedly at her four-legged tormentor who was busy jumping on Cole's back.

"Is Jackie taking the weekend?" Mrs. Foster asked.

"Yep, she's all set."

"What about me?" Tammy queried. "Am I supposed to work?"

"Ummm…" This eloquent response came from both Emma and Joanie.

"Oh, sure, dear. You can work with Grace and me on Friday." Aunt Agnes had jumped right in when her niece had hesitated. Give her an inch, she'd take a mile.

"Oh, good," Tammy chirped, clapping her hands. "We'll have fun."

"Emma…" Joanie hissed under her breath.

"Don't worry, Joanie. Aunt Agnes will have everything under control. Won't you Aunt Agnes?" Emma's piercing glare told her she'd better or else.

"Certainly, dear. Don't worry about a thing. Everything will be just fine."

Famous last words, Joanie thought, but she kept her mouth shut.

The revelers had just cleared out and the girls were closing up when Ben showed up with a gift for Cole. He made a fuss over the dog, gave him his gift, which was a beautiful leather leash that had his name engraved on it, spent a few minutes talking to the girls, kissed Emma briefly, but passionately on the mouth, and left.

"You want to explain that?" Joanie asked, her expression definitely perplexed.

"Explain what?"

"That," Joanie said, fluttering her hands in the direction Ben had taken when he left the store.

"What? It was Ben."

"No kidding, you shmuck. What was that whole thing about?"

"I don't know. Why don't you ask him?"

"Yeah, like that's gonna happen any time soon."

"So? What do you want from me?"

"An explanation?"

"Don't have one."

"Em... He comes in here, gives Cole a gorgeous leash that you know was custom made just by looking at it, he talks to us for a minute, gives you a scorching kiss, and then... leaves. "

"Yeah?"

"Did I miss something?"

"I don't think so."

"Are you sure?"

"I'm not positive, but if you did, so did I."

"You can't explain it."

"No."

"Do you think he can?"

"I don't know."

"Are you going to ask him?"

"I don't think so."

Joanie studied her friend for a minute. "Wanna forget it?"

"It might be best."

"All right; let's go home."

But Emma didn't forget it; in fact it bugged her for the rest of the day and was responsible for over two hours of restless tossing and turning before she was finally able to get to sleep that night. Ben, on the other hand, had a cat-ate-the-canary grin on his face all evening and had no trouble getting to sleep whatsoever.

*  *  *  *

Moira was lucid enough at the moment so that what she was seeing on her computer screen was finally registering. It had taken her a while to find the information she sought, and even longer to make sense of it. In fact she was stunned when she looked at her watch and realized she'd been sitting there for over four hours. She couldn't recall what she'd been doing all that time. She didn't want to try to figure it out; she needed to concentrate on what was on the screen.

She put her chin in her hands and stared at the monitor. She'd scrolled down through the list of shows until she'd found one that wasn't too far away. She was aware enough to know that she didn't want to travel too far in the middle of winter. Now she was reading the information provided on the show she'd found. The show site was just south of Buffalo, in Hamburg, and it hosted a four-day cluster.

The first thing that soaked into her consciousness was that the show ran for four days. Four days meant four chances. Her glazed eyes sparked. The second thing that penetrated her fogged brain was that the show was in *their* backyard. That had to mean they would be there. Her eyes widened and she grinned. So would she. She'd be there all four days. There wasn't any reason why she couldn't. She certainly didn't have a job to worry about any more.

She flopped back in her chair and started humming the same song as always. She swiveled the chair from side to side, pushing it faster and faster until she let it spin in a complete circle. The momentum carried her around five times, the humming getting louder with each rotation. When she stopped, so did the humming. She focused once again on the screen, then shut the computer down. She would be there, ready and waiting.

# Chapter Forty-One

Joanie had the great pleasure of working with Aunt Agnes on Thursday. How that came about wasn't exactly clear. The only way Joanie could figure it was this: everybody knew Emma was taking Cole to the vet's on Wednesday—that meant Joanie was working alone. Everybody knew Emma had a doctor's appointment on Thursday. Again, that meant Joanie was working alone. Aunt Agnes must have come to the conclusion she simply couldn't handle two days in the shop alone.

So there she was, all 58 inches of her. Cripe, she was barely tall enough to see over the counter. She had on her usual array of jewels, but Joanie couldn't tell if there were any new additions. To tell you the truth, she never looked too closely. All that gold and silver made her dizzy. She did notice though that her hair had been tinted a light shade of purple to match the voluminous dress she had on. Aunt Agnes was the only woman she knew who color-coordinated her hair with her clothes.

But don't let her appearance fool you. The lady may look like a cream puff, but she was a punishing taskmaster. Just ask Joanie. From the minute she'd stepped over the threshold she'd had Joanie hopping and she was still giving orders.

Joanie hadn't had a moment's peace all day. Some of the jobs Aunt Agnes had doled out, Joanie hadn't even been aware needed doing. Hell, she hadn't even known they existed. The end of the day could not come too soon.

Tank, on the other hand, thought she was great fun. Actually, he thought her dress was great fun. When she sat down, the billowing dress would drape on the floor and Tank would scoot under and hide in legions of folds. It took Joanie a while to figure out where he was when he disappeared and then it was a matter of extracting the little devil. Once she started to get him out he'd just keep moving around in the yards and yards of material until Joanie had to get up close and personal with Aunt Agnes in order to free her dress of one mischievous dog.

Aunt Agnes was a good sport though and thought the whole thing was rather funny. She even explained to Joanie that the poor dear had to do something to amuse himself since Cole wasn't there to play with. Joanie didn't comment. She thought if only Aunt Agnes knew what Tank was capable of in terms of amusing himself, she might not be quite so charitable. But that information would be considered a family secret, so best not to divulge it. Better yet, shove it in the closet with all the other family skeletons.

As luck would have it, wouldn't you know mighty-mouth Angie Newmann made an appearance that afternoon. Just what Joanie needed; it was the frosting on the cake. They'd only gotten about a month's respite after the Susie incident; they'd been praying for three, would have settled for two. Now that was all blown to hell. There was one bright spot Joanie saw as she watched her come ever nearer. Susie was nowhere in sight.

"Hey, Joanie," Angie called as she sashayed up to the counter.

"Hey, Ang."

"Hello, there," Aunt Agnes chimed in.

"Oh, hello." Angie turned to Joanie with a "who's this?" look in her eyes.

Oh, boy, Joanie thought, this should be good. "Angie, I'd like you to meet Emma's Aunt Agnes."

"You're Emma's aunt? My goodness, I didn't know she had an aunt."

"It's not that unusual to have an aunt, Angie," Joanie said and rolled her eyes.

"I know. I just didn't know Emma had one."

"Yes, dear, she has quite a few, but I'm her favorite."

"You are?"

"Yes, dear, I am."

Joanie rubbed her temples. It was starting; the marathon was on.

"Well, how come I didn't know about you?"

"I wouldn't know, dear."

"She never told me about you."

"She didn't?"

"No. Joanie, how come Emma never said anything about her aunt?"

"Maybe it never came up."

"Well, you'd think it would have come up some time if she's her favorite aunt."

"Well, you know Emma," Joanie hedged.

"I didn't know about you, dear," Aunt Agnes said.

"What?"

"Emma never mentioned you to me."

"She didn't?"

"No."

"Never?"

Aunt Agnes thought for a minute. "No, not one time that I can remember."

"See, that proves it," Joanie broke in. "Emma doesn't talk about anybody. She's very close-mouthed that way."

"You think that's the reason?"

493

"Has to be, Ang. I'm surprised Aunt Agnes knows about me."

Aunt Agnes's mouth twitched and she gave Joanie a poke. It hadn't taken her long to catch on at all.

"By the way, where is Emma?"

Uh-oh, round two!

"She had an appointment."

"What kind of appointment?"

"A doctor's appointment."

"What kind of doctor?"

"I don't know."

"What's the doctor's name?"

"I forget."

"What's wrong?"

"Nothing that we know of."

"Then why did she have an appointment?"

"A check-up."

"What for?"

"None of your goddamn business." It was out before Joanie could slap her hand over her mouth. *Oh, shit!*

"What?"

Aunt Agnes tried to smooth over Joanie's outburst. "It's really none of our business, dear. Emma's entitled to her privacy."

"Oh…You don't know either?"

"No, dear, and I would never ask." Yes! Chalk up a point for Aunt Agnes!

"Well…why are you here?"

Joanie groaned. Round three!

"Here?"

"Yeah."

"Here as in the shop or here as behind the counter?"

Angie looked confused. Damn! Aunt Agnes was good!

"I guess here behind the counter."

"I'm working, dear."

"Working?"

"Yes, dear, I'm working with Joanie."

"For how long?"

"For as long as she needs me."

"How long is that?"

"Till Emma gets back."

"When will that be?"

"I'm not quite sure, dear."

"You're not sure?"

"Well, no, dear. I don't know when she'll be done at the doctor's."

"Joanie, do you know?"

"Haven't a clue."

"And then, of course, there's the show." Aunt Agnes deserved a medal!

"What show?"

"Why, the dog show."

"What dog show?"

"The one the girls are going to this weekend."

"Joanie, what show are you going to?"

"The one over at the Agri-Center."

"It's this weekend?"

"Yeah…Well, actually it started today and runs through Sunday."

"Today? How come you're not there?"

"Does this ring a bell? Emma had a doctor's appointment."

"Oh, yeah. So when will she be back?"

"Next week."

"Next week?"

"Ang, listen to me carefully. She's at the doctor's today. Friday, Saturday, and Sunday she'll be at the show. Monday's our day off. Tuesday we open."

"Ohhh, I see. Well, that makes sense,"

"I'm glad you think so."

"So, how long are you going to be here, Aunt Agnes?"

Joanie excused herself and went to tackle one of the many jobs Emma's aunt had found for her to do. The old lady could handle things just fine all by herself without any help from her. In fact, they might have to put her on speed dial for whenever Angie came in. She lived close enough; she could be there within ten minutes. This could be a plan in the making, Joanie thought almost giddy with excitement. Bring in Aunt Agnes; stonewall the mouth that never stops. Perfect!

\* \* \* \*

Moira had gotten to the show around 8:30. The first thing she'd done was buy a catalog and check out the entry for Newfoundlands. When she didn't see the one she was looking for, she'd become so unglued she'd raced out of the building, heedlessly bumping into people in her panic to get outside. She'd blindly charged around the parking lot for several minutes before she calmed down enough to locate her car.

She'd let herself into the vehicle and then just sat there, staring through the windshield with her white-knuckled fingers gripping the steering wheel. Breathing hard, she tried to think and couldn't. Only one thing reverberated in her head. *They weren't there!*

It was so cold her breath condensed and the window fogged. Still, she sat, frozen in place. Gradually her breathing slowed and her hands relaxed their death grip. She leaned back against the seat. She looked around the car as if to get her bearings and saw the catalog sitting on the seat next to her purse. She didn't remember flinging it there, but there it was. She picked it up and absently thumbed the pages, her eye catching a word here and there. She frowned. Friday? Her attention caught, she skipped to the back of the catalog and found a judging schedule for Sunday. Then it dawned on her—the catalog listed the entries for each day of the show. She'd only checked Thursday's. Quickly she found the Newfie entries for Friday, then Saturday and Sunday. He was entered! He just wasn't there today!

Relief coursed through her as she let out the breath she hadn't realized she was holding. Tomorrow, she could still do it tomorrow. They would be there tomorrow and she could take care of it. Her anxiety eased, she relaxed and started to giggle. What was she doing out here sitting in a cold car? She had work to do. She stuffed the catalog into her purse and bolted from the car. Walking quickly, with a smirk on her face and eyes that held purpose, she went back into the building. She reached into her pocket and fingered the vial of poison, then she went hunting.

# Chapter Forty-Two

As it turned out the girls never made it to the show on Friday. Thursday night Cole came down with a digestive upset that didn't turn out to be anything serious, but he still wasn't in peak form Friday morning. He was a little lethargic and off his food a bit, so Emma decided to forego the show and let him lie low for a day.

Since Aunt Agnes and Mrs. Foster were all fired up about watching the shop, Joanie and Emma decided to go ahead and let them do it. Joanie and Emma both had plenty to do at home. Whatever mischief the two older ladies and Tammy got into, and they were bound to no matter what Aunt Agnes promised, the girls were sure they could set it to rights next week. It took a little convincing on Emma's part, but she prevailed and the girls stayed home. As for Sally, responsibilities at the restaurant never ended so it wasn't like she didn't have a million and one things to choose from to occupy her time, although she'd really been looking forward to getting away from it all. Now she had to wait an extra day to make good her escape. Well, she'd just have to make the most of her liberation on Saturday and Sunday.

While Cole was content to take it easy and enjoy a day of rest with Emma, Tank was another matter. The thwarted trip to the show had left him in bad humor. He'd been all set to go and then—boom!—nothing. They were staying home instead of hitting the road. This called for repercussions so didn't he make Joanie's day a living hell. Whatever she was into, Tank was too, literally. If she was dusting, wasn't he stealing the dust cloth. If she was vacuuming, wasn't he there barking and taking potshots at the vacuum. If she was reading, wasn't he climbing all over her making it impossible to read. If she was getting dinner ready, wasn't he grabbing the package of chicken out of the refrigerator when her back was turned.

This last incident resulted in a game of chase that Tank was only too happy to play. After leading her all over the house, he finally held her at bay under the king-size bed in her bedroom. There was no way she could reach him. Half an hour later when none of the usual enticements like food, cajoles, or threats brought him out, Joanie gave up and left. It was just easier to make something else for dinner.

Tank left his hidey-hole after what he considered a safe amount of time. He abandoned the chicken where it was since he didn't have any use for it any more and went to see what else he could get into. Little did he know that Sam had come home and was lying in wait for him. So when an unsuspecting Tank turned the corner, Sam swooped in and snatched him up, then quickly deposited him in his crate, thereby effectively ending his reign of terror. Undeterred, the little terrier looked at Sam through the bars of the crate's door for a moment, then turned his back and snuggled into the blanket that lined the inside. He blew out a big breath and closed his eyes. He figured he'd made his point.

Emma and Cole for the most part simply whiled away the day. Emma did a few housekeeping chores, but kept activity to a minimum because she knew Cole would follow her around and not rest the way she wanted him to. So they listened to some great music, she read and he played with

Heggie, she dozed and he dreamed of doggy treats and toys. Emma kept a sharp eye out for any other symptoms and monitored Cole's temperature regularly. By 5:00 he seemed to be back to his old self, so Emma felt confident they'd be able to go to the show the next day.

Jackie came around 7:30 and they had a light dinner of tuna noodle casserole, salad, and rolls. Emma had kept her on standby the whole day until she knew Cole was going to be all right. Frequent phone calls between the two had kept Jackie apprised of the situation and wouldn't you know everybody in the office where she worked was just as interested, including the doctor. Braces and patients could wait; they had to know the latest on Cole.

\* \* \* \*

Moira was barely holding onto her sanity on Friday. With her ability for clear thinking deserting her, she couldn't understand why the Newfoundland and his owner weren't at the show. They were listed in the entries, they should be there. In her mind there was no reason why they shouldn't be. It was simple. If they were entered, they should be there. But they weren't there. Why?

She'd stood at ringside before, during, and after Newfoundland judging, waiting for them to appear. They never came. She'd waited an hour after the judging ended before she'd moved. Then she'd wandered around the building, looking for them. She'd gone into the grooming area, around the concession stands, in the bathrooms, around the rings, in the rooms off the main hall, in the hallways leading outside, and in the front lobby. She'd looked for hours and didn't find them. She'd wondered if she had somehow missed them and had gone outside, going up and down the rows of parked cars, searching. She'd looked in every vehicle, sometimes encountering people who'd regarded her with apprehension. She'd left quickly then and gone on, coming back when the people were no longer there. She'd searched until her feet were frozen and her fingers numb. She never found them.

Finally, dazed and disoriented, she'd gone back to her hotel room. She'd taken off her outer garments, dropped them to the floor, and walked blindly to the window. Now, she stood there and stared. *Where were they?* She ran her hands absently down her legs and felt the vial in her right-hand pocket. She gave a snort of derision. She hadn't been able to use it. All that work, and she couldn't use it. Not anymore.

For some reason people looked at her strangely now. Before nobody had noticed her, but now they did. They stared even though they tried to hide it. She wasn't invisible anymore; she didn't blend in. She wondered what had changed.

Her hand moved lower and she felt the plastic sheath she'd sewn into her pants. It was stiff from the opened knife concealed within it. She put her hand into her pocket, nudging the vial aside and drew out the knife. The blade glistened in the sunlight, wet with the poison she'd poured on it. She still had this, she thought, she could still use this. If only they would come.

Holding the knife in front of her, she walked into the bathroom. She turned the hot water on and put the knife under it, rinsing off the poison. She put the knife down and soaped her hands working up a good lather with the water. She picked up the knife and cleaned the blade carefully with her soapy hands. She rinsed it again, then dried it off. She looked in the mirror and started to cut.

# Chapter Forty-Three

Saturday morning Sally picked Emma and Cole up first, then went over and got Joanie and Tank. Since it was a local show, the amount of gear they needed for the day was reduced to a minimum, although Sally had still needed to borrow her son's van.

The weather was cooperating with cloudless skies and no snow forecast. The roads were down to bare pavement, so they shouldn't have any trouble going over the hill. Upon leaving Joanie's they took Route 240 north to the center of Colden and turned onto the Boston Colden Road. They took it down to Boston State Road and then to Route 391 which took them into Hamburg. They turned right onto Pine Street which took them to South Park Avenue. They stayed on it for a few miles until they reached the main entrance of the fairgrounds. They turned in and headed for the Agri-Center.

Unloading was a snap because of what they *didn't* have and within a few minutes they were inside the building. They found a spot in the grooming area and quickly set up. Cole was in at 9:15, so that gave Emma about 45 minutes to get him ready. She was done with time to spare by the time they walked over to the ring.

\*   \*   \*   \*

Moira was standing at Ring Three, waiting for Newfoundlands to assemble. Mastiffs were being judged now, and Newfies were next, so they should be coming. She concealed herself behind other spectators and watched anxiously. She saw some Newfoundlands approaching, winding their way through the crowd, and prayed that he would be there.

\*   \*   \*   \*

Cole and the girls reached the ring and settled in to wait. Emma got her armband and did what she always did—got nervous. Sally and Joanie tried to distract her as usual, but she still got nervous.

Ringside was crowded as it seemed to be every time Cole was shown now. Joanie pointed out several people they knew and some they didn't, commenting on their various dogs or outfits depending on which was more interesting. During her perusal of the crowd, she noticed a woman flicking quick glances their way. She was almost totally hidden by the people standing in front of her; the only things visible to Joanie were her eyes and hair. Joanie made eye contact with her once and she hurriedly looked away. There was something about the woman's eyes that bugged her and Joanie continued to watch her surreptitiously. She pointed her out to Sally as innocuously as she could and asked if she knew her. Sally couldn't get a good look at her, but from what she could see said she didn't think so. Emma appeared to be in her own world, so Joanie didn't even bother asking her, although she should have because Emma was having those meaningful little shivers going down her spine. Her awareness of something was transmitted to Cole, but before either one of them could make sense of it, it was time for Cole to enter the ring.

*   *   *   *

Moira could barely contain herself. They were here. They were standing next to two other women, the ones they were always with. Her heart was beating so hard she could feel the blood pumping through her veins. Her hand automatically went to her pocket. She touched the vial and fingered the handle of the knife. She slid the blade partially out of the sheath, then let it slip back. She kept repeating the motion as she watched Cole and Emma enter the ring.

*   *   *   *

Emma tried to ignore the tingling as she stacked Cole. When she had him set up she gave a quick look around the outside of the ring. She didn't see anything that should be setting off alarm bells. Cole jerked his head up and her attention was brought back to him.

She repositioned his head and bent down to his ear. "You feel it too, don't ya."

Cole puffed air out his flews. "Let's worry about it later, okay? Right now let's show 'em what we've got." Cole responded by locking in position.

The judge, Mr. Bruce Clarkson from Charlotte, North Carolina took his first look, then sent the dogs around the ring. There were five Specials and Winners Dog and Bitch in the ring. Cole was the first Special in line. As soon as they completed the go around and were back in place, Emma stacked him. She dropped the lead and stepped back. Cole maintained the stack perfectly and only Emma knew his attention was focused on more than what was going on in the ring.

The judge examined Cole from top to bottom and then called for the down and back. Emma gathered the lead, gave

Cole's ear a little tug, and off they went. Emma moved him out showing off his front and back gait impeccably. Their stride was perfectly coordinated; the two were working as one.

They finished off the exercise with Cole's patented free stack when Mr. Clarkson signaled for it. Cole must have held it for a good 60 seconds before the judge had them do the go around. Mr. Clarkson seemed to be impressed as well he should be. The crowd was suitably so and showed their appreciation with impromptu applause.

While the other dogs were being judged, Emma went through the motions of playing with Cole, but neither one of them had their mind solely on what they were doing. Emma could feel the slight tension coiling in Cole's body and she certainly wasn't her usual calm self. Outwardly, of course, it wasn't apparent that anything was wrong. Only Emma and Cole knew there was a problem. And the only thing they knew was that whatever the problem was, it was right at ringside.

Individual examinations were over and Emma and Cole were once again at the head of the line set in a stack. The judge went down the line once more, then called for the go around. Emma and Cole led the group out and before they were halfway around, Mr. Clarkson gave the Breed win to Cole.

Applause broke out again while Emma was congratulated by her fellow exhibitors and given the Best of Breed award by the judge. Leaving the ring, Emma scanned the crowd, but nothing jumped out at her except Joanie and Sally and they jumped *on* her. Luckily, the area was too congested with exhibitors and spectators for them to have enough room to perform one of their crazy dances. At least Emma thought it was lucky until they were mauling her more than usual. Then she wanted to clear the place and let them have at it.

"Get off of me, you guys," Emma said, having endured all she could handle of the post-win celebration.

"We're not done yet," Joanie griped.

"Yes, you are. Get off."

"Party pooper."

"And glad to be alive to be called one."

"All right, we'll just hug Cole then."

"Leave the poor dog alone."

"He loves it."

"I wouldn't count on that."

"Come here, Cole. Let Aunt Joanie give ya a hug."

Cole hid as best he could behind Emma.

"Told ya."

Joanie eyed Emma suspiciously. "Did you teach him to do that?"

"Nope, he thought of it all on his own."

"Are you sure?" she asked skeptically.

"He's a smart dog. He knows who to avoid and when to do it. This happens to be one of those times."

"He wants to avoid me?"

"Yeah."

Joanie leaned forward and looked around Emma. Cole had his face burrowed up against the back of Emma's legs.

"I thought he liked me," Joanie said, her feelings obviously hurt.

"He does, you big dope. He just can't handle all that wild hugging and kissing you guys do after a win."

"I thought he liked it."

"He's been stoic."

"Oh… I guess we'll try to tone it down."

Emma rolled her eyes. Like that was going to happen. "Let's go back. I want to talk to you and Sally."

"Can't we talk here?"

"No, let's go back."

So with Emma and Cole in the lead, they headed back to their set-up. The tingles were no longer going up and down her spine, but Emma searched the sea of faces surrounding her all the way back.

\*   \*   \*   \*

Moira had watched them the whole time they were in the ring. She'd never taken her eyes off of them, not for a second. When the dog had taken the win and everybody had been congratulating his owner, that was when she had torn herself away. Any plans she might have had for taking her revenge right then and there had been forgotten. There were too many people around them. She would have never been able to get close enough. Instead, she'd released her grip on the knife and skulked off to the bathrooms. Once there, she locked herself in a stall and pulled the knife from its sheath. She switched it to her other hand and with her free right one took out the vial. She turned the knife one way and then the other, checking the wetness of the blade. She dribbled a few drops of the poison onto the surgical stainless steel and moved the knife so that the liquid coated the entire surface. When she was satisfied, she did the same to the other side. Then she pulled her pocket out away from her body and carefully slid the knife back into its plastic sheath. She put the vial into her pocket and sat down on the toilet.

Moira felt the knife laying against her leg and stroked her hand over it. Unconsciously, she began to rock back and forth while continuing to caress the knife. Then she started to hum.

There were no thoughts of other dogs. No more self-recriminations for having failed on Thursday. No more wondering where the dog was that had spoiled her plans before. Her target was here; the one who was supposed to be number twelve was very near. This time he wouldn't get

508

away. Today there would be no escape. This kill would make everything right.

Lost in the fog of her insanity, Moira never knew when she had stopped touching the knife and started to claw her face. Rocking and humming the endless tune, she scraped her nails down her cheeks until the blood was running freely. She was completely unaware of the shifting traffic outside her stall.

\* \* \* \*

When Emma told Joanie and Sally about her premonitions of trouble they wanted to leave right then and there. Nipping that idea in the bud, she asked them if they had noticed anything out of the ordinary at the ring. That was when Joanie volunteered what she thought had been strange about the woman she'd observed in the crowd at ringside.

"What'd she look like?"

"I don't know. All I could see were her eyes and hair."

"That's all?"

"Yeah. She was behind a bunch of people. But she has blond hair and kind of weird eyes."

"Weird? What do you mean weird?"

"Well, they're a real pretty blue, but—"

"What's weird about that?"

"They're… I don't know, kind of dead."

"Dead?"

"Yeah, like a… like a… shark's."

Emma rubbed her forehead. "Sally, did you see the woman?"

"Not really, I couldn't get a good look at her. There were too many people in the way."

"What do you want to do?" Joanie asked.

"Get Kirby ready for the ring," Emma answered.

"What about Old Dead Eyes?"

509

"What about her? All she did was look at us. That's hardly illegal."

"I know, but…"

"Let's just stay on our toes. Okay?"

"Yeah."

"Sal, get Kirby out. You're in the ring in…," Emma checked her watch, "…twenty minutes."

Team effort went into getting Kirby ready for her showing. Cole and Tank were shuffled into their crates so they'd be out of the way and the well-oiled machine went into action. When they arrived at Ring One they had five minutes to spare. As a precaution they'd brought Cole and Tank with them.

\* \* \* \*

Moira stared in the mirror, unable to understand what she saw. Where had those new scratches come from? They looked fresh, the blood hadn't even congealed yet. She looked at her fingers. Blood and pieces of skin were imbedded in her nails. When had she done this? She couldn't remember.

She quickly washed her hands and then her face. While holding wet paper towels on her face to stop the bleeding, she anxiously watched the door praying nobody would come in. For the moment she had the bathroom to herself. The bleeding finally stopped and she dried her face. Digging in her purse, she pulled out a compact and tried to camouflage the damage, patting the powder over the open gouges.

Deluded enough to think her appearance was normal, she left the restroom, brushing by three women who were just entering. It was time to find out where the dog and woman were.

\* \* \* \*

Kirby gave a good showing, but failed to take the Breed. Sally wasn't upset and Kirby couldn't have cared less. They'd only entered the show to bolster the Lab entry and have a fun day out. Kirby was, for all intents and purposes, retired from the ring; so this was just a lark, an expensive one, but still a lark.

Grabbing their coats, the girls took the dogs outside then and let them play. The parking lot was huge and a large part of it was empty, so they let the dogs act like dogs until the girls' faces felt frozen and their toes were in danger of falling off.

Back inside, a major cleanup was in order to get Cole presentable for Group competition. The machine went into high gear.

*   *   *   *

At first Moira couldn't find them and wondered if she'd somehow missed her chance. She'd checked everywhere she could think of and hadn't found them anywhere. She was close to hysteria when she saw them come in the main doors. They'd been outside with their friends. Her relief was so great her knees almost buckled.

From a distance she watched them make their way through the building. Moving parallel to the path they were taking, she kept the group in sight while she moved at a pace slightly slower than theirs so she would remain a little behind them. They stopped at their set-up. Moira moved closer, her hand going into her pocket.

*   *   *   *

Cole was standing on the table getting shampooed, dried, and brushed all at the same time. Each of the girls was working diligently to get the big dog ready for Group. Concentrating on their appointed jobs and inattentive to anything else going on around them, they didn't notice a group of people gathering near their set-up. Joanie was the first to become aware when she dropped her brush. Bending down to pick it up, she saw a whole lot of feet staring back at her.

"Hey, guys, we've got an audience."

Sally and Emma looked up, momentarily stopping what they were doing.

"Where'd all these people come from?" Sally asked.

"What are they doing here?" Emma whispered.

"I don't know, but there sure is a lot of 'em."

Leave it Joanie to find out. "Can we help you with something?" she asked, scanning the elderly group.

"No, no," people echoed.

"Then, what?" Joanie's diplomatic skills would never get her into governmental foreign service.

"We just wanted to watch," the obvious spokesman for the group said.

"Where are you people from?"

"We're from the retirement home. We came to gamble."

"Well, you've got the wrong place."

"Yes, we found that out."

"It's the building in the back."

"Somebody else already told us that, but we thought as long as we were here, we might as well see what was going on."

"Ohhh."

"What kind of dog is that?"

And so it began—the countless questions. Thank God the girls could chew gum and walk at the same time because they had to keep getting Cole ready while they politely supplied information to the inquisitive group. Not even Joanie wanted to be rude to an elderly person, unless, of course, they pissed her off.

\* \* \* \*

Where had those people come from? They hadn't been there a minute ago. All of a sudden they'd swarmed in like bees to honey. She hadn't taken more than five steps when the group had converged on Rogers and her friends. She couldn't believe it. She'd been all set to take the dog and woman out. She could have done it and been gone already.

Frustrated, she ran her left hand through her hair; the right was still gripping the knife, her fingers tightening around the handle until her joints ached. She shot furtive glances toward her target. There was no way she could get to them now. But time was running out. She had to do it soon.

# Chapter Forty-Four

The girls, Cole, Tank, and Kirby were standing at the Group ring waiting for judging to start. On the way over, Emma had experienced the tingling again, but was unable to define the reason for it. She'd seen nothing that would arouse her suspicions; she didn't even catch sight of the woman with dead eyes. If it wasn't for the fact that Cole seemed to sense something amiss, she'd have thought she was going a little crazy.

The ring steward called for the Group and Emma and Cole filed in with the rest. Emma found their spot between the Neapolitan Mastiff and the Portuguese Water Dog and set Cole in his stack. When she ran her hand down his back, she noticed how rigid he was and she shivered.

"Cole," she whispered, "relax, boy. Whatever's bugging you can't get to us in here. Let it go for now...Come on, big guy, relax."

Emma broke the stack and walked him in a tight circle, then restacked him. Sally and Joanie, watching from outside the ring, knew immediately that something was wrong. Cole never needed to be repositioned. Tank and Kirby, sensitive to Cole's moods, keyed into their friend's disquiet and became more alert. Cole held the stack, but the hair on the back of his neck went up.

* * * *

Moira had trailed them over to the ring, being careful to stay far enough behind and off to the side so she wouldn't be noticed. She'd dropped back a little when they'd been waiting outside the ring, but once they'd gone in, she'd moved up. She was standing behind the front row of people now and had a clear view of the Newfoundland and Rogers. There were too many people and dogs around them yet. She'd have to wait, but not for long. She couldn't; time was slipping away. She started to hum softly and reached into her pocket.

* * * *

The judge called for the go around and the dogs moved out, Emma and Cole moving with the group until they were back in place. Emma felt eyes upon her and searched the gallery. Nothing jumped out at her to indicate imminent danger. She brought her attention back to Cole and tried to placate him. He was growing more restless as time went on.

They kept moving up as the individual inspections were conducted. There were only two more to go before it was their turn to go to center ring.

* * * *

Moira watched their progress as they advanced to the head of the line. She was becoming more and more agitated the longer they were in the ring. The humming was getting louder and people standing nearby were giving her strange looks—not that she noticed. With her free left hand, she touched her face, increasing the pressure with every pass of her fingers. She had to do it soon.

\* \* \* \*

Emma and Cole were up next. She had him in a stack, waiting to go to the middle of the ring. The judge finished his inspection of the Neapolitan Mastiff and signaled for the down and back. As soon as handler and dog moved out Emma took Cole to center ring. She stacked him and waited for the judge.

\* \* \* \*

They were in the center of the ring and there was nobody around them. Moira's crumbling mind blocked out everything except the woman and dog. In her tunneled perception nothing else existed. All she knew was that finally her prey was totally alone and she'd never get a better chance. It was time to act. She drew the knife out of its sheath. Pushing an elderly man out of the way, she jumped the ring fencing.

\* \* \* \*

Watching for the judge to turn their way, Emma at first wasn't aware of the disturbance at ringside, but suddenly there was a woman in the ring running straight toward them. The startled judge tried to intercept her, but she screamed and pushed him away, brandishing the knife she clutched in her hand. Without thinking, Emma grabbed the lead and stepped in front of Cole.

The woman's bloody face was contorted with rage. Her eyes—her dead eyes—were focused on Cole. "Get away from him," she screamed. "I want him first. Then I'll take care of you."

Emma stayed where she was. Cole tried to move around her but she was holding him too tight. He strained against the lead and managed to get his head alongside her leg.

Every fiber in his being was taut with harnessed power waiting to erupt. He growled from deep in his throat; his lips curled back and his white teeth gleamed bright against his blackness.

Moira abruptly stopped her headlong lunge. The sight of Cole's drawn back lips and menacing teeth plummeted her back into memories she couldn't escape. For a second, now and then became one. Then she blinked, her eyes widened, and she charged. Screaming obscenities and slashing the air with the knife, she hurtled toward Emma.

Cole exploded into action. Wrenching his body away from Emma so hard he snapped the choke collar around his neck, he flew at the woman with deadly intent. He aimed for the hand that held the knife and grabbed her arm right above the wrist while his massive body collided with hers.

Out of nowhere came two more bodies, one yellow, the other white with two brown patches. As if rehearsed, the three dogs moved in a coordinated attack. While Cole went for the weapon, Kirby launched herself at a full run and hit the woman in the chest. Between her and Cole's momentum they took her down hard to the floor. Faster than you could think possible, Kirby's teeth were fastened around the woman's throat. Cole exerted painful pressure with his powerful jaws until the woman dropped the knife; then he just held on. A snarling, snapping Tank was right on their heels, posed for action between the woman's legs, his teeth already imbedded in the fabric. If she moved at all, he had her.

When the dogs had attacked, the scream that rent the air had been an ungodly sound, full of terror and mindlessness. It had bounced off the walls, echoing throughout the building, and bringing shocked silence to the arena. In the seconds following the dogs' defensive assault, a murmur began and grew in intensity. People rushed to the ring, others called for security, and still others called for the police. No one, however, approached the woman or dogs. They remained just as they had been. The woman though was no longer screaming.

Joanie and Sally had rushed into the ring to be with Emma. That was where the three were now huddled.

"Are you all right?" Joanie asked.

"Yeah, just a little shaken up," Emma replied, her voice not quite steady.

"Christ! I was scared shitless when I saw her coming at you."

"You and me both."

"I swear my heart stopped, Em," Sally said. "I could hardly breathe."

"Yeah, well, it's over now, thank God. I'm fine and so's Cole."

"Speaking of which, I guess we ought to call our heroes off."

"Not before security gets here we're not."

"You're right; why take a chance of something else happening. With our luck…"

"Say no more. The dogs stay where they are until reinforcements get here."

"Do you guys know who she is?"

"Nope, not a clue," Sally said.

"The only thing I can tell ya," Joanie said, "is that she must be the woman who was watching us at the ring."

"I wonder why she wanted to hurt Cole."

For once Joanie was a little quicker than Emma, but then Emma had had a severe shock. "Em, I know you're a little wobbly right now, but if you give this a little thought I think you'll come up with the answer."

Emma gave Joanie a questioning glance, then turned her attention to where the woman was being pressed to the floor by Cole's big black body. It took only a few seconds for everything to click into place. "She's the one."

"That's what I'm thinking."

"The one what?" Sally asked.

"The one who's been poisoning the dogs."

"Really? You think so?"

"Yeah, she has to be. I bet she's got some on her right now."

Security men had arrived at the ring, although they didn't look any too anxious to disturb the dogs. The girls went over to offer their assistance. With but a single word from their owners Cole, Kirby, and Tank released their hold on Moira and retreated a short distance away. Their attention, however, remained fixed on the woman.

Security was just getting Moira to her feet when the police arrived. They quickly took over. Unable to stand on her own, two officers braced her between them as they led her out of the ring, her movements jerky and uncoordinated. Her ruined face was blank, her eyes vacant. She was mute; the horrendous terror of so many years ago brought back to frightening reality so graphically by the dogs' retaliatory strike that she had retreated far into herself. Her mind had locked, holding her prisoner in her own body.

Still laying on the floor was the knife and the vial of poison, which had fallen out of her pocket when she fell. They were quickly bagged as evidence. After questioning by the police, during which the girls revealed their suspicions, they were allowed to leave the ring. Group judging was going to be shifted to another ring, but Emma and Cole declined participating. Back at the set-up, they'd begun to break down their equipment.

"What do you think's going to happen to her?" Sally asked.

"I don't know," Emma said. "It's pretty clear she's not in her right mind."

"That's for damn sure. She's crazy as a loon."

"Joanie…"

"Well, she is and God knows she's dangerous."

"She'll probably end up in some mental institution," Sally ventured. "I bet she never goes to trial."

"Maybe, maybe not," Joanie said. "She'll get a lawyer and there'll be a hearing to see if she's competent to stand trial and if not she'll be placed in a mental institution for however long and then there will be another hearing to see if she's competent and so on and so forth. If it happens at all, it'll probably be years from now."

"And you know this how?"

"Duh! My husband was an FBI agent for a good number of years, girls."

"Oh, yeah."

Joanie rolled her eyes, slightly exasperated. "Well, at least she won't be at any more dog shows."

"Yeah, thank God for that."

"I wonder whatever happened to cause her to want to hurt the dogs."

"I don't know and don't particularly care," Joanie said. "I'm just glad it's over."

"Amen to that," Sally agreed.

"Hey, the dogs did a great job, didn't they?" Emma asked changing the subject.

"They sure did. Couldn't be prouder."

"Cole charged right in. No way was he going to let you protect him," Joanie said.

"I know; he was terrific, wasn't he? I was terrified he was going to be hurt though. And how about that Kirby? I guess we know what her potential is now."

"Shit, yeah! She went straight for the damn jugular."

"Of course, then there's Tank," Emma said.

"What do you mean by that?" Joanie asked, her body stiffening, ready to defend her wayward pet.

"Well, what's with him?"

"With him?"

"Yeah, why does he do that?"

"Do what?"

"Go between people's legs? This is the second time he's positioned himself in that area."

"Oh, that. Geez, I thought you knew."

"Knew what?"

"He's a crotch man. Doesn't matter if it's male or female, he goes for the part he can reach."

Emma rubbed her forehead. "That makes sense in a twisted kind of way... and it's a little scary that I'm able to understand it."

"We're getting to ya, aren't we?"

"Damn, I think you are."

"He did a fine job, don't you think?"

"I'm gonna withhold comment on that one, Joanie."

"Oh, come on. He did great."

"All right, you dragged it out of me. He did do a good job."

"Are you proud of him?"

"Proud? Sure, why not."

"Me too."

"No kidding. You're practically bustin' your buttons."

"Well, yeah, but then I'm his mother."

And that explained everything regardless of the holy hell that Tank could make of Joanie's life. Totally enamored of her dog as she was at the moment, Joanie didn't hear Sally mumbling a heartfelt "Thank God" in regards to Tank's maternal parentage.

So, with the tables and crates broken down and the gear packed, they were ready to load up and be on their way. They left the building, piled everything into the van, and headed for home. They'd be there in no time and tonight Cole, Kirby, and Tank would be treated to a special meal, one deemed worthy of a hero to be sure. And the girls... well, they would be nothing less than compelled to raise a toast saluting one and all of their devoted and loyal canine knights.

# Epilogue

*Mid February*

Candlelight glimmered, creating fuzzy, ill-defined shadows on the walls. A CD of Frank Sinatra's love songs played softly in the background. The air was scented with the rich fragrance of blooming flowers arranged in colorful vases scattered around the room. Refreshment cooled in a silver ice bucket and cuisine fit for royalty waited to be served on a table clothed in white damask.

The gentleman stepped forward and gently kissed his ladylove. Her brown eyes glowed with expectation and she returned his kiss. He nuzzled her neck and brushed his body against hers; she leaned into his strength. He shivered; she trembled and quickly fell under his spell. His breath came in short spurts and hers was reduced to little pants. He gave her one hot, intense look and she was powerless to deny him. He kissed her once more with loving tenderness and they joined together in the age-old dance of mating.

"Hot damn! We're gonna be grandmothers!" Joanie whispered excitedly from their vantage point near the two lovers.

Emma, not taking her eyes off the two mating Newfoundlands lest she need to help with the process, elbowed her friend in quiet rebuke. "Be quiet for pete's sake."

"I feel like a voyeur," Sally said, peeking through the slats of the louvered screen they were hiding behind. "Don't people get arrested for this?"

"I don't think it applies here," Emma answered. "We're watching dogs."

"Besides," Joanie reminded Sally, "normally we'd be right out there with them. But this is a little different 'cause Cole and Molly are in love. It was only right that we make it nice for them; give 'em some privacy."

"Geez, Joanie, give it a rest. Don't make me sorry I went along with the arrangements."

"Em, lighten up, will ya? Look at 'em. Come on, you have to admit this is so romantic."

"Yeah, they do look kind of cute."

"Cute, smute. They're in love. It's as plain as the nose on your face."

"Maybe on yours it is."

"Never mind, smart-ass. Listen, guys, whether you believe they're in love or not, the fact remains we're gonna have babies on the way."

"It's a little early for an announcement, don't you think?" Bev Miller asked. Up until this point she'd refrained from commenting.

"Nope, I've got it on good authority."

"Oh, boy," Emma groaned.

"You do? Whose?" Bev asked, mystified.

"The Big Guy upstairs," Joanie said, pointing upward. "There's absolutely no doubt about it; we're having puppies."

"Uh-huh." Bev's skepticism was showing. "Listen, I don't think—"

"Don't bother arguing with her, Bev. It's pointless," Emma told her.

"Joanie thinks she has a direct line," Sally explained.

"Oh, really." Bev gave Joanie a disbelieving look.

"Don't look at me like that. On important stuff I do."

"All right then, wise guy," Emma said, "since you're the ones with all the answers, how many puppies are we going to have?"

"Eight."

"Just like that—eight."

"Yeah."

"That's a good round number, Em," Sally stated.

"Whose side are you on?"

Sally managed to look a little shamefaced. "I got caught up in the moment."

"Well, don't. She doesn't need any encouragement. I suppose now we're going to hear it's divine intervention again."

"How'd you know?" Joanie asked, looking very pleased with herself.

"Lucky guess, since the average number of puppies in a Newfie litter is six."

"Well, there you go. That proves I got it straight from the top."

"You know what? Tammy's got nothing on you."

"Hey, I resent that."

"Too bad."

"That wasn't very nice, Em."

"I'm in a mood."

"I'll give you a mood."

"Uh… girls?" Sally had to break this up really quickly or she had a feeling they'd be going at it right up until the expected puppies were born.

"Yeah?" Emma and Joanie asked at the same time.

"We've got 63 days before we find out if Joanie's prediction is right, so why don't you cool it."

"I'll be right," Joanie shot back.

"We'll see," Emma said, not wanting to let her friend have the last word. It was the principle of the thing.

And so with a dubious truce declared, the wait began.

# Author's Note

I would like to take this opportunity to offer my sincerest apologies to all Schipperkes and their fanciers for the unfortunate mistake made in *Tricked*. Despite the care I took to avoid errors and in spite of the fact the pertinent information was right in front of my nose, I still categorized Schipperkes in the wrong Group. Doris Scott, a longtime Schipperke owner, was the first to point out my mistake and I thank her for alerting me to the problem. Schips are in the Non-Sporting Group, not the Toy as I stated on page 171. *I knew that and still got it wrong!*

Unable to come up with a reasonable explanation as to why I goofed and since I am of the age for "senior moments", I'm going to blame it on that. But be assured that I am terribly embarrassed by the blunder and will redouble my efforts to avoid any future ones. However, if they should occur, they are purely unintentional and strictly my own.

# About the Author

Diane Bridenbaker has had a life-long love affair with dogs and has been involved with her canine friends in one way or another for over thirty-five years. She's experienced in both conformation showing and obedience training and was fortunate enough to successfully assist in the delivery of several healthy litters.

She recently moved to West Seneca, New York after closing her country gift shop in Glenwood. In addition to writing, she works part-time as an orthodontic assistant.

Ms. Bridenbaker is the proud mother of three grown children and loving grandmother to their three offspring.

She is also the author of *Tricked*.

Diane loves to hear from her readers, and may be reached through e-mail at: *thistle99@earthlink.net*

Printed in the United States
66729LVS00001B/55-498